JITTERBUG LIFT

BY
OLIVER FLYNN

Copyright © 2012 Oliver Flynn

All Rights Reserved

ISBN: 1479259136

ISBN 13: 9781479259137

"With this signature the German people and the German Armed Forces are, for better or worse, delivered into the hands of the victors.

"In this hour I can only express the hope that the victor will treat them with generosity."

General Alfred Jodl
on signing the surrender for Nazi Germany
to end World War II in Europe
Reims, France

May 7, 1945
2:41 A.M.

CHAPTER 1

Treptow District, Berlin,
November 9, 1938, 9:21 P.M.

"We're too late!"

Her voice was hoarse with the cold and a whisper just above the staccato, racing footsteps. She glanced down at her part of the treasure, her whole world in a bundle pressed against her breast. Elsa Neumann stumbled.

Michael Neumann's urging grip held her up and Max spun back to the young couple at the break in the desperate rhythm. Even in the dark, Michael saw the Communist street fighter's blazing eyes and knew why the conspirators called him *der Magier*.

"Shut up," the Magician hissed.

A louder crash of glass and a cheer meant they were heading straight for the riot. Elsa's terror slowed her. She saw the same in Michael's face in the light of a radio store, its window full of red and black swastika flags to ward off the coming destruction up the street.

Max pulled them on, away from the island of light. Ahead, they could see the flickering orange glow of the torches. The Nazis had singlehandedly resurrected an ancient industry, practicing their dark religion of street theater by the pure light of fire.

Monster shadows twitched on the tidy stucco walls. A shriek echoed off the windows shielding the Berliners' *Kaffee und Kuchen* dessert ritual from the destruction. A drawn out wail followed, lost in the enraged mob's roar.

Elsa shielded her treasure from the violence with her shoulder. She looked to Michael again. Max scouted on a few steps and trotted back, framed by the torchlight. The entire square seemed to be in flames and Max was leading them right into the mouth of the furnace. His arm whiplashed at them.

"Come on! It is the only way."

Elsa felt Michael's pull at her arm. They moved on, hypnotized. As they entered the square that should have smelled of bread, they choked on the diesel oil soot from the torches and could even feel heat on their faces.

Elsa focused on Max's back, trying not to provoke the demon by looking it in the eye as they hurried in the shadows at the edge of the *Junkerplatz*. Michael darted around to her right, putting himself between his wife and the Brownshirts. Still, a violent motion caught Elsa's eye. She turned instinctively. Michael was already staring.

Ziegler towered a full two meters in the doorway of his bakery, a bull tormented by a pack of jackals. The six-foot-four half-Jew raised the oven scrape over his head again, blood running down his contorted face. He swung down and to the right. A torch arced up and back into the mob. There was a squishy thud and another cry of pain slammed into the nineteenth-century façades. The mob spasmed a groan and recoiled. Then they bellowed with one voice and one primal mind, surging toward Ziegler.

Ziegler stabbing at the brown-black sea with the shattered and blood-red oven scrape burned into Michael's mind before the corner of Kerner's clothes shop eclipsed the square. He knew this was part of the conspirators' plan, but he hadn't calculated the cost.

"Poor Sonya," whispered Elsa.

Michael worried that the sounds of the riot did not fade as they moved up *Göthestrasse*. The chaos chased after them until they reached the house in the middle of the block. The sound almost kept him from thinking about the loss they were about to face. Elsa was looking down at her treasure. Her lips were moving, but he couldn't hear her above the not so distant noise. Elsa's face creased at the crash of more windows and she pulled the bundle closer. Michael could tell she was repeating something. It was drowned by a disintegrating shop window.

There was a pause and Michael heard what she was saying.

"Your name is Sarah Neumann. Your name is Sarah Neumann. You must not forget. Your name is Sarah Neumann."

Max took the steps two at a time and rapped on the window to the left of the door. A light in the hall went out and the door cracked open.

"Dear God!" escaped from the woman's lips as the door started to swing back closed. On the steps, the streetlight revealed Max's brown shirt and trousers. A brown bicycle cap topped his short-cropped hair. Even this close he could pass for a jackal.

Max kicked the door back and shoved Elsa inside. Michael glared at the magic eyes, silently protesting the offence. Max ignored him and checked the street.

Everyone who knew Joshua "Max" Fäder was always struck by his eyes. Their steady, targeted gaze gave Max the air of a military officer. But many said there was something else. Michael saw it immediately when he met the man months ago as they sketched out their plans for what they were all sure would never happen – all but Max. There was a magician who was a sensation at the *Theater Hohenmarkt.* Max had the look of the illusionist as he made a lit candle disappear. Moments later it reappeared – still lit.

Michael had mentioned it to his wife and she told everyone. Soon all the conspirators were calling Max *der Magier* behind his back.

Michael saw the parlor door slide partway open. He recognized the young girl, perhaps sixteen, who flinched back into the shadows as a car lit up the entryway before Max closed the door. Her hand was holding the door with long, delicate fingers. The girl's dress was simple, but her figure defied being hidden.

Michael smiled. She did not smile back. Instead she watched Max.

"Clever, Herr Max," she pronounced evenly. She sounded like one of the lawyers at Michael's firm congratulating another on a fine court brief.

Max only glanced at the girl before disappearing into the house.

"Sonya, be quiet! And take the baby," the woman scolded, pushing Sonya forward.

Sonya Ziegler reached out to take Elsa's baby. Elsa met her eyes.

"We saw…" she stuttered before Michael cut her off with a tug at her elbow.

"Don't worry. You will see it again before we put it on the truck," Sonya said softly, cradling Elsa's part of the treasure.

"We are out of time!" Max rammed into their conversation and pulled them toward the back of the house.

The cellar smelled of old furniture, stale perfume and bodies: the stink of a dozen men and women who had been waiting too long and now were trapped. A man gasped as Max's brown trousers and boots came into view. The small crowd recoiled away from the stairs and surged back after bouncing off the walls.

"He's one…" started a woman's voice.

Max pushed his way to the center.

"Good evening, Herr Fäder…" the Rabbi tried to begin a short speech.

"Shut up," spat Max. "Is it all here?"

Stung, the Rabbi adjusted his spectacles as he had a thousand times when some young boy had mispronounced the Bar Mitzvah Hebrew reading and proclaimed that the Almighty was an ass instead of in the burning bush. "Yes, finally," he whispered, seeing Michael come down the stairs followed by Elsa.

The Rabbi turned to a young man who looked out of place for two reasons. First, he was formally dressed and wrapped in a prayer shawl, which also draped over the torah he cradled in his arms. Second, he looked completely unafraid.

"Did you bring it here like that?" Max hissed.

"Of course. I will not disrespect it," lectured the Rabbi.

"You might as well have put an advertisement in the *Berliner Morgenpost*. What am I supposed to keep this in?"

The Rabbi stared blankly. "We thought you would think of something."

"It might be years," Max railed at them. "Give it to me," he barked.

The young man looked to the Rabbi for confirmation.

"We are wasting time."

Max seized the treasure, shawl and all. He put it under his arm like a load of laundry. The Rabbi reached out to steady it, but *der Magier* was on the move.

"The rest?"

The small group moved, each revealing a suitcase or steamer trunk. One had a potato sack. Max shook his head.

"We brought it inside because it might rain."

"Until the *Wetterdienst* uses something other than Hitler's astrologers, we follow the plan. Out."

A truck started up in the alley.

"Damn! We're late. You want Ziegler to die in vain?"

All froze. Michael knew how secretly glad they were when the half-Jew baker volunteered to hold off the jackals. Each had their own version of the rationale. The baker had once told Michael softly the real reason. When this was over Michael would tell them all. Not now. It would waste more time and only shame them. He only hoped that, when this was over, there would be any left to tell.

"Move!" Max threw open the rear door to the stairs.

Obediently, the small crowd shuffled out. Michael stepped back to let Elsa go up first, but Max thrust him back onto the short steps. The outside door was already open and all could hear stomping feet and singing. The Brownshirts' coarse choir kept perfect time, punctuating each stanza with crash of shattering glass.

It was not a night for civilized behavior.

Someone murmured overloud, "How do we know we can trust him?"

"We don't."

Max whirled on the speaker. It was the Rabbi.

The mob's torches flickered off the end of the alley as the window at the back of the house bounced open.

"They're coming up *Göthestrasse*. Toward the *Vogelallee*," whispered Sonya.

Max looked for the driver and footsteps running up the alley told him the worst. He saw the others following the sound, tempted to follow.

"Everything in now!"

"Let me say goodbye to my child!" Elsa pushed forward with the desperate knot of six other mothers. The infants had been loaded while they were in the basement to make the separation sharp and quick.

"Too, late!"

Elsa screamed as if she was in labor again and clawed at Max. He started to shake her off, but saw Michael charging at them and had the good sense to let him pull his wife's convulsing body back.

Max grabbed the potato sack, heaved it with one hand into the back and placed the treasure on the top of one of the trunks of gold and silver adornments from six other temples.

"They must have seen us," cried a woman.

"Take us with you," panicked a man in even a higher register.

"Let me have my baby back!" screamed Elsa.

"Not in the plan," said Max. "Go home."

"Home? Through them?" The man's face was inhuman with panic.

"You'll think of something."

"Come inside. Quickly!" It was Sonya. Michael realized she was imitating Max. She learned fast. She'd survive. He was also relieved not to be tortured by urge to snatch their baby back.

Elsa flinched as Max slammed the tailgate of the old Mercedes truck. "Say Kadish for us." It was only a hopeless whisper.

Michael urged her toward the house with the rest of the sheep heeding their new shepherd.

The Rabbi lingered at the back of the truck. On tiptoe, he reached over the worn wooden gate to see the treasure one last time. He felt around the one open crate, patting one of the seven babies. They were the seeds. The Torah and adornments were merely fertile ground. *Der Magier* pushed the Rabbi toward the house's rear door and climbed in the front of the truck.

Still, the Rabbi couldn't resist touching the religious part of the treasure from seven synagogues again. The truck started with a cough and began to move. The Rabbi tripped a few paces after it.

At the end of the alley behind the truck, a Brownshirt scout turned the corner. He had heard the truck start. A truck at this hour was not so suspicious, but a truck with a Jew tripping behind it was a new target. The scout whistled to the others.

The Rabbi darted back toward the safety of the shadows and stopped. The Brownshirt scout was screaming to the others, pointing after the truck. The mob surged up the alley after it. It would have been a hopeless chase but the old engine gasped and died. The Rabbi saw the truck stop as the starter ground slower and slower. The jackals would be on it in seconds.

The venerable religious leader of over a thousand Jews in southern Berlin stepped out in front of the Brownshirts pouring around the corner. He straightened his tie and removed his hat, revealing the dark yarmulke on his bald skull. The mob stopped, confused. The Rabbi walked toward them squaring his shoulders to keep the jackals from seeing him tremble.

They used no clubs and it would take them some time to tear him apart.

The truck's starter had almost given up when Max saw another pack of Brownshirts blocking his escape to the street at the other end of the alley. He yanked the choke wide open and punched the starter to clear the flooded engine. The engine finally caught. He rammed the truck into gear and accelerated at the mob.

The jackals trampled each other to get out of the narrow alley, surging to the sides to avoid the charging truck. Even in the dark, Max could see the dark stains on their clothes. Some even had it smeared on their faces like war paint. If they were injured, they didn't act like it. Max steered toward the bricks at the back of an apartment building. The truck shuddered as it hit something soft and watery. A scream scraped along the wall.

He veered back to the center of the alley and put the end of the steel baton through the front teeth of the first jackal stupid enough to climb on the running board. He dropped the bloody metal between his legs and downshifted, turning right into the main street. He stomped the accelerator hard and popped the clutch. More bloody hands tore at the thin door. The engine wheezed but caught again. For a moment Max saw his own death, but the *Göthestrasse* ran downhill here and the truck accelerated.

Torches flew as the jackals scattered. The flames bounced off the shattered glass in the street, turning it into a sea of sparks that would give the night its future name.

The sparks outlined a figure too slow to move out of the way. Gunther Mährad stumbled in his torn *Gauleiter* uniform. The zealous Nazi leader of Treptow wanted to be in the front of the action, hoping it would be in the papers. Ziegler had caught him in the thigh with the oven scrape. The half-Jew baker would have split the Nazi's head, but his own blood had gotten into his eyes.

Max accelerated toward him and the *Gauleiter* went under the truck with a shriek. Max heard him dragging on the cobblestones across several streets until he reached the road south. The thuds of Mährad's body bouncing against the floorboards became softer as it turned into pulp. But it gave *der Magier* no satisfaction. Ziegler, the *Gauleiter* and the frightened Jews were the past and Max would stop thinking about those left behind in the past.

He had the future.

CHAPTER 2

26,500 feet over Berlin,
March 14, 1945, 2:16 P.M.

He tried to follow the speck and lost it for a moment. The sub-zero slipstream stabbed his eyes. Chauncey "Chance" Mitchell winced away tears, which froze instantly on his unfeeling cheeks. He concentrated and focused as the speck reappeared from behind the red icicles.

"109, eleven o'clock level," he tried to shout.

He prayed someone was still alive back there and heard him on the intercom. The enemy fighter would dive under them and swing up at the last second to rake the belly of APPLE PIE with cannon fire aimed at the B-17G's heart.

And there wasn't a damn thing he could do about it. Except watch, facing a firing squad at five miles up.

He tried to look left and it made him dizzy again. Something bad had happened. But he was still alive and wanted to stay that way.

The Nazi wingman was right where he feared it would be, attacking from the side to split their fire. The fighters should be firing by now. It was happening too fast. Why couldn't he think? He was cold and there was a constant thundering roar.

"Nine o'clock high!" He heard his own voice yelling in the distance.

The jackhammers started. The airframe vibrated then buzzed as all of the Browning 50-caliber machine guns opened up.

All but one. No sound came from the nose, except the roar.

Hot brass casings hailed behind him from the top turret. He lost the front fighter diving under them and twisted left for the other. The nose cannon flickered and APPLE PIE reeled, slammed from the left. Two massive concussions heaved him upward, dazing him for the second time on this run. The world drifted away and then screamed back.

"Oh, God!" The scream trailed to a moan.

It took Chance a moment to realize he wasn't the one screaming. He choked on the biting smoke. An electric whine behind him ground to a stuttering stop.

"The ball turret's jammed!" Jimmy Vernon, the radioman, still sounded like a boy. "I can't get to Joey."

"Jimmy, come on!" Joey pleaded over the intercom.

"Six low!" Satch's Minnesota twang warned softly.

"I'm bleeding. I can't find the bleeding! Oh, God, no!"

"Seven high!" Nebraska was calling in too.

"Where?" a calm voice intruded.

"Please! Please, it's bad!"

"Joey, shut up! Everybody calm down," Chance commanded. "Jimmy, do what you can."

The jackhammers rattled to life again.

"Fucking bastards!" Joey screamed.

"Where are they now?"

Chance knew that voice. At least he thought he did. He saw George "Nevada" Post's eyes smiling over the oxygen mask. Nevada reached over and felt around the back of Chance's head.

"Bingo."

He held up his glove smeared with blood.

"Not too bad."

Chance's mind wandered and the noise faded.

"Stay with me, buddy." Nevada shook him and held his gaze.

Joey screamed again and shuddered into sobbing.

"Somebody gonna help Joey?" Satch begged.

"I'm trying!" Jimmy hollered back.

"3 o'clock."

"Can't see him."

"It's stuck."

"I can't make it!"

"I'm coming, Joey."

"Use the fire ax!"

Shells hitting APPLE PIE drowned out the riot on the intercom. They tore at the airframe, splintering the thin aluminum. They stopped for only a second before someone yelled a warning over Joey.

"Coming again!"

"Where?! Where?!"

"God, it hurts!"

"Jimmy, get up here." Chance forced himself to be even.

Jimmy poked up in the cockpit as the jackhammers started again. Chance heard the attacking Messerschmitt ME-109 roar past with APPLE PIE'S 50-caliber breath hunting after it. A Nazi 17 mm shell punched through APPLE PIE, nicking the rudder control cable.

Chance tore off his oxygen mask and pulled Jimmy to him. The thin, cold air smelled of blood and hot metal.

"Jesus! You're hit!"

"It's nothing. Cut Joey's intercom."

Jimmy's child face showed every bit of the agony between duty and loyalty.

"But..."

"You can't help him. Cut the wires and get on the nose gun."

"It's gone."

Chance craned forward to look out the front windshield but the spider-webbed glass and red icicles made it impossible.

"Flak got us. It's what knocked you out," Nevada pronounced, searching through the shattered Plexiglas before he saw the fighters again. "Two low!"

Chance started to unbuckle and Nevada grabbed his arm.

"Oxygen. Before you pass out." His eyes caught something behind Chance. "Ten o'clock high!"

Chance yanked himself away and climbed out of his seat. It was against all regulations. The pilot stayed in his seat even if the plane was crashing – until everyone else was out.

The slipstream was a freezing blowtorch. The nose was gone and so was most of Kevin Shanley, his bombardier from LaGrange, Illinois. Kevin's legs were splayed on the shredded wall of the forward compartment, as if he had done a somersault and landed upside down on his head. Except there was no head. His bomber jacket held a frozen sack of gore that had been everything above his navel.

The nose of APPLE PIE was burst like a lily and Chance could see one of the arcing Messerschmitts rolling over and firing on the smoking BAILING WIRE, the only other plane left from their group. The machine gun jackhammers started again, sounding miles away.

He wasn't scared and realized he was altitude happy. He turned back to Jimmy.

"Cut the wires." He started to push past the radioman and stopped. "Tell him we'll help him as soon as we get clear. And try to get a bandage in to him."

Jimmy stared at him and then nodded.

Chance crawled back up to the seat and plugged back in to the intercom.

"…went left. Coming around."

"Got 'em."

"Seven level! Two of 'em!"

The chemical taste of the oxygen was better than the smell of the guns and Shanley's freezing body. He cleared his mind and started to remember.

"DROOPY DRAWERS spinning out of control," Shanley had calmly eulogized just before yelling about another pair of fighters coming in. The B-17 heaved up out of formation, inertia forcing it into a graceful arc as it rolled on to its back and started twisting down. Even diving full throttle, it would take several minutes for the plane to auger into a meadow. After two turns the men inside were trapped. The plane's spin would make them feel as if they weighed 400 pounds. They would whirl, unable to move, thinking about God knows what, knowing they were dead.

Then he woke up staring at the red icicles. They looked like Arab daggers. Bright crimson with flecks of yellow. Something out of a two reeler. In fact, they were out of Shanley's head. Blood and brains blasted out of the nose on to the shattered windshield and flash frozen at 30 degrees below zero into a graceful curve by the 140-knot thin air.

Chance wondered what memories he was looking at. He grabbed the shuddering control yoke. The jittering meant one of the tail control surfaces was shot up or one of the control wires was cut.

A speck dead ahead sprouted stubby wings and disappeared again below the shattered cockpit window, refracting in cracks around a ragged hole. No gun flashes. The Germans were almost out of bullets. They were almost out of everything now. They used what they had left carefully. Lethally.

Chance waited for the hammer blows and more screams on the intercom. Their group had been hacked down to two planes. They were alone and shot up. Easy prey.

"Five high!"

"Two of 'em again."

A jackhammer stuttered from somewhere in the back. Another and still one more joined it. APPLE PIE had three out of its six gunners left. Two 109s roared past. They were pressing closer, smelling two more kills.

"Jesus, that guy had brown eyes!" Satch with jokes again.

"They'll get us next time sure."

"Shut up!" Chance barked. "Call 'em and skip the chatter."

Chance's mind wandered drunkenly. He willed it to focus. The crew was shot up, inches from panic. Panic spread like clap in a plane. It was as deadly as the fighters and flak.

"How soon to primary, Jimmy?"

"Three minutes to primary," shuddered the radioman.

Jimmy was probably staring through the small hatch to the front of the plane and whatever was left of Shanley.

"How are we gonna know when t' drop?" the eighteen-year-old's voice lowered an octave, but still sounded like the barmaid at the Stave and Crown that Chance banged once in a while in Middle Wallop, England. "Kevin would..."

"We drop when BAILING WIRE drops. Count us down."

Chance made another effort to concentrate. If he passed out now, it would rattle the crew. They didn't really need Jimmy to count down. He just needed him busy studying his watch and the charts and not looking at half a man ten feet away across the bomb bay or thinking about his buddy in the ball turret, who was probably dead. Anyway, this stopped being a precision raid when the Nazis killed his bombardier.

Not that precision made any difference.

Half of Berlin was already flat. They were pummeling a country down on its face, but still not ready to surrender. Some had welcomed the Allies as they crossed the Rhine, glad the nightmare was over. In Berlin they were still driven by a mad demagogue and a terror of the approaching Russian tide.

American B-17s hit Berlin every day, followed by British Lancasters at night. Chance wondered who decided that. Maybe it was a toss of a coin.

"Two minutes." Jimmy sounded calmer now.

"109 six low." Nebraska spotted a speck coming out of the suburbs below.

"Where's the other?"

"Can't see him!"

"Look high, other side."

"Negative."

"Jesus, where..."

The guns started again. The fighter shot out ahead of them from under the plane. Two whacks punched through the aluminum skin. Some of the 109's wing gunfire had found its way into his airplane. *His* airplane. *Bastard.*

"Jimmy, you okay?" Chance knew the bullets had to have come through the radio compartment.

"Everything passed through." Jimmy was a soprano again.

Chance concentrated on the speck arcing left about two miles ahead of them. "He's gonna finish BAILING WIRE this time." Only one waist gun and the top turret on BAILING WIRE had tracked the fighter. The rest of her gun crew was dead or wounded. Heavy smoke was now trailing from the number two engine, which ground to a stop.

"Satch, put your gun on the left side."

After a moment Satch's Minnesota accent sang over the intercom. "Nevada, is Chance okay?"

"Right as rain," Chance tried to sound cool. They had less than ten seconds now. "My aircraft."

Nevada's eyes stopped smiling. "Okay. Your aircraft." He slid his hands off the control yoke, resting them on his knees just inches from taking control again.

Chance hadn't taken his eyes off the turning 109. The wingman had formed up on it. They would overwhelm BAILING WIRE. They were counting on the Americans staying true to formation tactics. BAILING WIRE would hide the fighters from APPLE PIE until the last seconds, only able to put two guns on them, one almost blinded by the smoke from the number two engine.

"They'll be coming on the left."

Chance was intent on watching the two growing spots. He thought he had lost them for a moment. He didn't see Nevada inching his hands back toward the yoke.

The spots disappeared behind BAILING WIRE. Chance waited a split second before pushing the throttles and yoke forward together. His left foot pushed on the rudder pedal. The nicked control line snapped and the pedal flopped uselessly.

"Kick left!"

Nevada obeyed and his hands twitched as APPLE PIE did a diving sideslip – a maneuver hard enough for one healthy pilot to coordinate.

APPLE PIE was dancing on the knife-edge of control and Chance pushed her harder, rolling the B-17 slightly. It wasn't really flying, but slicing through the air with all the elegance of a brick moving under BAILING WIRE.

"Got 'em. Ten high!" Satch understood the ploy.

The fighter pilots suddenly faced five guns: two on BAILING WIRE with the top turret and two waist guns pointing left out of the careening APPLE PIE. The sight of the slipping B-17 blocking their path must have startled the fighter pilots. No gun flashes appeared on their wings or noses.

Seven 50-caliber Browning M2 machine guns each sent 20 rounds per second across the quarter mile of thin air at the 109s. After just three seconds of the jackhammers, two orange cauliflowers erupted ahead and to the left of them. In a heartbeat they were behind them.

"Guys, those Krauts ain't gonna bother us anymore. BAILING WIRE owes us a round." Chance was shaking as he cleaned up APPLE PIE, bringing it back to level behind BAILING WIRE. It was like trying to dance with a drunk B-girl. They never let you lead. Nevada pitched in with the rudder control almost unconsciously. He was shaking his head when Chance finally looked over at him.

"We'll never collect. This is thirty-one."

After this mission, the crew of BAILING WIRE was headed home. They'd done their bit. Some accountant had figured out that after that many missions, crews were flying on borrowed time. It did no good for public morale to have no one go home in one piece. It was a secret, but anyone good at math could figure out that after just eight missions, they were all on borrowed time.

"Thirty seconds." Jimmy's one-boy choir was still counting time.

"Your aircraft," Chance whispered to Nevada.

Chance flipped a switch and a motor whined behind them. A pounding roar filled the bomber almost as loud as the howling hole in front of him. The plane slowed a little as the bomb bay doors opened. A green light showed the doors were all the way open. But Chance never trusted his life to little green lights.

"Jimmy, check the doors."

"Doors open, chief. Any time now." Jimmy was impatient.

Chance held the bomb release and watched BAILING WIRE. Slightly above them, he could see their doors were open, too. The engine fire seemed worse. The plane gave birth to twelve

500-pound bombs. Each was enough to level an apartment building. Once on a quiet trip back to England, Chance had started to figure out the casualties. A five story building with twenty-five apartments. Each with three people. He had stopped there.

He pulled the bomb release. APPLE PIE lurched up, suddenly free of three tons of steel and explosive. Chance had never seen his bombs hit. Or anybody's bombs. Sometimes the bombardier would. Maybe there was a memory of that hanging in front of him. Through the shell hole at his feet he could watch BAILING WIRE's stick as it took 72 seconds to reach some *Strasse* or another. This time he wanted to watch. Too bad nobody could be left alive down there.

He wished it were a virgin run with acres of tidy red or gray tile roofs that he could rape with his bombs. The steel would barely slow when they punched through. Even the detonator wouldn't notice. Chance imagined some Nazi huddled in the basement with his whore would hear the weapon boring through the five or six floors above them. The fins would strip off the bomb on the top floor; a clean shaft would hit bottom and...

"Shit." The plane lurched again as Nevada rocked the plane right and climbed.

Chance looked up to see BAILING WIRE's two wings flying in opposite directions, engines still turning. Between them was an expanding black blotch with a fading orange fireball center. Chance felt something hit his face as they flew through the edge of the debris. He thought he saw a man or part of one tumbling in space over them.

He looked back down for their bombs. He had lost them against the splotchy gray clutter of the ruined buildings. A flash of yellow caught his eye to the right. Rows of whitish flowers bloomed soundlessly on Berlin and crawled for the city's heart.

Chance looked ahead. It wasn't like he had imagined.

"We're done. Let's get out of here."

Nevada banked left for the rest of the formations, following their white contrails. There would be more fighters. They were alone and a long way from home.

And APPLE PIE's bombs still had thirteen seconds before they hit.

CHAPTER 3

*Friedrichstrasse, Berlin,
March 14, 1945, 2:31 P.M.*

It was the best time, but one had to be careful. The raid had already lasted an hour. Sonya could tell it was winding down. The drum beat anti-aircraft fire from the battery in the *Tiergarten* had stopped cracking and echoing off shattered walls. But there were always straggling bombers and the danger from unexploded anti-aircraft shells raining down. Once, a B-17 had spiraled into the street by *Unter den Linden*. The flaming fuel incinerated everything for one hundred meters. Just the heat had scorched her last dress. It was the first thing she had seen from America.

Sonya wiped a matted strand of black hair out of her face and knew there would be others waiting. The horse had been pulling a streetcar and was left hobbled in the madness. It had tried to run when the first stick of bombs stomped through the ruins across the wide boulevard. A supersonic shard from one of the bombs had caught it in the flank. The concussion of the same bomb had stunned it and knocked the animal over.

The horse's head moved, flicking off some of the dust that gave it a ghostly look. Sonya looked at the five other starving women sharing her cave, the steel arch of the collapsed department store entrance that gave them a false sense of safety.

"You will have to kill it." The older woman was polite, using the formal *Sie* address because Sonya would not tell her where she was from. She had spent the last six years living in the woods, sleeping in barns or cheap apartments. Always moving, she wasn't from anywhere. But the mystery impressed the old woman. She stopped asking. Either she had given up or she had made a guess about the unafraid woman from nowhere.

"Those of you who want eat have to help." Sonya was not polite, talking to the strangers like children, fixing each of them with dark eyes. They weren't really strangers. Each knew the other's mind. Hunger had a way of uniting people.

Still, no one volunteered. Sonya knew they had to start, before what sirens were left blew the all clear and the others came out of the shelters. Looking across the jagged, smoldering ruins, she had to wonder why anyone would come back up at all. At least she had a reason. A desperate hope and a promise.

She ran toward the horse ignoring the new rubble cutting through her shredded shoes. It was hard to see the animal. *Staubnebel,* the fog of dust hung in the air. Bomb impacts half a kilometer away would lift it from the street as the earth convulsed. It mixed with acid smoke swirled up from tires, furniture and bodies.

Sonya crossed the street. The horse turned to her, flopping its dust-gray head over to one side. Red mucus drooled out its muzzle. She would be doing it a favor. At least someone would be out of their misery.

She hid the knife, trying to move around behind the animal.

A bomb landed in the next block, the concussion pounding her chest. The next was farther away. The stick moved up the street, distracting the horse. She lunged.

Her first stab missed, sliding off the cut skin. The horse made a violent gurgling sound and tried to get up. Sonya straddled the neck as it came up between her legs, holding on to a fistful of mane. Her forty-five kilos was just enough to slow the animal. She stabbed again, unleashing a crimson fountain.

The thuds of more bombs fell on her ringing ears. One of the women called, but her voice was lost in the drawn-out roar of another blast.

To the devil with them if they won't help! She twisted the knife, widening the flow, soaking her bunched trousers. Weeks ago, Sonya took them from a body she had found outside the ruins of the *Gestapo* Headquarters in *Prinz-Albrecht-Strasse*. *Gestapo* or not, looting could get her shot by pimple-faced youths who still believed in the fairy tales spewed over the airwaves backed by scratchy phonograph recordings of martial music played by men long dead in lost lands. Not looting meant a certain death by starving.

Sonya had seen a man caught stealing from a storeroom of a fine department store in the *Alexanderplatz*. The troop of Home Guard, Hitler's last-ditch, child soldiers, was led by a boy of just seventeen. The man bargained for his life, offering each boy a share of the loot and more in the future. The boys agreed. Unfortunately, a less hungry SS officer arrived and the boys shot the man with their bellies full of caviar and tinned fish. The ones who survive this will be tough negotiators.

The horse defecated and stopped breathing.

Sonya moved quickly to the flank. She gouged into the flesh with the dull knife, pausing only to be sure the animal was dead.

Then her body was squeezed like a grape. Spit and dust flew out of her mouth as an anvil of hot air came at her from all sides. Orange and white glows played outside her closed eyes. Something brushed her cheek.

There was no sound. Only crushing pressure. Then it was gone.

Her emaciated breasts hurt and she couldn't breathe. She felt the burning sting of explosive smoke. The world was suddenly silent except for a ringing in her ears.

The first of APPLE PIE's twelve bombs had landed only a hundred meters behind her. The blast was partially deflected by the pile of rubble from a collapsed office building.

Sonya thought she was dying. Still she cut into the horse. The dazed knot of nerves in her solar plexus began to unravel as the second bomb hit the building across the intersection. She felt the impact through her feet as 500 pounds of steel and explosive burrowed thirty meters below the basement of a furniture store. And stopped.

Time slowed. She waited for the blast. It never came. One of thousands of duds that would terrorize Europe into the next century, it might explode tomorrow or years from now when someone disturbed the sleeping giant.

She realized she was breathing. Mostly smoke and dust but some air. She kept cutting as another blast threatened to rob her breath. Even at 150 meters around the corner, brick shards still ricocheted off the lamp posts.

A letter topped with a swastika landed in the dirty blood. More papers fluttered down. She noticed a word or two on the records as she used them to wrap the meat. Not exactly manna from heaven, but it would do. Little bits of lives useless to anyone.

The *Ausweisamt*, the Identity Bureau, had controlled those lives, processing the identity papers of the millions in the Greater Germany and their newly annexed lands. The papers determined your destiny. A typo could kill. A "J" only a few millimeters tall in a tiny box meant death as the Nazi state sought to cleanse itself of *Unmenschen*, non-humans. Birth and marriage records were searched and cross-indexed for any taint of Jewishness. A mistake could wipe out whole families.

Or save them.

The dust leapt from the cobblestones as another bomb from APPLE PIE pounded the city. Sonya heard only the ringing in her ears. She coughed, gagged and choked in the semi-darkness. What spit she had left was tinged with gray and black streaks. A drool of blood fell from her face. She touched her cheek and found a gash. Pittsburgh steel had sliced her face just below her left eye. It felt big and bled fast.

So this was hell.

She took another retch-producing breath. *Fine, I must live in hell.* She dug back into the horse as the street shook, threatening to open up. *But, how deep will I fall?*

The Berlin night sky had its perpetual orange glow. Not from gay streetlights but from huge fires burning until only stone was left and thousands of little fires. Each tiny fire meant a ration of light and warmth for about a dozen beings. The big fires belched smoke that reflected their light in a perfect setting for Wagner's *Götterdämmerung*, the twilight of the gods.

Sonya didn't think of the figures around her as people anymore. She avoided looking into their faces across the flickering sphere of hope. They had all become *Unmenschen*. They were competitors.

Sonya and the women had built the fire and barely singed the meat, before gulping it down. The smell of cooking flesh was everywhere. But the stench of bodies cremated in the rubble made the aroma of horseflesh that much sweeter. There were new gaunt masks around the burning desk.

Sonya's stomach didn't claw anymore. It was a numb ache that drove her. The ache was sated for tonight. A few of the ghosts chatted. There was another rumor the generals had killed Hitler and were suing for peace. People without hope had to counterfeit it. One fool still believed Germany would win.

"Impossible. It is simply impossible. Clay-headed Slavs will never overrun the pinnacle of human power that is Germany." The young woman spoke as if she was sipping coffee in her parlor after a creamy dessert.

"That *was* Germany." The grammar expert was out in the darkness.

"You'll be shot!" chirped the young woman, stabbing a finger toward the sound.

"Perhaps. But not by a German." The voice was male.

The young woman turned. A few people sat up. The after dinner floor show had begun.

"Why aren't you at the front? Fighting?"

"I am at the front, you cow."

The woman stood. The fire heightened her face, lined beyond its years.

"Come here where we can see you."

"Come here where I can touch you."

The woman froze. The grins were gone from the others. Fear opened eyes and flared nostrils. Sonya felt for the knife.

JITTERBUG LIFT

A figure moved in the darkness, just outside the glow of civilization. Sonya caught a glimpse of the man's eyes, but he would not come all the way into the light. She thought the eyes did not need the fire to work their magic. She had come all this way, risking everything to find him. She couldn't believe he would just walk out of the night.

"*Bitte Verzeihung.* I did not mean it that way. I simply do not believe you are real." The man's voice had authority, genuine regret and humor. He came into the light of the fire. Sonya's heart slowed. It wasn't *der Magier*.

"Good night."

Several women automatically replied. The figure moved again and was gone.

No one spoke until a splinter of wood cracked in the fire. The young Nazi woman gasped and everyone laughed. Sonya was amazed she could laugh too.

The rumble came out of the east. Some looked to the sky, hoping for a spring shower to give fresh water, but expecting the British Lancasters. The rumble growled around at the edge of their hearing. Sonya still couldn't hear anything softer than a loud conversation.

"What do you hear?" she asked the fire.

"Rain, I hope," said the polite old woman. She had treated the gash on her cheek and told Sonya she would have a scar.

Others around the fire said it was anti-aircraft guns. A young girl was certain it was a raid on a distant heap of rubble that bore a city's name.

"It's the Russians." The man's voice of authority came out of the dark again and ended the talking for the night except for a whisper from the polite old woman to Sonya.

"If they find out who you are, they will hang you."

CHAPTER 4

*US Army Air Corps Field Middle Wallop,
England, April 26, 1945, 6:08 A.M.*

"Gear up."

Off to Chance's left, the sunrise was warming from red in the ground fog to full yellow as APPLE PIE TOO bumped off the mud ruts into a velvet blue spring sky. The last jolt was the filled-in crater at the end of the long grass strip. THREE'S A CHARM had plowed in two days after Chance had flown in from Africa in 1944. The battered plane had limped back from Schweinfurt on two engines and a shot-up rudder only to pitch up and stall seconds from safety. A 500-pound bomb stuck in the bomb bay had exploded in the fire, vaporizing the rescue crew and any survivors. Two days later, a pilot who had returned from a raid with his headless copilot next to him had gone into the woods at the edge of the air base for some peace and found a fire suit helmet with one of the rescue crew's head still in it. He calmly brought it back to the base hospital and asked if there was anything they could do for the poor guy. Maybe sew it on his dead buddy's body.

The gear motors whined to a stop and Chance banked toward the circling formation that was his group. The newly-healed wound at the back of his head nagged him with the drop in air pressure as they passed through 1500 feet. He had discovered that on his first mission back on duty and wondered how long it would last.

After the routine checks of the B-17's engines, controls and systems, Chance gave Nevada the yoke and allowed himself the luxury of looking out at the English countryside. Fog undulated across the deep green Hampshire downs. A smoky finger pointed out a red brick farm house, its slate roof mottled in yellow moss. They banked toward Winchester Cathedral. The spires had often provided a bright yellow beacon in the morning light to line up the group. The town council had requested that the hordes of bombers not fly directly over the medieval relic. The daily thunder of a thousand Wright Cyclone engines was too much for the delicate stained glass.

Chance caught himself thinking about life after the war. It wasn't that he was superstitious. He could control what happened to him. But to do that, he had to keep his mind on his job. The war was thundering to a climax. The Russians were knifing through the Berlin suburbs. Rumors had Hitler fleeing to South America or Switzerland. The Nazi Luftwaffe had all but vanished. All but. One of the few surviving ME-262 jets had cost Chance's group two planes three days ago. He did not want to have the honor of being the last casualty in the long and bloody war.

Still, his mind wandered again. He had always dreamed about his wheels touching down for the last time, keeping an even number of takeoffs and landings. The last engine would stop and the plane would be quiet after eight hours. He would look around the cockpit for his things and be the last one off.

Strolling away from the oil and plinking of the cooling engines, he would find a place in the grass and sit down. He'd stare at nothing, seeing everything for the first time. He had no idea how long he would be there, but it would be a while.

The chalk cliffs marked the south coast of England with a white ribbon only ten minutes after Winchester slipped under the left wing. When Chance and Nevada had arrived in England after D-Day, this had been the edge of the war. Now, they were still out of range of enemy fighters and flak, heading for newly liberated France, Holland and Belgium. Even most of western Germany was under Allied control. But there was still shooting. And people were still dying.

"I'm thinking a nice fat Dakota would be the ticket." Nevada barged into Chance's thoughts, acting as if he owned them.

"How do you figure that?" Chance felt the updrafts along the cliffs through his seat.

"Cargo. New way of gettin' things around. Everybody only thinks a' trains now. I heard one of those babies can haul in four tons."

"What do the railroads charge for four tons?"

"Dunno. But we'd be faster. New York to Frisco in a day or so. Not three or four. And there's mail. Maybe Mexico and South America."

Chance liked the idea of that. Nobody shooting at you. Drinks and steak dinners in some beachside cantina, charming the local girls. It also meant hours of long-haul flying, bad weather and getting out of airports that have no more than a suggestion of a runway.

"Where's home base gonna be?" Nevada's smile said he'd at least let Chance pick that.

Chance's face froze. "Let's win the war first."

Nevada winked and flashed his eternal grin.

"Sure."

Chance shook off Nevada's nagging question. They were passing through 10,000 feet. He took back control of the aircraft with a nod to Nevada.

"Oxygen, boys," he put on his pilot's voice with the oxygen mask. He must never scream or yell. It would only come out garbled over the intercom and it would rattle the crew. They had to do their jobs knowing there was somebody up front who was in control. Watching over them. Making sure they got home safe.

They were almost at the turning point, out over the English Channel. They could see the church spires in France dead ahead. The towns appeared undamaged. Sometimes Chance could see roofless houses or rubble in the streets. But he could never see the cratered lives and shattered people. It was miles away and in another world down below.

"Check your guns." Chance settled into the routine, hoping it would keep away the tantalizing thoughts. The Nazis had nicknamed B-17s *fliegende Stachelschweine,* "flying porcupines." APPLE PIE TOO shuddered as the crew fired a few short bursts to check their barbs. The intercom stuttered a litany of "Checks" and "A-Okays." Chance only recognized Jimmy Vernon, their radio man's voice. He and Nevada were the only ones left. Chance had never seen the horrible things a bomb could do. Only how his crew had been ripped apart one by one a few feet away.

"Turning point." Mike Olson, the bombardier, was all business. He had survived 28 missions in five other aircraft. Chance thought of him as *the* bombardier. Not *his* bombardier.

Chance brought the B-17 left to 070, straight for the Reich Chancellery in downtown Berlin. A few months ago there had been dozens of waypoints in between as the river of TNT snaked around flak and fighter strong concentrations.

For some reason, Chance thought of Shanley as they crossed the French coast at Sainte-Cécile Plage. The beach town looked untouched. At 26,000 feet, Chance was cold despite his heated flight suit. Dazzling white contrails led to the rest of the raid. He and Nevada would not say much, keeping the intercom clear. He had heard of other pilots who sang or told stories and jokes. But they were all dead.

Overcast began to hide the spring fields below. On the last raid Chance could tell where the war was. The fields were not plowed and had a rough green-brown look. He welcomed the clouds, the climbing fighters would stick out against them.

The navigator, Eddie Nazar, had just reported they were fifteen minutes from crossing into Germany near Wesel, when Jimmy popped up into the cockpit, breathless from the thin air and the news he had.

"We've been recalled! The Russians are in Berlin!"

"Are you sure?"

"Yeah. They sent it in code. And now they're sending it over and over in the clear!"

Nevada slapped Chance's shoulder. "Look."

Ahead and all around them the arcing, white contrails showed the formations turning left for home.

"Eddie, get me a course back to base." Chance tried to keep the elation out of his voice. There was an indescribable feeling surging out of his soul and he knew it was dangerous.

"268, chief." The navigator only took a half second to answer. Evidently, word had spread around the plane faster than the intercom.

"Get back on oxygen and tell everybody we're coming to 268."

Jimmy ducked out of the cockpit. Chance keyed the intercom.

"Okay. We're heading back. But let's save the party for Beebee's."

A chorus of screams and hoots turned the intercom into a painful, raspy howl.

"Can it!" Chance's bark was lost in the din.

It was so unbelievable that, for over a second, Chance's mind could not register what was happening. SAYER PRAYERS was leading his formation across APPLE PIE TOO's nose. In seconds, nine B-17s in loose formation were filling the windshield. In another second Chance and his group were in the formation. The cheering on the intercom turned into a riot of calls.

"Jesus! B-17! He's right..."

"He's diving!"

"...coming up."

APPLE PIE TOO lurched violently left, twisting right with a loud bang followed by a grating roar. The yoke was ripped forward out of Chance's hands. It felt like Gene Krupa was doing "Sing, Sing, Sing" on the airframe with pile drivers. A shadow blotted out the sun passing over the cockpit and the overhead exploded.

Chance ducked instinctively as shards of metal ricocheted off his head and the instrument panel. A giant sword sliced between him and Nevada. He could feel the air slammed out of the way. When he sat back up, the other B-17 was twisting left away from them. The number four engine tore away as the bomber pitched up and over to the right. The rest of the right wing beyond the number four mount snapped away. The broken Fortress went over on its back and began to spiral down. Chance wrenched his fascinated attention away and scanned his instruments.

Nevada saw it first. "Three's flying apart." The gaping hole over their heads made it hard to hear.

"Feather three." Chance craned past Nevada to see the prop wobble to a stop. Two blades were badly mangled and one was completely gone. The nacelle was torn off the top and the engine was obviously hanging down. Behind it a ten-foot gash tore through the wing to where the right aileron vibrated, ripped from its support. White fuel vapor streamed out of several points on the gash.

"Pull the bottle on three." Chance focused on keeping control of APPLE PIE TOO. The flapping aileron wanted to violently yank Chance's plane left.

"Find out what else is hit and get back here."

Nevada unbuckled and headed aft.

Chance keyed the intercom. "Check your chutes, boys. But sit tight. Jimmy, get up here."

Jimmy leaned into the cockpit ducking around the shredded aluminum. "Tony's hurt."

"Listen up. Get on to the group and tell 'em we're hit, but still flyable."

Jimmy ducked out without a word. He had grown up. His face showed none of the terror it should have.

"Ernie, start checking our position every minute. And give me how far to the coast."

"Coming up, chief."

Nevada pushed the torn metal from the screaming gash out of the way to climb back into his seat as the navigator answered.

"Ten minutes."

"Okay. Any alternates before that?" Chance knew he was fishing. Most airfields on the Continent were still picking up the pieces. There was no radio set up yet and the solid overcast below ruled out searching for a runway.

"Nothing before Manston. It's right on the English coast. Come to 266."

Normally, Chance would just have to touch up the bearing, but APPLE PIE TOO steered like a dazed prizefighter.

For once, Nevada sounded grave. "One and two are running okay. Not sure about four, but we're holed on both sides. Tony was in the top turret. He caught Plexiglas in the face. Pretty bad. He can't see."

Chance looked left to see a propeller blade from the aircraft that hit them stabbing into the wing between the two engines. A sheen of leaking fuel was visible on the top of the wing.

"Pappy says it's pouring out the bottom," Nevada added.

The ball turret gunner had a front row seat to watch APPLE PIE TOO bleed to death.

Chance let Nevada take control of the bucking B-17. He needed to think and knew he didn't have to ask his copilot. Bailing out was always the most dangerous. With the overcast they would have no certain idea where they were coming down. But if they sunk below 5,000 feet, that was out and they were committed to staying with the plane. The fuel gauge was ticking steadily down. The clouds still blocked finding a field to land in. Chance saw it was thinning back toward the coast. If the wing snapped they would have only seconds to get out.

"Ernie, give me minimum fuel to make Manston."

"88." The navigator had anticipated the question.

"At the coast?"

Chance imagined his options like girls primping before him. The ugly one was ditching in the Channel. Big and buxom was landing at Manston with fuel to spare. But her bust line was deflating as she aged fast.

"75 from the coast if we lose the bomb load and you land on fumes. It'll be 27 minutes."

Chance tapped the fuel gauge. It showed 100 if he looked at it from the right angle, but was dropping fast. Ahead, only gray water showed beyond the overcast. The right wing was holding but number three was wobbling. Chance wondered what it would take with it if it tore away.

"We got to slow down."

Nevada throttled back to 175 knots and Chance hit the bell twice.

"Bail out stations. But keep the hatches closed. When can we jettison?"

"Five minutes."

Losing 4,000 pounds would help things a lot. But dropping now could obliterate some village just getting used to peace. Turbulence shook APPLE PIE TOO as it sank. Chance thought the right wing fluttered more than the left. Jettisoning the bombs would lessen the stress on it besides lowering their fuel consumption.

"Think we're gonna get wet?"

"Don't get your bathing suit out yet." For once Chance was the optimist.

"Fuel's going." Nevada nodded at the instrument panel.

The fuel gauges were flirting with zero when number four sputtered.

"Feather four."

The overcast was still solid below them. One and two began to choke.

"Feather one and two."

"You're over the coast." Ernie's voice was clear as APPLE PIE TOO died and became a 19-ton glider.

England was tantalizingly clear, 80 miles ahead. Chance keyed the intercom.

"Jettison." Landing in Manston withered to an old crone.

"Roger, Chief. Bomb doors." Mike was the old pro.

APPLE PIE TOO slowed and sunk faster as the bomb doors entered the slip stream. The altimeter was a crazy clock.

"Bombs away."

The B-17 lurched up as the bombs fell out of her belly. Chance was expecting the whine of the doors closing but there was loud bang and grating noise.

"Christ, what was that?" Chance checked the right wing. It was still fluttering and attached. In the almost silent aircraft, Chance heard Mike clambering aft to the bomb bay. There was some shouting before Mike appeared in the cockpit.

"A 250 is stuck. The collision warped the bomb racks."

"Can we close the doors?"

"No. Its nose is in the slipstream and it's armed."

Normally a small propeller in the bomb's nose would spin as the bomb fell, arming it. That propeller spun in the air roaring past the mortally wounded B-17. It and the bomb doors were dragging APPLE PIE TOO down at 500 feet per minute.

"Jimmy, tell Command we're ditching and get everybody in there ready. Ernie, give Jimmy our last position."

Chance punched the bell six times. Most of the crew moved to radio compartment just behind the upper turret. The tail gunner would join them. But the radio operator would remain at his post. Nevada checked his window making sure it would slide open. Chance did the same. He could make out the white caps on the Channel coming up fast and banked the plane to land parallel to the wave crests. The right aileron was becoming fidgety. If APPLE PIE TOO landed with one wing down, it could cartwheel.

The white caps were racing past now.

"It won't blow," Nevada pronounced.

"Even if it doesn't we'll still sink fast." Chance fought with the yoke. "Jimmy, open the hatches."

"On it, Chief. Make it a good one."

"Flaps." Chance was now wrestling with the plane. It lurched, banking hard right.

"No dice on flaps. Right one's jammed." Nevada pulled the lever back. They were going to land fast.

"Help me." Chance had his eyes fixed on the horizon.

Nevada pitched in with the yoke. The two men flew the plane as one. A glance at their airspeed told Chance they were going to hit very hard. He held the bell down for several seconds.

Sea spray hit the windshield. They heaved back on the yoke. APPLE PIE TOO's nose came up slowly and there was the first impact. The plane's tail hit the water and it wanted to pitch back forward. But Chance was determined to be the master of his aircraft. They held the nose up as long as they could.

APPLE PIE TOO stalled and slammed into the water.

CHAPTER 5

*25 Miles Off Domburg, Holland,
April 26, 1945, 9:12 A.M.*

Chance couldn't remember how he got out the window. He met Nevada crawling up on APPLE PIE TOO's back near the shattered top turret. Hands were stretching out the radio compartment escape hatch and Nevada took one, pulling out Ernie. Chance grabbed the next pair and hauled out Pappy, the thirty-year-old ball turret gunner. The two rafts were already in the water but the men waited on either side as Tony was lifted out. His face was crudely bandaged and he felt for arms and hands to grab onto.

As Pappy and Ernie eased him down to the raft, the radio compartment hatch was clear for a moment and Chance could hear water flooding in. He could also feel the plane rapidly sinking. Yelling echoed inside, but no one else came out.

"Come on!" Chance screamed down.

"Jimmy's trapped." The face of Kaminsky, the engineer, briefly appeared in opening and then disappeared. Chance could hear Jimmy panicking, giving short cries of terror.

"Everybody out! Now!"

The water was over halfway up the sides of the fuselage. Air was blasting out the windows and gun turret. The rest of the crew scrambled out and into the rafts.

Chance swung his legs into the opening.

"You only got seconds, Chance."

Chance damned Nevada for stretching the truth and jumped inside.

The water was up to his waist. As his eyes adjusted to the darker interior he could see Jimmy pinned against the left side of the radio compartment with the radio equipment rammed into his lap by the 250-pound bomb. The impact had thrust the bomb backward through the rear of the bomb bay and into the compartment. Jimmy's eyes were twin searchlights in the gloom.

"Don't leave me."

"I won't. Can you push against this shit?"

Jimmy tried and Chance grabbed on the raw, torn metal, cutting his hands deeply. The water was at Jimmy's chest and rising. The plane groaned and shifted left sharply, putting the water under his chin. He screamed. Chance grabbed Jimmy by his life preserver and stretched him out of the water.

"Nevada! Get me the ax."

It was a long second before the handle appeared in the hatch and Nevada swung his legs down.

"Stay out and get clear if she goes."

Nevada only nodded and pulled his legs back out.

"Don't leave me! Don't leave me!" Jimmy struggled against the metal cutting into his chest through his vest. Blood filled the water. He didn't seem to notice the blood.

Chance hooked the sharp end of the ax head into the shredded bulkhead and heaved. The bomb moved a fraction but seawater also poured in faster. Jimmy was choking and thrashing. Chance hacked at the bulkhead, ignoring the sparks as the ax banged the steel shell surrounding 150 pounds of high explosive.

The first wave came through the hatch.

"Chance! She's going!" Nevada was at the hatch again. He grabbed at Chance, who shook him off. He took two more cracks at the wreckage.

"Chance!"

Water began to pour in the hatch. Jimmy screamed.

Jimmy was staring right at him when Chance caught him on the left side of the head with the ax handle. The boy was instantly still. Chance turned to face Nevada who had his hand out, almost underwater himself. Chance let himself be delivered from APPLE PIE TOO.

They ran up toward the turret and jumped into the raft with Tony, Pappy and Ernie. The other raft was paddling some fifty feet away. They cut the line tying them to the sinking plane and rowed to get out of the suction.

APPLE PIE TOO gasped and was gone. Chance saw her damaged wing slip below the surface.

"Let's get to the other raft." Nevada's whisper was swallowed by the waves.

"Did Jimmy get out okay?" Tony stirred in the silence.

No one answered.

"Jimmy?"

Nevada leaned over to Tony.

"No."

"Aw, geez. He was a nice kid. A real nice kid."

Chance looked out to sea. Nevada put himself between Tony and Chance.

"Why didn't he get out?" Tony was persistent.

Chance saw Nevada grab Tony's arm and whisper something. Tony nodded and didn't mention Jimmy again.

It was early afternoon when a Dutch fishing boat picked them up. The crew was mostly girls and two young boys. The crew was happy to see the girls. The weather-beaten captain offered his best beer to the men and was very curious about what had happened. Unfortunately, his English was good and he pressed Chance for the story. Nevada kept the girls at bay and deflected the old man's questions until they got to shore.

A British Army officer picked them up and they were back in England when it was announced that Hitler had committed suicide. The celebration delayed Chance's debrief.

When he finally sat down with a jovial lieutenant it was a lovely spring day with the trees blooming. The windows of the Quonset hut were open and the scent of the flowers drifted inside. It was over an hour before they got to the hard question.

"What happened to James Vernon?"

Chance told him the truth.

CHAPTER 6

*Reims, France,
May 7, 1945, 2:41 AM*

Admiral Friedeberg and General Jodl arrived at the schoolhouse headquarters for Allied Supreme Commander General Dwight D. Eisenhower, expecting to see him. The German general's boots scuffed the plain wood floor as he strode into the assembly hall and snapped to attention. Eisenhower was not there.

After a brief exchange of salutes, the general addressed the Allied commanders in excellent English, "We have not seen the terms of surrender."

"There are no terms." One of the commanders nodded toward a brief document with a pen lying beside it.

The German general scanned the faces of the American, British and French officers on the other side of the table. He did not dare to look into the eyes of the Russian witness. He stepped forward smartly and signed. The Admiral signed after him.

General Jodl asked for permission to speak. "With this signature, the German people and Armed Forces are, for better or worse, delivered into the hands of the victors. In this hour I can only express the hope that the victor will treat them with generosity."

No one answered him.

The General was running scared for good reason. After Hitler's suicide at the end of April, the rump German government had quibbled over terms, hoping to get as many refugees fleeing the Russian onslaught to the relative safety of areas captured by the US, British and French. Soldiers were still dying and Eisenhower's threat to close Allied lines to refugees dragged Jodl to the schoolhouse to face the four powers.

The French had borne the brunt of two invasions by their belligerent neighbor to the east in the last half-century. They planned to relegate Germany's industrial might to the scrap heap and history books. Germany would become a purely agrarian land. It would have to fight the next war with butter, cheese and flour.

The British ambivalently planned to go home. Nazi bombing had crippled industry and her empire was not able to support the sceptered isle. Rationing would last for years.

The Americans also had a hankering to go home. They had been yanked across the ocean for the second time in less than fifty years to shove the German evil genie back in its bottle. There were calls, shared with all the other victors, for punishing reparations. The calls became a riot as the sordid details of the Nazi *Endlösung*, the "Final Solution," redefined barbarity.

That would leave Germany to the Russians. They had suffered terribly. From Leningrad in the north, to Stalingrad on the Black Sea, the Nazi war machine had plunged deep into the Soviet heartland.

The Soviets had their own ideas about punishing the Germans. After the surrender, Stalin joked that his Army had fought hard and "deserved a little fun."

CHAPTER 7

*Felsenstrasse 17, Soviet Occupied
Berlin, July 20, 1945, 6:22 P.M.*

"Anna Niederhauer?"

Sonya heard the floor creak inside the apartment. Knocking had produced no results. The floor squeaked again near the door.

"I have been sent by the Housing Authority." Sonya spoke closer to the door, trying not to sound desperate.

The other side of the door remained silent. Sonya played her trump card.

"I have food."

The lock clattered and the door opened a crack.

"Are you alone?" The voice was girlish, almost melodic, but fear soured the melody.

"Yes." Sonya held up the document. "I have an order."

Anna reached through the crack and snagged the paper with two fingers. With almost half of the city's population homeless, the occupiers had set up a system of assigning those without a roof to those who had one. Anyone with an apartment, home or even unused office had to take someone in. They weren't asked. The defeated were told by the victors.

"Ziegler?" Anna uttered the name with one blue eye pressed to the crack.

"Yes."

Sonya knew why this would be the stumbling block, but she had to operate in the open, under her own name. It was her only hope.

"I do not know…"

"Do you want the Russians to come here and tell you? They may want to find someone as pretty as you."

"Do not be disgusting." The door closed a fraction.

Sonya weighed her options. She could force the door, but it could be useless if Anna was not the one. Still she had to know.

"I just do not want you to be in trouble with the Russians." She played her last trump card. "They find Nazis even where there are none."

The door waivered and opened. Anna glanced out in the dark hall, still wary. Then she stepped back. She was the picture of defeated Aryan purity. Unwashed blonde hair was plastered to her pale skin. Sapphire blue eyes made an effort to scan Sonya. Anna's wide hips promised many children for the fatherland, but had not lived up to Hitler's demand.

Sonya saw it as soon as she entered. The telephone was set on a table just around the wall from the door. Clean finger holes in the dial, free of dust, revealed recent use as did the wires tidily connected to the wall socket. In most of Berlin such an extravagance had long been sold on the black market or traded for food.

"You said you had something to eat."

Yes, Anna must have a very good reason to have the phone. She was the key to everything.

It was almost a week before the first call came. Sonya was closest to the telephone, but Anna pushed her away and answered it herself. Her hand over the mouthpiece, Anna told Sonya she wanted to have some privacy. In the small apartment, it was not hard to hear the code words. The second call, a few days later, confirmed the code. Anna took messages and relayed them when others called in.

Sonya practiced Anna's high pitched sing-song voice, learning her accent and slang. She deftly probed for information on where Anna had grown up. It took some doing as Anna made it clear she did not like living with a Jew.

One steamy afternoon in August, Anna lost her temper over Sonya spilling the water they had hauled up from the street hydrant. Her rant quickly turned from the spilled water.

"I never believed you were sent here by the Housing Authority. You lied! Just like all the Jews! I am going to check on you!"

Sonya already knew how Anna got to her job at a hotel for the Allied military leaders and the press. She had learned Anna's schedule and when she would pass a particular stretch of bombed out buildings.

Sometimes alone.

CHAPTER 8

*Felsenstrasse 17, Soviet Occupied Berlin,
August 21, 1945, 11:08 A.M.*

The hand crushed her right shoulder again, dragging her back down the stairs. Sonya lashed her arm behind her, slamming solidly into sweaty flesh. The hand relaxed slightly and she broke free. The Russian slurred a curse and lunged after her. Despite being drunk, the officer was able to snag her ankle. She crashed forward into the wooden stairs. He twisted Sonya's ankle, wrenching her hip and flipping her over.

She had lost one shoe but her bare heel broke the giant man's nose anyway. He bounced down the wall, snapping the banister. Sonya clawed her way back to her feet, but her twisted ankle slowed her. She made it to the next landing before he tackled her, all 120 kilos mashing her into the floorboards. Splinters bit through her summer blouse into her breasts. He was tearing at her bottom and her underwear cut into her vulva before giving way. She felt his hard penis poking at her. Her fingernails chewed at the wood, trying to get out from under the bull. She kicked backwards, mostly hitting the wall and only allowing him to spread her legs further.

Then he stopped.

"*Nyet*," he pronounced, final, like a death sentence.

Sonya was only confused for a moment. His arm speared under her waist, seizing the shreds of her dress and spinning her over. Her arms and legs lashed out. His smile only flinched when she punched him. He jammed his knee into her groin, splaying her legs. His full weight crashed down on her and blood poured out of his smashed nose onto her face. His left hand clenched her throat pressing down on the arteries to her brain.

The world receded, surrounded by a black haze. Her thrashing weakened as his other hand grabbed his penis. He stopped, loosening his grip on her throat just a little.

"Ny…ny…" he tisked.

As she was coming around, he leered and thrust.

The world exploded back into Sonya's mind. A relentless pressure stabbed into her groin. A wave of pain rammed between her legs and twisted her body, shrieking out of her mouth. He laughed and thrust again.

"Petrov! Yuri! Cerilli!" He pounded her pelvis into the floor and slurred each name from a bloody mouth. He started a fourth name and roared. The Russian arched backwards, spasming.

Sonya was finally able to throw him off. He fell back against the wall, laughing. Her gut convulsed and she doubled over as the vomit surged toward her throat. He stopped and stared at her. She tensed.

"Ivan." He held up a finger and counted out the four names. "Petrov. Yuri. Cerilli. Ivan." His eyes turned sad for an instant and then he laughed again. He pushed himself up the wall and fumbled with his pants. He did not look back at her before lurching back down the stairs.

Part of Sonya fled. Her mind split in two and most went to a safe place she had developed during the years of cold, hunger and fear during the war. The fields were blooming. Trees swayed in the wind as waves of grass hurried to the horizon. The warm sun bathed her skin.

The other part of her mind carried her battered body up the stairs.

The Russian officer picked his way through the ruined *St. Maartens Krankenhaus*. The path ahead was blocked by a huge crater. At the bottom, rain water reeked of burned wood and rotting corpses. He stopped to hike his trousers again. Wiping congealing blood from his nose, he accidently moved it. His head lurched back from the punch of pain. He detoured left around the crater and hurried across a clear path in the broken bricks that was *Barken Allee*, brushing past a pair of armed Soviet soldiers before they could salute. He moved better now. The drunk was wearing off, but it was bringing pain.

He stopped when he heard a noise in a maze of broken walls and scorched concrete. He was lost. Rubble was piled like snowdrifts against the ruins. It looked the same no matter where he turned. He tried to get his bearings from the sun, but he had forgotten where it was while he was chasing Sonya. This part looked familiar, but he wasn't sure if he had run this way before the rape or if he was only going in circles. Still, the large officer moved on until he heard the noise a second time. He cocked his throbbing head, listening. After a moment, he snorted a laugh through his mashed nose and instantly regretted it.

The Russian saw the woman as he stepped around a wall that had enclosed a child's bedroom. Dancing elephants and a giraffe were painted over bright green trim. She was curled on her side in a dark overcoat. A babushka covered her head. All was covered in mortar dust. The overcoat was too heavy for the summer weather and it flapped in the slight breeze revealing bare feet. The Russian stopped, studying her. There was no sign of life and the woman's face was away from him, buried in the red and gray shards. The Russian had seen plenty of the starving and dead since arriving in Berlin. The heavy coat said she had been there since the spring. He had no desire to abuse his nose further, and moved downwind around the body, giving it only one glance before hurrying on.

He took one step beyond the form and screamed. Sonya twisted the knife in the back of his left knee and ripped it sideways, cutting the officer's tendons. He toppled forward as the knee buckled out to the left, the joint tearing to the side instead of front to back.

Her weight was on his back for only a second. The Russian heaved himself, trying to throw her off, but she was already gone. He twisted over despite the pain and fumbled for his holster. He found only the cut leather lanyard that had held his pistol.

Sonya ripped the babushka from her head, shaking her hair free. Her first shot hit him in the upper thigh. She had missed her target, but the impact rippled out, crushing one testicle. The Russian folded up, grabbing his groin with one hand while the other flailed around to ward off more bullets. His mouth gaped but could not scream. The shock had paralyzed his diaphragm.

Sonya was careful and followed her training. But she would allow herself one personal act. Something to tell the rest of her when it came out of hiding. The Russian rolled on to his right with his left leg flopping uselessly below the knee. He was trying to get up and she kicked him back over at the shoulder. He landed half on his back and half on his side with his left foot under his buttocks.

Sonya aimed at his forehead. He tried to lift his arm, but the shock was fighting the adrenalin.

"*Nyet.*" She mimicked his pronouncement perfectly.

The gun swung down. Her aim was perfect as she counted out six shots. The first obliterated his penis. The second emasculated him completely. His body lurched back as the next three chewed up the gore. In no hurry, she fired each shot carefully, waiting for him to squirm to a stop after a new round slammed into him. She flicked the Tokarev TT-33 slightly up and to the left and sent the last 7.62 mm round into the Russian's navel. Anything but a *coup de grâce*, the shot ensured that the rapist would die slowly in agony.

Sonya dropped the empty weapon at gurgling man's feet and made her way through the ruins. She was twenty meters away when the Russian tried to scream. It faded quickly to a whimpered plea.

The Soviet colonel marched up the wooden stairwell of *Felsenstrasse* 17 as if on May Day parade. His new adjutant kept pace, two steps down and just to the left of the colonel's swinging arm. The adjutant's eyes were locked forward. It was his first hour with the colonel and he had already learned to not be caught staring at the back of his superior's neck and head.

The noise sounded like a platoon to Sonya. She had been expecting the Russians to question everyone within a kilometer of the newly-minted Russian eunuch. When no one appeared after three hours, she knew there would be no questions. The Russians would never ask about things they already knew.

A horse-drawn streetcar rumbled by as she passed the open window to the north. For over fifty years it had never seen the sky. The Allied bombing had demolished *Felsenstrasse* 27 and provided the apartment with an instant view of the Berlin warscape. An old man shuffling down the rubble-lined street toward her building stopped suddenly and darted across the roadway. He didn't like something in front of her building.

She scanned the apartment again. Everything was ready. She had already jeopardized her mission. Now she had to save it.

The marching stopped. The knock was two sharp raps. Something hard, maybe steel. Sonya froze in the center of the room. A fetid breeze moved the curtains, bringing the scent of undiscovered corpses.

Two more raps. Louder.

"*Aufmachen!*" The accent was perfect and conveyed no irritation. Only absolute power.

"Soviet Military Security. Open the door at once."

The shadows under the door shifted as Sonya reached for the key. She opened the door and stood back, favoring her twisted ankle. The colonel leaned forward to charge in, but hesitated. Sonya was by the window. The daylight highlighted her form. A glittering diamond of sweat ran down her throat to linger on her chest before plunging down between her breasts.

The colonel finally strode in with the adjutant at his heel. As the adjutant closed the door, a look of terror convulsed Sonya's face.

"Not again, please."

The adjutant did not understand German and looked to his commander. Sonya backed toward the tiny kitchen area. The adjutant spotted a knife on the counter and drew his pistol.

"Help!" she screamed.

The colonel barked in Russian, keeping his gaze on Sonya. The young officer obeyed at once. He holstered his pistol and reopened the door, coming to attention on the right to leave it unblocked.

"There," the colonel pronounced. "You have nothing to fear."

"Women have been raped on the street in broad daylight." Sonya's terror hardened.

"Yes. The streets are very dangerous. When a fire has blazed so hot, one can be burned by even the ashes for a long time."

The poetic colonel moved carefully through the apartment, glancing up and down. He stopped where Sonya's underwear was folded on the dresser.

"I am Colonel Basily Ivanoff of Soviet Air Security." He took off his cap and Sonya flinched at the lunar landscape of scars on the back of Ivanoff's neck and head. His cap had gouged a long, horizontal welt that gaped purple in the blue-gray hide that passed for skin.

Ivanoff turned, raising an eyebrow.

"Sonya Ziegler."

"You are..."

"Jewish. Yes," Sonya finished his sentence, raising her chin slightly.

"...packing to leave?" Ivanoff finished his own question, touching the dresser top next to Sonya's neatly folded intimate clothes. Behind him, more hung from a piece of twine strung across the archway leading to the bed. Sonya could see more scars on his hand. His little finger was partially eaten away. He flicked the edge of a tattered piece of linen.

Sonya limped back into the kitchen area and picked up the wooden bucket out of the sink. She brought it to the dresser and swept the clean underwear into soapy water. Ivanoff brushed aside the hanging clothes and stepped toward the bed. A stained mattress was partially covered in a loose sheet. The tattered horse blanket folded carefully at the foot waited for the inevitable winter. A sack stuffed with old newspapers and wrapped in a towel stood in for a pillow.

"I found some clean water and they were filthy."

Sonya set the bucket down and waited for Ivanoff to turn back to her before yanking down the drying wash he had touched. She threw it into the bucket, splashing soapy water on his boots.

"Is this your apartment?"

"Yes. I was given it by the Housing Authority."

"Then someone else lives with you."

"Not anymore. The woman with me went to find food and never came back. That was two weeks ago."

Ivanoff growled in Russian to the adjutant. The young officer saluted and hurried out, leaving the door open.

Ivanoff snatched Sonya's hand, twisting it back to show Sonya her own fingertips. Black splinters from the floorboards were surrounded by angry, red blood clots under Sonya's fingernails.

A horde of boots thundered on the stairs. Ivanoff dropped her hand.

"They found what was left of Lieutenant Oleg Karopofski two and a half hours ago."

Four soldiers with slung rifles came to attention behind Ivanoff. The new adjutant circled behind Sonya.

"He was my adjutant and a drunken oaf. He lived long enough to tell me what he did. Everything. He also said you were so beautiful that he almost did not notice the scar."

Ivanoff reached out to touch Sonya's wounded cheek. She did not shrink back and he held his scarred forefinger millimeters from the torn skin.

Suddenly he whipped his hand back and carefully screwed his cap back on. Sonya noticed a mere cloud of pain as the stiff leather bit into the scars.

"You should have shot him in the head."

The adjutant forced a black hood over Sonya's face. Two strong hands grabbed her while others wrapped a belt around her arms, pinning them behind her. Her feet never touched the stairs. She heard the sound of boots change as she was carried outside. A woman was crying and the sobs moved around to her right. The hands pushed her against a wall and the boots moved away. A young voice yelled a single Russian word and there was the metallic rattle of weapons. The woman's sobs became shrill.

It was an eternity. Sonya heard everything and thought of her father. Her breath was short, but she forced it to slow. She tried to think. Thoughts blurred into a panic.

The command and the sharp cracks came together. The woman's sob was cutoff by a thud followed by a raspy breath and someone slumped against Sonya's thigh before sliding down to her feet. The labored breathing continued. It sounded like someone was drowning.

The boots came back and the hood was ripped from her head. Ivanoff was in her face. He looked down to Sonya's right. A middle-aged woman was writhing, bleeding from the mouth. Her chest was bright red with blood surging out of multiple wounds. Her eyes begged Sonya as Ivanoff's pistol flashed out. It jerked and the woman's forehead split. One side of her face bulged and her left eye popped partially out. Her mouth opened and closed, then was still.

"She was caught stealing food from a Soviet soldier. She tried to run away."

Ivanoff jammed his pistol into his holster and snapped the flap back in place.

"Even before this you knew we were liquidating members of the Resistance. You had three hours to flee."

He loosened the belt pinning Sonya's arms.

"But you did not. You must want to be in Berlin very badly."

CHAPTER 9

*Tiergartenstrasse, US Occupied Berlin,
December 28, 1945, 7:56 P.M.*

"One of the trees is walking," shivered the MP stomping next to the jeep.

"Hope he don't topple over here." His partner sat in the rear seat by the radio. The glowing tubes and electronics gave off some warmth, so they took turns sitting by it with the earphones keeping the bitter cold at bay. Since starting their shift, they had found four frozen bodies. Each required a long report on how they found the corpses. Together they had come up with a plan to minimize the paperwork. They had stacks of reports, each filled out for a particular location on their patrol. They would use the one closest to where the dead was actually found, fill in the time and date and call headquarters to alert the German city government. The cause of death was common to all forms – starvation.

The ghost-tree materialized out of the silent snowfall. A thin form mimicked the trunks in the park near the heart of Berlin denuded by the blasts of the summer fighting and picked clean in winter by freezing Berliners for firewood. The frail man glanced at the soldiers briefly as he passed. Hatless, he was hunched against the cold. His light coat would not be much against a spring shower much less a winter storm.

The stomping MP unfolded his arms and pointed at the figure.

"Halt."

"Shit. Why'd you go and do that for?" protested the warmer MP huddled in the jeep.

"Somethin' to do." The shivering MP motioned with his arms to the figure shuffling toward him. "*Hände hoch.*"

The MP murdered the umlaut but the figure understood and put his hands on his head. The MP almost regretted his command when he saw the pain with which the man moved.

"I assure you I am unarmed." The figure's English was far better than the MP's German.

The MP was thrown only for an instant. "We'll see."

"Oh, come on, Charlie. Leave the nice Kraut alone."

The MP patted the man down briskly at first and slowed. The coat was held up by the man's shoulders. There was almost nothing underneath except a boney trunk lost inside the coat. The MP stopped.

Raising his arms had pulled back the man's coat sleeves. The MP saw the tattooed number on the ghost's arm under the melting snowflakes.

"Sorry. Go on."

The man stood there, gazing at the MP with deep-set eyes that carried a cold sadness into the MP's chest as he tried to move. He took so long to lower his arms that both Americans thought he would spend the rest of the night with his hands held over his head.

"Thank you." The figure bowed slightly and hurried on. He slipped in the snow and the cold MP reached out reflexively to help him. The figure noticed the gesture and paused before bowing again. He was swallowed by the snow in a few steps.

The MP in the jeep adjusted the earphones to better cover his ears.

The colder MP watched the ghost vanish into the white gloom.

"Hey. Don't get comfortable. It's my turn."

Sonya did not recognize the slow footsteps on the stairs. The reports of rapes had fallen off with the cold, but she still worried. She also had reason to feel protected now – but she still worried.

The footsteps stopped. There was a knock at another apartment. One of the other three doors on the landing creaked open. Sonya relaxed until she realized the neighbor's door had stayed open. Voices murmured in the hall and then the door closed.

Sonya listened for the footsteps and heard only one as a shadow shuffled to a stop under her door. The knock was very soft. She did not answer.

The knock came again, barely louder.

She stood still, afraid the floorboards would creak. The apartment was mostly dark. A single candle flickered deep in the kitchen. She hoped it wasn't visible under the door.

"Sonya? Sonya Ziegler?" The voice was a rustle of crumbling paper.

Sonya was sure even the sound of her widening eyes was giving her away.

"I have come for the treasure."

Sonya threw open the door and held it, ready to slam it closed if this was a trick. Her face swirled between shock and searching. The ghost-tree shivered audibly.

"I am Michael Neumann."

Sonya went back a thousand years to another life that happened to another girl on another planet.

"Beth Ysrael Synagogue. Treptow District."

Sonya could see the effort he was expending just to remember.

"My wife and I…"

"Come in. Please." She wanted to add 'quickly', but the ghost threatened to crumble to dust if he did anything quickly. The cold from the hall followed Michael in. Not that it was much warmer in the apartment.

Sonya went to the fireplace.

"Please do not put on any coal for me."

It had become the standard greeting in Berlin that winter. Coal was more valuable than food. You could survive a week without a meal, but a single freezing night could claim you without coal.

Sonya added two lumps anyway. An impressive pile waited next to the grate. She turned to find Michael drinking her in. His arms came up and he embraced her. Sonya froze, feeling Michael's trembling ribs poking through his coat and hers. She let him sob on her for a long time before she returned the embrace. He gave a soft, long-stifled cry and she felt him sag.

"Please sit down. I will get you some coffee."

Michael stepped back, looking down. He let her guide him to the chair. It barely creaked as he lowered his frame to it. He sat twisted toward his right side.

"Are you hurt?"

Michael only waved his hand. Sonya lit the alcohol stove and started the coffee, watching Michael from the kitchen. Melting snow dripped from unkempt, gray wisps that hung down over his haunted eyes. He was a misshapen heap tottering in the chair. She grabbed a towel and hurried to steady him.

"When did you last eat?" She dabbed his drawn face. The skin taut over his cheekbones gave him a fierce look. He looked at her as if not believing she was really there.

"I thought…"

He swallowed a shiver with effort.

"…I was alone."

He seized her hand holding the towel to his face and held it before him in both hands. He seemed to be squeezing with all his strength, afraid to let go, but she barely felt any pressure.

"I am so…"

He stopped, his eyes searching space. He brightened, having found the forgotten word.

"…happy."

His gums were bleeding when he finished chewing the bread crust. It had taken him fifteen minutes to nibble on the single half slice. He talked about finding her through the Red Cross and forced back tears when she told him no one else had responded to her message there.

He stared at the other half of the slice that lay untouched on the chipped china saucer.

"It is all I can eat these days. Little meals." He pointed at his bloody mouth. "It is the same inside. Nothing works."

She noticed some flicker of life had come into his eyes.

"May I take this with me?"

Sonya was reaching for the coffee pot and stopped.

"Of course. Please take the loaf."

"I could not do that."

"Herr Neumann, please!"

Michael held up his hands in protest and she decided not to force him. He would never stand the strain. He studied her for a moment. She saw his eyes flick to the scar. And he noticed he had been caught.

"You are doing well. You have coffee, bread and coal."

He turned toward the fire.

"Quite a bit of coal."

He let the statement stand, glancing at Sonya out of the corner of his eye. She moved a saucer on the table for no reason.

"I am staying with Mathaius Beddendorf. We met in…"

He motioned with his head to the south and stopped, pain creasing the tight skin.

"He is a politician with big dreams for Berlin. He thinks the Allies will let us run things. He is not so sure of the Russians. I am sure they will not."

Michael picked up the half slice and carefully wrapped it in a stained handkerchief.

"Politicians with dreams do not eat very well these days."

He pocketed the bread and leaned forward with his hands folded, elbows resting on his knees. It looked like two broomsticks were inside his pant legs.

"Is *der Magier* alive?" He said the name as if invoking the Almighty.

"Yes."

Despite expecting it, Sonya was stunned by the effect on Michael. Although only ten years older than her, he looked like ninety. Now he leapt up, a huge weight off his feeble frame. He had been afraid to ask the question and joy spread on his face. She stood when he swayed.

"But I cannot reach him. I have no idea where he is. He has a price on his head."

Michael shook his head as the nightmare returned, then he quickly brightened again.

"But the treasure…?"

"I do not know where it is."

The man imploded.

"But you fought with him in the Resistance! He never told you?"

"No. I saw him only a few times."

"We must find him!" Michael trembled, tensing as if ready to hurl himself into the task. "Every day that passes means we may never find it! It is all I have now!"

"We will find the treasure."

He stared at her. She feared he would see the truth.

"I promise."

It was a long time before the call came. The leaves of the few trees left in Berlin were budding for the third time since the war. Sonya recognized the voice immediately. They had stalked him and he had hunted them.

And caught many of them.

CHAPTER 10

*Approaching Tempelhof Airport, US Occupied
Berlin, March 12, 1948, 10:48 A.M.*

Nevada spotted the rivulet of rain leaking through the windscreen onto the instrument panel as he brought the four-engine Lancaster onto the runway heading. Tempelhof's grassy oval among the ruins popped into view as they came out of the spring shower.

"Now we're taking on water."

Copilot Martin Glasdon's bushy mustache twitched up as he glanced over at the aging, converted British bomber's newest problem.

Nevada tapped his chin with his finger. "Now let me see, when landing on two engines in a four engine bomber, how much flaps do we use?"

He pulled the throttles back to let the bomber and its three tons of food and medical supplies sink too fast for comfort. He looked over at Glasdon, who took a breath.

"Same as bloody yesterday." His heavy Yorkshire accent made Nevada feel like he was speaking a foreign language.

Nevada cranked in 20 degrees of flaps and pushed the throttles forward to compensate for the drag. Tempelhof was a giant mottled lawn with a brown stain stretching ahead, marked on either side by white paint lines. The spring rain had softened the ground and it looked like a long version of a football field after Notre Dame had slugged it out with Navy.

The landing was gentle with the youngest member of Empire Air Freight's fleet sinking slowly into the mud. They taxied across the grass toward the large terminal building, passing the baseball diamonds set off the apron by the 232nd Wing of the US Army Air Corps. The two diamonds would do Yankee Stadium proud, even if they were set at crazy angles. Several bomb craters had been filled in shortly after the war. The unsettled earth would not take the weight of larger aircraft, so they were relegated to the occupier's national pastime.

Number one engine was also stuttering before the Army private crossed his flags at the terminal, signaling the end of Nevada's fiftieth trip to Berlin – not counting the ones when he didn't land there.

"Looks like we're gonna be stuck here a couple of hours," Nevada grinned.

"You are an optimist, Yank." It was obvious Glasdon was not.

With the end of the war, Berlin was divided into four parts between the British, French, Soviets and the United States. It was a miniature version of Germany itself, which was also divided among the victors. Berlin was an island in the Russian Zone. Each occupying power's military ruled their own zone, with local governments being left to the Germans under the stern gaze of the occupiers. The Russians had the sternest gaze of all.

The victors met regularly to coordinate the occupation, but agreement was becoming more and more elusive almost three years after the war's end. Just a month before, the Soviets had toppled the Czech government. It was advertized as a popular Communist uprising, but everyone could see Soviet dictator Josef Stalin's fat finger pushing things along.

There were rising fears of something brewing in Germany. Berlin could easily be cut off by the Russians and slowly starved into seeing that "Uncle Joe" really had their best interests at heart.

Nevada noticed the man following him wasn't trying to be sneaky. He had appeared the moment Nevada stepped out of the airport grounds. Nevada passed the German and waved back at the MP at the small post guarding the entrance from *Columbiadamm*. About forty, the man walked quite erect, not hunched or furtive. He looked like he knew where he was going, which was anywhere Nevada was going.

Nevada kept walking, listening to the footsteps behind him. The pace quickened and Nevada turned. The man stopped at once, bringing both his feet together, his heels tapping with a soft click.

"I beg your pardon. I have given you fright." The accent was thick. The man slowly removed both hands from the neat overcoat, showing they were empty, except for a leather wallet.

"You don't frighten me, bub." Nevada glanced around, checking if the shadow had friends. The man's gaze never wavered.

"You are American."

"As of this morning."

The man moved a half step toward Nevada and halted again, coming to attention.

"I believe you have perhaps lost this." He pushed the wallet toward Nevada. It was thick.

"Ain't mine." Nevada didn't bother to look.

"Perhaps you know a pilot who has lost it."

"How d'you know it's a pilot's?"

The man unfolded the wallet and delicately removed the black and white photo with two fingers. A teenaged girl in a pair of shorts posed by the gear of a DC-3.

"Nice. Her number in there, too?" Nevada grinned at his own joke.

The German merely raised one eyebrow and tilted his head slightly.

"Forget it. Look, bub, take it right back there and turn it in." Nevada jerked a thumb toward Tempelhof.

"Pardon. I am forbidden on the airport," the polite German explained.

Nevada started to walk on. "Give it to the MP."

The man fell into step. Nevada was sauntering, but the German marched.

"I had the hope there was a reward."

"It's in the wallet. Fish out some cash and turn it in then." Nevada checked his watch and hoped the mechanics would not be too quick to fix the old Lancaster's problems.

"I do not need money."

Nevada stopped and the German did, too, his heels coming together with the same soft click.

"I have much money already."

"Lucky you."

The German looked over his shoulder. "We should walk on."

"Why?"

"I do not wish to keep you from your appointment."

The German smiled. Nevada had seen more sincere smiles on car salesmen.

"See ya." The man moved to go with Nevada. "Tempelhof is still back there."

The man smiled again. "I had the hope we are going to a place where there is many pilots."

"You know any bar within a mile of here?"

"Many."

"Pick one. There you'll find many pilots."

Nevada walked on, determined not to stop again. The man marched next to him. In the silence, Nevada sized up his new friend and figured it would be easy to toss him into the nearest rubble heap.

"I am jealous of pilots. Borders do not stop them."

The German paused and took a breath as if he was to jump into ice water.

"So many Berliners want to be leaving this city."

"Seems like a nice town." They had moved into a sea of small heaps where blocks of apartments had once stood. The irony was not lost on the German.

Nevada spat his gum out. The man winced at the sullying of his ruined city, but swallowed his disgust.

"Some want to pay in gold the equivalent of one thousand dollars. Ahead of the flying."

Nevada pulled out the pack of gum from his pocket and slipped out a stick.

"You must want to get out of Berlin pretty bad."

"It is inevitable that the Russians will force you out and take the city. My daughter and I wish to be in a warmer climate when that happens."

"Maybe. Want some?" Nevada offered the gum.

"No, thank you."

"You better take it. Cause it's all you're gonna get from me."

The German thought about it and took the stick.

"My daughter likes it. Good day."

The man executed a sharp *volte face* and marched off.

Nevada didn't like turning down a big payday, even if it did fit Chance's and his dreams. But he told himself he wasn't going to get involved in something so risky.

It took the woman only ten seconds to change his mind. She had someone named Max who would pay a lot more than the German who had escorted him partway to the bar.

Despite the scar, she was gorgeous. The dark eyes were nice, but he liked what was below them a lot more. Her whole person had a fire, a hunger.

It never crossed his mind that it was for anything but him.

CHAPTER 11

*Somewhere over US Occupied Germany,
March 20, 1948, 1:28 P.M.*

"We're lost." Nevada almost sounded excited.

Danger, certain death and destruction brought out the little boy on a backyard adventure. Chance loved that about him – sometimes. It meant Nevada didn't panic. It also meant he had a tendency to get into these situations much too often and with much too much zest. Nevada flashed his searchlight smile. Chance hoped it would burn off the clouds.

Chance scanned the solid floor of cloud tops a thousand feet below. Hills should cause swells, with the clouds breaking open on the leeward side as the winds stretched them over the rises in the land. Whatever part of Germany they were over was flat or gently rolling. No breaks could be seen in the unending whitish-gray. Heat rising from factories would also thin the overcast. But three years after the end of the war, operating industry in Germany was still on an eighteenth-century scale.

Chance dialed the automatic direction finder to 265 kilocycles. A gentle hiss instead of the repeating Morse code "FD" meant the Fulda beacon was off the air again or the surplus Douglas C-47's direction finder was not quite to manufacturer's specs.

"You sure you want to buy this crate?" Chance tried the beacon at Rhein-Main. More hiss.

"Sure. We can fix it up."

Chance tuned up to the Armed Forces Radio Service (AFRS) in Frankfurt on 601 kilocycles. He should have heard *The Breakfast Show* sponsored by Toni Crème Shampoo, recorded three days ago in Chicago and flown over. Some private would hack up the most popular show on the radio and cut in bulletins on the latest move by the Communist Russians to grab another country in a Europe still on its knees. Under the Potsdam agreement between the victorious Allies, the Russians occupied half of Germany but unashamedly lusted for the industrial western half.

But Chance heard no cheery jingles or rumors of war riding a carrier that would point the lost fliers to Frankfurt and the Rhein-Main Airfield. Instead a growl became a screech forcing him to tear the headphones off.

"Found a guy named Rossi. He knows everything about these tomatoes." Nevada was doing a sell job, which meant he had already bought it. "*Nichts*, huh? *Kaputt*."

"Yeah. Broken." Chance added that the direction finder was inoperative to the long and ever-growing gripe list.

"You should learn the language. A little *Sprecken Sie Deutsch* goes a long way with the *frawlines*."

"Yeah, let's stop and ask for directions." Chance willed himself to see through the clouds. "You know how to use the sextant?"

"Ain't one." Nevada was enjoying this.

Chance looked at the fuel gauge. It still read zero, bringing back nightmares. They had no real idea how much fuel they had left. They had taken off in the twin-engine transport an hour ago with 1,500 pounds of gas – if the broker could be trusted. That should give them just under three hours flight time – if there were no leaks.

Nevada could fly him back to England. It would violate a bazillion regulations, but at least Chance wouldn't be AWOL. His leave was up tomorrow midnight. Nevada had been mustered out six months ago, but the Army had managed to mess up Chance's paperwork. With Russians getting nastier, there was scuttlebutt about learning to fly B-29s, the atomic bomber, to Moscow. For a moment, Chance liked the idea of flying all the way back to England. Nevada would do it. And Nevada would take the heat for it. Chance would be just riding along.

He smelled something burning. The mixture of hot metal and Bakelite that could come from any one of a thousand places in a Dakota. Chance looked behind Nevada for the fire extinguisher. The holder was empty.

"What do we have on the grill today?"

Nevada took a whiff. "Oh, that. It's probably one of the dynamotors."

"The one that runs the ADF?"

Nevada shrugged. Chance thought about his optimistic friend flying this death trap for the coming four months that Chance's commander had assured him would be the last of his military flying career. He flipped out the breaker for the ADF.

"Why should I learn Kraut? I thought we were going to find a plane and go home."

"You don't like this one? We'll call it PIE IN THE SKY."

"Oh, she's a honey. You're not planning to go home."

Nevada grinned. It reminded Chance of when he woke up after being hit in APPLE PIE. He rubbed the back of his head, feeling the scar.

"Where's home gonna be, anyway?"

Chance's eyes paused in their scan of the instruments and then kept going. Nevada pretended not to notice.

"The money's here. Hell, boatloads of flyboys are already home. They're not letting the Nazi's fly…"

"So they can walk. Hitch up their horse carts."

"War's over, buddy. There's money to be made. We won't be dealing with the Krauts anyhow. Uncle Sam all the way."

"The Russkies tune up and Uncle Sam should be back home where he belongs. Let these jokers learn to solve their own problems."

Nevada tweaked the right throttle. The engines were running fine. It was just something he did to fill time.

"Let me take it for minute." Chance did not sound enthusiastic.

JITTERBUG LIFT

Nevada pulled his hands off the yoke. "All yours. Tends to pull right and wants to yaw when you climb."

"Among other things." Chance took the yoke. It felt stiff and sticky. But he pushed forward easily. The plane went into a gentle dive. He pulled back and the yoke wouldn't move. He upped the pressure and all he felt was a stubborn, grating resistance. The altimeter said they were losing fifty feet per minute.

"How she feel?"

"Yoke's stuck."

Nevada tried. He didn't seem surprised. "He said it might do that. Just push ahead and pull back." Chance pushed. The dive steepened to one hundred feet per minute and the yoke stuck in its new position.

"Anything else he said it might do?" Chance was mentally calculating how long they had before they hit something. He shoved the image of *Died from Corrosion* on his tombstone out of his head and ran down his options. He worked the trim tab wheel and cranked in positive trim. The nose came up and the descent slowed to seventy-five feet per minute.

"Trim tabs work." His command voice had kicked back in. The elevator trim tabs gave them some measure of control, but it was still downhill all the way. Normally trim tabs were used to adjust for minor imbalances in the aircraft.

"I'll check the cables." Nevada was out of his seat and heading toward the tail. "You got a flashlight?"

Chance wanted to chew Nevada out for being totally unprofessional, unmilitary and dumb as most dead pilots are. But that would eat up more altitude.

As Nevada felt his way aft, Chance thought of turning and starting to circle. They could be heading toward a section of Germany that was higher elevation. But any turn would lose altitude.

The yoke shook. Nevada had found the right set of cables.

"That's them," Chance yelled. Nothing came back except the steady – *thank God* – rumble of the engines in the nearly empty fuselage.

The yoke jerked forward and stuck.

"Wrong way."

Chance pulled back on the yoke. No joy. He saw the cloud tops were moving faster below him. They were only five hundred to a thousand feet from going into the soup. He felt a slight bump. Hopefully there would be more updrafts than downdrafts.

The yoke shuddered again and then began to bounce rhythmically. Chance could just hear Nevada banging on the cables with something. Chance wanted it to be his friend's head.

The plane lurched up again and a wisp of cloud whipped past. The bouncing turned into a rough road of air as the cabin darkened. He yanked on the unyielding yoke.

Nevada yelled something lost in the engines.

"What?"

"Fire!" echoed out of the back. Black smoke rolled into the cockpit.

"Fix the cable!" Chance yelled, trying to keep any panic at bay. It was always there, paralyzing and final.

Chance thought he saw something below. It was too indistinct to give him a sense of altitude. If it wasn't the sea, he had less than twelve hundred feet left – if he could believe the altimeter.

More smoke filled the cockpit. Chance coughed. He slid open the left window. The air was damp and cold but breathable.

"Nevada?"

Nothing came back. Chance checked below. He saw a stretch of dark green that immediately burst into view. Trees. Trees whipping past at 140 knots. Trees only few hundred feet below. Chance looked for which way the land sloped and turned left. He could not see far ahead. Praying there were no mountains, he followed the terrain.

A man looked up from a small herd of scattering sheep. Chance would recognize him if he ever came back here. He could lower the gear or come in on the C-47's belly. But he could be landing into anything. There simply wasn't enough visibility.

Everything went gray again. Smoke was stinging his eyes and throat. Part of him braced for the violent slam that would finish everything. Most of him kept flying.

JITTERBUG LIFT

Something silver caught his eye to the right. A river. He turned and realized there was a hill in front of it. Trees framed the ridgeline. A gap beckoned at the highest point. Chance tried the yoke again. He thought it moved. Ground effect would have to do the rest. A wonderful pillow of air hugs the earth and has nowhere to go, so it pushes back on landing – and crashing – planes just a little.

Something hit something as the plane hurtled the top of the hill. It was slight but he felt it. He checked both engines. The smooth, even blur of the props told him they were intact.

The river was in a gentle valley. The ground seemed to lower and Chance checked the altimeter. Still going down.

"Nevada?" He heard only the echo of his own smoke-hoarse voice.

The blast of air from the cockpit window increased, clearing the cockpit and his head. Either Nevada had opened the rear door or the fire had burned through the skin of the airplane or the tail had fallen off. But he'd already know if it was number three.

The ground fell away steeply and Chance felt he could make the turn over the river. He scanned the instruments. The twin cyclone engine indicators showed everything was okey-dokey. He kicked the rudder and banked, trying to keep the turn as slow as possible. But the other side of the river was coming up fast. He turned harder and lost a few feet, but it was better than ruining the pretty, steepled town on the other side.

The river was about a quarter mile wide and snaked through the hills. He could see the land coming up on either side. He was committed – a pilot's word for trapped in events completely out of his control. He prayed the river didn't have a great big dam on it to end his misery.

He was still going down. In less than sixty seconds he would have to ditch.

"Nevada!"

Nothing. *Probably knocked out by the smoke. Never'll know what hit him. A thousand girls at his funeral; he has all the luck.*

Chance followed another bend in the river. A single barge whipped by, drying clothes strung from the mast to the stack. At least someone will be able to explain what happened.

He started running down ditching procedures. It would be real fast. Drop the flaps and the plane will balloon up a little. *Damn Nevada!* Bring back the power and let her settle in to the water while keeping the nose up – he had done it all before.

"How the hell am I gonna do that? Fucking Nevada!" he yelled.

"You better pull up or you're gonna hit that bridge." Nevada leaned into the cockpit, coughing.

The railroad trestle stretched across the river at the level of the surrounding land or about a hundred feet above the water. Problem was it had been bombed and the center span had tilted over into the river, leaving a small triangle. Chance had no idea whether the plane would fit. But there was no time to pull up.

Chance did not think. He banked the plane and pushed the rudder opposite to hold it straight. Chance's hands wiggled the freed yoke mere fractions on an inch. Canted parallel to the trestle, the Dakota closed the distance in a half second.

Chance heard the engines echo off the ironwork as the C-47 sailed under the ruined span. It sounded like metal tearing. He thought they were crashing, but was going to fly this thing until he couldn't. He yanked back on the yoke expecting resistance and the nose jerked up. He pushed back, keeping the plane out of a stall. The airspeed bled off and he shoved the throttles forward. In seconds they were in the clouds. A heartbeat later sunshine burst through the window.

Chance leveled off and Nevada got back into his seat. It was an eternity before Nevada spoke.

"Miltenberg."

Chance stared at him blankly. "What the hell does that mean?"

"Miltenberg. It's the name of the town we just passed. Saw it on the hotel. Guess we're famous there now."

Chance's hands were hurting. He relaxed his grip on the yoke. Nevada pulled out an air chart.

"Nice flyin'. Here we are."

"What about the fire?"

"I opened the rear door and it blew out. Just some wires, I guess. Come to 318."

"And what do we do when we get there?"

"Overcast'll be gone. You'll see."

Chance banked the aircraft. He pulled back slightly on the yoke to keep the nose up. He still expected it to lock. Something about Nevada's optimism was just infectious. Clap and dysentery were infectious, too. They had cures for those.

"Who's your first customer?"

Nevada looked up from the chart and grinned.

Chance felt the tension in his shoulders and arms easing away. Adrenaline made his jaw feel like it was one of those chattering teeth toys. He looked Nevada in the eye.

"You didn't almost kill me to sell me the plane. You've already bought it. You're selling me on staying here."

"Just for a while. We do some hot jobs and go back with enough to set us up with a fleet. Most of the guys already home are fighting over short-haul stuff with one plane. We'd clean up." Nevada's tone was the same as when he told Chance the yoke might stick a bit.

"What's the hot job?"

"I call it Operation Jitterbug. Fly a little cargo out of Germany…"

"Out? From where?"

"Some place. East."

Chance sighed. "No, no, no."

"Come on. It's cash up front. One trip for ten thousand Yankee dollars."

"That's why you call it PIE IN THE SKY. You'll be lucky to get out of there with your hide, much less the airplane. Wise up, Nevada."

"I ain't no dope. I got hooked up with this Max guy…"

"He's a Kraut?!" Chance banged his head back on the head rest and groaned. His old wound twinged.

"Met a girl in Berlin and she hooked me up with Max. They gave me the down payment for this Dakota."

Chance felt like a father explaining to his daughter that there was no Santa Claus and the other three famous lies. "It's a set-up. There are thousands of Nazis dying to get away from the Russians – and us – and you're flying one out."

"No Nazis. Max promised. Some risks. Nothing I can't handle. I'll be in and out in less than five hours."

"Promise me you will find something, anything else to carry. A load of nitroglycerin."

"Deal's made, pal. I just thought you'd say okay. I'll be careful."

Chance stared at the huge expanse of blue. Nevada could have just as easily done this crazy run without him knowing. But they were partners; one of the thousands of duos forged by battle and blood during the war. When APPLE PIE had been shot up, it was Nevada who had kept the crew together and the B-17 flying. Chance found out at the debrief that the flak that wounded him and killed his bombardier was only the beginning. In the ten minutes Chance was out, a fluke concentration of 109s had pounced and the formation lost sixteen aircraft. The survivors praised Nevada for his cool thinking and invincible attitude that shamed the rest of the crew into not panicking.

"Overcast is breaking up. Told you we'd do okay." Nevada settled back, smiling. The clouds thinned to a shelf over brown spring fields.

"Yeah, you did." Chance throttled back, starting their descent.

CHAPTER 12

Russian Railroad Checkpoint Marienborn,
April 1, 1948, 12:15 A.M.

The British captain had had enough. He and his men had been sitting in three cars of the 11:46 P.M. *Deutsche Bahn* train for Bremerhaven and points west. The captain had refused to allow Soviet soldiers to board the train and search the British soldiers to check their identification. It just wasn't done.

Under the Four Power agreement, the western Allies had unrestricted access to and from their occupied zones in Berlin through three rail and highway corridors. There was also a brief mention of three airways, each ten miles wide. But the day before, the Soviet Deputy Military Governor in Berlin had demanded that all Western nationals traveling to or from Berlin be prepared to show their identity papers at Russian checkpoints. Also anything going in or out of the enclosed city required a Soviet permit.

The captain thought about his coming leave being eaten away and that it was bloody cold. All because a Soviet sergeant kept repeating the only two words of English he barely knew.

"*Dok-uments pleez.*"

As he walked toward the head of the train, the captain began mentally jotting his protest which he vainly hoped would be passed all the way up to the Allied Control Council, the government council of Berlin formed by the representatives of the four occupying armies.

It was in vain because the council had not met since March.

The chairmanship of the council rotated monthly and it was customary for the chair to play host to his counterparts with a sumptuous lunch following hours of haggling over some detail about money, refugees and the like.

It had been the Soviets' turn in March. The Soviet Military Governor of Berlin, Marshal Vassily Sokolovsky, gave no indication of the bombshell he was about to unleash. At the end of a rambling statement accusing the West of not living up to the Potsdam Agreement, Sokolovsky abruptly adjourned the meeting. When the French asked when they would meet again, Sokolovsky did not reply.

And there was no lunch.

The British captain saw a figure wearing a visored military cap coming out of the steam with the Soviet sergeant trotting behind it. The Soviet captain planted himself in front of the British captain and spoke much better English.

"Documents, please."

The Russian saluted with a smile, did a smart *volte face* and was gone, leaving the captain with the verbally-challenged sergeant.

As dawn broke, the Allies realized they faced a complete blockade of the city of Berlin. "Technical difficulties," document checks, and permit requirements thwarted every land route in or out of Berlin. Despite Soviet shrugs that it just couldn't be helped because of the need to protect the city from "subversive and terrorist elements," many felt it was really the prelude to war. The garrisons went on alert and quickly assessed how much food they had to last out the siege. It would not be long.

They would hardly have to worry about re-supplying their troops since a starving civilian population would capitulate to the Russians on any terms in a few days.

The Russians repeated their mantra of "technical difficulties" and sat back to wait for German stomachs to empty. They were confident until their radars showed the Allies still flying in and out of Berlin.

To test Allied resolve, the aggressive head of Soviet air security ordered a YAK-3 to fly "maneuvers" in the approach pattern to Tegel Airport in the British Sector.

The action produced immediate results.

At about one in the afternoon and in clear visibility, the YAK collided head on with an approaching Viking airliner from British European Airways. Both planes crashed with no survivors, the Viking in the Russian Zone and the Soviet fighter in the British Zone.

The next day, General Sokolovsky met with his opposite numbers and railed against the foolishness of the Allies. Shamefaced, he then added that the rail lines and roads had been reopened to the west; the technical difficulties had been miraculously sorted out overnight.

He did not promise that they would never return.

CHAPTER 13

*Rhein-Main Air Base, Occupied Germany,
June 4, 1948, 8:09 P.M.*

"Dakota 243, cleared for takeoff," drawled an even voice over PIE IN THE SKY's new radios as Nevada locked the tail wheel in place.

"Roger. 243," Nevada replied, already pushing the Dakota's prop pitch controls all the way forward. Two RPM needles worked their way solidly to 2700 and held. The power throttles followed in one-second steps to 48 inches of manifold pressure. He switched the mixture to AUTORICH and felt the plane pushing on his back. No burps or fiddling with the mixture. Nevada liked that feeling. Flying light, the plane leapt forward. In seconds he eased the yoke forward to lift the tail. The rudder was mushy for a second before Nevada could feel the air trying to push it back. The Dakota wandered right of the centerline and he corrected. The plane responded to his control. Nevada liked that feeling, too. He waited until the airspeed read 85 knots and pulled back on the yoke. He suddenly became a blur of arms and hands, doing all the things the copilot should be doing. He pulled up on the landing gear lever on the floor on a positive rate of climb. Two red landing gear lights caught his eye as he adjusted the prop pitch and trimmed out the aircraft, pleased that the newly lubricated cables and controls all worked smoothly. Max's bottomless pockets had seen to that.

The C-47, owned by International Airlines, was fresh from the hangar and Nevada had filed a flight plan for a check ride to test the aircraft. International Airlines was an impressive name for PIE IN THE SKY and whatever chair Nevada was sitting in.

The Air Force sergeant, who had given him the weather rundown, had stopped picking his teeth when he read the flight plan.

"We're thinkin' big," Nevada had said, pointing to the owner entry.

The sergeant was unimpressed and uninterested. "Who the hell does a check ride at almost sundown?"

"Got an important run first thing tomorrow. They just got it finished in time." Nevada jerked a thumb over toward the hangar at the other side of the airport south of Frankfurt.

The sergeant had eyed Nevada and started picking bits of cornbread out his molars again. "Your funeral," he had droned, punctuating his opinion with a time stamp on the flight plan.

Nevada had been almost out the door when the sergeant snorted. "Won't be today. Nobody'd be caught dead in that get up."

The pants he had bought at the black market by the Frankfurt *Römerplatz*, a wool jacket with different color patches in both elbows and a moldy worker's cap purchased at the same made Nevada a sorry sight for less than a pack of cigarettes – the going hard currency in Germany.

"Uniform comes later. After this run, I'll look better than Goering," Nevada had slowed by the door.

The reference to the flamboyant former Nazi air marshal had also failed to impress the laconic sergeant. He had slammed the file drawer closed on Nevada's flight plan with his hip. "You do. But Goering's already dead."

Nevada climbed to eight thousand feet, throttled the props back to 2050 RPM, adjusted the power and set the mixture to AUTOLEAN. He turned north and departed the flight control area for the main U.S. airbase on the European Continent.

Traffic was light and he had the fading orange to sapphire sky to himself.

"Rhein Control, this is Dakota 243."

"Go ahead 243." The flight controller sounded young; it was Friday night second-string.

"I'd like to do some maneuvers. Any restrictions?"

"243, remain below ten thousand. No other traffic except the Russians sixty miles to the east."

"Roger, Rhein." A comedian was all alone, staring at an empty radar screen and an equally empty eight hours of duty. Nevada hoped the funny kid wouldn't watch the radar too closely as he turned west and throttled back over a Europe that had settled back from the jitters of almost two months ago.

It was twenty minutes before Nevada keyed the radio again. "Rhein Control, this is Dakota 243 declaring an emergency!"

Nevada's frantic voice had an immediate effect on his minder. "Dakota 423, ah 243, Rhein Control. What is the nature of your emergency?"

Nevada was relieved that laughing boy was a by-the-book flight controller when the chips were down.

"I have lost one engine and the other is running rough. I think it's the fuel. Shit, it's quitting too." Nevada put the aircraft into a steep dive. "What is the nearest emergency field?"

"Stand by, 243." The carrier dropped for two seconds and came back on. "243, this is Rhein Control. Nearest is Alsfield. Correction Alsfeld. Repeat, Alsfeld. Ten miles at heading oh-niner-eight."

"Roger, Rhein. Will try to make it."

This kid was on the ball. Two seconds to come up with an alternate field and he only had trouble with the German name.

"243, be advised, Alsfeld is abandoned and unlit. Runway heading is 120. Field is north of town center about two miles."

"Roger, Rhein. Thanks. Gonna be busy here." Nevada watched the altimeter creep below three thousand feet. Desperately looking for landmarks, he already knew what the next transmission would be.

"243, lost radar contact."

"I said, I'm busy, kid," Nevada whispered without keying the radio. The horizon was totally dark and Nevada was fighting deadly disorientation which could make him believe he was climbing when he was diving or even fly upside-down. He was flying into total blackness and fought the urge to look out the window when he must trust his instruments.

His instruments told him he had only one thousand feet left. Nevada scanned the way ahead and caught a dim red light to the left.

The Nazis had had a radio station at Alsfeld silenced by Patton's advancing tanks at the end of the war. But the antenna still stood and its dim anti-collision beacon was Nevada's ticket.

Oriented, he pulled the plane level and turned. He watched his artificial horizon and relaxed as the nose came up.

Nevada was flying straight and level as he passed directly over the abandoned Nazi fighter airfield. He wondered if he and Chance had faced Messerschmitt ME-109s based here in APPLE PIE as he noted both RPM gauges still showed a solid 2050 revolutions.

He reached up and turned off his navigation lights. Only the indigo pulsing exhaust from both engines gave him away.

"Dakota 243, how do you read?" The signal wavered, blocked by the same 2300 foot *Vogelsberg*, literally Bird Mountain, that now hid Nevada's aircraft from the Rhein Control radar.

"Dakota 243, please acknowledge."

Nevada smiled. The kid was genuinely worried about him. He pulled out the carefully marked flight chart. Some town with an unpronounceable name beginning with G was his next waypoint. No radio antenna, just the bright lights of the military prison run by the occupiers. After that, things would get interesting. He could only fly as low as possible, not knowing where the Russian radar stations were. He hoped Max's information was current.

After twenty minutes of flying through the Fulda River valley, the prison was difficult to miss. Just as easy to spot was the border with the Russian occupied zone. At the end of the war, the Soviet Army had descended like a Mongol horde and taken everything of value – nailed down or not. The booty included several complete power stations, each carefully dismantled and shipped east on rail cars. The resulting power shortage made the Russian zone an expanse of ink at night.

Max had chosen targets that were sure to be lit. Just over the border was a hospital, an island of light. One mile beyond the hospital, Nevada picked up the red and green lights of the rail line heading east to Halle. Max's list set out precise altitudes and times for Nevada to fly a few hundred feet above the low mountain range. He would be able to correct for wind by counting the signal lights along the line. Max's instructions warned of a point where the rail line passed through a thin cut in the Harz Mountains. There would be no lights to warn Nevada; he would have to time his trip after the hospital. At precisely twelve minutes and twenty-eight seconds, he would climb to two thousand feet. He would hold that for two minutes and seventeen seconds while he passed over the hill and then descend back to five hundred. The Dakota would appear briefly on Soviet radar, but by the time anyone noticed, he would be gone; another spook or ghost reflection. Maybe the Russkies also had their Friday night water-boy squad on.

Nevada counted the last few seconds then pulled back on the yoke while shoving the throttles up to a full twenty-five grand. The plane responded like a fighter flying through oatmeal. Nevada tried not to worry. He had a full mile either way, depending on winds. And this was the easy part.

He was at two thousand in less than a minute. He checked his watch in the dim red glow of the cockpit. The radium dial told him time was up. He could wait longer and risk a visit by a dozen Russian YAKs eager for target practice. Sooner toyed with a full-throttle dive into the trees or whatever was down there in the ink.

He pushed the yoke over and powered back, not bothering to look out the window. If something went wrong, he would be the first to know.

The altimeter sunk to five hundred feet and Nevada leveled off. He was sweating in the cold cockpit. The hard part was over, but he would have to do it all in reverse in a few hours, when he was much more tired.

A dull orange glow on scattered clouds told him Halle was dead ahead. He began a wide turn around the city to pick up the rail line heading toward Berlin on the north side.

The instructions warned about a Soviet airfield south of Halle. There was no radar installation there. The Soviets centralized everything, concentrating their radar stations at their area commands, not at individual airports. Still, Nevada pressed PIE IN THE SKY as low as he dared. As a town flashed underneath, he smelled baking bread. Low enough.

He picked out the rail line signal lights twenty miles north of Halle. They were all red, warning him to stop and go back. He began to count. The last half-hour was straight and level. Just don't lose count.

His sweat made him smell the three people whose clothes he was wearing. The pant owner had been partial to the *ersatz* lemon cologne that shortages had forced on the Fatherland. Nevada wished the jacket owner had been as fastidious.

He peeled the cap off, finding it sticky and...

There was the light. White and dazzling in a land of dull orange points. It came and went. He was focused on it when it flashed again: long and short. Things were okay.

When Sonya had relayed Max's instructions about the signal, she seemed really concerned about him. She made him repeat it several times. Long – short everything is okay clear to land. Short – short – short: wave off. He was to keep checking the lights until the moment he landed.

He checked his watch. It was a minute and two signals early, but there plain as day. Maybe he had picked up a tailwind. That meant he was a minute late pulling up over the hills. Nevada decided not to think anymore about that.

The light flashed again as Nevada skimmed over it. The pulse was wrong this time: short then long. Maybe the person he was meeting was excited or something obstructed the beam. Maybe Nevada was just tired of hedge-hopping a few feet from destruction.

Nevada banked around. There was no doubt. A long open meadow was just visible under the moon beyond the light, exactly as Max promised and Max seemed like a guy who could do anything.

Nevada adjusted the props to 1800, throttled back, quickly lowering the flaps to a full forty degrees. It was a nice meadow, but not Rhein-Main. He started a short field approach. He dropped the landing gear and compensated with the power. The yoke started shuddering as the plane flirted with the stall speed. The rudder began to ignore him.

Nevada closed the throttles, shoved the props all the way forward and pulled full back on the yoke. PIE IN THE SKY was threatening to splatter like a banana cream pie in a Three Stooges short.

A tree was a dark blur off to the left as Nevada brought the wallowing Dakota over the edge of the meadow. The plane yawed left – a nasty habit, thought Nevada, as he kicked the rudder hard right. The rudder wasn't interested. The whole plane was becoming belligerent.

The first bump was hard. Nevada started applying the brakes right after the second. He held the nose up to keep the tires from digging in and pitching the Dakota over, making a new water hole in the soft ground. Something dark flicked by on the right. A cow? Alright, Max wasn't perfect.

The Dakota slowed and Nevada was able to wheel it around well before the trees. He was smiling as he cut the ignition and squinted out in the dark. That landing was one for the books. He couldn't wait to tell Chance about it. He noted that it was just after eleven o'clock on the cockpit clock and climbed out of his seat.

Five minutes later, Nevada was sprinting back toward PIE IN THE SKY, already visualizing the start up procedure as the sticky workers cap flew off his head into the dew slick grass. He slipped and scrambled on all fours until he was running upright again. When he looked back over his shoulder, he wasn't smiling.

CHAPTER 14

*Soviet Army Headquarters, Karlshorst,
Berlin, June 5, 1948 2:27 A.M.*

Colonel Ivanoff hated when the phone stuttered. It would give one of those short dings and he had no idea whether some fool was working on the miles of damaged wires or if Stalin himself was trying to reach him. At this hour it was more likely the man the Americans had named "Uncle Joe" than an illiterate, *dinyah* private trying to sort out the telephone system for the thousandth time.

Given the recent blockade attempt, it was very likely. Moscow had been digesting the Allied response; a process that was as long as it was unfathomable. Colonel Ivanoff expected a decision soon. They would try again and no one would sleep for months.

Any other colonel in the entire Soviet Army was not expected to be at his desk at this hour. But Colonel Ivanoff still answered before the second hesitant ring. He took a deep breath to be sure he did not sound like he was sleeping. Little things like that got people shot.

"Security Section. Colonel Ivanoff," clipped the scarred officer, instantly reaching for a pen to make notes. He measured his tone. To inferiors he must sound authoritarian. To superiors, he must sound ready for immediate action; never annoyed or harried.

The captain at the other end was not so careful with his voice. He could not hide that he was surprised to get the head of Air Security at almost 2:30 A.M. on a Saturday morning. At least not sober.

"I am sorry to disturb you, Comrade Colonel, but…"

"Report!" snapped Ivanoff.

The captain identified himself and the section under his command. Ivanoff knew all of the sections in the Russian Occupied Zone, but the town the captain mentioned was new to him. He turned to find it on the large map behind his desk, steel gray eyes scanning thousands of names written in both Cyrillic and Latin script. What was left of an eyebrow raised when he saw how deep into the Russian zone the incident location was.

When the captain's report was finished, Ivanoff scratched a few notes.

"What about the pilot?"

The captain gave a short reply.

"Touch nothing. I am coming myself."

He held down the cradle and let it up. The operator was also wide awake. He had put the captain's call through, of course. What Ivanoff did not know was that the telephone staff paid particular attention to his line. They knew he never slept. If the insomniac Colonel picked up his line at any hour, the operator on duty was jolted awake by a fire bell liberated from Tempelhof Airdrome while the Russians had briefly controlled it before turning it over to the Americans. Such a heroic officer required their respect.

Ivanoff did not wear the Order of Lenin that Stalin himself had pinned on his chest. He did not have to. His reputation and the burn scars climbing up the back of his neck said more than any medal.

The last time Ivanoff had slept was July 6, 1942. July 7 dawned hot and muggy. Ivanoff took off in his YAK-2 for the sixth time since midnight. The Nazis were perfecting their newly-invented *Blitzkrieg* or lightning war. They had bypassed his airfield – really a stretch of pasture and some tents – on their way to besiege Leningrad. His air group was down to three planes. They had not even enough fuel for full tanks; his commanders had abandoned holding their field as hopeless and there had been no supplies for days.

That did not stop them from ordering Ivanoff and his comrades into the air one last time. A wave of Nazi bombers was heading for the defenses of Leningrad. They were to intercept. The line went completely dead after that.

Not quite at seven thousand feet, Ivanoff easily found the cloud of bombers and their fighters. He searched the sky for any other Soviet fighters to join the assault. There were none.

"Attacking," was all he said over the radio. He never knew if his wingmen heard him. To claim he was attacking when three ME-109s were already screaming down on him was more than stretching the truth.

Ivanoff's world collapsed down to the bubble of sky he was fighting in. There was no war, just three enemy fighters for each of the Soviets.

His first burst caught one of the attackers in the wing. The enemy Messerschmitt flicked away and Ivanoff skidded head on to the next one. He saw the gun flashes had already started and his windshield exploded. Ivanoff jammed the stick forward and right, diving out of the lethal stream of shells. He could feel the YAK shudder as the rounds slammed into the airframe. Smoke immediately boiled up between his legs and something whanged through the cramped cockpit from the left, ripping a gash in the instrument panel.

Ivanoff lost orientation and found he was upside down and diving. Flames lashed out from under the instrument panel. He pulled back on the stick and pushed it left, trying to right the YAK. It sounded like a mad woodpecker was eating at the plane and something punched through his left shoulder, spinning him to the right. His left side went numb with shock.

The burning insulation and wire dropped from the instrument panel and his legs sizzled from the heat eating through his flight suit. The fire also gnawed around his back. Holding the stick between his knees, he tried to release the canopy with his right hand, but the fire distracted him.

He would not allow himself to scream.

Ivanoff could feel his cooked skin sloughing off his legs as they rubbed against the stick. He pounded on the canopy. Finally, it gave, slid back a foot and stuck. A shard of the broken airframe behind him would let it go no further.

He felt next to him for the fire extinguisher and yanked on it. It was already hot from the fire and he could not drag it out. He pulled the ring and the white foam sprayed forward into the instrument panel. The fire did not die away completely and the chemicals ate into his legs.

For a several moments, Ivanoff did not know where he was. Shock and pain pummeled his being toward blackness. He willed his mind forward; back into the world of agony. He refused to accept the mastery of the pain and assessed where he was. He was at only a few thousand feet, but straight and level. He tried the throttle with his right hand and found it worked. The rudder pedals were sticky, but also responded.

Believing he was dead already, he turned the plane around and climbed.

When he caught the Messerschmitts, they were lazily strafing fleeing Russian troops. Focused on their play, they did not see Ivanoff pouncing from above.

The official report said the planes he shot down were the same three that had almost killed him. Ivanoff never claimed they were. He concluded that his still-smoking YAK confused the Germans and they could not believe the wounded plane was the one attacking them.

When Ivanoff bounced into a field nearby, the troops had demanded to carry him off as a hero. Instead, it took an hour for the doctor with them to separate Ivanoff's charred back from the remnants of his cockpit seat.

He never truly slept again. His life became a dark, eternal dance with pain. The tightening scar tissue threatened to deform him into a warped freak.

Unconsciously flexing his back to stretch the leathery tissue that served as skin, Ivanoff barked an order to the operator for his personal YAK fighter to be standing by. He pulled out his sidearm from the desk drawer and gave his second order. The operator repeated both orders back, ending the second order with a rising note to his voice.

"Immediately!" hissed Ivanoff. He grabbed his field coat and, his march echoing through the empty halls, thought about his future.

Perhaps the Americans were testing their air defenses in preparation for a preemptive strike. If so, Colonel Ivanoff had failed. In fact, someone had most likely been asleep at one or more of the radar stations. But blame bubbled up in the Soviet Army. Reaching higher until it hit someone politically connected who pushed it back down. Usually by personally dispatching the "guilty" with a bullet in the base of the skull. Ivanoff himself had become head of air security in April when his superior had been executed for ordering the YAK to harass the British airliner. But Ivanoff had had no time for politics. He had been busy defending his homeland and proven himself more than worthy during the Great Patriotic War.

He clenched his teeth as he stepped into the hulking, black Horch luxury staff car that had been confiscated from the Nazis. The driver spun the vehicle and floored the accelerator. The driver did not have to be told the colonel was in a hurry. He drove down the center of the nearly empty streets of Berlin's eastern outskirts. The only other cars he might have encountered were other Soviet officials and officers – also in a hurry.

People, politically connected people, were beginning to forget the war and its great patriots. The Kremlin had its eyes hunting West, about to play a delicate game. The stakes were all of Europe and blunderers would not be tolerated.

Four floors below Ivanoff's office, in the basement of the former German Army Engineers School, the questioning private carefully tore out the page of his phone log. He transcribed the evening's calls back into the logbook, leaving the last two entries out.

But he was also under orders by someone connected much higher than the impatient Colonel. He slipped the torn log page into an envelope.

He knew the address by heart.

CHAPTER 15

*Frankfurt am Main Bahnhof, U.S. Occupied
Germany, June 13, 1948, 4:33 P.M.*

Chance began to realize what the man really wanted to know. He was about fifty, wearing a black Homburg with a frayed brim.

"If I may introduce myself? I am Doctor Heinrich Klempnock," he had precisely enunciated about fifty paces from where Chance was still trying to lose him on the train platform.

The little German's English was fairly good and he had put undo emphasis on the *Doctor*. Chance had expected the hand on the elbow any second, followed by the well-rehearsed plea for food, occupation scrip or cigarettes. If the beggar was imaginative, the speech would include mention of a daughter or sister, dangling sex in the distance.

While stationed in Tripoli, Libya in 1943, Chance and Nevada had made the mistake of cutting through a bazaar to get back to base. Beset by beggars and children, they were an hour late and down a month's rations of candy, gum and cigarettes.

When Chance had traveled to meet Nevada in March, he had expected much the same. But the Germans had held their eyes downward or away, shamed by the well-fed, victorious American. Chance liked it that way. He had to admit that he had felt a twinge of embarrassment when an old woman, her life wrapped in newspaper bundles, stood to give him her seat. Then, he had turned his eyes away with a short shake of his head. He had waited comfortably dry on the same platform with a group of loud, back-slapping GIs as the locals had consigned themselves to stand apart under the rain that poured through the wounded nineteenth-century roof.

Spring sunlight now made a dazzling archipelago through the same holes. Chance noticed the doctor winced every time he crossed one of the bright islands. Chance used an old fighter pilot's trick as he stopped and stood so Dr. Klempnock would have to press his interrogation to Chance's face wreathed by the sun.

Undeterred, eyes narrowed to painful slits, the smiling doctor had started all his questions with "Do you not think…?" The interview wandered from the life Chance had left behind in Tulsa. Chance had said he didn't have much time to see the sights in Tulsa. He had been there only a few months working in the oil fields when the Nips bombed Pearl. He made sure the good Doctor understood that. Klempnock had only smiled and nodded. He continued to probe deftly. Fed up, Chance was about to tell him to go fuck himself and teach him and any other Krauts in earshot some of the lesser-known American invective.

Then he understood what Klempnock had really wanted to know. The questions about home. How did Chance rate the Russian soldier? Was Truman a good president and as widely loved as Roosevelt was? Had he formed any attachments to a German girl?

Klempnock couldn't see the anger pinching Chance's face. The taller man's finger stabbing into his chest told him plenty.

"Listen, bud. You jerks started this mess. You clean it up and you get whatever's coming to you. I'm done saving people's asses. The Russkies can have what I haven't bombed flat. I'm going home."

Klempnock staggered as if punched. The same fear on his face would have been there if Chance had told him he was going to break his neck. He took off the worn Homburg and was pleading to the big American's back as Chance went for a swim in the shadows.

"And where is home?"

Chance's face changed briefly as he headed for the *Ausgang*; Fraktur typeface inlaid into oak with a regulation GI "EXIT" stenciled crooked in red above it on the ornate trim.

The street outside was a wide boulevard with the *Bahnhof* opposite jagged ruins jutting out like a skeletal hand from a pile of masonry. A group of *Trümmerfrauen*, or rubble women, crawled over the mound of broken stones. Gray shadows who neither sang nor spoke brought two bricks at a time down to where others chipped off the mortar and stacked them in neat rows on a horse cart. Everything about them was gray; perfectly camouflaged until they moved against the dusty jumble.

An olive US Army Packard with a white star on the door raced past, throwing up more gray dust. When it was gone, silence settled like the dust, weighing everything down.

Chance could not believe he was in one of Germany's major cities. The random tock-tock of the chipping hammers fell clearly on his ears. No car horns or church bells came from any direction. No one yelled or spoke above a whisper. Chance could see almost a hundred people from where he was standing. A few rode bicycles or pulled carts made from anything like tires and anything like a box. Baby carriages were amazingly popular, but few had enough faith to have babies. One carriage was buckling under a load of gaudy light fixtures recovered from some bombed out building.

The shadows moved past as if trying not to disturb something. They picked their way carefully, footfalls muted by the dust.

One of the *Trümmerfrauen* brought her two bricks to the chippers and paused. Chance would not have noticed her if she hadn't taken off her head scarf. Underneath, her blonde hair caught the sun like a beacon. She was briefly part of the blue sky and white spring clouds. She wiped her face with the rag and tied it back, returning to the rubble.

The procession stopped when a distant siren wailed. Instinctively, most of the shadows looked to the sky. Chance couldn't help joining them. He hoped the Russians would make their move when he was not in Germany.

The lone siren died away, but the people still searched the sky. Chance felt an underground hammer blow through his feet. He pulled his head down, hunching his shoulders before he consciously heard the loud concussion two seconds later. The blast echoed through the ruins, dying to a roar that boomed around in the hollow train station behind him.

A woman reflexively screamed behind him. Chance could see her raw terror trying to burst from her face as she covered her ears. A man put his hand on her shoulder, whispering something soothing. The woman's tears turned white, gathering the dust on her cheeks.

"*Pass auf!*" shrieked another woman across the street. He didn't understand the words, but the tone was unmistakable. Chance whirled again.

The *Trümmerfrauen* were stumbling over the stones toward the street. Three stories above them, a section of someone's office with a map of Germany on one wall started to collapse. It moved very slowly, holding its shape at first. By the time it hit the two women, it was a blur of dust and bricks. The noise was deafening as dust shot across to the train station.

Chance choked, unable to open his eyes. He stumbled in the gritty cloud, something moving him toward the scene. He found he was with the others, also choking, but crossing the street.

A fresh breeze cleared most of the dust. Voices screamed and shouted back and forth in a guttural mish-mash. Chance stopped at the back of the crowd in a small sea of baby carriages, carts and bicycles left where the crowd had dropped them. He saw a man picking through the possessions. The thief pulled out something shiny from one cart and kept glancing at the crowd fixed on the building collapse. He froze when he saw Chance.

Chance did not move. After a moment, the thief put the object back and moved on.

"*Ist zu schwer! Bitte, Hilfe!*" It was the woman with the blonde hair, now caked with plaster and mortar. She was pleading with the crowd who had formed impromptu chains, passing bricks from the mound to the street. The man in front of Chance handed him a brick. Chance tossed it behind him. Another followed.

Someone was bound to spot him. They would think he caused this. Maybe he had. He would move away and leave them to it.

"*Sie!*" It was the blonde pointing her raw finger directly at Chance. "*Grosser Mann!*"

Chance looked for a weapon. All he had was the bricks. They had them, too.

"*Sind Sie taub? Helfen Sie!*" she screamed again.

The man in front of Chance pointed toward the pile and grabbed for Chance's arm to pull him forward. Something in Chance's eyes made the man stop.

"*Lieber Gott, sie sind begräbt!*" he pleaded. "*Begräbt!*"

Chance moved toward the front of the pile where everyone was pointing. He climbed up to the blonde and saw a large wooden beam with a pair of skinny legs poking out from underneath. Two bigger women were trying to shift it. One of the legs moved and Chance heard a moan. He slid down to the beam and looked around for anything to use as a lever. A pipe stuck out from a wall and Chance ripped it loose. He gave it to one of the big women and bent down to lift the beam as she wedged the pipe underneath.

Chance's overcoat was restricting him and he took it off revealing officer's khaki, tie and trousers.

The crowd stopped talking.

"*Ein Ami,*" half-whispered the blonde.

Chance saw his coat was covered in dust. He had been one of them until he took it off. He couldn't read the blonde's tone – a curse or just matter of fact.

He bent down to get a grip on the beam and heaved. The big woman with the pipe pried the beam to the left and it tumbled down the pile.

The form underneath made an animal noise, an airy shriek. Blood gushed from the left side of her head, until now held back by the weight of the beam. There was no real left side of her head, only a mass of gore mixed with dust, hair and a kerchief pressed to the thickness of a potato pancake. The form twitched into a seizure, hands clawing the air and legs dancing to a frantic tune. Mercifully, the seizure was short. The woman stopped, her remaining eye staring at Chance.

Someone was praying. Chance couldn't understand it, but he knew the rhythm.

The tock-tock of the brick chippers started again. The crowd drifted away to squeaking baby carriages and groaning carts. The big woman took the pipe to the edge of the pile where it joined tons of iron already picked from the building.

The blonde picked up Chance's coat and shook off the dust.

"Hang on." He reached for it.

"*Für die Leiche,*" the blonde moved back, clutching the coat and tottering on the constantly shifting bricks. She pointed at the graying form of the girl.

Chance snatched the coat back.

"*Die Leiche,*" she sobbed at the top of her lungs. The procession stopped again. The blonde looked at the dead girl and shrieked at Chance, pointing.

Chance came off the pile of rubble. The man who had handed him the bricks stepped in front of him.

"*Bitte, für die Leiche.*"

The crowd was forming again, whispering. Chance looked at his escape options. The train station? Then where?

He caught snatches of the German. He could recognize some of the words. "*Bomben*" and "*Pilot*" stood out despite the foreign pronunciation and emphasis. Could they have read his insignia? He kept his coat off, planning to throw it at the crowd if they attacked.

"*Für die Leiche!*" shrieked the blonde, a siren call from the top of the rubble.

The crowd was closing in. Chance could not read their faces. A small man held up a fist. Chance stopped and got ready for the worst.

CHAPTER 16

*Frankfurt am Main Bahnhof,
June 13, 1948, 4:42 P.M.*

"*Polizei!*" raced through the mob and everything stopped.

"Captain Mitchell?" The young MP pushed through to Chance. "We wondered what happened to you." The words and accent enveloped him like a warm blanket.

Chance let the MP lead him to the waiting jeep. The Germans pressed the MP, hands outstretched. Some pointed at the rubble and at Chance. The MP moved them out of the way. They murmured "*für die Leiche*" over and over. The MP only nodded.

Chance and the MP were blocks away before Chance stopped looking over his shoulder.

"What does *fur dee lieke* mean?"

"Fur what?" The MP cocked his head as he beeped at a group of men pushing a pre-war Mercedes with two well-dressed women riding in back as if the car was still being propelled by its diesel engine.

Chance repeated the phrase, trying to imitate the rasping consonants.

"Yeah, yeah. *Für die Leiche.*" The MP's German pronunciation was perfect. "'For the body.' They wanted your coat to cover the body. They figure you can get another one. Hell, over here a skid row bum from Milwaukee would be a rich man, sir."

Chance said nothing more for the mile ride to Supreme Allied Command Headquarters. The building was the modern, seven-story, concrete and glass, former headquarters of Germany's largest chemical company, I.G. Farben. Built in 1931, the chemists must have had an invisibility potion or a link to the Allied bombing target committees. Only a few rough patches spoiled the immaculate white exterior. Chance noticed the biggest wound as he walked in. The arm of an obliterated lamppost had been driven into the massive right pillar of the entryway. The Army engineers evidently thought it was too much trouble to remove. The trail of rust bled down the concrete.

The outer office of Major Thomas McKane boasted a view of the city center. Despite being over a mile away, Chance could clearly see the train station across a landscape of butte-like ruins. A better piece of scenery in the office was a WAC secretary. Even in the regulation uniform and spartan makeup, she was a sight for starved eyes. But something about her told Chance she could also break his neck. He could expect that with these intel types.

"Hey, beautiful, can you get me 32nd Bomb Disposal?" sang out the MP as if talking to his wife while he closed the door behind Chance.

The WAC gave a warm smile and made the call. A second later she handed him the phone.

"Hey, Fred. You guys working over in *Bahnhofsviertel*?" The MP offered the WAC a cigarette which she demurred. He whistled softly. "Really? That big. The blast shook down a building across from the *Bahnhof*. Two dead." He lit the equivalent of ten minutes with a German prostitute for himself and took a deep drag. "Nobody's blaming you. Just give us the word and we can get these *Trümmerfrauen* clear when it goes up. Sure, thanks." He handed the phone back to the lethal looking WAC and nodded to Chance. "Captain." He blew a kiss at the WAC and left.

Chance got up. "Where's the gents?"

"Please sit down, sir." The WAC was smiling.

"I'd like to clean up." Chance dusted off his arm for emphasis.

"Sit down, sir." The *sir* was almost forgotten.

"Come on."

"Sir, if you leave, my orders are to have that MP bring you back using any means necessary." Chance was amazed at the ugly images the WAC's beautiful, upturned face conjured up. "And he'll do it, pronto. 'Cause he likes me." She smiled.

"I can't even go to the gents? What's all this about?" Chance let a little menace creep into his voice, too.

"Sit down, sir. Major McKane will be with you shortly." The WAC wasn't buying. The small part of Chance that wasn't annoyed was aroused.

He threw his dusty overcoat into a chair, raising a small cloud. The WAC found something pressing to read on her desk. Chance found President Truman grinning at him. It was a small picture. The grime on the wall outlined a larger frame that it had replaced. That one would have invariably been one of a corporal with a small mustache who rarely grinned.

Despite the American flag, presidential picture and the former bobby-soxer turned watchdog, the office was all German.

Chance missed odd things about home. Fire hydrants that looked like fire hydrants. Mail boxes, barber shops with *The Hit Parade* on the radio, gas stations with liveried attendants and movie theaters trimmed in neon with big yellow cabs pulling up in front. Big stores with names like Walgreens and Kresge. Ma and pa stores with a potbellied stove inside and big boxes of fruit outside, where you could buy a steak for twelve cents a pound. A soda fountain staffed by a dame like the WAC in a blue uniform, a checkered apron and one of those silly white hats. Newspapers with baseball scores – anything but *Stars and Stripes*. The smell of hot dogs.

"Captain," The voice sounded like a radial engine burning its bearings.

Major McKane was well over six feet tall and could have been half the front line for Notre Dame. Chance saluted and barely squeezed by him into the large office. He heard McKane whispering to the WAC.

"Anything?"

JITTERBUG LIFT

Chance didn't hear the WAC's reply if there was one. The floor trembled as McKane barged back into his own office, slamming the door behind him.

Chance recognized bluster when he saw it. Like a bull pawing the ground before it charges. The bull hopes just the pawing and snorting will make its adversary go away. It would rather not have to charge.

"Sit down, captain."

Chance recognized where the WAC got her tone and sat in large leather chair that was amazingly stiff. It smelled like somebody had spilled coffee or milk on it and not bothered to clean out the diamond pleats.

McKane lumbered around to the other side of his desk, but did not sit down. More bluster. He picked up a brown file folder and studied it, flipping one page back and forth several times.

Late two nights before, Chance's CO had given him a set of orders to report to USAIG, U. S. Army Intelligence Germany. No reason given. He was on the first train down to the coast and got some sleep on a Navy transport out of Dover for Ostend, Belgium. Three trains got him to Frankfurt by 4:00 P.M. so he could run into the inquisitive doctor. Somebody either had the wrong guy or…

"You did thirty-one missions?" McKane's voice had managed to find an even lower register, something between meat grinder and cement mixer *profundo*.

"Yes, sir." That was a question that could be answered by telegram or telephone. Chance wanted to add *almost*, but didn't. Everything that had happened was in the file. Right down to the fact that he and Nevada were the only ones left of Chance's original crew.

Satch had caught a round over Berlin on the next mission after Chance had been wounded. Another pilot had been flying Chance's crew in an unnamed, brand new B-17, with Chance getting checked out at the base hospital. Satch hadn't made a sound except to say he had been hit. Nevada said the waist gunner had uttered the words with quiet disbelief and bled to death before anyone could help him. Later they found out that it was a 50-caliber round. The Nazis didn't use 50-caliber ammunition.

Mick, the other waist gunner, had been killed on Chance's first mission back in APPLE PIE, TOO. Mick was cut in two by cannon fire from one of the Nazis' new jet fighters.

He tried not to think about how he lost his radio operator, Jimmy Vernon.

"Do any debriefs, Captain?" McKane was asking questions that were answered in Chance's file.

"Two weeks. While I recovered." Chance nodded toward the file in McKane's catcher's mitt hands.

McKane shrugged. "This isn't yours. We don't have yours. Yet." He came around the desk and bored into Chance with the greenest eyes he had ever seen.

"I think we got the file on the wrong guy." McKane sounded relieved. "I'm sorry, captain. It happens a lot now. Guys are mustering out at the rate of a thousand a day. Paperwork flies all over the place and this guy's file ended up here."

Chance noticed McKane didn't smile. He just kept staring at Chance.

"We're doing a project comparing bomb debriefs with actual damage surveyed on the ground. We sent for you to help us sort out the bullshit from the useful info. Easy duty until you ship home."

The WAC came in after a soft knock. McKane hadn't pressed any button or intercom that Chance could see.

"Make sure Captain Mitchell has a place to stay tonight, Beverly."

"The TOQ is full, sir."

"Well, think of something," roared McKane.

"Yes, sir."

McKane hadn't taken his emerald eyes off Chance. "You'll be with us a while, captain. We'll make you comfortable."

McKane finally broke his gaze and went back to studying another lost file. The WAC held the door open. Chance took that as a sign the interview was over. He left without saluting.

Five minutes later, Chance was on his way to Rhein-Main Airfield in the back of one of the white-starred Packards with a silent sergeant at the wheel.

When they reached the airfield, the sergeant showed him where to check in as a transient pilot and left. The sergeant behind the desk of the transient pilot billet took a full ten minutes before he said he couldn't help him.

"You don't have an aircraft. You're not a transient pilot without an aircraft. Try the TOQ."

"It's full. Major McKane sent me over here." Chance was tired and it was becoming a struggle to keep his voice from yelling. It wouldn't help. Contrary to popular belief, it's the sergeants who hold all power in the Army.

"McKane? What section's he with?"

"Intelligence. Command Section, USAIG."

The sergeant phoned and after a long wait determined that they had gone off duty. There was no one there who knew about any homeless Captain Mitchell.

"You're out of luck," pronounced the sergeant as he answered the ringing phone. Chance leaned over the desk and pressed down the hook.

"I'm a captain in the US Air Force. That's the outfit you work for. It means we're on the same side. I'm tired. There's gotta be a GI regulation rack someplace."

"How much money you got?" The sergeant still had the dead receiver to his ear.

"Ten dollars."

"U.S.? Pictures of Lincoln and Washington?"

Chance nodded.

"Then I respectfully suggest the captain quit beefing, sir. All we get is occupation scrip. You can walk out that door and grab the next transport into town. Two dollars gets you a room with a bed and a private bath in the best hotel left standing in Frankfurt. A buck-fifty gets you something like a steak dinner with all the trimmings. And five pictures of General Washington gets you someone to make sure you sleep well and wake up with your ashes completely hauled. Sir."

Chance stepped out into the cold spring night. Somehow his overcoat wasn't warm enough. A drizzle started as he made his way toward the transport stand where a car waited. Only steps from it, a pilot still in his flight suit trotted past him and dove in the car to the welcoming cheers of the riders already in it. The Chevy took off before the door closed.

Chance waited alone for a few minutes before he spotted the gate to the flight line. It swung freely in the rising wind. He walked toward it.

A fuel truck jockey pointed out the hangar where Nevada kept his plane. He took pity on the soaked captain and gave him a ride the two hundred yards down the flight line.

INTERNATIONAL AIRLINES was scrawled across the door, the chalk slowly eroding in the rain. The door was locked and the hangar empty.

The fuel jockey regaled Chance about the good life back in Seattle as he drove him over to flight operations. There another not-so-helpful sergeant informed Chance that he couldn't find any flight plan open or closed for anybody named Nevada or any C-47 belonging to International Airlines.

Two other pilots checked in and asked about transport into Frankfurt. The sergeant told them they were lucky. The last one was leaving in a few minutes.

On the fifteen-minute ride to the Hotel Tivoli, the two pilots fielded Chance's questions about when Nevada and his C-47 might be back.

"I wonder if it's that guy they were calling for last night," yawned the redheaded Californian.

"It was two nights ago."

"We've been flyin' too fuckin' much, Billy. Getting my days all mixed up."

"They've got us running supplies day and night into Berlin. Somebody thinks the Russians are gonna make a move." The lanky Minnesotan had his flight cap pulled down over his eyes. "They were looking for somebody last night. And they found him. Just hadn't closed his flight plan."

"Back here?"

The hot shot from Los Angeles was already breathing slow and deep.

"Back here. Wake us when we get to the hotel, buddy," the Minnesotan sighed.

The sergeant at the Transient Pilots' Billet wasn't kidding. By 1:00 A.M., Chance was trying to sort out the day's events, well fed, washed and warm – but alone – in his room with a private bath.

At 2:10 A.M., a click at the door let him know he wasn't going to be alone much longer.

CHAPTER 17

Tivoli Hotel, Frankfurt am Main, Occupied Germany, June 14, 1948, 2:11 A.M.

Chance rolled onto the floor and closed his eyes before the orange light from the hall spilled into the room as the door opened. Instinct had taken control. He would have the advantage of being adjusted to the dark if the intruder closed the door behind him.

He heard the door click closed and peeked over the bed. The intruder was hatless, squat and looking down at the bed waiting for his eyes to get used to the dark. If he had thought about it, Chance would have guessed an American – but he wasn't thinking.

Chance planted one foot on the bed and lunged across. The intruder heard the bed squeak under Chance's weight and tensed just before Chance's shoulder caught him under the chin. The pair continued into the hard plaster wall.

"Shit," expelled the intruder in perfect American vernacular.

Chance's head bounced against the wall and he saw a flash as his retinas registered the shock that stunned him.

"Take it easy…" The accent was New York.

The sentence never finished. Chance was not listening and took a swing at the voice that met nothing but the damp air.

The intruder caught him under the rib cage with a hard left that felt like a sword as Chance's bottom ribs bent very unnaturally inward.

Chance staggered back against a wardrobe, pushed himself left and came at the intruder again.

"Idiot…" started the chatty intruder again before Chance's right connected badly between his chin and chest. The intruder gurgled and lashed out with a kick to Chance's stomach.

Chance fought the urge to double up, knowing it would bring his head in range of another kick, which usually ended all the other bar fights he had seen or been in.

He was trying to target the intruder again when the door opened, blinding him as the squat man bolted and went left. Chance followed, picking up speed as soon as he found he could breathe again.

Chance could just catch that his attacker had dark hair before he darted into the stairwell. Chance pushed the stairwell door back open before it closed and started down, steadying himself on the rail. He thought he heard rapid footsteps below and charged down. He slipped on a turn and went sprawling on the tile floor. He got his footing and found it was remarkably easy to get up. The hand grabbing a hunk of his shirt was helping a lot.

He was pulling back to swing when he saw the white leggings wrapping the ankles of the man behind his benefactor. Five years in the military made even his instinct stop.

"Whoa!" the big major with the cement mixer voice barked. The MP who drove Chance from the train station was behind him, already drawing his baton. McKane pushed the MP back with a hand the size of a tennis racket.

"Captain Mitchell won't give us any trouble."

Chance pointed past them down the stairs. "Some guy busted into my room. He ran down this way," he panted.

The sound of a door closing several floors up made Chance a liar. McKane cocked his head at the MP, who immediately ran into the floor they were on.

"Knows what he's doing, your friend." The cement mixer dropped into low gear again.

"I don't have any friends here." Chance rubbed his forehead. It was bloody.

McKane grunted. "We'll talk about that. Let's talk about everything."

A vice circled Chance's arm as McKane pushed him back toward his room. A few minutes later, McKane tossed Chance's key at the sleeping night clerk. The MP came down the stairs on the other side of the hotel and met them in front of the lobby desk.

"*Nichts.*"

McKane made a noise that could only be disapproval.

"Maybe the other guys got 'im."

McKane made another noise that told Chance he was not a positive thinker and pushed Chance toward the front door.

The WAC looked up wearily as McKane led Chance in. She didn't smile at the MP from Milwaukee or the other two that had ridden behind McKane's Packard in a jeep back to the huge building on a hill above the city.

"They said you guys had gone home," Chance growled before he got to McKane's office.

"Coffee and something to clean him up." Chance noticed McKane softened considerably when he spoke to the WAC. Still gruff orders, but the edge was off.

McKane closed the door and slipped out of his coat. He sat down behind the desk and briskly rubbed his face. Chance moved toward the smelly chair.

"Stand at ease, Captain." The cement mixer was gone, replaced by a tone Chance couldn't place. The band was tuning up, but he had no idea what the dance would be.

Chance's training as a B-17 pilot had included interrogation by the enemy. This had all the hallmarks of the "bad Fritz." Chance stood as straight as his aching belly would let him.

The WAC came in with a cup of fine china that smelled of even finer coffee. An eighteenth-century couple was in mid-prance in royal blue around the cup, which the WAC set on McKane's desk. The china was so delicate that the dark coffee was clearly visible through the flawless white. Chance guessed rightly there wasn't a second couple coming for him to make it a foursome.

The WAC smelled of stale cigarettes and wiped his face with a very soft piece of linen. She handed him a towel. Chance noticed she had just put on her lipstick and her lips parted slightly. He shook the idea she was "good Fritz" with a smile that almost made it to his face. He dabbed his neck and she held out her hand for the towel, looking him straight in the eye. He handed it to her in a wad and turned to McKane.

Chance's voice was as raw as the hour. "What's this...?"

"You've forgotten your military courtesy, Captain. You speak when spoken to."

McKane had taken half the cup in one gulp and proceeded to drain it. Chance hadn't heard the door close and now heard the WAC's stockings swishing together as she brought the pot in to refill the prancing couple. The image of silk-encased thighs heating up with friction made it half way up his brainstem, only to be turned back as Chance tried to think.

The door sealed closed with an airy click.

"Don't try to think, Captain. We're way ahead of you. The more you think, the more we'll tear you apart." McKane gulped more coffee and banged the cup down cockeyed in the saucer, leaving the couple in a tilted minuet.

"Have I been spoken to, sir?" Chance kept his voice even. He resented McKane's reading his mind. What made him mad was that the lug did it so easily.

McKane stared at the window. The blackout curtains were pulled back and the east was warming from blue to red. "We've been at this since before the shooting stopped. You're buying into a game where all the tricks have been tried. Yet you hot shots think you can try them again. Your way is better. You won't get caught. This is all a dream. You're really sleeping in the TPB."

"The TPB sergeant wouldn't let me bunk there, sir. I don't have an aircraft."

"Never underestimate a sergeant, Captain. They're always right. You don't have an aircraft. You don't have any aircraft, at all. All you have now is your hide, your uniform and what I let you have."

The office trembled again as McKane got up and moved behind Chance.

"Who was Nevada flying out?"

"I don't..."

"You know! These are the guys who killed your buddies. Nazis! And you're gonna be the dope 'cause they waved some Swiss Francs or gold or some stolen art under your nose."

"The plane was barely flight worthy. Nevada wasn't going to fly anyone very far."

McKane reached past Chance and snatched a file off the desk, flipped it open and stuffed it at Chance's face. "We're not blind, Captain! He had eight thousand dollars worth of work done. Cash! You guys take up a collection or were you squirreling away your allowance? Try again, Captain! Don't look surprised, 'cause you're not."

Chance was surprised. Not only at the amount of money, but at something that had finally dawned on him as the sky outside turned evenly gray with morning fog. They didn't have Nevada. If they'd caught him, they didn't need Chance. But if they didn't have Nevada, where was he? A C-47 is not easy to hide.

Chance faced McKane squarely. "I don't know who Nevada was flying out or if he was flying anybody out. We test flew the Dakota in March. We almost crashed. He said he might have a job. That's all he told me."

"He might have a job. You two faced hell and gone together. You and your plane were shot up and you lost your entire formation. He flew you home. Christ, you fucked the same women and all he told you was 'he might have a job'? It's getting light, Captain. The time for bedtime stories is over."

"I don't know who it was, if anybody."

"Tell me!"

"I don't know."

"Captain, the Russians are looking for any excuse to take Germany. They're already squeezing Berlin. Anything could set this off. If they think we're smuggling Nazis, they could sweep to the Rhine and the whole world would say 'Bravo'."

"I don't know."

"He's dead. You know that?" McKane whispered.

Chance stopped breathing. It had been nicely done. McKane had called up all the love and loyalty, priming Chance. McKane wasn't a bull. Quite the opposite. Like a bullfighter, he had held the rapier behind the red cape of the political situation.

"The plane crashed on takeoff in a pasture ten nights ago. Someplace called Ziewald. About two hundred kilometers into the Russian zone. Russian patrol found the burning wreckage. One body on board."

CHAPTER 18

*USAIG Headquarters, Frankfurt am Main,
Occupied Germany, June 14, 1948, 4:01 A.M.*

Chance swayed.

McKane became almost human. "Please sit down, Captain."

Chance flopped into the leather chair. It was the first round and he had already had his bell rung.

"Are you sure?"

"The Russians got real excited about a week ago. Lots of radio chatter. They can't pick their noses unless somebody high up approves it. We learned enough."

McKane lunged off the desk.

"Somebody is looking right now for another sucker to be his ticket out. A fuckin' Nazi. Help me get 'em."

"Nevada wouldn't tell me. He said it was some*thing* out of the East. That's all he said. We'd be set up for when I mustered out. I told him not to do it."

"Then who was the guy in your room?"

Chance could only shake his head. His whole world was a mess. He wanted ham and eggs at the Kresge lunch counter.

"The Russians will try to choke off Berlin again. And this time for keeps. They could use Nevada's simply flying into their zone as an act of war. They even got one guy over there whose sole job it is to make life hell for anything that flies in or out of Berlin. As Berlin goes so goes Germany. And then Europe." McKane's voice had settled back to just above a whisper. It was several seconds before he spoke again. The light seeping in had brightened to lifeless gray, but no further.

"Give me the guy that attacked you." A big hand grabbed Chance's shoulder. "Just the name. He was Nevada's German contact, wasn't he?"

"We didn't talk much." Chance stared at the streak of blood on the back of his hand. "You're gonna bring him back, aren't you?"

McKane's grip tightened to the threshold of pain and was gone. "No. The Russians can't prove anything now. If we go ask for the body, we might as well admit we knew what he was up to." He reached over to his desk. "Get out of here." A flimsy single sheet of typed paper landed in Chance's lap.

Chance didn't read it until he was outside the I.G. Farben building. He was ordered back to England. If he wasn't back there by noon the next day, he was AWOL. The rest was train and ferry times.

His favorite MP pulled up in a jeep, the tires skipping to a stop on the damp cobblestones.

"Ten minutes, sir." His face betrayed nothing. No sympathy or recognition. Chance got in and held on to the dashboard.

Chance had met Nevada in Libya. Chance's copilot had gotten drunk and rolled a jeep, breaking his back. Nevada had lost his pilot on his first raid. A run on the Romanian oil fields had put a piece of flak through his skull.

Their CO had assigned them other replacements, but a typing error threw them together. They built up a crew that eventually went to England after D-Day.

"I understand you need somebody to teach you how to fly this thing," had been Nevada's way of introduction.

That led to a gut-wrenching (for the crew) flight where they tried to outperform each other with what a B-17 could do and still come home with the wings mostly on.

Chance stood at the entrance to the *Bahnhof*, watching the women working on the collapsed building. After a minute he spotted the blonde trudging back off the pile with two more bricks.

The MP waited, too, until Chance was on the train to Belgium.

Chance expected the rest of his time in the Air Force would be hell. He would be watched every moment, given little or no leave and shipped home.

A late spring storm made the Channel crossing bleak. A very short, spectacled assistant to some French Red Cross group tried to make conversation at the coffee bar. The Russians were making repatriation very difficult. Whole areas were being sealed off. People with technical backgrounds were being shipped east in the Soviet occupied zones never to be heard of again. Poland was very bad.

Chance ignored her and went on deck. He didn't want to hear about the refugee problems or how millions were trying to make their way back home – those that still had homes to go to. Somehow it was easier to watch a deck chair sliding back and forth as the ship rolled in the driving rain.

The gate sentry told him to report immediately to Major Witten's office where he got the second flimsy sheet of paper in as many days.

"You're out. We could be going to war any day now and some madman has decided you should go home. You wouldn't mind giving me his number?"

Whitten didn't expect an answer and went back to figuring out where to put the new B-29s being flown over to intimidate the Russians. The newer bomber was the same that had dropped two atomic bombs on Japan to end the war in the Pacific. President Truman knew that the United States had no more nuclear weapons ready to bluff the Soviets out of marching all the way to Paris. But the Russians didn't know that. They were to see the scabbard and assume the sword was in it.

Chance was used to seeing the light come through the cracks in the walls of his hastily-built quarters. The whole Quonset hut shifted in the wind, threatening to come apart at the seams.

Little puffs of air fluttered his orders to report to Southampton at the end of the week for a ship home. They were keeping all aircraft in Europe. Ham and eggs at Kresge's in New York waited at the end of ten days.

He never made it.

CHAPTER 19

*Rhein-Main Air Base, Frankfurt, US Occupied
Germany, June 19, 1948, 4:47 P.M.*

Chance recognized his late-night attacker immediately. The dark-haired man returned the favor.

The cowling was off the C-47's left engine. Oil had hemorrhaged from the main bearing, forming a small puddle around the work stand. The fuselage boasted "Empire Air Freight," obviously painted over US Army Air Corps markings. The mechanic wiped grime from the wrench in his hand, looking down at Chance, who was still trip-rumpled in second-hand pants and a cardigan he had picked up in Winchester.

"Some bean brain jockey let it glide with the power pulled back. Starves the engine for oil. Lucky for him the bearing didn't seize." The Brooklyn accent stood out like the Statue of Liberty. "You look like a jockey who'd know that. But youse should dress better."

Chance took a step back as the squat fashion critic jumped down, still holding the wrench.

Chance's 2:00 A.M. dance partner reached into the pocket of old Army overalls that had mustered out with their owner. Chance glanced at the open tool box two steps away. The rest of the hangar was dark. Voices echoed indistinct from far off. If the squat man made trouble, there'd be no witnesses.

"Want some chocolate?" The mechanic held out the half-eaten Hershey bar. "Most guys trade 'em for women and stuff. You could get a whole harem for a month's ration. But I can't help it." He took half of what was left in a single bite and worked it into a ball in his cheek. "Nick Rossi." *Rossi* came out *Roshy* as he stuck out an oily hand.

Chance eyed the wrench. "We've met."

"Yeah, but you skipped the proper introductions." Rossi walked around the oil and carefully placed the wrench back in its box. He was a grimy mess, but his toolbox could have been in an operating room. "Don't worry. I wouldn't hit youse with that. Might hurt a perfectly good tool." He flashed a brown grin.

"Why would you want to hit me?" Chance watched Rossi's hands disappear into the black-streaked, olive overalls.

Rossi shrugged. "You started it. I just wanted to tell youse what I knew about our friend."

"Our friend." Chance hated song-and-dance routines. And this one didn't even have shapely legs to make it endurable.

"Not here. I gotta rebuild this and it's too late to start that. I'll meet you by the machine shop."

The small glassed-in area had received a coat of paint since the end of the war, but "*Der Feind hört mit!*" and other Nazi war slogans bled through. Chance heard the British manager yelling after Rossi as the mechanic threw a wave over his shoulder.

"Tomorrow. If youse don't like that, tell yer idiot jockeys to read the manual."

The manager grumbled something back which Rossi ignored, already smiling at Chance and jerking a thumb towards the base exit. "Guy thinks he runs this show."

Chance still felt like he was being set up when they went into the basement *Kneipe* which had boasted being an all-American bar in whitewash on the cracked wall of a burned-out building. Inside there was nothing American about it. A pair of very well-dressed and well-fed Germans whispered in the corner as Rossi shoved a beer at Chance. A crank Victrola played "Moonlight Serenade" for the second time since they had arrived. Maybe for the thousandth time since the owner had gotten the old record. The groove was so worn, the clarinet solo sounded like a train whistle.

Chance couldn't place the pattern on the wall behind the Germans. The wall had fifty small doors in it, each almost three feet square. The hinges were still there, but the handles had been removed and painted over.

Rossi caught Chance glancing at the two Germans.

"Don't stare." The New Yorker licked the head off his upper lip. "They're black market. Territorial as lions. Just as dangerous. *Prosit*, as they say."

Rossi banged the old table which served as a bar. "Hey, flip it over, will ya?"

The barkeep looked confused until Rossi turned his hand over several times.

"You got it, Joe." He cranked the box and flipped the record. It crawled back up to speed.

"What's the matter, you don't like the song?" Chance remembered standing dirty and hungry outside an Omaha dance hall hearing Glenn Miller's 1939 classic for the first time.

"I didn't like the company." Rossi cocked his head toward the two black marketers, now deep in conversation, ignoring the Americans. "If we was MPs, we'd try to be real quiet."

Rossi looked over his almost empty glass at Chance. "You don't seem real interested in finding anything out."

Chance stared into his beer. Dust was riding the bubbles up to the top and falling back to the bottom when they popped. He set the beer on the bar. "Where was he going?"

"Who?"

"Come on."

"Who?"

"Nevada."

"Just bein' sure. Wouldn't want to steer youse wrong with the dope on some other jockey. Confuses things."

The mechanic looked at his hands. Black delineated every split nail and scratch in his hands. Oily dirt was under his nails and even etched in his palms' lifelines.

"Why do youse want to know? You want to do the job?"

Chance hesitated. "I don't know yet."

"Whaddya gonna use for an airplane? See, I'm smart. I know everything that flies in and outta here. And you walked on the base, buddy. If you wanted the job you'd have to get a plane first. Don't get riled."

Chance was beyond riled. He had been clenching his jaw since Rossi had started playing coy again.

Rossi held up his road map hand. "Easy, buddy. You ain't getting anywhere without me. If you just want another shot at me, then get it over with." He took a step back.

"I want to know where Nevada was going. What – or who – he was picking up and where he was taking them."

"So I tell ya. Then what?"

"I don't know yet. I just want to know."

Rossi thought until the record started to skip. The barkeep hadn't noticed. He was talking to the two well-dressed men.

"Jitterbug. Something called Jitterbug. I don't know what it is. He wouldn't tell me. Plunked down a wad of cash to have the plane fixed up. Told me he was gonna take it up fer a check ride and never came back."

"When did you last see him?"

"Friday two weeks ago. Checked it out before he took it up at sundown."

"Was everything working on that crate?"

"Don't get insulting. He coulda flown me home with that."

"How much gas did he have on board?"

"Full tanks. Whatever he was bringing out was far away."

"Or he didn't want you to be able to backtrack where he was going." Chance almost smiled. "He was pretty smart, too. He crashed in a place called Ziewald. It's about 120 miles into the Russian zone. How can I get there?"

Rossi belched. "You don't. Unless yer name's Ivan."

"What if it was Fritz?"

"Papers. Krauts can't cross the street here without papers."

Chance nodded toward the trio in the corner. "They could help with that."

One of the men noticed Chance nodding at them and the conversation stopped. Faces were set in stone.

"Hey. You try that you'll end up in a place like this."

"I'm already in a place like this."

"I mean before. Use'ta be a morgue. Thick walls." Rossi paused dramatically. "Say you get these papers. It's a 120 miles; it'd take you days. And I don't think you speak much German."

"Ziewald's only thirty miles south of Berlin."

The bar creaked as Rossi leaned against it.

"You know what you should do? You should find the first MP you see, steal his weapon and put a bullet through your thick skull."

"Thanks for the advice."

"So it's near Berlin. How are you gonna get to Berlin?"

"You'll take care of that."

Chance walked over to the two Germans and the barkeep. The barkeep decided it would be marginally safer behind the bar.

"What's your names?"

"Peter und mine name is Harald." The more frightened of the two pointed to his partner.

"And yours?" The calmer German fingered his cigarette.

"I want papers."

The nervous German looked at the other, incredulous. He said something which Peter, the harder man, whose eyes never left Chance, cut off with "*Stumm!*"

Rossi sighed as Peter reached into his pocket. The New Yorker stepped toward the group, picking up a mismatched stool with one hand without pausing. The nervous Harald flinched and the braver Peter sucked in a breath as they saw the beefy American hefting the stool.

Peter's hand whipped out and slapped a small paper, folded in quarters on the table. Harald immediately followed suit.

"What the hell is this?" Chance muttered.

Rossi laughed, "Dumb fuck, they think you want *their* papers."

He dropped the stool with a sharp crack. The Germans managed weak smiles.

CHAPTER 20

*Over Occupied Germany,
June 21, 1948, 6:32 A.M.*

Shanley's head exploded.

Sun-bleached blonde hair came off first in slow motion, torn away as if an invisible demon was clawing at the scalp from the inside. Bits of light showed underneath, like a city under broken overcast at night. Chance's navigator wanted to tell him something. Shanley turned to Chance, eyes pleading as the top of his skull opened and words came out.

The words were in red blood and gray gore and Chance couldn't understand what they meant.

Shanley's eyes went their separate ways in tears as his face swelled and ripped into red, curved Arab daggers pointing in toward an orange cauliflower.

And it all made sense. Chance didn't want it to make sense, but it did. He just couldn't figure out the words.

The drone of the engines made his fingers tingle as he tried to catch the shreds of Shanley's mind before they flew off. He willed his arms to move and they refused. If they would move, he could glue the pieces back together. Chance tried to lean toward the daggers. They struck his head, feeling like ice.

He had to tell Nevada something. He tried to crawl forward, but the plane was full of bombs. They were soft bombs. Big and stacked in neat rows almost to the ceiling. Chance could see the light from the cockpit. Headphones were over an Army Air Corps cap.

He had to tell Nevada, but he couldn't make it; it was too far.

"It wasn't my fault"

Nevada turned, but his face was wrong.

"Flaps ten," repeated Rossi to the unseen pilot.

Chance smelled something like paste. The drone of Dakota's engines matched the sounds of his dream seamlessly. Chance was staring at a word. Pillsbury. Now nothing made sense.

He had fallen asleep after they took off from Frankfurt. Weather had delayed the flight where Chance was aboard as one bag of flour in plane that carried mail, spare parts and almost a ton and a half of the makings for bread; enough to feed almost three thousand people. The Army insisted that every flight into Berlin carry full loads. Chance's extra weight would mean that over a hundred would wait until the next day for their ration if the Soviets blockaded Berlin again.

The Allies had been laying in extra food by rail and truck since the Soviets' abortive April siege. At first, people in the East and West wondered why some idiot in Allied Command even had the Air Force bring in anything by air. A single freight train could bring in what a hundred Dakotas could barely carry. The West wasn't wondering anymore. As the plane had taken off, Berlin was holding its breath after the Soviets had walked out of the *Kommandtura* – the Four Power military occupation government of Berlin – again.

And the Soviets were quietly smiling, confident that all the planes in the world could not keep Berlin alive very long.

Chance had crawled over the bags in his sleep. His hands and arms reminded him of the ghost women in Frankfurt.

He shook off the sleep fog and slid forward to the cockpit and found he was staring into a graveyard.

"What wasn't your fault?" Rossi threw over his shoulder.

"Can it. Flaps twenty." The pilot was tired. Bad for landings on a good day.

The graveyard filled the windshield. It was unnerving enough to see the endless stones. But huge crosses of perforated metal stood in a straight line, each with a light on top. The hastily erected runway approach lights fit the decor perfectly.

The Dakota's nose came up and the field was on the horizon. The graveyard lay in a canyon of bomb-damaged apartment houses. At the end, the buildings ended at a large open space with a line that looked more like a bike path in the grass than a runway.

"Full flaps," sighed the pilot. Rossi's hand was already moving.

Chance watched Rossi's control yoke. Connected directly to the pilot's, it twitched, jerked by the nervous plane jockey. Rossi was busy with throttling back the engines.

The pilot spat a curse. Chance knew the pilot was trying to make the aircraft do something it didn't want. Like doing a two-step with girl who wanted to waltz. Somebody was going to hit the floor hard.

"Let 'er crab," kibbitzed Rossi.

"Wind. Fuckin' crosswind. Every time."

"It'll be worse when we come out from these buildin's."

A pilot has to accept certain things. Gravity, wind, fatigue, bad coffee, fuel limit – in no particular order. When he ignores one, they get mad like a bitch at a dance. But these can kill you and get away with it.

Rossi had underestimated the wind. The crosswind punched into the Dakota as soon as they cleared the last apartment house. The plane yawed as the props made the all too familiar rasp of not facing the wind.

"Power!"

Rossi made a slight of hand with the throttle. It looked like he was pushing the power up. But he wasn't stupid or suicidal. Chance almost laughed as Rossi put his left thumb on the yoke, pulling it down, just before they hit. The left wing dropped slightly so the left wheel would land first and straighten out the Dakota that was pointed southwest but flying west.

They hit. They didn't land, not in any self-respecting pilot's opinion. Chance remembered flak that pounded softer. An indicator lamp popped out of the instrument panel and an oil gauge cracked with the impact. The load shifted as the pilot braked and the daily bread began to slow.

Rossi had half a Hershey bar gone before they reached the terminal.

Tempelhof was an oblong open field, about three and a half miles south of what was left of the center of Berlin and almost a mile wide from east to west. The massive terminal swept an entire quadrant from west to north. Architect Dr. Ernst Sagebiel under the guidance of the chief Nazi architect, Albert Speer, had designed the building with one purpose: intimidate. The modern gateway to Nazi Germany had belittled the foreigner and reminded the native of the absolute power wielded by his master.

Speer was in Spandau Prison now with the remnants of the masters; really their petty acolytes.

Chance could see the missing windows and blotches where swastikas had been shot or blasted away.

"We're lucky anything is still here," chewed Rossi. "Fuckin' Russkies even took the toilets."

A US military truck pulled away from the corner of the building and moved to meet them. Seven German laborers bounced like sticks stacked on end in the back. The pilot braked and Rossi killed the engines. Chance could hear the Germans' quiet, tired chatter outside.

He had been hearing the language for a few days and was beginning to catch the tone of phrases. There was a sharp cough and what was unmistakably a curse.

The rear door banged open and a German climbed aboard to direct the truck driver backing up to the plane.

"*Komm... Komm... Halt!*"

Chance understood that. Maybe this German thing wouldn't be too hard to crack. Just that, in about an hour, any mistake would be fatal.

The pilot went into the terminal to whine to anyone who would listen about the crosswinds, bad runway, and the coffee.

Rossi and Chance waited for most of the flour sacks to be off before they started their little theater with an explosion from Rossi.

"Jesus fuckin' Christ! Get out! *Raus!*"

The Germans stopped, wide-eyed as Rossi dragged Chance aft from the cockpit area. Covered in flour, Chance looked like any of the laborers. Except his cheeks were a little fuller.

The squat mechanic kicked Chance out onto the half-loaded truck bed. Chance swallowed a Yankee expletive. Rossi had caught him on the top of the pelvis, just below the kidney.

No one helped Chance as Rossi chewed out the German driver who was the titular leader of the laborers.

"Stowaway. *Fersteh'n Zie?* Stow-a-way. Your fault." Rossi used the common method of translating thoughts to non-English speaking people: shouting, with his finger pointing at the nose of the driver.

"He is not with us. *Nein. Es gibt sieben.*" The driver held up seven fingers and counted out the laborers. Rossi was screaming again before he hit three.

"Aw, go screw yourselves. Lousy Krauts. I'm gettin' the MPs." He muscled his way through the thunderstruck laborers like a buffalo in reeds.

The driver went white. Rossi was threatening him and whomever depended on him with death by starvation. Food was already rationed. A job with the *Amis* meant a hot meal once a day and occupation scrip. The laborers were also threatened. The occupiers had all the power and there was no appeal. The Germans had had years of that already and guilt by association was the norm.

The little German grabbed Rossi's arm. The New Yorker flung it off with a boxer's grimace, his jaw leading as his head came around. The driver pulled his hand away as if Rossi was charged with ten thousand volts.

"*Bitte.* Please." The words gasped out. "No Empeez."

The driver turned on Chance who was half sitting on a bag of flour.

"*Verfluckter Idiot! Einsteigen!*"

Chance didn't understand or move.

"*Sind Sie taub?*"

The ghost woman had shrieked that at him. The driver kicked Chance in the thigh. The hard boots were standard issue German Army. Chance flinched and started to leap up to wring the filthy Nazi's neck. Rossi fell out of his belligerent character long enough to shoot his eyebrows up.

"Lock him in the cab and get him off the base!"

Chance caught himself and rose slowly.

"Ja. I do dat." The driver turned back to Chance. "*Schnell! Sonst ruft er die Polizei 'ran.*" He yanked Chance's arm, jumping off the truck bed and pulling him after him. "*Bevor die Polizei ankommen, verprügel' ich Sie,*" he hissed as he shoved Chance into the truck cab and slammed the door.

The little Fuhrer then went back to Rossi to report his success in managing the problem.

"Every-ting oh-kay." He made an exaggerated gesture to Rossi and clapped his hands to the laborers. "*Los wieder!*"

Rossi waited as they off-loaded the rest of the cargo. He signed a small chit which the driver folded carefully and pocketed. It was worth eight hot meals.

The driver never spoke to Chance again. He stopped near the gate at the edge of the field. An MP came out of his little hut to check what was happening. The driver made a noise and cocked his head. Chance climbed out. The truck sped off, the seven laborers staring at Chance. There was no hate or pity.

Chance turned toward the street outside. He remembered the Germans he had seen and dropped his head, not meeting the eyes of the conquerors. But he could feel the MP's stare all the way until he crossed into the city of Berlin.

He finally remembered what Shanley was trying to say. It was the standard navigator's warning to the crew that they were entering enemy territory. Death could come without warning. A few minutes later it came for Shanley.

It was the last thing Shanley said to him.

"We're crossing the coast."

CHAPTER 21

*Russian Sector Checkpoint, Sonnenallee,
Berlin, June 21, 1948, 5:47 P.M.*

The woman behind Chance was praying again.

"*Vater Unser...*" she whispered in gasps. The rhythm was familiar enough. Chance had heard his crew praying on the intercom. Some quietly, some alternating curses with screaming pleas as they died. The hopeless whisper was a distraction. He was deep in enemy territory and death was nearby. But he couldn't cut the intercom this time like he had on his dying ball turret gunner, Joey Carn.

The line of Germans at the checkpoint shuffled forward again. Two Russians soldiers were spot-checking and searching every few people. They were boys really. One's cap would wobble side to side on his small, shaved head. He would search with one hand, holding his rifle in the other and pausing to steady his cap as the Germans shuffled forward. He turned to look across the street and the cap refused to turn with his head, the red star remaining fixed on the line of Germans.

Across the street, older veterans did the searching. Chance spotted two men in suits smoking in a doorway a few feet into the East from where people were crossing into the American Sector. They didn't have the pallor of the Germans and weren't waiting for a streetcar. Black marketers would not be so careless. The Soviet *Ministerstva Vnutrennikh Del* (MVD) secret police goons were stalking someone coming out of the East.

The woman choked off the last part of her umpteenth prayer. They were close now. The larger of the two boys, a blonde with acne and one eye sown shut, waved the line quickly forward. He had already picked his target.

The woman wore a tattered scarf, really a dirty rag. Chance thought it was a shred of vanity or an obvious way to hide something. It was out of place in the summer heat.

A smile twisted the boy guard's maimed face. He waved Chance through without a glance.

"Halt!" The guard took a step to his left and blocked the woman. Chance turned back on the word, thinking it was meant for him.

The other guard grinned as he motioned Chance and the line forward. The smaller guard gawked as his friend searched the woman, knowing exactly what he would find. The one-eyed boy mauled the woman, clawing one breast then the other. The woman dropped her bag and swayed like a boxer out on his feet. The boy groped lower.

The other Germans moved on as if the woman and the Russian were chatting like friends. They studied the sidewalk like a well-behaved, defeated people.

"*Vater Unser... Vater Unser...*" She contracted the prayer to a basic plea.

Fall down! Chance willed her to take a dive. For some reason she stood there, eyes searching heaven for help that would never come. The one-eyed boy leered and cocked his head for the other to get a piece.

Most of Chance decided to walk away. Not all. His head moved first as he took a step toward the half blind-boy, eyeing him, lowering his brow as if he had horns. He was doing the unthinkable and the boy reacted. The other guard's hat spun off as he whirled on Chance, bringing his rifle up.

"*Rauz!*" barked the boy, fumbling with his weapon.

Chance felt a hand on his arm, pulling him away.

"*Sie können es nicht ändern.*" Low voices pulled at him, too. "*Bringt nichts.*"

Chance stood his ground. The two MVD men paused in their smoking. One moved to the curb, catching the single eye of the boy already twitching in anger. He threw the woman at Chance.

"*Rauz!*"

The woman didn't seem to be there. A *Hausfrau* swept her up. Another joined her as the mauled woman's knees finally gave out. They moved past Chance as the crowd pulled them away. One of the women smiled at him.

They had gone only a few steps when the shooting started. Two shots almost together and a third. Chance dove instinctively, pulling the smiling *Hausfrau* to the cobblestones. The woman with the scarf stumbled on.

One of the two goons walked slowly into the center of the street and fired twice into what looked like a heap of clothes. Something red splattered in the street.

The suit screamed at the crowd. "Nazi! Nazi!" He pointed his still smoking pistol at the corpse.

Chance and the crowd recovered and began to shuffle again.

The dead man was a clockmaker. The closest he had been to being a Nazi was listening to Hitler vent on the radio.

Unfortunately, he also looked like a man who was about 100 kilometers farther east, waiting for a chance to escape to Argentina. The people who had tipped the Russians were loyal Nazis. They had sent the clockmaker into the West on a fool's errand. No one would look for a dead man now.

For the next several hours, Chance played the day's events over in his head. He had been a complete idiot. The woman was nothing to him or Nevada. She neither acknowledged nor thanked Chance.

One of the *Hausfrauen* had taken the mauled woman's scarf to wipe her face. The woman had a recent wound that cut an ugly smile across her neck. The *Hausfrau* came over and blathered something to him. She lowered her voice on a familiar sounding word: *hangen*. Chance nodded as if he understood.

JITTERBUG LIFT

By nightfall he was in the outer suburbs of the city. Whole blocks of houses stood untouched by the bombing. He found a place to sleep in back of a bombed-out building that was a complete exception. Across the road was an open field with a row of craters wandering off toward a small woods.

Somebody had jettisoned their bombs as a last-ditch effort to survive. Most likely it was as useless as when he had tried to dump his bomb load over the Holland coast. The bombs had to go somewhere. The back of his head began to throb.

Sometime in the middle of the night, he woke to trucks. His fear rose until he realized they wouldn't send a division for one man. A whole convoy raced through the village, heading for downtown Berlin. He counted fifteen trucks before he fell back to sleep.

Chance saw a few people on the road the second day. He skirted the villages to avoid possible check points. On the third day a Russian military truck growled over a hill a half-mile ahead, giving Chance plenty of time to get off the road and into a shallow ditch.

That night he slept in an empty hay barn. The cold wind brought the smell of something sweet baking. His belly ached, but he couldn't risk stealing or begging for a meal.

He saw a rusted road sign for Ziewald late the next afternoon as it began to rain. The land had become mostly flat with low rolling hills. It reminded him of Oklahoma, but not quite, the ground here was soft loam dotted with old world cottages. There were lots of little clues he wasn't home. The fences were wrong. The fields weren't square. He sure as hell couldn't stop for directions or ask who was number one on *The Hit Parade*.

The rain let up as it began to get dark. Chance was shivering. He was wondering if he had passed Ziewald. He also thought about why he was risking his soaked skin. He couldn't believe it. That was the heart of it. He couldn't believe he had lost them all and Nevada was dead.

He thought about what he would do when he got there. Prayers weren't his style. He shook some rainwater off his coat and saw the tail of PIE IN THE SKY.

CHAPTER 22

One kilometer north of Ziewald, Soviet Occupied Germany, June 24, 1948, 9:08 P.M.

Chance moved off the road, his feet squishing in the damp grass. The perfectly upright tail looked strange, as if the plane was parked at Rhein-Main. The rest of the plane was blocked by a low rise and trees. Chance had to see the rest, but didn't want to. Still, he moved forward.

There was no sign of fire. Unless there is someone there to put it out, a plane usually burns to smoldering, molten metal.

Another step brought the whole meadow into view.

The plane was intact.

It sat at the end of the meadow as if poised for takeoff clearance.

A man laughed far to his left.

Chance ducked down and swiveled his head, trying to pick out the source. The trees rimming the meadow were thick enough that he could not see more than fifty feet.

A splattering of Russian and another laugh echoed in the woods. Chance saw a blue layer of smoke between the trees. In the deepening gloom he could just make out the flickering of a fire.

Another man called out. Chance fought the instinct to run. Maybe they thought he was a curious farmer. Then the back door of the Dakota opened. A soldier in the same green uniform he had seen in Berlin hopped down. He had been sleeping in the plane. He slipped his cap back on against the cold. He was no boy. A veteran.

The two by the fire called to their comrade again. Chance smelled something like onions. Soup was on.

Obviously someone who knew about planes had ordered them to keep the fire away from the aircraft. The natural – and stupid – thing would have been to build the fire under the wing.

The soldier left the door open on the aircraft, but no one else came out. Usually guard patrols are in pairs. *So where was number four?*

Chance decided to wait until dark. The guards had their fire close to the road. There was no way into town without passing it, except across open fields.

He could just make out a dim light or two down the road as the world turned deep blue. He ran down his options. The best plan started with simply slipping away. At the end of a long, tortuous route was the Kresge lunch counter – if he was extremely lucky. All the others were suicidal.

Dizzy with hunger, Chance tried to remember when the moon would rise. He hadn't seen it the night before. When he flew, he knew the rhythm of the heavens like a mariner. The sky had cleared after the storm. If the moon rose while he was moving, he would be an easy target.

The last blush of twilight was not quite gone when Chance crossed the road. Hunched over, he picked his way through the field across from the meadow. The guards' fire blazed clearly to his right about fifty yards away. They really weren't expecting anyone. All three of them stared into the fire. Chance knew that even if they looked right at him, their eyes would take minutes to adjust to the dark.

He made the village in about ten minutes. It was a collection of five houses and a small chapel. He smelled manure. In the German style of farms, the barns and outbuildings were all in the village.

An angry German voice echoed, muffled by the stucco house. Movement caught his eye in the house near the chapel. Chance edged toward the small window with a flickering light. The man barked again, demanding. Curtains hid anything inside. Furious, the man screamed something. Furniture or a body boomed on the floor.

The house door flew open. A woman came out in tears. She sobbed less than six feet from Chance. The man bellowed and was at the door behind her. He grabbed her and she tried to run, taking a step toward Chance. The big farmer yanked her back with a curse and she gave a squeak before he hauled her inside. Chance was certain she had looked right at him.

She shrieked out something fast that was cut off by the sound of flesh on flesh. She wailed and there were more punches and slaps, which the ape farmer used to keep time with his lecture.

It made Chance sick, but he was done being stupid for this week.

Chance searched the rest of the farmhouses. All were silent. He noticed there were no vehicles and concluded Nevada was already in Soviet-occupied Berlin or worse, farther east.

If he could convince McKane, maybe they would raise a stink to get him back. Nevada got lost, instrument failure. That plan was a dead in the water. How would he convince McKane?

He noticed the houses and sky seemed brighter. As he headed out of the village, the moon rose higher. A few days past full, the pilots' friend was a lethal searchlight.

He really didn't have a plan. Chance plotted out a series of gambles with ever-worsening odds. Once started, he had to go through with it. No options, no contingencies nor alternate landing sites.

Chance smiled at the edge of the village. Maybe he wasn't through being stupid, but Nevada would love it.

The guards' fire belched up a blossom of sparks as one of the Russians tossed on another log. Chance froze half-way across the field. The wet log dampened the flames to almost nothing. With the brightening moonlight, it would be less than a minute before he was visible. He could clearly see the features of the guard facing him between the heads of the two others. They weren't talking anymore. They were alone with the cold. The rain had brought a freak chill to the midsummer night.

One of the guards kicked the fire with a short comment. It swelled up. Chance moved when the fire brightened so the guards were squinting.

Chance worked his way around the woods to the other side of PIE IN THE SKY. He slipped under the right wing and felt for the fuel drain. Set at the bottom of the wing tanks, the drain was designed to let out any water that had settled in the tank. He opened the small door, cringing at the squeak of the stiff hinges.

The valve wouldn't move. His fingers refused to grip with cold and hunger. He tried again and thought the valve gave. He tucked his hands under his arms for a minute and checked the guards. He had no idea if they were on some kind of rotation or if they had orders to check the plane periodically.

The valve protested but opened. Chance heard the fuel stream hitting the ground as he felt his way past the landing gear. He estimated the wheels had sunk a few inches into the soggy meadow.

The valve on the left wing opened without resistance. He was busy being satisfied when he noticed the guards had stopped talking. He heard something in the grass and saw one of them was walking toward the plane.

One of the guards by the fire called out and the nearest guard stopped. The fuel ran free out of both drains, rasping into the grass. The noise sounded like Niagara Falls.

The near guard called back to the others and a short argument followed. Chance let the fuel flow. Even if he closed the valves, the fuel would reek. He tried to gauge the wind and could feel none.

The argument sputtered to a stop. The guard took another step toward the Dakota and stopped again. Abruptly, he turned and headed back. The other guards laughed.

Chance felt the plane shift. Maybe the fuel loss was unbalancing it. He checked his watch. He figured an hour to lose half the remaining load. He looked toward the far trees, estimating about a thousand feet. He could do it – if the wheels didn't sink in the mud, if Rossi wasn't just bragging about his work, and if the Russians would give him thirty seconds.

For the second time in three days Chance was doing something he knew was absolutely wrong. He wasn't done being stupid this week by a long shot.

Chance began to wonder as the Russians let the fire die away to embers. Had they fallen asleep?

He checked his watch. Five minutes to go.

The sound of the truck almost didn't register at first. Chance scrambled across the grass slick with fuel to close the right valve. It certainly wouldn't be Germans out on a late night hay ride.

He got to the left side when he saw the three guards moving back toward the plane. One of them was calling out something. He left the valve open and darted back to the rear door. He smelled vomit.

Chance hopped up as the Russian military truck pulled up with the relief guards. In the darkened plane he heard a groan.

The fourth guard asked him a groggy question and tried to get up. Chance felt for the soldier's rifle and poked it into his ribs.

The sick guard swore and stumbled to his feet. He tried to focus on Chance in the scattered moonlight. Chance shoved him toward the door. The guard evidently thought Chance was a superior and began to mumble something that had the tone of an apology. Chance hit him at the base of the skull with the rifle butt and he tumbled out the door.

The other three guards were heading out from the edge of the trees where the truck was pulling up. They were not quite a hundred yards behind the tail of PIE IN THE SKY.

Chance ran forward, slipping on a puddle of partially-digested onion soup. He jumped into the pilot's seat and flipped on the instrument lights. They glowed brightly, but the battery showed the voltage was down.

He quickly adjusted the fuel mixture. He was about to hit the starter, but stopped. He reached behind the copilot's seat and grinned. Nevada had been a very good boy. Chance pulled out the emergency flare pistol and slid open the pilot's side window.

He punched the starter and the number one engine groaned into motion much too slowly. The idiots had been running the heater to keep the sick guard warm.

He could hear the shouts even before number one caught. Sparks flew out of the exhaust but none found the fuel soaked grass.

Chance tried to start number two, but the battery was flat. He needed seconds he didn't have for it to recharge.

The shooting started as he tried to get the plane to move forward. He had to jam number one to full power before the wheels clawed out of the muck. He was trading precious takeoff space for time. The plane rolled a dozen feet and Chance fired the flare pistol up and behind him.

A bullet shattered the Plexiglas window and rattled inside the cockpit as the flare burst above them. The soldiers stopped firing for a split second, confused as the area was bathed in a red glow. But then they found their target was much easier to see and opened up with everything.

The plane sounded like it was in a hailstorm. Chance punched the starter again, setting the flaps with the other hand. Number two caught just as the flare landed. Something banged off the cockpit doorframe near his ear.

He could see the whole ring of trees turn orange, reflecting the inferno behind him, with the prop wash blasting it at the soldiers. The shooting stuttered and fell off. The plane lumbered up to thirty knots, but Chance couldn't see the rivulet of fire that was chasing the open, left drain valve.

He had both throttles fire-walled as he crossed the midpoint in the field. The plane bumped hard as he hit Nevada's landing ruts. The trees looked enormous. The meadow sloped downward to a low point just in front of them.

Chance didn't even look at his airspeed when he pulled back on the yoke. The plane shuddered. The grass seemed to be slowing him down, refusing to let go.

There was no low point in the trees to shoot for. He pushed the yoke forward until the shuddering stopped. The plane left the grass behind in one bump. The trees filled the windshield. He had no choice. He hugged the yoke into his lap.

PIE IN THE SKY stalled at fifty feet.

The air moving over the wings separated from them, giving up the losing battle of pulling against the plane's weight.

All of Chance's future hung on two whirling propellers. The Dakota pitched up, gaining fifty more feet as the airspeed bled off. The propellers were giving up, too. Their thrust was no match for gravity and the aircraft began to fall like a brick.

But it was just enough.

Chance cleared the trees and brought the nose down. It was more by force of will than anything he did with the yoke, because there was so little air moving over the control surfaces.

PIE IN THE SKY moved like an elephant at a steeplechase. In slow motion, the plane headed down, nose first. Chance couldn't see the ground in the dark. The yoke shuddered violently as the air searched for a grip on the wings and let go again five times a second.

There was nothing to do. He had no more power and no more altitude. It was the worst feeling in the world.

After an eternity, the shuddering stopped. Maybe it was ground effect, maybe somebody said a prayer for him. PIE IN THE SKY flew. Chance felt the plane lifting him.

Now it got hard. He had one hundred twenty miles of enemy territory to cross and the entire Russian Air Force would be looking for him.

CHAPTER 23

*Over Soviet Occupied Germany,
June 25, 1948, 12:17 A.M.*

The Russians had taken the maps. Chance was left with a compass and the dim blue, moonlit horizon. He saw the same sky Nevada had seen a few weeks before, devoid of lights or landmarks. Without the maps, he could only steer a course west and hope.

The Fulda beacon. He tried to remember the frequency as he twisted the dial on the RDF set. The signal swished in with its robot Morse code identifier. The needle steadily pointed the way home. McKane was right; Nevada had had everything fixed.

The maps would have told him how low he could fly to avoid the Russian radar. Russian YAK fighters weren't equipped with radar. Instead, they were directed by their ground stations.

Chance couldn't even guess the minimums. The last time he had flown over this part of Germany, there was no minimum safe altitude. Hell, there was no safe altitude, period.

He eased the Dakota lower, hoping that a sudden cloud or fog bank wouldn't rob him of his horizon or hide a mountain. He didn't bother to search for the Soviet YAKs. They would be on him before he knew anything.

And he would be completely at their mercy. And he doubted they had any.

He checked the fuel. The left tank was still draining. It would take another hour to empty and by that time he would be home or not needing the fuel anymore.

His heart stopped when a bright light flashed off to his right. Tracer fire? Chance relaxed when there was no more. It was probably a meteor. He hadn't done a lot of night flying, but had seen a few. It was amazing what you saw when the sky was your home.

A sliver of light appeared on the western horizon and crawled much too slowly toward him. He peered out, looking for any sign of the ground. A river of silver moonlight wound to the southwest. Chance knew many of the German rivers were in deep valleys hemmed by steep hills. Still he pushed lower.

He tuned the radio, hunting for Rhein-Main traffic control. Once he hooked up with them, they would guide him home. A Russian voice pounded in his ears. It was loud and urgent. The hunt was on.

Chance tuned up higher and found the Rhein-Main frequency. He stopped before keying the mike. If he started talking to them, it would give him away. The Russians would be listening and no doubt had people who spoke English. His call to Rhein-Main would have to wait until he crossed out of Russian airspace.

He scanned the skies looking for the pulsing exhaust flames of the YAKs. Chance had flown two night raids on Germany during the war. He and the gunners had tried to track the enemy fighters by the yellow and blue exhausts. It hadn't worked very well. Chance looked out at his own exhaust, dim blue on number one. Number two engine flickered orange. He leaned the mixture to dim it as much as possible.

The lights on the horizon had become an ocean. Chance estimated they were about fifty miles. Against the darkness below him, a diamond-white column flicked on just ahead and to the right. The searchlight rapidly tilted toward him. They were trying to light him up for the fighters.

He did the only thing he could do and dove hard for safety of the ground. The searchlight gave him a reference of the ground at its base, but that assumed the terrain was relatively flat. He stopped diving when he could see trees silhouetted against the bottom of the accusing finger of light. Tree shadows merged into a solid line as a hill rose to obscure the beam.

The cockpit lit up as if struck by lightning and went dark. Chance was blinded as the searchlight caught the Dakota just before the hill blocked it. He didn't think about whether they had seen him – he couldn't see anything.

It would take minutes before his night vision returned. He had no idea where the horizon was. He locked on to the artificial horizon in the cockpit and flew by feel. Soft bumps of turbulence bounced him higher. Wind rolling up or down a hillside. He pulled up slowly, coming out of the turbulence and flirting with the deadly, white spear that he could just make out scanning the air above him. He was guessing and he hated that.

The ocean of warm lights was closer now. They came back into view as Chance's vision cleared. He was in a valley, with the searchlight over the rim to his right. The lights ahead gave him tantalizing comfort.

The first shell caught the wingtip. PIE IN THE SKY banged like a tin drum. They'd found him.

The rest of the tracers arced ahead in the darkness and flashed briefly as they struck the hill in front of him. Chance pulled up on the stick and twisted the cow he was flying until the airframe groaned. The YAK overshot him and turned off to the right to come around again. Where were the others?

Chance dove for the ocean of lights, skimming through the neck of the valley. He could only guess the pilot had been looking where the searchlight had reported him and was surprised when he caught up with Chance. The Russian had fired a quick burst and was lining up for another try. Unless the radar station was right below them, the Russian would have to guess where Chance had gone.

He crossed the border and was in the ocean of the brightly lit West. He still couldn't risk that the Russian wouldn't follow and skimmed the tree tops.

More tracer fire flashed overhead. The Russian hadn't crossed into the West and had tried a long shot at the buzzer by angling his guns up to give them greater range. It wasn't very accurate, but they wanted him dead badly.

He flew an evasive course for several more minutes before coming up to three thousand feet.

He heard a crowd of planes calling Control. It sounded like the Allies had everything in the air at once. He couldn't believe it was for him. It took him several tries before he was able to break into the constant stream of radio traffic.

"Rhein-Main Control, this is U.S. aircraft requesting approach vector."

"Unidentified aircraft say again."

Chance repeated and there was a pause.

"Unidentified aircraft state your position."

"Rhein-Main, I have no idea."

Another pause.

"Unidentified aircraft, come to course 256. Stay this frequency."

That's what he was going to be: Unidentified Aircraft. He steered the course and entered the pattern about forty minutes later. All of the radio calls were normal; as if he was an afterthought. As if they were expecting him.

A large volume of planes were flying in and out of Rhein-Main. Control landed seven planes ahead of Chance before he lowered his gear for final approach.

The Dakota ahead of him was still on the runway as Chance touched down. It turned off toward the terminal building joining dozens of other aircraft.

The tower told the C-47 behind him to go around. Chance heard the fatigue in the pilot's voice as he acknowledged.

A jeep appeared in front of Chance with a large FOLLOW ME sign lit up behind the driver. The Pied Piper led Chance off into the darkness on the far side of the field. A ground crewman with lit wands took over, waving him to a stop. As Chance killed his engines, he could see a ring of soldiers surrounding PIE IN THE SKY.

He also saw McKane's unmistakable hulk charging toward the rear door.

CHAPTER 24

*Rhein-Main Airport,
June 25, 1948, 1:28 A.M.*

"Say nothing," growled McKane even before Chance had the aircraft door fully open.

"I'm leaking fuel."

"Shut up."

McKane dragged Chance toward the Packard. Chance actually needed the help. He hadn't eaten in four days. He had almost been killed several times in the last two hours while doing the impossible and it hit him that he wasn't as young as he used to be.

Chance was crammed between McKane and his faithful MP. They had to wait twice as the car tried to cross the runways behind the Pied Piper. The FOLLOW ME jeep had a radio and was in touch with the tower. Chance wasn't too tired to notice the chaos. The jeep started across one runway and then stopped, waving the Packard back frantically, just before a C-54 roared over. They barely crossed the same runway before a Dakota bounced in behind them. Whatever was going on, it was near panic.

The folding chair in the former Nazi customs office boasted it was made in Fort Wayne, Indiana. Its brothers stood in the jumble against the wall between two desks on end. There was barely room for McKane to close the door on the MPs outside. The big man was in a hurry. No minuetting couple on the coffee cups. No distracting secretary.

"When did you cross into the east?" McKane sounded tired, but the well-rehearsed questions came as if he already knew the answers.

"Sunday... Monday," Chance wasn't so well-rehearsed.

"Where?"

"Little checkpoint by Sonnen Alley. The Russkies shot a Nazi trying to sneak over. I need something to eat."

"How'd you know where the plane was?"

"I didn't. You told me it crashed at Ziewald. I went to see the crash site."

"Why?"

"I didn't believe you."

McKane paused. A plane flew over, climbing out, engines straining.

"I didn't believe Nevada was dead," Chance tossed in.

"He's indestructible? Like Superman?"

"Yeah. He believes that. And he's good."

Another plane rumbled over, catching Chance's ear. One engine was running rough. The pilot should turn back.

McKane's next questions were about what Chance saw in the east. What color where the uniforms of the Russians guarding PIE IN THE SKY? What did their insignia look like? What military did he see on the road? Chance remembered bomber crews shot down over France getting the same debriefing after they were smuggled back by the French Resistance.

An alarm started nagging what was left of Chance's brain. He'd sparred with this matador before. What sword was behind the cape this time?

Chance's exhausted mind wandered after that idea like a drunken roughneck stumbling forward to keep from falling flat on his face. McKane seemed to take it for genuine thought.

"You don't get it, do you?"

"What?"

"You fucked up the whole deal. Let's say Nazis hired Nevada to fly them out."

"He wouldn't…"

"Shut up. This is my story. Nazis hire Nevada – 'cause he's good and can land a Dakota on a match head. He flies over and either gets forced down or," he paused for emphasis, "he lands where he's supposed to and something goes wrong. We hear that his plane crashed and he's bought the farm. But they say nothing out loud. Stay with me." McKane pushed the tottering Chance back into the chair with a finger that felt like a broom handle.

Another Dakota droned over.

"Now, I don't think your buddy's all that hot, but that story smells like a whore's crotch on Sunday morning. He gave them the perfect propaganda coup. Just what they would love to tell the whole world. Especially now."

Chance waved the jumble of words away.

"Where's Nevada?"

"Probably standing in front of some Russian intel guy. Answering the same questions he has for a week. If they haven't shot him."

There was a knock. McKane cracked the door as wide as he could without sitting in Chance's lap. The MP mumbled something lost in the roar of another transport echoing in from the hall.

McKane slipped out and exploded into an argument with whomever was unlucky to be bringing him a message. Messenger boy was losing. He asked about the plane just sitting outside doing nothing. McKane gave him the military equivalent of "go fuck yourself" and the messenger boy quietly played his ace.

"General Clay's orders. Sir." He had invoked the name of a man who only answered to President Truman: General Lucius D. Clay, Commander in Chief European Command, affectionately known as "the Kaiser."

Light dawned on Chance. He looked up as McKane opened the door completely. A corporal stood with the MP.

McKane came back more unhappy than a minute ago. Chance didn't think it was possible.

"When did the Russkies invade?" Chance tried to sound smug.

"They haven't. Not yet. They've blockaded Berlin."

CHAPTER 25

Citing "technical difficulties," the Russians simply ended all access to Berlin just before midnight on June 23rd, announcing it over the wires of *Allgemeine Deutsche Nachrichtendienst* (ADN), the only press agency allowed to operate in the Soviet occupied sector of Germany.

Tensions had been rising for a week as the Western Allies tried to introduce their own occupation Deutschemarks to replace the old Nazi Reichsmarks, and hopefully stop the dizzying inflation and curb the black market. The beginning of the end had occurred on June 16th, when Colonel Alexei Yelizarov led the Soviet delegation out of the regular meeting of the *Kommandatura*. It ended what was left of the cooperation between the victors forever.

The April mini-blockade had shocked the Allies. They had rapidly calculated how long the western sector of Berlin would last without basic food supplies. Unfortunately, the spring had been cool, so coal was needed for heat and to generate electricity.

The Allies estimated that, without resupply, the industries in the blockaded city would grind to a halt in days. Workers would be on the streets where pro-communist marches would entice them with promises of food and work – if they cooperated.

The western powers also calculated how long it would take before Berliners' stomachs started thinking for their owners. It was the Nazis who had provided the answer. Meticulous studies done at the death camps showed that the average adult could barely survive on 800 calories per day. The Allies' arithmetic told them that Berliners would be able to do little or no work to help themselves. The Soviet calculating machines had already ground out that desired answer.

Berliners would listlessly come to the inescapable conclusion that their only hope awaited in the east; bread and milk offered in an iron fist.

And as Berlin went, so went Germany. And perhaps Europe, one day.

CHAPTER 26

*Leipzigerstrasse 181, Berlin,
Soviet Zone, June 25, 1948, 3:27 A.M.*

Nevada was certain the man had a twin.

The questions had been coming for...he could not count the hours. He had never seen the interrogator. The crisp voice came from behind him as he faced the green brick basement wall, not allowed to turn around. He was not allowed to sit either. He stood in a puddle of his own filth, not permitted to go to the bathroom. The voice was as razor sharp now as it had been when they started. *Was it yesterday? How could the man last that long without having a twin?*

The last face he had seen was that of the Russian officer in Ziewald who jerked the black hood over his head. He had noticed the man's insignia had wings. Deprived of information, he had begun to notice little things. Like a man in a cave who begins to hear the blood pulsing past his ears in the silence.

He imagined his interrogator wore leather. He could hear it crinkle as the man moved. The man was about his height and walked with a slight limp. It was more of an offbeat rhythm. The man's voice was even. He never shouted, but always conveyed menace. But still, this time was different. Something was up. In all the...*how many times has it been?* In all the previous sessions, he had never heard the voice so strained. It was something to think about alone in his cell.

There was something about the hands that brought the food that was nagging him, too. Something else to do back in the little cell.

"Why were you off course?"

It was like a dance. The voice measured out the beat.

"I was lost. I told you." Nevada's own voice sounded farther away to him than the voice of the pacing man in leather.

"Tell me again."

"I was on a check ride and got lost."

"But why did you land?"

"I was low on fuel."

"You had enough fuel to fly to Berlin."

"I wasn't sure. I told you."

"So you were concerned about the fuel. And you made an emergency call."

"Yeah. But I lost altitude. The engines weren't running right. I think it was the fuel pump."

"You called over the U.S. Zone and your engines were in excellent condition."

"I got it working again and kept going, but then the pump went nuts."

"Why are you lying again?"

"I'm not." The words were the last air out of a flat tire.

"You should have called us."

"I did. Must have had the wrong frequency. Nobody answered."

The sound of the leather reminded Nevada of cowboys shifting in the saddle in some second feature.

"Who would want your plane back?"

Ivanoff saw Nevada's head go up. The pain of stretching the shrinking scar tissue had clouded the Russian's mind. He jerked his head at the exhausted sergeant and Nevada was yanked out of the cellar room as Ivanoff reached for his shirt. In the silence he could hear his own skin snapping as he moved. He had failed again. So focused on his goal of finding the man who had stolen the plane, who had humiliated him, Ivanoff had given Nevada the unforgivable gift of the one thing he had spent days trying to strip Nevada of; the one thing the pilot would be helpless without: hope.

He would have to break the American soon.

He was at the Karlshorst Soviet Army Headquarters just ten minutes later. He barely noticed the dawning sky. He was looking west. A line of aircraft lights flickered one behind the other as they approached Tempelhof. Other lines made for Gatow and Tegel. The lines stretched as far as he could see, fading to reddish orange near the horizon.

Ivanoff almost didn't hear the sound in the headquarters change as the day brightened and warmed. Although the staff had been on alert around the clock since the beginning of the blockade, there was a definite change as the night staff gave way to the day team. Ivanoff was part of neither group.

Before interrogating Nevada again, he had spent two hours interviewing everyone connected with the latest incident – except for the sick guard who had been sleeping in PIE IN THE SKY. He had been shot by his captain in a futile attempt to foist blame. The private from the vastness beyond the Urals, where there wasn't a road or a railroad, was executed while still unconscious.

The captain was unsure as to the number of men who stole PIE IN THE SKY back. It may have been as many as four. Or as few as one. And everyone was just as unsure where they had materialized from.

In short, all Ivanoff knew was that the American plane was gone, last seen flying through the Soviet air defenses, *his* air defenses, into the West.

Whoever had pulled this off had balls, big ones. Or they were completely insane. Ivanoff had to admit that they had done the unthinkable. Just as he had six summers before.

General Zukushev tapped on Ivanoff's open door and was about to try again to get the attention of the obviously distracted war hero, when Ivanoff leapt to attention in one motion. Zukushev knew that the agony of that move would bring Ivanoff's focus to crystal clarity.

"Comrade General."

"Good morning, Colonel," flowed smoothly from the General's thin, ashen lips as he slowly closed the door behind him. Anyone seeing the Zukushev for the first time could be forgiven a gasp. Zukushev looked like a man who had frozen to death.

Zukushev would never send a minion to summon Ivanoff to his office. He would always come personally to the young man. Everyone who knew of this habit said it was out of deference to the wounded patriot. In fact, it was because Zukushev had committed a secret act of cowardice in Spain.

The Spanish Civil War had been the opening sparring match between the Soviet Union and Nazi Germany. Supporting opposite sides in the war between the Fascists and the Republicans, they had tested weapons, aircraft and even sent pilots to fight. In 1936, Zukushev had led a group of twenty men and two women against the newly re-formed Luftwaffe pilots flying for the Fascists. All were confident their youthful Marxism would wipe the skies clean of the Nazi trash.

They lost half their number in their first engagement with the better trained and equipped Germans.

In their second action, the Battle of Brunete, near Madrid, Zukushev failed to attack when Nazi Heinkel He51 biplanes appeared over the Republican lines. Instead, he led his squadron into a rain squall "in search of the main wave." The crime was lost in the confusion of the Republican collapse and Stalin brought his people back to Mother Russia as heroes anyway.

Zukushev rose quickly through the ranks for two reasons. One, he was among the few pilots in the Soviet air forces with combat experience. Second, no one questioned the reputation about someone Stalin had made a hero.

Zukushev knew that was the only thing now keeping Ivanoff from the fate of the sick guard in Ziewald.

Normally, Zukushev would smile and deferentially motion for Ivanoff to sit, but he let the colonel stand at attention as he unhurriedly sat in the barracks chair opposite the desk.

The door lock was sticky and it finally clicked in place as Zukushev regarded the maimed man's face. A phone rang somewhere down the hall and Zukushev drew a breath.

"You will take personal charge of hunting down those who have invaded our hard-won territory. Twice." Zukushev's voice barely rose above the bureaucratic din seeping under the door. It was the party line and both the General and the Colonel knew it.

Ivanoff's eyes never left the wall behind the slow-moving General. The General sat forward, rubbing his hands.

"Reach across and destroy them. You will have anything you need." The General spread his hands, forgetting them for the moment. "Except my protection."

Ivanoff realized the room contained two dead men – if he failed.

Zukushev rose slowly and made for the door, never looking at Ivanoff.

"And you must not let this foolish…" he paused, searching for a Russian word that could approximate the hopeless insanity the Allies were trying to pull off. He gave up and used English. "This *airlift* action by the Americans and British must not succeed. You must do everything to stop it – short of shooting them down. But just short. Even if you cannot erase this…" He paused again. Then he whispered, "This shame."

He opened the door and left, leaving the door slowly swinging back toward the wall.

Ivanoff still stood at attention. An army secretary hurried down the hall, tossing a worried glance over her shoulder.

Word was out.

He remembered he had been dead once before and picked up his phone.

CHAPTER 27

*Marienplatz, British Occupied Berlin,
June 26, 1948, 10:32 A.M.*

Chance felt like the villain walking into a movie saloon. The Babel of a dozen languages died to a murmur in the stifling International Red Cross office as Chance moved to the edge of the open floor separated by a low rail from twenty desks piled high with tottering files. He had been given a number by a Mr. Barek, who spoke English as if he had learned it at garden parties with the King of England.

Chance tried to tell him the layover was only for an hour because the airlift was having teething trouble. Planes were backed up over a rainy Rhein-Main in Frankfurt so they were not being allowed to take off from Berlin. If the Russians had the guts, they could capture most of the US air cargo fleet in Europe stacked up at Tempelhof.

His khakis cut no ice with the Swiss as they would be fed by whomever was bringing in food and it was twenty minutes before his number was called in the baking-hot room. Still, his khakis or his accent did pull some weight; he was well ahead of most of those clinging to their hope of finding family and friends in their little slips.

"Do you know what *Stalag* your friend was in?" The woman was already filing out the form and did not look up at him.

"He wasn't captured by the Germans. The Russians got him."

The pen faltered, but Miss Bonache did not look up.

"When?"

"The fourth or fifth."

"This month?"

"Yeah."

Bonache put the pen back in the stand and folded her arms on the desk. She glanced over at him and then back down at the blotter. Her expression remained bureaucratic.

"Is your government not handling this?"

"No."

A frown tangled her unplucked eyebrows for a moment and she pushed forward in the chair. Her breasts heaved up like a wave, threatening to spill over her sweaty forearms. She seemed lost as to where to go next.

"How was he captured?"

"He landed in the Russian zone by accident. It didn't make the papers," Chance added, anticipating the next question.

"One moment."

She was up and the badly laid linoleum popped as she headed off to a doorway in the back of the room.

Chance noticed several of the others waiting were staring at him. He couldn't quite tell their expressions. He looked down and spotted a small piece of paper peeking out from under Miss Bonache's desk. It was one of the forms. Under a name and address was a long list of other names, maybe a dozen in all. The survivor searching for the dead. They were probably dead because next to each name was "Dachau."

"The Soviet Government has not updated their prisoner of war list for several months." Miss Bonache was back empty-handed.

"Can I look someplace else?"

"I am sorry, no." She looked out at the crowd waiting. "*Nummer zwo, acht, sechs. Zwei hundert, sechs und achtzig.*"

An old man tottered to his feet and headed through the barrier as she looked down at her blotter.

"Is there some way to reach you? Perhaps if you left your name."

Chance stood up and looked out at the crowd pressing at the barrier and the old man with bad teeth coming at them.

"That would be tough."

The old man arrived, clutching his scrap of hope as Chance stood up.

"Can I check back here tomorrow?"

"I do not think things will change that fast. Perhaps after three or four days I will know something."

"What about just asking the Russians?"

"That is done by the diplomats. And takes time. If I could have your name."

"Mr. American." The old man seemed impatient, annoying Chance.

"Hang on, bub. Nevada – no, George Post. We called him Nevada. That's who you're looking for."

"I thank you." The man put it hand toward his mouth as if holding a piece of bread.

"Yeah, sure." Chance headed for the barrier.

The room was still jammed but at least cooling off when Miss Bonache finally made the phone call. She simply said Nevada's name and hung up.

CHAPTER 28

Tiergarten, Berlin, British Zone,
June 26, 1948, 6:28 P.M.

The shouting started again when Michael paused. He did not like to stop and it was not for dramatic effect. He was out of breath and tired. He hated that the Nazis had stolen his family and robbed him of his energy for the rest of his life.

The agitators had shoved their way to the first rows of the crowd, right on time. Michael was almost done.

The Social Democratic Party (SPD) had refused to be absorbed into German Communist Party (KPD) two years before – at least in the British and American zones. A plebiscite had been called for, but the Russians had refused to let anyone vote in their sector, citing the inevitable "technical difficulties." Vote or no vote, the SPD had disappeared into the Communist party in the East anyway. In the West, the SPD survived to put up candidates for the mayor of Berlin – whom the Russians promptly vetoed.

With the city now split in two, the SPD led the resistance to the siege. They were the fire. The Allies were supplying the fuel.

The party had found Michael to be a convincing speaker. They organized hit and run speeches all over the city. On trucks, cars or even on the shoulders of two men, he would begin to speak unannounced. This time he climbed onto a broken park bench in the middle of Berlin's bombed-out zoo. The denuded, cratered landscape served as a flea market, which masked for the black market. Crowds were looking for clothes and shoes. Others hunted for soap, medicine and liquor. Cash was acceptable but American cigarettes from the occupying troops were king.

Michael had spoken long enough for the crowd to gather. Now he needed to finish, before the Communist goons started doing more than just shouting.

"Traitor!"

"Fucking bastard!"

"Nazi!"

That one always hurt. He finished his speech, looking that man square in the eye as the agitator shouldered his way at him.

"Without food, we die one by one. But maybe a child is born to take our place. Without our freedom, we cease to exist at once. And our children are born as nothing."

The crowd cheered, drowning the agitators who had other things on their minds. They surged forward, clawing for Michael. The SPD had given Michael some larger men as security, but they were outnumbered and the cheering crowd was not cheering enough to help them. One SPD man pulled Michael down and pushed him forward as three others fought a rearguard action to keep the Communists at bay.

Michael was fifty meters away before he felt he was safe. The SPD security did not think the middle-aged man trotting after them was a threat and they let him catch up as Michael caught his breath.

"Herr Neumann. If you please. I would like to ask you some questions."

Michael stopped. The man was plainly dressed in a light shirt with the sleeves rolled up. A short tie was loose around his neck. He loosened it more.

"Klaus Farber." He bowed slightly and added, "ADN."

Michael snorted, but held back the SPD man who moved in protectively.

"Which way will you twist what I said this time? I am a neo-Fascist or an old Nazi?"

"We print what you say."

"Yes, but often have trouble with the word order."

"Just a question. I wanted to verify that you were married."

"My wife died in…1943."

Farber ignored the pain in Michael's face. "Was there not a child?"

Michael shifted his weight. It looked like he might collapse and the SPD man took his elbow.

"We tried to protect her, but I have no idea where she is."

"Perhaps we can help. If we found her, would you not like to know about it?"

"Have you found her?" Michael straightened, but knew the answer already.

"Not yet. Perhaps soon. We are trying to because you are such a public figure now. Our readers would be most interested."

Farber made sure the threat had reached its target.

"Thank you, Herr Neumann."

Farber turned to go, but stopped.

"I am surprised you do not spend more time trying to find her yourself. And not waste your time in a hopeless cause."

Michael watched Farber melt into the crowd, now focused on its more tangible and immediate needs.

"There is time for one speech more before dark." He was moving as the other SPD men fell into step. "Let's try the *Potsdamer Platz*."

It would be full of early evening strollers and that much closer to Sonya.

CHAPTER 29

*Tempelhof Airport, Berlin, U.S. Zone,
June 27, 1948, 9:13 A.M.*

It would be Chance's third attempt at suicide in one day.

The briefing had warned of visibility less than a hundred feet. Meaning that, at takeoff speed, the average non-exhausted pilot would just have time to say "shit" between the moment he saw something ahead and his brains splattered all over it. Chance knew the weather guru had not actually come out to the runway to measure the visibility. He could barely make out the runway lights fifty feet away in the fog as Rossi pushed PIE IN THE SKY's throttles forward.

They had made two hops from Rhein-Main Airport since 4 A.M. today. The cockpit floor reminded Chance of the old joke about the waiter totaling a bill by tallying the stains on the customer's tie. Little dunes of coal dust merged into clots of flour. The gray outline of a boot print showed where the dust stuck to a smear of butter.

The briefing had also warned of a crane working off the end of the runway. A larger four-engine C-54 had overshot the runway on landing, the pilots coming in blind. The plane ran into the softer part of the rain-soaked field and stopped abruptly. The partially assembled bulldozer it was carrying didn't. The crane was there to recover the bulldozer. The pilots were mostly a permanent part of the field.

Predictably, PIE IN THE SKY yawed right and Chance corrected, feeling the rudder bite sluggishly in the accelerating slipstream.

"Eighty," intoned Rossi, calling off the airspeed.

Chance started to pull back on the yoke and realized a second later he was completely disoriented. The runway had faded below him as the unloaded plane lifted. They were in zero-zero visibility fog.

"Altitude?" he demanded, unwilling to tear his eyes from the cotton-bale sky, searching for anything to tell him up from down.

"How the fuck do I know? Still on field elevation." Rossi was no help.

"Positive rate of climb?"

"Yeah."

"Gear."

As the landing gear motors' whine echoed in the empty aircraft, Chance wrenched the yoke over. Rossi made a noise, but never said anything. The crane flashed past just under the right wing. Chance wasn't conscious that he had seen the derrick until it was behind them. He had reacted instinctively to a vague shape slightly darker than the fog, his mind saving itself, willing his arms without thought.

He allowed himself the luxury of a check of the compass. He had not completely corrected PIE IN THE SKY's characteristic yaw and they had turned right of the runway.

"We gotta turn." Rossi croaked his New York accent back to life, *turn* coming out *toiwn*.

Seconds after takeoff, they were in danger of crossing over the Soviet Sector in Berlin. They needed to make a tight turn to the left to stay over the Allied portion of the city, away from the harassing Russian YAKs and threatening anti-aircraft fire.

"They can't see us," sighed Chance.

He was tired. Tired of Russian blinding him with searchlights and jamming the air traffic control radio. Tired of Air Force ineptness at organizing the stampede of aircraft. Mostly he was tired of trying to kill himself seven times a day.

He pulled the yoke back over as the radio came alive.

"Departing aircraft, your slip is showing." Some wag in the tower had come up with that code yesterday. Originally the Air Force had coined the tactically dry *Alert Blue*. But so many pilots were joining the airlift daily, that many were confused. Humor had a way of making them pay attention and few misunderstood the meaning. The newly-arrived pilots hearing it for the first time knew what they had to do without having the phrase explained to them.

Chance wanted to tell the tower controller to look up somebody else's ass, but he was spent. Besides, it would violate radio procedure.

They popped above the fog layer into a surreal world between the lead overcast above and the featureless sea of white below. The only other signs of human life were a C-54 diving into the sea for Tempelhof and the Dakota ahead of them that had departed three minutes before PIE IN THE SKY.

The coming hour of numbing boredom weighed down on Chance. He looked off to his right. Nevada was out there, drowning in the obscuring ocean. The Red Cross was useless and the U.S. Military Government had no interest. Except McKane.

After Chance had snatched PIE IN THE SKY back from the East, the Army and the Air Force were unsure what to do with him. His only sin was not filing a proper flight plan. And he was a civilian.

On top of all of that, the Allies were drawing anything airworthy into Western Germany. Military transports were coming from as far away as Alaska to form a conveyor of aluminum to feed the besieged island of democracy.

Despite the McKane's growling, the military told Chance he was flying the airlift. He would make as many trips as he could in an eighteen-hour day. They would give him fuel, oil and parts for his plane. He and his crew would get food, a bunk and one hundred dollars a week.

If Chance didn't like the terms he could go home. But he had to leave PIE IN THE SKY behind. And Nevada.

All Chance had was a name – Max in Berlin. A million Germans could have that name. One thing he had in his favor

JITTERBUG LIFT

was the fact that some ten percent of male population was dead or still in prisoner of war camps in the Russian East. That still left 900,000 Krauts to ask.

"We're going to have engine trouble," Chance said flatly.

"What?" Indignant, Rossi scanned the instruments, tweaking the mixture for effect. "Everything's fine."

"Not now. When we get back to Berlin." Chance rolled fatigue out of his shoulders. "Something that'll keep us there a day or two."

Rossi couldn't read Chance's face. He'd given up trying long ago. But he thought he saw something like determination for a moment.

"Your aircraft."

Rossi took the yoke as Chance released it, tension draining from his body. He ratcheted his seat back, wondering if Rossi ever really learned to fly. The mechanic's ham-fisted grip on the yoke bounced them all over the sky, constantly overcorrecting. If a pilot lets go of the controls on most any aircraft, it will fly just fine. All a pilot has to do is guide the plane and keep it out of trouble.

It occurred to Chance that his decision to ground PIE IN THE SKY in Berlin for two days would cost the fledgling airlift 200 tons of coal, flour or powdered milk. Some Germans might go hungry, even die. But Nevada was behind him somewhere. The Germans had started this mess and deserved what they got.

He and Rossi had worked out a system where Chance caught a half-hour snooze on the way back while Rossi napped on the way in. Usually he was asleep before they entered the narrow airway to Rhein-Main. But something was eating at him, something way down in the dark.

"My aircraft."

Rossi turned the control back to Chance with a look of surprise.

CHAPTER 30

*Tempelhof Airport US Occupied Berlin,
June 27, 1948, 11:49 A.M.*

PIE IN THE SKY was mortally wounded – at least according to Rossi. The plane's landing gear had barely settled on the runway when Rossi killed the number two engine. The fog was gone and the tower noticed immediately, despite the fact there were almost a dozen other aircraft demanding their attention.

"5534, be advised. Ground procedure is to taxi with both engines," intoned the controller with a twang that could only be from Green Bay, Wisconsin.

"Tower, 5534. Number two is overheating. Unless youse want a bonfire out here, we'll limp 'er in," Rossi played the part to the hilt.

"5534, do you need the trucks?" The controller played his part straight.

"Tower, 5534. Negative. T'anks." Rossi didn't want to have their "problem" scrutinized too closely. As a private carrier, he could insist that he alone work on the aircraft. Although they were entitled to have the Army mechanics do it.

They had chosen the fault carefully. Overheating could have hundreds of causes, all hard to track down. It would give them the time they needed.

It took the German ground crews twenty minutes to off-load the tons of powdered milk PIE IN THE SKY carried. Meanwhile, a brass band and a spread of sandwiches and donuts reminded Chance and Rossi of an Independence Day picnic. The bunting on the mess tables set up in the sunshine was either lazily rippling in the warm breeze or snapping in the passing prop washes. A team of WACs in summer uniforms kept the table stocked and chatted with the half-dozen jockey crews who had time to stand there while their planes were off-loaded. Someone had given the WACs permission to doll themselves up way beyond regulations.

For some it was a nice break. For others it was a painful reminder that they should be home at a picnic or ball game with an ice-cold beer, eyeing their girlfriends or soon-to-be girlfriends in gauzy dresses. One pilot joked he had seen the same sandwich when he came through two and a half hours before.

Chance was hungry. The sun-dried mess bread and something that vaguely hinted at baloney quieted an ache in his belly. Rossi grabbed two sandwiches and took alternate bites out of both, asking for mustard with his mouth full. The mess orderly brought out a stainless steel pot of lemonade and poured it into a porcelain bowl on the table. A lump of ice, frozen in the shape of a coffee can bobbed in the middle.

"Where ya from?" The female voice had Texas laced through it. The WAC smiled when she had Chance's attention.

Mouth full, Chance cracked a grin and pointed the half-eaten sandwich toward PIE IN THE SKY.

"I mean back home."

Chance forced the lump of food down and glanced off to the side. He turned back to the WAC after a moment's thought.

"That's it." The sandwich still pointed at the plane.

The WAC was sensitive enough to notice the change in Chance's face. She forced another smile and offered him some lemonade. Whatever was in the sandwich was salty and Chance gulped it down.

A C-54 started up, obliterating a tiny voice behind him. He felt something touch his shoulder; so lightly he thought it was a napkin blown by the prop wash of the four-engine giant. The

WAC looked over his shoulder at something as Chance jammed the rest of the sandwich in his mouth. He turned.

It was still a shock to see them up close. There were seven of them. Their sunburned skin was drawn tight over their cheekbones, where a thin sheen of sweat served as makeup. Old dresses with the sleeves cut away sacked breastless bodies with ribs and hip bones protruding as if broken.

The lead *Trümmerfrau* approached with her raw hands clasped as if to deliver a well-rehearsed grammar school speech. Two of her fingers were bandaged together with a strip of dirty cloth.

"Vee…" she gestured to the other women arrayed behind her with attentive faces. "Vee con-gratoo-late you on dee Day ov Inde-pen-dence." She nodded to the others.

"Hoppy Fort ov Dschuly," chorused the *Trümmerfrauen* on cue.

Several of the jockeys smiled and one even clapped. Chance was unmoved. They were obviously after the sandwiches and lemonade. They had sung for their supper, but he still didn't think they deserved it.

"Thanks. But it's next week."

"Ja. But you make party now with…" She pointed a stick-like arm at the bunting and food.

"Picnic. We're having a great time." Chance stopped the sarcasm when he saw how Miss Texas was eyeing him.

Chance waited to see if the *Trümmerfrauen* would scoop up a sandwich or some donuts. All they stole were glances at the expanse of mess hall food with the imagination of the starving. In their minds they put the bread in their mouths, feeling its texture and tasting its sweetness. They gorged themselves on the fantasy, but not one touched a stale slice.

Rossi offered some of them chocolate. Smiling, they refused, looking to their leader to explain.

"It is zu varm… too warm. It will…" She waved a raw hand at the summer heat and hunted for the word. "…*schmelzen*…"

"Yeah, melt." Rossi turned to the WACs. "Youse guys gonna be here all day?"

"Some of us."

Rossi fished out eight bars of Hershey's best from his flight bag.

"Hang on to dose for dem."

The WAC smiled and took them. It was an uneasy smile.

"Youse pick dose up when youse finish," Rossi explained to the lead *Trümmerfrau*. "When youse go home. *Versteh?*"

"Yes. Is clear. Thank you." The lead woman turned to the others and explained in a burst of German. The others brightened with an outburst of "*Dankeschön*" and hefted their shovels and pickaxes to their shoulders. They marched away, single file.

"All they want is chocolate. Sandwiches ain't good enough," grumbled Chance.

"They don't eat it. It's for their kids," Rossi said to the bar he was unwrapping.

"The children don't get a full food ration like the adults," tossed in the WAC. "We're probably keeping half of Berlin's children alive with chocolate. The women will do anything for it." Her face clouded as she realized what she was saying and she forced another smile at Chance before finding some out-of-place slice of bread that needed adjusting. She spoke as if she understood the common desperation of motherhood, although there was no way she could know herself just yet.

Chance watched the women marching off onto the field. They waited for a Dakota to touch down and then trotted across the runway, evaporating into rippling mirages lost in the expanse of the airport.

Chance didn't shower before hurrying off to the *Tiergarten*. He found the obliterated flak towers. The massive four-story concrete monsters had held the anti-aircraft gun emplacements to defend the city. Chance wondered if any of them had fired the shells that killed some of his crew or gutted BAILING WIRE.

Chance passed lamps and scissors laid out on tablecloths on the ground. He wasn't interested in the small-time sellers. He wanted the ones who moved cases of liquor, medicines and gold. The ones who would know Max.

The Germans were perceptive enough not to try and sell Chance anything. Some asked if he had smuggled any goods in or had cigarettes. They never said what he might get for the cigarettes. He didn't have any so Chance tried to explain he wanted to find Max. Shrugs were all he got until he pulled out a dollar bill. The Berliners exploded into gestures and some English, pointing out someone or trying to give him an address that probably didn't exist anymore. One woman was repairing shirts as her customers waited, bare-chested, studying the American. She told Chance that he would have better luck finding black marketers in *Potsdamer Platz.*

As he walked across the city's carcass, Chance struggled with the huge expanses of broken buildings. Frankfurt was a scratch compared to this. He had seen the newsreels of Hiroshima, and the heart of the Nazi Reich reminded him of that level of devastation.

After a few streets he found himself staring at the cobblestones. He would only look up when he passed a group of *Trümmerfrauen.* The rhythm of the chipping hammers was slower here and faltered like a dying heartbeat.

A whole crowd of them scavenged the buildings across from the *Columbushaus* in the *Potsdamer Platz.* They were working just below and east of a turning point for aircraft coming into Tempelhof. Every three minutes, a plane throttled back and banked to the south over the army of ghosts. Occasionally, one would blot out the sun, giving a split second of shade.

The British, American and Soviet occupation zones all met at the large square. It was a favorite haunt of black marketers because they could choose which police force was particularly lax at any moment and set up shop. If conditions changed, a few meters' stroll brought them to another jurisdiction. Since the start of the blockade, they had concentrated on the Allied side of the boulevard. There was no real marked border, but it seemed everyone knew where it was.

Chance immediately spotted two Soviet soldiers, rifles slung on their shoulders, walking along the curb in front of the ruined *Hotel Fürstenhof* on the east side of the *platz.* Three Limeys in their berets, pulled up in a jeep on the north end. On their arrival, a small wave of men and a few women made their way south. It reminded Chance of the call for last dance at Nora's, a stable-turned-dance hall in Tulsa.

Chance searched the faces for someone to ask about Max. He rested his foot on the remains of an iron fence that has once surrounded a tree. The fence now marked the edge of a bomb crater filled in with rubble. He saw no one in the new arrivals from the north.

He was surprised that, despite the blockade, the border to the workers' paradise was extremely porous. A large red banner facing the west proclaimed something cheery or threatening in German with lots of exclamation points. There was no checkpoint here and the Russian soldiers patrolled lazily, more intent on talking to each other than on watching anyone in the square. Chance guessed that if a starving Berliner wanted to head for the welcoming arms of Uncle Joe, the soldiers wouldn't stop them.

It struck him that so far no one seemed to be taking advantage of it. If Berlin was starving, the Berliners were sure as hell not acting like it.

He wondered if he could ask one of the soldiers about Nevada. Maybe they would take him to their command HQ and he could see him. Or bail him out. Maybe he could explain that Nevada was just stupid and they'd let him go.

It all seemed so bizarre. It was like Nevada *was* dead. Or, he could be only a few blocks away. Chance could walk there. But the whole world seemed to be in the way. He was searching for a man named Max, the needle in a haystack of needles. His only other hope was Adolph and Hermann, as Rossi had nicknamed the pair of black marketers they had met in the Frankfurt morgue-turned-bar, who had provided him with fake papers. They had said they were based in Berlin. Chance realized he wasn't even sure of their names.

He was flying over Germany again, lost in the clouds in the junk heap that was to become PIE IN THE SKY. Except he had no idea where Nevada was this time.

A shout snapped his attention to the women working. It was nothing this time and he watched from the relative cool of the shadows across the street. Chance tried to see progress, but it was lost on this scale. Running the back of his hand across his forehead, he glanced up and down the street. There were buildings waiting for the women as far as he could see. They were emptying an ocean of bricks with teaspoons.

Maybe they felt the same as he did.

One of the women stood still, holding two bricks and looked up. Rivulets of sweat streaked the dust on her face and arms like grotesque makeup. Chance glanced elsewhere, thinking it was only a personal break. He found another woman staring at the sky. A third joined her. The pedestrian traffic had stopped too. Everyone was turning to the sky, standing where they stopped — even in the middle of the street.

The silence was heavy with the heat. The Germans were clustered in groups, talking. In one little group that had moved into the American zone, a man motioned the others quiet and they all stood silent, listening. The man shook his head and the conversations resumed.

Chance noticed the group was looking over at him. The Germans were careful not to make it obvious they were staring and stole looks at the American pilot. Chance realized that, despite his civilian dress, he still stood out.

Chance turned back to the street and saw one of the German men coming toward him, the others in the group watching their emissary.

The wind shift had blown the rumble of a Dakota away until it was almost overhead. The sun winked out for an instant and the plane banked. Chance saw they were on one engine; number one was feathered and still, making them late.

The *Trümmerfrauen* pointed and smiled. The emissary stopped and turned back to the group, looking over his shoulder at the descending plane. A giddy party fever bubbled through the crowd and faded away with the sound of the C-47. The silence returned and the smiles twitched.

The Germans turned toward a growing thunder in the west. A *Trümmerfrau* clapped her hands together and beamed. A Skymaster loomed over the buildings, the explosive sound of four engines pounding on chests. If the Germans cheered, it was lost in the roar.

An old man gaped at the C-54. Chance watched the Germans as the waltz time of the airlift returned. The city was breathing again. The tock-tock heartbeat started up and the flow of people moved on.

The boy who found him could hardly have been fourteen. He spoke fair English, punctuating his sentences with a nervous tic – a head-jerk down to the right and then up over his shoulder with his jaw jutting out until the cords in his neck showed. It was the time-honored way of thieves to use the innocent in areas of uncertainty and danger. For them it was insulation against the authorities. For the innocent, it was an entry-level job.

"You could bring some-ting in, not?" The boy got right to the point after asking bluntly if he was a pilot.

"You want chocolate?"

"Is for *Kinder*. I am too old. Maybe cigarettes?"

A few other boys descended on them and there was some not-so-gentle pushing and shoving.

"Can it!" Chance barked. "Anybody know a guy named Max?"

The chorus of "*ja*" was too enthusiastic to be believable. One boy did not answer with the others. He stared at Chance warily as he slipped away.

"In the east." Chance pointed across the border and the enthusiasm vanished.

"Okay. How about Peter and Harold?"

One boy volunteered to find them but no one knew them. Chance described the black marketers as best as he could remember.

"*Ach, ja. Peter und Harald!*" The boy with the tic gave their names the German pronunciation with Peter coming out "Pater."

The boy introduced himself as Karl and led Chance south on *Potsdamerstrasse* across the Spree River to an alley off *Dennewitzstrasse*, just west of the rail yards. Chance had seen shell-shock victims with a similar tic while he was in the hospital. He had wondered if they were reacting to the same blast over and over.

The trip was short. Chance and Karl were able to cut across whole blocks, cleared of buildings. Once, Karl pointed left where a large hole was hidden in the rubble. Bricks and broken concrete partially filled the basements of bombed buildings. Karl knew a boy who had died falling into this particular hole.

The area was nearly deserted and Chance got the feeling he had 'sucker' written all over him. He saw fewer people on the streets and couldn't remember when he had last seen a U.S. military patrol.

Karl knocked on the large wooden door several times before it cracked open. The voice inside did not seem happy to see Karl. Twitching, Karl argued something back. Chance wondered if he was saying "I have brought you this great, big, dumb American. And he has cash!"

The door opened wider and a slightly older boy peered out at Chance. The older boy took a step back inside and grumbled something. Karl smiled and cocked his head toward inside. Chance stepped into the garage.

Karl tried to follow, but the older boy shoved him back outside with a curse. Karl whined an appeal to Chance, but the heavy door slammed in his face, plunging the garage into darkness. Only a few shafts of sunlight lanced through the peaked roof.

The older boy motioned Chance to stay put and left through a groaning metal door. Chance could make out a few older cars without wheels and something more intact under a canvas tarp. The cobblestoned floor was puddled with oil and little balls of excelsior. Snatches of German voices whispered behind the metal door. An older man was unhappy and then there was silence.

The metal door groaned again and a large man unfolded himself from the passage. Chance thought he could have tossed McKane around like a doll. The giant ambled past Chance as if he was invisible and checked outside the large doors, looking in both directions.

On the way back he paused to look Chance over and headed toward the metal door with a sniff. Chance went on alert. The giant turned. An enormous hand lifted him up. It felt like a huge jaw had clamped down on his neck.

"I Max," announced the giant with a grin. "Why you want me?" Contrary to all of Chance's experience that often a man's size is inverse to his smarts, Max realized that the choking American could not answer. He tossed him at the canvas-covered car. The curved fender sliced into Chance's back and he fell on his knees.

Mercifully, Max was physically slow, but was still able move to the groaning pilot in one step. A boot pinned him to a tire.

"Why you want me?"

"Nevada," Chance forced out.

Max paused. Chance felt something under the car.

"Where's Nevada?"

An elephant sat on Chance's chest as the hulking German pushed himself back. Chance knew that opportunities to breathe may be few and far between and inhaled deeply.

Max cocked his head to the right trying to figure out the question. He gave up and the boot headed back for Chance's head.

"*Max, hör auf!*" The voice coming from behind the malevolent German was familiar.

Chance swung the wooden pole out from under the car and connected with Max's knee, ducking the boot at the same time. Max howled, dropped down hard on the wounded knee and howled again. Chance scrambled to his feet and wound up with the pole.

Peter, aka Adolph, rushed up and grabbed Max.

"*Hör doch auf, Idiot!*" He cuffed the giant roughly in the ear giving him new pain to think about.

Chance recognized the black marketer who simply glared back at him. Harald rushed in. He was particularly glad to see the American, ignoring his comrades.

"Herr Chance! It is very nice to see you! I knew you would make it." He turned to Peter who was helping Max up. "*Es hat geklappt! Der Ausweis war perfekt!*" he gushed. "My papers is excellent, not?"

Peter and Harald took him to the optimistically named *Café Hollywood* on the *Schöneberger Ufe* just over the railroad tracks on the Spree River. A sign in the window promised a special for any American servicemen. It did not say what would be special.

Harald thought Chance had had to show the false papers at every checkpoint and was supremely proud of his product.

He kept pressing Chance to remember if he had ever given the forgeries to the Russians and was disappointed every time when Chance reported he hadn't.

"You guys know somebody named Max? Works in the East and brings stuff out." Chance was tired of repeating details about his self-guided tour of the Soviet Zone.

Harald choked on his coffee. Peter simply stared out the window at the bomb-damaged apartment buildings across the river.

"Max is a very common name." Peter squinted a little. "You have already made a mistake."

Chance resisted following his gaze and did his best to make Harald more nervous. Peter ran his thumbnail in a scratch on the table top.

"Come on. You know him. Hermann's coffee almost came out his nose." Chance watched the thinner, nervous German dab his lips with a frayed napkin.

"Mine name is not Hermann," he managed to squeak out.

"What is it you want? Perhaps we can help you." Peter still found the partially-collapsed structure fascinating.

"I want Max. Does he have a last name?" Chance shifted his attention to Peter, much to Harald's relief.

"This is nonsense. Max, Max. Go out on the street and shout it. Hundreds of peoples will answer you." Peter turned back, throwing an arm over his head and speaking to the table top.

The outburst caught the attention of the young waiter who had just brought Chance the special – three small glasses of Schnapps. Chance caught the waiter staring at him. The waiter – not more than twenty – forced a smile and looked at Peter for some reason. Peter had ordered in German so Chance doubted he understood more than the name.

Peter grabbed Chance's wrist. Chance didn't like it.

"Go fly your plane in this ridiculous air operation. Maybe you do some good." He let go of Chance's wrist. "Otherwise, if you ask about Max, you are just committing suicide."

"If I may..." Harald leaned in, lowering his voice.

"It will be suicide. *Punkt.*" Peter slapped the table top for emphasis.

JITTERBUG LIFT

"If I may," Harald pressed on. "Max fought against the Nazis for six years. They hunted him. He was here in Berlin and they could not find him."

Peter was less wide-eyed. "*Amt Sechs Sicherheitsdienst*. Office Six of the SD. More feared than the SS. They could not find him. Or stop him."

"They were clairvoyant!" exploded Harald. "They could find anyone. It was amazing. Anyone!"

"Max does not care about Russians or Americans." Peter glanced at his fidgeting partner in near disgust. "He goes where he wants. Takes what he wants. And kills who he wants."

"I gotta talk to him." Chance was unmoved.

Peter sat back and shook his head. "You Americans think you can do anything. Close the borders and you say 'OK, we drop chocolate from the air.' Your friend goes missing in the east and you think you can talk to Max. *Wahnsinn*. Craziness. If you bring him something he wants, then maybe you have a chance. Otherwise, *kaputt*." He slapped the table again.

"Your friend met a girl in Berlin," Harald said almost absentmindedly.

Peter winced.

"You saw Nevada?!" Chance was almost on his feet.

"Calm," Peter commanded. "Sit down. Please."

Chance sat slowly. Peter waited for the staff and other customers to return to their own business.

"We saw him once. We did not say something because it would do no good." Peter glared at Harald and turned back to Chance, holding his hands wide, offering the thought. "He came to Berlin flying for the British and was eager for some, how do you say…special jobs. He wanted a lot of money and we could not do business. We did not know what happened to him. And you had not told us why you were going into the east."

Ever helpful, Harald thought of something. "He had a lady. At *das Löwenmaul*. The Lion's Mouth."

CHAPTER 31

*Soviet Military Headquarters, Karlshorst,
June 27, 1948, 1:56 P.M.*

Ivanoff had not stood when the pair came into his office. He never stood for their kind. They had presented identification but Ivanoff ignored it. Two plainclothes men who walked in unannounced and without an appointment could only be working for one organ of the government. Perhaps the MVD men had noticed the slight. The taller of the two, who called himself Balankiya, had rattled off prepared questions. The smaller man had allergies and kept sneezing, apologizing to Balankiya and not to Ivanoff as he wrote down the answers. Ivanoff realized that they had missed his prisoner interrogation training in his file.

The questioning ended with, "Where is the American pilot?"
"He is secure."
"Perhaps it would best if we could process him."
"No."
Balankiya stood and leaned over the desk. He could almost put his head over Ivanoff's.
"You have failed in your duty twice, Comrade Colonel." Balankiya stood up straight. "The second time was worse than the first. How do we know there will not be a third time?"
The sniffling man's pencil scratched across the notebook.

"My record answers that."

"I am not impressed with trinkets. Nor do I pity scars." Balankiya's finger aimed right at Ivanoff's nose. "We will ruthlessly crush our enemies. And we will crush you, too, if you are in the way. These are dangerous times. We cannot let sentiment or false gratitude influence us."

Balankiya strode to the door and was out in the hall. The smaller man leapt up, nodded to Ivanoff and was at the door frame when he turned back.

"Frankly, I do not know how you have survived this long."

He turned left to follow Balankiya. That meant they were not done with his section. Ivanoff wondered how many of the secretaries, enlisted men and women, even including his own adjutant were on the MVD rolls as "patriotic helpers", the euphemism for informer.

He could no longer count on help from his own section. Fortunately, he had other assets.

CHAPTER 32

*Das Löwenmaul, British Occupied Berlin,
June 27, 1948, 11:13P.M.*

The woman seemed to know him.

She didn't say anything as she floated through the smoke haze of the modest bar, looking directly at him. She didn't wait to be invited to sit down. She pulled out a chair, almost elegant in her poise. The wounds in her tan raincoat were neatly stitched. She had opened it before she got to Chance and Rossi's table. A simple black skirt was brushed clean and a faded green cotton blouse was buttoned to the top. Her legs were bare, leading to suede shoes. If Chance had looked further, he would have seen a scrap of newspaper peeking out of the top. A headline of the *Tägliche Rundschau,* proclaiming happiness was descending on the workers in eastern zone. *The Daily Observer,* the Soviet Army mouthpiece in the Russian zone was now filling out her oversized shoes that one of the happier members of the proletariat had sold for a kilo of bread.

The woman's worn clothes failed to hide her beauty. They muted her form but the promise passed through unscathed.

Chance thought she looked different than the other whores who seemed to be in every corner of the room. Half of Berlin was on the edge of starvation. A few marks or – better yet, dollars

– could spell the difference between life and death. The Germans sold anything they had. Even themselves.

For a population sinking into hunger and despair, little things had begun to matter. Vitamin deficiencies meant minor wounds wouldn't heal. A paper cut could easily become infected and kill the starving in days. A missed meal spelled a slower death. The victim's mind became clouded; bad decisions were made. That led to more missed meals. The victim would spiral out of control, dragged down by an invisible force like **DROOPY DRAWERS** or hundreds of other B-17s that had seeded the Fatherland.

Chance had had a nightmare of a million Germans hanging on a cliff by their fingernails. He watched them slip one by one over the edge for a long time, not feeling a thing. He remembered the dream when he woke up. And was annoyed that he felt something then.

He had brought Rossi along because he didn't want a repeat of this afternoon's foolishness. His mechanic had laughed when he saw the giant, oil-stained boot print on Chance's chest.

"Youse been asking some indelicate questions."

Chance decided that Rossi's knowledge of Berlin's customs and neighborhoods and his smattering of German might be useful.

He had a name and now he had a thread. A frayed thread, but something. It was odd, with Berlin bombed flat, Chance could see a mile. There seemed nowhere that someone could hide or be hidden.

He had started asking indelicate questions again as soon as he entered the club. *Das Löwenmaul* was populated by Berliners only. The foreign press and Allied government officials stuck to the more comfortable and better-stocked hotel bars. Chance got a couple of blank looks, but mostly frightened glances, as if he was asking for Satan himself. Chance was surprised that even with such a common German name, almost everyone knew exactly who he was talking about. After one angry near-argument, Rossi thought they should take a break until the late night crowd came in. Word was out: they wanted Max. In a city where five dollars was two week's wages, anyone who knew Max in *das Löwenmaul* would find them. Chance hoped they would be helpful and not out to break their necks.

The three-piece band had wound up a bluesy and barely recognizable rendition of "Don't Sit Under the Apple Tree" as the woman arrived at their table.

Rossi waved off the scuttling waiter, whose gaunt neck swam in the white livery shirt. The waiter had timed his arrival to coincide with the woman's. Perfect timing, Chance thought, reminding him of the curtain coming down at the end of the hootchie-kootchie shows back in Tulsa to keep things decent.

"We ain't buyin' fer her. Beat it." Rossi defended their table with his thumb toward the door.

"Hang on," Chance enjoyed studying the woman. "What do you want?"

She looked him in the eye, not enjoying being studied.

"Coffee. Very sweet." The accent was refined, the pronunciation perfect. Not the usual guttural German trying to be English. Chance had heard of professional women, doctors, psychiatrists, and teachers now trolling the streets to survive.

But they usually didn't order coffee. It was a common trick, though, the very sweet part. A tablespoon of sugar had 25 calories and in blockaded Berlin little things like that mattered.

"That's not what I meant."

"You asked me what I wanted."

The woman's voice and gaze never wavered. The whores usually were quick-tempered or ashamed.

"Have a seat."

The woman sat like a princess.

"Should I leave youse loverbirds alone?" Rossi was drunk, but Chance suspected he had already picked out a bedmate for the night. He didn't answer. Rossi pushed back from the table and stood up, trying to look less drunk than he was.

"Hap-py landings," and he vanished in the smoke.

"You are pilots?" The question sounded more like a royal decree.

"Yeah, we're lost. Any idea which way is Tulsa? It's in Oklahoma. That's in the U. S. of A."

The woman smiled. It was genuine and warm. For a moment, the hardened exterior dropped. Chance liked what he saw. But then the defenses returned. Thick like flak around Frankfurt.

He noticed she had a scar on her cheek. Small, but there, a crack in the flawless statue. The perfection surrounding the blemish made it all the more noticeable in the dim light. Chance wondered if she had gotten it when she was raped, as thousands of Berlin women had been. She seemed like a fighter. A survivor.

"Chance Mitchell."

The woman's eyebrow lifted slightly. Another unguarded moment.

"Sonya." She said the name oddly as if she didn't expect him to believe her. "An interesting name. Chance. It is a nickname, no?"

"Yeah."

"Nicknames are often very descriptive."

The cadaverous waiter sidled up with the coffee, giving Chance a second to think. He was finding that difficult at the moment. His mind cleared as the waiter leaned in to set the cup on the table, blocking Chance's view of Sonya.

Her focus was on the coffee cup as the waiter stepped back, waiting. Chance touched his glass. The waiter nodded and was gone.

He studied her again while she stared down at the 25 calories waiting tepid in the cup. Fuel was at a premium out on the Berlin *Strassen*; coffee was only hot at Tempelhof.

"Thank you for the coffee." Her voice stayed even. Her gaze was somewhere between a starving animal and a high priestess about to perform a sacred ritual. She lifted the cup and sipped, leaving her lips wet. She dabbed them with a handkerchief produced from nowhere, an extravagant waste of precious calories. Chance only registered the wet lips.

"So what's it going to be?" Chance drained the last of the liquor from the small glass.

Sonya looked genuinely surprised. "I am not what you think, Mr. Mitchell." She avoided the ubiquitous German *Herr* address.

"What do I think you are, Sonya? And it's just Chance."

Her nostrils flared. Chance had finally met a German who would not bow and scrape in deference to the victors. Chance realized he desperately wanted to know just what Sonya was.

"You are not a military pilot."

"How would you know?" Chance caught a shadow watching them at the bar and forgot for the moment she had ignored the question.

"You are asking about a man named Max. You own your airplane and cannot be military. Smuggling for the black market would get you court-martialed and put in prison if you were still in the Army." The words flowed effortlessly from the wet lips.

Chance was annoyed that she had figured out so much about him in such a short time. Yet, he still knew nothing about her. McKane had done it, too. But he had his file. He wondered if everything about him wasn't stenciled on his forehead.

"Close, but no cigar."

Sonya's eyebrows tried to meet for an instant, then widened and rose in satisfaction as she decoded the expression.

"It is very dangerous to ask about this Max. He is not someone who wishes to be found."

"I know a little about dangerous things and people."

"As do I."

She had been looking down at the coffee cup. She lifted her face with her chin slightly elevated.

"I was in Berlin during the war." Her chin lowered slightly. "And after it."

Chance badly wanted to clear the alcohol out of his head. He was a tired drunk and Sonya would be a handful even if he was wide awake and sober. And she seemed to know something about Max.

"You know where I can find this Max?" he said, wincing his eyes into focus.

"No, I do not." She adjusted the coffee cup so the handle was straight to the right. "I have overheard two men at the bar who have done work for him. They know you are asking about Max and think you are a stupid American military policeman. They would like to teach you a lesson."

Chance checked out the shadows at the bar. One had not moved.

Sporadic notes and drum tattoos announced the band was back. As they started "Little White Lies", Sonya turned her head slightly toward the corner crammed with the trio and looked back at Chance. His attention could not resist the pose.

"Would you like to dance?"

Up to now, only B-girls had ever been forward enough to ask him to dance. He never liked them. "If I had wanted a date I would have brought one," was a favorite jab to send the cocktail sirens running.

"It would look better," she said. "Policemen would not dance."

She had laid it out all nice and tidy. He was way behind the curve and still falling back. He liked being in control – of an airplane or a budding romance. But somehow this didn't bother him.

He got up carefully, testing his balance that hadn't been dissolved by whatever they called whiskey in Berlin. A few couples were swaying out on a section cleared of tables. Chance caught sight of Rossi with a much older and taller blonde who was bending over to plant her head on his broad chest while trying to two-step out of time. The blonde stood to full height and cocked her head toward the door. Rossi saluted Chance and left with her. The shadow at the bar took no notice.

Sonya led the way and turned. She was a figure that had escaped some art museum. Her right hand waited, suspended languidly at shoulder height. Her left had brushed down her skirt as she walked, hiding the move from her partner. It came up, perfectly anticipating Chance's arrival into her open, inviting space. Her turn was on her toes and her skirt flared slightly. The outline of her hip trailing into her leg hinted that more perfection waited out of sight. The entire maneuver had the appearance of being rehearsed, but was still relaxed and unstrained.

Chance felt her for the first time. His left hand slid under her right. The warmth and softness exploded in him. His right arm encircled her waist, her light blouse revealing the lithe strength in the small of her back. The beginnings of her hips and the rise of her behind tantalized him in the flexing muscles at the bottom of the curve.

The heat from her face caressed his as she moved closer, her eyes never leaving his. Her eyes were dark, with slight upturns on the outsides, the eyebrows and lashes accented her gaze and held his. He could detect no makeup.

Not even to hide the scar.

He tried not to look at it. Not out of revulsion, but he figured she would be self-conscious about it. Yet it fascinated him. He wanted to reach back in time and undo whatever brutality had damaged this vision.

Something was wrong. She stopped and he did, too. She adjusted her hold on him and smiled, again that look of satisfaction.

"Americans all dance differently."

He pushed back the thought that he was probably a whistle stop on a long line of Americans and others.

"I just picked it up places."

"Tulsa?" The oil boom town sounded so romantic when she said it. He remembered dancing at Nora's. The girl had been rich and slumming in the muck and derricks. Her finer tastes were artificial and worn like her gaudy party dress. And were just as quickly shed.

He pulled Sonya a fraction closer. She pulled back, keeping the distance between them proper, but not too far.

"Yeah, Tulsa. Little Rock. Kansas City. Dallas. Galveston." Each city rolled off with some memory.

"What happened in Dallas?" The eyes bore into him.

"Nothing."

"Dallas was different."

She had read him again. The memory was painful. His feelings for Lisa were still a train wreck. He decided that if she could read his past so well, his present should be a piece of cake. He would not make her guess.

The band was in the last refrain of the song and he pulled her very close. His right hand moved down instinctively toward her center of gravity and he pulled her right hand in. His chest registered the impact of her breasts.

Her lips parted, still slightly wet. Her eyes flared, their blackness threatening to pull him in.

"Thanks for the warning. About Max."

"I must go."

"How about another dance?" He leaned very close. She turned her face, moving her jaw and the scar opened up. The cut had not been stitched closed and gaped bloodlessly. Chance shuddered and pulled back, letting his arms flop to his sides.

She planted her feet, snapping her head back to face him squarely. Her eyes seethed as the lights went out.

A butterfly caressed his left ear. The words did not register as much as her warm breath on his ear and the pull of her hand.

"Come with me now."

CHAPTER 33

*Das Löwenmaul, British Sector Berlin,
June 28, 1948, 12:33 A.M.*

The drizzle felt cold on Chance's face as they got outside and he started to think.

The Allies were using rolling blackouts to conserve fuel. In some other part of West Berlin, Berliners were getting up to cook and wash while there was power. The waiter had appeared with a candle seconds after *das Löwenmaul* went dark. Sonya led Chance quickly away from the light toward the door.

He had gotten a better look at one of the shadows at the bar tracking him as they hurried out. Something was familiar about the silhouette. Despite the security at Tempelhof, Germans had access to the field. Thousands of workers repaired the runway and muscled food they would be eating in less than a day off of the non-stop conveyor of aircraft. Chance placed the memory as someone he had seen there.

They charged into the street. Chance slowed when he realized they were more vulnerable here than in the bar. He heard a riot of German as the door to *das Löwenmaul* opened. He ducked into the doorway of the corpse of a building across the street, pushing Sonya on ahead. She seemed to understand the tactic immediately.

His leg brushed something soft. Flowers pushed up through the cracks. This time of year Berlin tried desperately to hide its disfigurement with blossoms that sprouted magically and tenaciously from every crack and crater. A pretty scab on a gaping wound. A crisscross of floorboards reminded him that he was on a precipice, inches from plunging into the crater.

The path of candlelight paved the wet street for an instant, lighting up Sonya walking quickly away from him.

Chance watched her with a part of his vision. A trick he had learned to keep track of pouncing Messerschmitts a few miles above their heads and an eternity ago. He watched the bar door intently, too. The familiar shadow paused as if checking how hard it was raining. It searched the skies for some sign, caught sight of Sonya and stopped, just for a moment. The shadow either had an appreciation of women or was wondering what had happened to Chance. It turned and moved slowly in the opposite direction into its brother shadows who embraced it.

Chance headed after Sonya. Some streetlights remained on, but they were few and far between. After almost a block in the darkness, Chance caught up with her.

Her breath was fast, convulsing her chest. She forced a smile and looked behind him. Chance checked too and fell in step with her into the night. He felt protective, even if part of him was acting like a predator.

They moved through areas of drizzle and even fog. The city was almost silent. The weather and hunger kept people inside. Chance and Sonya came out of the anonymous street into the broad *Leipzigerstrasse* and turned east. The dark forced them to pick past heaps of bricks lit only by the scraps of light from single bulbs in the apartments above them. She seemed to know the way well. A few other people hurried past. They would have business out on a night like this. One did not waste calories on an idle *Spazierung*.

That occurred to Chance, too. Why had Sonya come in bad weather? Just to warn him? She had walked right up to him. Had she been sent?

After several more blocks – if you could honestly call the expanses of rubble and ruin between streets "blocks" – even the streetlights went out.

They walked in silence, crossing the Spree River. Chance thought it was strange that the sidewalk was meticulously clean. Berliners had cleaned up what they could. If they were going to have to live in ruins, they would be the tidiest ruins.

Ahead was the sound of a mobile generator and bright lights flooded the intersection with its matching US and Russian checkpoints. The demarcation line snaked through the city, arbitrarily separating the hungry free from the not-much-better fed workers' paradise. Here it was marked by a white line in the center of the street, occasionally decorated with bales of barbed wire. The Soviet-occupied side was a blaze of lights and if any Berliners were out they would smell the aroma of bread and sausage wafting over the line from a Russian field kitchen purposely set just out of sight near the border.

In Berlin, little things mattered.

Chance realized another block would be the end of the line. The blockade had been only a day old when a British pilot had taken a short cut across what he thought was an open field. In reality, it was a flattened block of buildings that had been hastily leveled. It was also in the Russian zone. The Soviets held him for two days, grilling him about the airlift and the Allied intentions.

Chance took the time to look behind him. The street was nothing but ink.

Sonya stopped. "Good night and thank you for accompanying me. I live just on the other side."

The smile warmed her face for a moment. Despite the calendar saying it was midsummer, the cold made her shiver.

"Look, I'm…"

"The Russians can see us." Sonya cut off the fumbled apology. "Good night."

She hesitated a moment. Something was supposed to happen, but Chance wasn't sure what it was. Sonya smiled again and turned toward the checkpoint. Chance watched her a few steps and she stopped.

"Please go now. It is not good for me to be seen with you."

"I want to see you again."

"Go. Or you will not."

Chance turned and headed away from the checkpoint. She waited until he had disappeared in the blacked out street before continuing on.

Sonya looked over her shoulder one last time at the empty darkness behind her before turning left down a side street away from the checkpoints and along the gutted stores on the U.S. side. Their show windows yawned like empty eye sockets. They had long been picked clean of anything that could be sold or burnt. She paused at a darkened storefront, grabbed a glassless window frame and swung her leg up. A second later she was gone.

Chance reached the same window less than a minute later. He climbed up after her and found himself plunging into a cavern of black. Scattered light from the street gave up quickly.

Chance figured she had to be following a memorized route. Her tan coat was still slightly visible for a few steps, but then the blackness swallowed that, too. Chance strained to listen, trying to track her. But her footsteps were irregular, stopping and starting, crunching through debris and then clicking on the hard floor.

He seemed to be moving through a narrow passage; Chance could hear the closeness of the walls and ceiling. Then he heard nothing. He stopped. He felt his way forward, hands ahead, testing the floor with his foot. The echoes of his own breathing and footsteps had changed. He felt like his left ear had gone deaf.

A hand grabbed his, jerking him to his right. He resisted, but found himself quickly pressed against a familiar warmth. His face was inches away from Sonya's. Light from somewhere lit up her eyes. The terror was clear. She nodded back over his shoulder. Chance looked up and saw where the light was from. They were on the edges of a large atrium. Several stories above, the skeleton of the skylight let in some light. Chance looked down to see he had been a step from a two-story drop into the basement.

Chance sensed the sound; he never really heard it. It came again from behind them like a fluttering piece of paper; just the air moving. He turned back to Sonya, cocking his head toward the sound. She still held his hand and pulled him forward, deeper into the dead building.

They moved quickly now. Chance tried to follow where they were going, but gave up. He had to surrender to this woman and trust her, something every bit of him loathed. Almost every bit. He could feel her hand. The warmth was familiar but the texture was new and foreign.

There was a loud bang of wood on stone behind them. Sonya never stopped, but kept going with Chance in tow. He felt like an idiot. The only things his mind could register were her hand and the floor below them.

It was imperceptible at first, but it rapidly became clear they were starting to head down. Chance felt the angle getting steeper. They weren't running as much as falling forward. Chance felt like he was in one of PIE IN THE SKY's permanent dives again – before it was repaired. Sonya began pushing back on him, as his momentum carried him faster. He heard Sonya hit the wall with a soft "uh." Not a cry of pain, but as if she expected it.

A fraction of a second later he hit the wall, too. His left hand was out and took most of the impact. His left shoulder took the rest. His head just bounced off the brick. And then Sonya was pulling him on.

It was only two steps and then the store released them. The echo and darkness fell away like a heavy canvas. They were out on the street.

They were completely away from the building before Sonya slowed. And some steps beyond that she let go of his hand. Chance was looking at her face at the time. She did not meet his eyes, but took her hand away to brush back her hair. Her hand did not return to his. He kept his there, waiting as they walked another block. Then he slipped it into his pocket.

They turned left up a nameless *Strasse*. After another block, ill-defined by the heap of rubble at one end, Sonya stopped abruptly.

"Good night." There was warmth. "You were foolish." The warmth was spent in the night.

"What's this about? Why couldn't you cross there?"
"I will explain another time. Can you find your way back?"
"Yeah. Sonya…"
"Go!"

She ascended the short stairs to the apartment block and vanished inside.

Chance waited for a light to come on in the windows above. He saw none. He noted the address and turned to head back, pausing to check the windows above once more. It was raining harder and he hurried.

Sonya stood at the dark window until she saw Chance turn the corner. The walk had left her skin cold. She pulled off the wet raincoat and turned on the light. Her face hardened.

"*Wurdest du aufgehalten?*" hissed from a dark corner in impeccable, but familiar German. "You were delayed?" Colonel Ivanoff spoke like an impatient, jealous lover.

"A blackout." She faced away from him as he came out of the dark.

"I want you to do something for me."

It took him a few minutes to explain what had happened with the American plane landing deep in the Soviet Zone all the way up to the MVD visit, mentioning no names. Sonya clung to the shadows, afraid he would read her face.

"The American is resisting interrogation. Perhaps he will eventually break. But we do not have the time. His friend is looking for him. I believe it was he who stole the plane back. I must find him quickly. You must help me."

She saw him searching for her face in the dark as he stood by the window.

"If something happens to me, you will not be free. I have ensured that my fate is yours."

He came across to the black space sheltering Sonya. His tunic was already open. He ran his hands up the sides of her arms.

"You are cold." He turned away abruptly. "Help me out of these things. Then get warm." He headed into the bedroom.

She began unbuttoning her blouse, pulling it out of her skirt. She emptied herself, her mind closing massive inner doors and sealing herself in. She began to think of the mountains. A meadow where she could be all alone. It was very familiar, though she had never really been there. There was no sound. She could not imagine the birds or the wind. But it was safe.

She had gone there when she was raped, but that is not why she needed to go there now.

CHAPTER 34

*Tempelhof Airport, Berlin,
June 28, 1948, 1:18 P.M.*

They wouldn't be flying today for lots of reasons. Rossi's hangover meant he couldn't even fake working on PIE IN THE SKY's sham overheating problem until after three in the afternoon. The unusual European summer weather helped out with another damp fog and zero ceiling. And there was no way Chance was leaving the besieged city without seeing her again.

Her face would not leave his mind. There was the scar, a flaw that made her fragile but perversely added to her beauty. Her eyes had him more than anything.

Chance had laughed to himself at what was breakfast for him and some of the three dozen other pilots wolfing down coffee, powdered eggs and pancakes at the Tempelhof mess. For others it was lunch and for a few haggard mouths, it was dinner. For anyone outside Tempelhof, it was an obscene orgy of food in a starving Berlin. The set of huts thrown up near the runways was far from where any ordinary Berliner could get to. Field kitchens nearby disgorged coffee, donuts and whatever the Army said a man running on no sleep should have.

The pilot across from Chance slowed his chewing on a shingle of toast drowned in butter. Chance caught the man looking at him again and found himself smiling. He was an idiot. Sonya and he had hardly spoken a dozen words to each other. He knew nothing about her except an address in the Russian Zone.

And it didn't matter. Women were like flying. He had an instinct. It drove him without thought; reactions and passions surfaced from a blind abyss inside. Chance recognized only the hunger and the need.

He'd faced more than enough dangers flying. But he'd had more than his share of near tragedies with the other instinctual pursuit. And he had bailed out more than once – with women, that is. It was the safe thing to do and the decision came from the same place as the desire that had gotten him in trouble to start with. In a plane with one wing, the altitude never bothered him. It was his friend. With women it was just the opposite and he was climbing again.

Nevada had been – and hopefully still was – his buddy. He wanted to find him desperately and Sonya could find out something about Max. At least she had heard things about him. His twin needs converged on her.

Chance noticed the scrabble-bearded pilot opposite him was not staring at him, but at the ceiling, listening. So was everyone around him. The room was silent. The engines of an approaching C-47 rumbled through the battens of damp air. With the fog, no one had attempted a landing for several hours. Now some poor jockey low on fuel, exhausted and frustrated – maybe with mechanical trouble – was trying to feel his way down. If he made it, breakfast, lunch or whatever was over and twenty tired crews were back on the job.

Even so, the men in the mess were up there with him. Everyone knew the wrenching terror. Radar and instruments could get you close, but that last quarter mile you were on your own.

The engines throttled back. The pilot thought he was over the field. Several crews turned toward the large windows to see nothing but a gray shroud. Others knew better or didn't want to see.

The engines revved, one missing badly. Chance tensed involuntarily. The eggs of the boyish copilot down the table slipped unnoticed from his fork, spattering in the ketchup on his plate.

The engines sputtered closer, reverberating in the mess hall. They throttled back again. The pilot was hunting and picking out ghosts of the ground from the fog. He used his instruments to tell him if his wings were level and if he was climbing or diving, otherwise his eyes hungered in the emptiness ahead and down for a light, a patch of color or a shadow.

The engines wound up rapidly. Both missed, the copilot was behind on the mixture. They were losing power. One man stood in the mess hall as if to lend a shoulder to the doomed plane. Chance knew the odds. A plane loaded to capacity, one engine on the ropes and the other starving for fuel and air, trying to claw away from the unseen ground. The pilot pulling the nose up, but the power isn't there. Chance saw the trees at Ziewald. The pilot had to fight instinct and push the yoke forward to keep the plane from convulsing into a flat iron, soon-to-be coffin.

The good engine roared back to strength, then screamed. Chance braced. The tables creaked as other crews joined him and the men fighting for their lives.

It was imperceptible at first, but the sound was fading. Maybe they would hit downfield. Slowly, the sound climbed away. The plane passed through the temperature gradient that was holding the fog to the earth and the sound died.

Dry throats coughed, cups and cutlery clattered and the low, tired murmur returned, knowing there was more sleep in their future.

And more nightmares.

Chance walked by the ruined store twice in the fog. He wasn't sure he was even on the right street. He couldn't read the Fraktur script someone had painted on the corner wall announcing *Waldstrasse*, although he could make out the "*strasse*".

But his biggest problem was getting inside. The street was full of Berliners on their way to work or in search of food. He finally realized they were all intent on their own problems and the well-fed American loitering in front of a bombed-out department store was not worth the calories to even think about. And the fog helped isolate him even more.

Picking his way through the collapsed floors was only marginally easier during the day. The building was in its death throes, rain-fed waterfalls eroded cracked concrete pillars barely supporting shifting floors.

Chance relived the brush with death from the night before as he edged sideways along the atrium. The floor ended with splintered boards bending downward. The whole floor tilted down from the wall behind him, making it all too easy to plunge onto the jagged debris forty feet below.

In the narrow passage on the other side, Chance stopped dead. A hand lay across the opening ahead. He watched it for almost a minute and it did not move. It was curved upward, away from the floor in an unnaturally elegant gesture. The bare arm vanished around the corner. Chance inched forward and suppressed a laugh. The dismembered arm ended at a crumble of plaster.

He could see the wall this time as he made the headlong run down the collapsed floor. The floor bounced as he ran down, many times feeling as it would simply give way to the unknown depth below.

Coming out onto the street on the Russian side was an entirely different matter. There were few happy workers out and a Russian jeep parked a fifty yards down the street. The patrol had their weapons slung and one was lighting a cigarette, entertaining his comrades about some night exploit or joke. Chance waited for the fog to thicken and slipped onto the sidewalk. He startled a couple coming the opposite way. For a moment they regarded him as if he had just landed from Mars. Then, with a word to the woman, the man steered them across the street. The woman would not stop looking at Chance until they disappeared in the gray gloom.

He climbed the stairs through layered aromas. Something smelling like burnt rice joined the scent of toasting bread. A radio softly played RIAS, Radio In the American Sector.

Hastily set up, RIAS promoted the free-world side of things and was a propaganda outlet largely controlled by the three western victors. However, the control was loose and the media outlet was the first almost free voice in Germany in almost twenty years. It was still not forbidden to listen to it in the Soviet Zone, but doing so could bring Colonel Markgraf's *Polizei* looking for any shred of one's Nazi past – real or imagined. Markgraf was a former German prisoner of war in Russia who had returned to enthusiastically serve his warders.

Chance slowed when he heard laughter from the radio, joined by a chuckle from the apartment. The pattern was familiar enough, a hen-pecked husband pleaded with his wife. It sounded like *Fibber McGee and Molly* in German.

Chance slowed again when he got to the top floor. He had tried all the other floors. She had to be here.

What was he going to say? He imagined the scar looking out at him through a cracked door – if it opened at all. Hopefully the small bag of sugar smuggled from the mess would at least get him that far. Another pilot had caught him pilfering the sugar pot. They stared at each other until the pilot asked Chance where he got the paper bag. Chance told him.

He stood in front of four doors on the third floor. There were no names, only numbers and the directory showed only last names. He cursed himself for not knowing Sonya's. Five seconds of Eeny-Meeny-Miney-Mo settled him on the third door from the left. A knock produced instant results.

"*Wer ist da?*" The voice was reedy and old.

"Sonya?"

"*Neben an. Nummer dreizehn.*"

"No…um…sprecken. No sprecken." For once Nevada had given good advice. In fact, he seemed downright clairvoyant.

The door lock squeaked. At the same time the door behind him opened. A middle-aged man peeked out, letting laughter from the radio spill into the hall. The door opposite him opened wide. An old woman headed a gaggle of occupants crowded in the 120 square feet.

"*Lieber Gott. Noch ein Ami.*" The little, wrinkled *Hausfrau* made her pronouncement barely above a whisper, her eyes widening to what they were when she was twenty. Then they darted past

Chance to the cracked door across the hall. "*Lass es,*" clucked out of dry lips and bad teeth.

The door behind Chance closed. The old woman smiled. Chance could not tell if it was friendly or derisive. She pointed to the door to his right.

"*Sonya wohnt da.* Sonya here."

"Thanks. Um… *Danke.*" Chance found himself bowing slightly. The woman smiled again and turned back into her flat. Chance could see pre-war furnishings and pictures. Delicateness curiously unscathed by years of war.

Chance raised his hand to knock.

"*Vorsicht.*" The *Hausfrau's* tone was hard to place. Mocking? She smiled to herself and repeated it. "*Vorsicht. Unglück.*" She wagged a finger at him and closed the door.

"*Danke,*" Chance mumbled. He knocked on the door marked thirteen and heard the blood pounding in his ears. He heard nothing else for several moments and knocked again.

"*Wer ist da?*" Sonya's voice hit him like a thousand volts.

"Chance." His own name came out hoarse.

There was an eternity before the door cracked open. Her unscarred cheek and eye were all that was visible for a moment. Then the door opened completely. She did not step back, turning her scarred cheek toward him.

"Yes?"

"I brought you some sugar."

"How did you know I needed it?"

"You like your coffee sweet." Chance hated waltzing, even with someone as lovely as Sonya. "A bad habit when half of Berlin is starving." He instantly regretted his harsh tone. A cloud crossed her face, replaced quickly by the even gaze that had proceeded it. Something was off. Chance was too involved in realizing how beautiful she was in what passed for daylight in the hall. Diffuse light seeped in through a half boarded up skylight above them. But something nagged him.

He held out the bag of sugar. Her eyes flicked to where some trickled out of a tear. He shifted the bag to stop it, but the tear widened. He held out his hand to catch it as she did the same.

"Inside. Quick," she commanded.

She backed in, bringing him and the bag inside to a table in the center of the apartment.

The room was full of her scent. She pulled a cracked plate under their hands and the leaking bag from a tiny table. The plate was china and matched nothing else in the apartment.

"It will be all right."

Chance still held the bag.

"You may let it go."

"Sorry. It was a bit of a hike getting here."

She swept the grains of sugar out of his hand onto the plate with delicate fingers. Something caught her eye in the hallway and she strode to the door, closing it quickly on the nosy middle-aged man across from her.

"It is very bad that you have come. And to offer me a gift in the hallway. What will people think of me? And if the Russians find out…"

"You're welcome." Back in the States, Chance would have pulled the rip cord on this not-so-budding romance long before he had offered the sugar. But something about her made him too mad to do that. That and she might somehow, at the end of a very tortured road, lead him to Nevada.

She stood at the table, fingers resting on a lace cover. It was stained with candle wax and frayed. It reminded Chance of Dr. Klempnock at the Frankfurt *Bahnhof*: dignity shredded at the edges. The dignity was there, even disdain. The dark black eyes stabbed into him.

His instinct wanted her, finally catching up with the baser parts of him.

"Where did you learn your English?" He groped for neutral ground. "It's pretty good."

"I learned it at school and it is excellent."

"Yeah, better than mine. Are you always such a…?" He let the sentence trail off knowing it would end all hope – for Nevada or any more immediate progress.

"I did not ask you here. You may take your sugar and go."

"No."

"Get out!" The eyes flashed into anger.

He had found it. Her Highness liked to be obeyed. He sat on the sofa, which should have looked out on a city of lights. Now the gray fog hid the corpse. He knew this was a dead hand, but he was driven from somewhere in the dark abyss to keep playing. He sat back on the sofa.

"Got any coffee?"

"*Ersatz.*"

"The fake stuff."

"If you wanted real, you should have brought it." Her face returned to the even gaze. He was playing hide-and-seek. Mostly seek. Chance's experience with women made it easy to read them. But Sonya was a challenge. And if he had to get her mad to have her reveal herself, it was going to be a short relationship.

Sonya disappeared behind a curtain and in a few minutes the stink of burnt rice filled the apartment. Sonya presented him with a tray holding a single cup.

"Sugar?" Her voice had softened.

"No, I take it black."

"You will want the sugar."

The first bitter sip convinced him she was right, but he wasn't about to drink his own gift.

"What does *Vorsik* mean?"

"I charge a half-kilo of butter and a kilo of bread for German lessons."

"Really? You got some then."

Her face showed otherwise.

"Business must be bad."

He was pleased to see her struggling to keep the smile from rising to her lips.

"*Vorsicht* means 'be careful'."

Chance forced another swallow of the ersatz coffee down. "And what about *Onglick*?"

She frowned at that one. "*Ach so, unglück.* You have learned some useful words. Most *Amis* only want to know how to haggle with the whores. It means unlucky."

Chance smiled. The old lady was telling him Sonya lived in Number 13. Unlucky.

Sonya looked out the window at nothing. "It also means disaster. Or tragedy."

CHAPTER 35

*Felsenstrasse 17, Soviet Occupied Berlin,
June 28, 1948, 7:40 P.M.*

She hadn't spoken for several minutes. Chance was worried she was going to hustle him out when it got dark and that there was a boyfriend or pimp to make sure he left. The awful coffee had gone cold, forgotten in the conversation. In the last two hours they had talked about their distant childhoods. She asked quite a few questions during his stories of riding the rails across the U.S. and Canada. He asked about life before the war. At one point she watched him carefully when she told him she was Jewish. Chance asked how she survived. She told him a little about being on the run and working for the Resistance in Berlin. And how she got the scar during a bombing raid. Chance wondered if he had been on that raid and she read his mind again.

"It was the fourteenth of March, 1945." She let that hang in the gloom for a moment. "During the day," she added pointedly.

Chance tried to remember and stopped. The back of his head throbbed and he ran his fingers through his hair over the scar.

He didn't ask about life after the war. That part of her life remained a black void. He had heard enough stories about what it was like for women in Berlin after the war and decided that it would be better not to press.

"I lost every one of my crew, except Nevada. And I'm not going back alone."

He told her about Nevada and that he was missing in the East. When he explained how he got PIE IN THE SKY back, he noticed her eyes widen.

"Yeah, it was crazy. I never thought I'd get away with it."

Sonya put Chance's cup back on the tray.

"Why'd you come to the Lovenmal?"

Berlin was turning deep blue in the fog. She stared at the velvet nothingness at the window.

"*Das Löwenmaul*," she corrected. "I stop there sometimes. I was looking for a warm drink and I had not eaten all day. You *Amis* are very generous; you will give a woman a drink if she sits with you. Chocolate if she dances with you and cigarettes if she sleeps with you." The tone never wavered. Almost as if she had said the litany a thousand times.

"What does sugar buy me?"

She turned, flashing anger. "Two cups of ersatz coffee. And I do not smoke." Her black eyes went through him again. He had no armor against those, but he was relieved at the answer.

"Neither do I."

"Then you will be very popular with the ladies."

"How do you figure that?"

"You are issued a ration, no?"

"I'm civilian, not in the Army. We get to eat in the mess, but no rations. So, no cigarettes." He moved to the window with her. "You were lucky. Rossi and me were the only Americans in the bar."

Her face softened a fraction and she nodded almost imperceptibly and turned back to the royal velvet fog.

"If you like Americans, why not just stay in the Western Zones?"

"I do not like starving."

"You don't have much faith in me and my friends."

"You are here and your friends are on the ground. I am good at arithmetic, too. Your newspapers say that every plane brings in enough food for 100 people for two days. This happens every three minutes." She turned to him. "When was the last time you heard a plane? This morning? Hundreds of planes have not landed. It is summer. What will you do when winter comes and this lasts for days?"

"I'll be long gone. I just want to find Max and get my friend back."

"Is that all?"

He thought he heard sadness in her voice. He still couldn't read her. Maybe she was laughing at him. Still she was a treasure that he badly wanted to open.

"Almost all."

She frowned again like she had when he had used the slang "Close but no cigar." Then her face relaxed and she stared out at nothing. His instinct was screaming at him what to do next when he heard it. It was a Dakota, climbing out. The jagged city had begun to reappear. Another Dakota climbed out after the first. She turned back and faced him, moving a fraction closer.

"I will do what I can to help you find Max. I can find things out. They will know I am not a policeman."

Every nerve closest to her felt like it was trying to jump out of his skin. "Anything I can do for you?"

She smiled for a moment. He was beginning to live for that smile.

"The sugar is nice. And perhaps I would like to ride in your plane one day."

The smile faded and Sonya held his eyes with hers.

"For now I ask two things. You must stop asking after Max. It is too dangerous. And you must never come here again. It is also dangerous."

Chance pulled her slightly toward him.

"You will need to get back. You and your friends are very behind." She turned her head ever so slightly, offering the scar.

The fog had vanished by the time he hit the street. Warmer air moved in from the south. Days before it had left the Sahara and headed north.

Chance had not gone far when knew he was being followed. The shadow was smart, walking on the other side of the street. It paused several times but always was in sight. Ahead was the back end of the bombed-out store. A few more paces and he would turn right and lose the tail in the ruins.

He stopped and listened. The following footsteps were gone. The door to the store and the American Zone was to his right. He could be through it in a second. But what if the hunter knew that way – and better than Chance did?

"It is not a good idea, tonight." The accent was German, the shrill delivery, excited.

Chance spun to meet the voice and found a gaunt face with wild eyes. They darted toward the store.

"A very bad idea." A hint of a giggle.

Chance glanced into the building and saw flashlight beams ricocheting inside. Snatches of Russian echoed off the crumbling walls.

"One street that way." The crazy eyes had hands but they stayed in the pockets of the leather jacket. Only a shoulder shrugged back down the street in the direction of Sonya's building. "They are drunk." The eyes became euphoric. "In the morning, they will be shot." The man blurted an idiotic laugh and caught himself. "Shot quite dead. They are good at that."

This had trap written all over it for Chance. But he had no choice.

The eyes lost their glee and became commanding. "You should hurry. They will be relieved any minute." The tone was confident, as if the owner was in charge of everything.

Chance found himself moving in the suggested direction.

"*Gute Nacht.*" The eyes smiled sanely.

Chance checked several times to see if the eyes followed him. The figure stood still, unmoving, haloed by a streetlight in the damp air. Then Chance turned one last time. The figure and the eyes were gone.

He turned to corner and found a small Russian checkpoint. A strand of barbed wire crossed the street. Chance slowed and heard singing. In an empty shop front, four Russian soldiers were trying to out-shout each other. There was no opposite U.S. checkpoint and Chance edged his way to the wire. He took a few steps back and jumped. He landed on the other side, attracting what was left of the attention of one of the doomed soldiers. The Russian shouted and stumbled to the door.

"Halt!" A stream of Slavic curses followed. His comrades laughed and went back to enjoying their last night on earth as Chance ran into the darkness.

He slowed as he came onto a wider boulevard and realized his lunatic benefactor had spoken to him in English. How could the crazy man have known so well in the dark?

The boulevard was deserted. The summer night was cool and the smell of rain was in the air – even if it was drowned by dust, decay and the stink of a disabled city. Chance moved on, convinced he was alone. But two sets of eyes tracked his stride, each not knowing about the other.

Their methods were different. One set leap-frogged ahead of Chance, calmly anticipating his route and simply verifying that he was not deviating from it.

The other set took no chances. Dimitri's target was new to him. He was glad his first shift to tail the American was on the deserted streets. It would be hard to lose someone who stood out as much as the tall pilot. But his superior had made it clear that the penalty for failure was well beyond a negative report or even demotion. Dimitri had asked if the goal of the surveillance was to intimidate the target, in other words, let Chance know he was being watched. Dimitri's boss had yelled a sharp *nyet* over the phone.

As Chance walked ahead some 50 meters, Dimitri took a step after him. A jolt of pain shot up his leg as a piece of Krupp steel brushed against a nerve in his calf. Only two and a half millimeters across, it was all that remained of over a half-kilo of shrapnel that had changed his life outside Stalingrad. His whole company had been wiped out by the German 88 round that had ended their first meal in days. The field doctors had removed what they could see by candlelight, but the tiny piece was overlooked. When he complained about the pain, they told him he was lucky to be alive. The soldier's current employer had promised to have it taken care of, perhaps even here in Germany – if Dimitri did a good job. In these times it was good to work for a boss who could arrange anything. Dimitri rubbed his leg, cursed the departing damp soundlessly and limped after the *Americanski.*

Both men trailing Chance stopped when he cleared the MP at the gate to Tempelhof. The limping soldier noted the other tail. Someone else was interested in his target. Did his superior not trust him? Or did his superior not trust the other man? He thought about it as Chance retrieved his papers and disappeared inside the chaos of trucks and planes. He was right about the other tail, though. As soon as Chance was gone, the other pair of eyes turned and slowly shuffled off in the direction they had come. The soldier toyed with the idea of trailing him for a moment. But he had not been told to. Perhaps he would be compromising some other operation by one of several secret organs in the Soviet government. His mind ached and his leg throbbed. And then what his superior counted on won out. Dimitri was a good soldier. His limp was more pronounced as he headed south around the field. He mentally dismissed his counterpart as an amateur. A good tail never doubles back.

Circling the field, Dimitri noted the aircraft arriving and their timing. Every three minutes, another plane landed. He could see their lights as they taxied to the terminal building and more lights as trucks raced to the plane before the engines stopped. One had to hand it to these Americans. Whatever they did, they tried very hard. But they were stupid.

Did they not realize it would never work?

CHAPTER 36

*Brandauer Allee, Berlin, British Zone,
June 28, 1948, 10:27 P.M.*

"How did you find this out?" Michael's eyes searched everywhere in the room for hope and found none.

Sonya put her hand on his arm. "An American came to me and asked about him. He got the plane back. It did not crash."

"If he talks…" The eyes went wide. "Perhaps he has already."

"No. There is still time."

"How do you know?"

Sonya forced a smile. "I know Nevada."

Michael quieted and looked away. "Some of the members of the city council are talking about making peace with the Russians. There are the beatings. The Russians know about my child. One of their parasites asked me about her." He sank down in the tattered sofa. "Will this new American do this for us?"

"Yes."

Michael whirled. "How do you know? Does Max have any more money?"

Sonya noticed the door to the other half of the apartment was open. Brahms' *Hungarian Dance Number 1*, echoed spiritedly in the orange candlelight.

"He is asleep." Michael turned back to her again. "When can we try again?"

"As soon as I can convince the American."

Michael stared at her. "Surely Max has more money."

"Not so soon."

"Please do not..." Michael broke off, the hoarse whisper dying to a rustle of leaves.

"But your child."

"Not for that price."

Michael pulled her to her feet with him and held her tightly. "You are all I have. Perhaps I can talk to the American."

"No. If he is caught, I am dead. But you will be safe." She touched his lined face. "It is better this way."

"Sonya, I will not lose you."

"You will not."

"When this is over..."

"When this is over, you will have a daughter."

"She will be eleven. A tender age for a girl. She will need a mother."

Sonya had feared he had been thinking that way. She could not blame him in the least. Until yesterday, she would have considered it.

But not now.

"I may not see you until we are ready."

CHAPTER 37

*Soviet Military Headquarters, Karlshorst,
Berlin, Soviet Zone, June 28, 1948 11:43 P.M.*

Ivanoff caught the porter staring at his scarred head.

"Comrade Private." Ivanoff let the syllables crackle.

The porter snapped to attention. But it was not as practiced as it should be. It was obvious the man had not done it very often. Privates in the Soviet Army can expect to snap to at least several times an hour unless they are on guard duty in the Arctic.

"What happened to Private Malogska?"

"He was reassigned, Comrade Colonel."

"Did he not speak to you about your duties before he left?"

Ivanoff noticed the man's confusion.

"No, Comrade Colonel."

"There are some things you should know. Tell your superiors to brief you better."

"Yes, Comrade Colonel."

Ivanoff did not expect to see the private again. The MVD would realize his cover was blown.

His driver waited by the Horch with the engine running.

"I will not need you."

The driver suppressed his surprise and stepped aside. Ivanoff got in with pain. The driver closed the door and leaned in the window.

"I obey only the colonel's orders, sir."

Ivanoff merely nodded and accelerated away. The lack of traffic made the tail stand out. It was a Russian auto, which made it stand out even more.

Evasive tactics in the air involve getting your enemy to commit to a path which will force his weight and momentum to carry him away from you. It is the same on the ground, but it is not so much weight and momentum as foolish pride.

Ivanoff raced for the safe house in *Leipzigerstrasse*. The tail hung well back, apparently confident of his destination. Only 100 meters from the house, Ivanoff turned abruptly down a side street when he was briefly out of sight of the tail. The MVD men would pull up at an empty house, wondering where Ivanoff had hidden the car. They would find no one. Nevada had been removed one hour before.

Ivanoff checked his rearview mirror several times as he raced out of the city, satisfied with his first attempt at evasive maneuvers. He had never practiced them before. He had only attacked.

The Russian pilot was frightened even before Ivanoff barged into the tiny office at the same airfield that held his private YAK fighter. Despite his civilian clothes, the young man leapt to his feet as Ivanoff placed his cap and gloves on the desk and faced him.

"Where did you land in the West?"

"Gilfheim, Comrade Colonel. I only wanted to bring back things my comrades would like."

"Answer only what and when you are asked. There is no airfield at Gilfheim."

"I landed on a road, sir."

"Were any American or British pilots involved?"

"*Nyet!*" The pilot sounded insulted.

"You are a dead man. We both know that."

Ivanoff gauged the pilot's height as anguish exploded on his twenty-five-year-old face.

"The evidence is clear and we both know that it is true."

He waited for the pilot to sniff away tears, turning his back on the smuggler.

"There is one way you can still serve, however."

"Be careful," Rossi yelled at Chance's back as Chance dashed out the gate at Tempelhof just after noon.

Chance hadn't really heard him. They had learned about the rumors about the pilot as soon as they landed. No one could be sure who he was. Just that he had been found someplace in the east. Chance didn't worry about finding some false engine problem. He simply headed for the gate.

The Soviet officer studied Sonya's papers for an eternity in the tiny shed at the checkpoint crossing. At one time he was on the phone. Sonya had missed whether it had rung or he had made a call. She watched the other guards and whether they looked at her or away.

"Our friend has appeared. Main hospital," Michael had cryptically whispered over the phone just before dawn. "Basement," he had added with finality.

Sonya scanned the soldiers around the checkpoint and searched for anyone in plain clothes that lingered there. One man, tall with an ocean of sweat on his white shirt, faced away from her. He had his suit coat hooked on a finger over his shoulder and was fiddling with his tie. He turned and looked right at her.

"*Sie dürfen gehen.*" The border guard's German was very good. Perhaps he had a girlfriend.

As she crossed into the U.S. Zone, Sonya felt a short-lived twinge of relief. If Nevada had been found, it was only because Ivanoff had gotten what he wanted from him. Everything he wanted. Hurrying through the ruins, cutting across town, she asked herself what Ivanoff had asked her two years ago. *Why didn't she just run?*

When she got to the hospital, she saw Chance presenting his papers to the British sentry. She called to him across the lawn in front of the gray block. Intent on getting inside, he didn't hear her.

He tried to follow the signs in German. Occasionally there was a sign nearby in English. He finally saw a sign with a word he partially recognized: *Leichenschauzimmer,* and remembered the screaming blonde *Trümmerfrau.* Ten minutes before someone had understood he was looking for the morgue.

The British corporal was neither cheery nor somber. He might as well have been giving Chance a new part for PIE IN THE SKY.

"All you have to do is nod, sir." He was poised to pull back the sheet, which he promptly did and then watched Chance carefully.

The man had been savagely beaten. Chance stared at the almost unrecognizable face.

"Where was he found?"

"In *Bernauerstrasse.* Soviet Zone." The voice was behind Chance and the accent was a rattlesnake's rasp.

Chance turned, expecting to see some German official. He hadn't counted on the Red Star.

"This is Colonel Ivanoff of the Soviet Forces." The corporal handled the introductions like a diplomat.

"Is this your friend?" Ivanoff pointed at the body, his own scars disappearing up the sleeve of the dark green tunic.

Ivanoff moved next to Chance, as if studying the body. Then he looked at Chance with a hard, unblinking gaze, waiting, the way he had waited for the enemy to come into his sights.

Chance was sick of looking at the body. "How do you know he was a pilot?" He was looking at the corporal.

Ivanoff produced an aeronautical map out of his tunic and offered it to Chance. Chance did not take it. He could see the U.S. Army markings on the border. The map was folded, but the part that was visible was Berlin and the area south of it. The southern air corridor was marked in blood red.

Chance resisted looking for Ziewald and forced any reaction as far from his face as possible. He nodded only slightly. In all his time in the war, he had never faced his enemy. Now he was and there still wasn't anything he could do about it.

"I don't know him."

"Are you completely certain?"

The corporal hesitated covering up the mangled face.

Chance faced Ivanoff squarely. "Yeah. I'm sure."

"Then whom are you looking for? Perhaps we might be able to assist in finding him."

"Shanley. Kevin Shanley. He was my bombardier."

"During the Great Patriotic War?"

"Yeah. I didn't know this was somebody new."

Ivanoff held his gaze. Chance turned to the corporal. "Thanks."

He could not help but glare at Ivanoff one last time before heading out.

Chance would have spotted her in a crowd at Yankee Stadium from 10,000 feet. Sonya was watching the hospital and pacing nervously in the shadow of an optimistic tree that had sprouted leaves from a single remaining branch.

She seemed to see him but turned away, running toward the large boulevard curving past the hospital. A streetcar had slowed at the curve and Sonya jumped on the jammed car. She clung to the outside with other Berliners. One steadied her with an arm around her waist.

"Sonya!"

She turned. But it was only to smile at the man holding her waist. The streetcar accelerated with the boulevard empty of cars.

Ivanoff came out of the hospital. He zeroed in on Chance easily an instant before being drawn to Sonya's form nearby as she raced toward the streetcar. The American seemed to be hurrying after the same streetcar, but gave up. The sun burning on his scars distracted him from following that thought.

He had a face and soon he would have a name. It would be easy to have the record of Kevin Shanley dug up in England. A relative would be looking for members of the dead bombardier's crew and some sympathetic clerk would be all too eager to help.

He started down the steps and noticed a short man with a limp trying to keep up with the American. The American crossed the street and the tail moved immediately to keep him in sight at a constant distance.

He scanned the hungry Berliners, ignoring obvious hate in their stares, looking for others who had no hate in their eyes. Only interest. He glanced again after Sonya and went around the side of the building to his car. He had ordered the military ambulance that had brought the body of the Russian pilot away long before.

CHAPTER 38

*Potsdamer Platz, U.S. Occupied Berlin,
June 29, 1948, 9:23 P.M.*

Music travels a long way in a gutted city. A small band had set up on the edge of the large triangle of hollow buildings that outlined the *Potsdamer Platz*. The stage was the bed of a U.S. Army truck, the white star on the driver's door covered with a RIAS banner. Loudspeakers propped in the empty windows bordering the square and lashed to bent lamp posts made the band sound like it was playing in a tin can, but in thirty minutes they had drawn over five thousand people from the British and American zones and the curiosity of the Soviets a few steps away. The Russians had hastily closed the border, turning back several hundred music lovers from the East, including a few of their own troops.

The black marketers stayed, melting into the gathering crowd, joyously adapting to the windfall of customers.

The RIAS station had set up the impromptu concert and announced it over the airwaves. The occupiers on both sides recognized it frankly for what it was: a propaganda stunt right under the Soviet noses to show that West Berlin may be starving, but they still were having a good time. The Russian translation meant something like "whistling in a graveyard."

Chance saw Sonya looking behind her again. The *contradiction* had been following them since they left the *das Löwenmaul* a few minutes before. This one didn't look anything like the maze of beautiful confusion and conflicting emotions that strolled beside him. The man behind them stumbled like a drunk, but there was something odd about him; odd about how he tripped and just caught himself on a sign post. He was a man who made no sense. Chance had spotted the odd Berliner coming out of the bar moments after Sonya had hustled him out. He had gone straight there from the hospital and never got past the foam on his beer when she raced in.

Chance had never let a woman lead him anywhere. It bothered him that it was okay when Sonya did it. She said she was in a hurry to get to the music and was sorry she had missed him at the hospital. She was curious why he was there and was genuinely relieved that the body was not Nevada. Now, she seemed nervous about the man bumbling behind them.

In his brief time there, Chance had come to realize that nothing happened by accident in Berlin. The city was being strangled and every cell reacted with a purpose. He had begun to believe that every Berliner – right down to his madman guide of the day before – he encountered for a reason. He was even uneasy that his meeting Sonya may not be just luck.

The *contradiction* wore a cap low over his face in spite of the humid evening. It was a worker's cap, but the suit coat spoke of higher station. When they had waited to cross *Prenzlauerstrasse*, the drunk paused behind them to light a cigarette in a doorway, but there was no wind. And despite all his weaving and tripping, he was still only thirty meters behind them.

Sonya whirled quickly back around and found Chance staring at her. She smiled.

"That's a relief. I was beginning to think you weren't glad to see me anymore." Chance returned the smile, forcing it just a little.

He had to be careful. He had discovered two things in the short time he had known Sonya. One, she was not a fool or easily fooled. His usual charms and ploys that had worked so well on

B-girls in Tulsa and wide-eyed English girls in Middle Wallop she dismissed with something approaching boredom. The second thing he was not so sure about. She seemed to be beginning to like him, but she often retreated behind the shielding, scarred poker mask below those penetrating eyes.

At first it had been a game to play to maintain the tenuous link to Nevada. Now he felt a twinge of guilt as he realized he was beginning to enjoy it. And he had begun to care about how he and Sonya would play out.

He had plainly seen her looking back this time. She tried to camouflage the gesture with brushing her hair out of her face. Her chin was forward and slightly up. Her eyes closed, she let her hair catch the breeze and she shook it off her face. It exposed her neck and lifted her breasts in the plain blue summer dress. Some lock of hair did not cooperate and she turned back to wipe it from her face. Chance noticed her eyes were open and searching behind her.

She caught Chance also looking behind them out of the corner of her eye. "We have gone the wrong way. I am sure of it now."

She turned abruptly, grabbing Chance by the arm. The grip was firm, almost desperate.

The *contradiction* looked surprised for a moment, then brightened.

"*Gnädiges Fraulein.*" The cap was off a slightly bald head. The nonsense man bowed deeply and took a hard step forward to keep from landing on his nose. The cap swung like a courtier's plumed hat.

Sonya led Chance past the doubled over drunk. He stood and noticed the couple moving behind him. He turned and bowed again, sweeping the cap back and forth with an unsteady flourish.

"*Gnädiges Fraulein.*"

"Okay, okay. I'll come quietly." Chance wasn't sure he liked being dragged by Sonya anymore. "What's a 'gnaydiz frawline' or whatever he said?"

"He is drunk."

"Not what I asked."

Chance took a step back and bowed, sweeping an imaginary hat. "Gonadig Frawline."

Sonya looked after the drunk who was stumbling on, carrying the cap. She laughed at Chance as he stood back up.

"It's something funny, right?"

"When you say it, it is ridiculous."

"What's it mean?"

"Nothing."

Chance moved closer and pulled himself up. His smile vanished and his voice took on the practiced tone of an officer. The game was over and he was tired of playing anyway.

"What's it mean?"

Sonya's face hardened and her eyes found their mark.

"Just tell me what it means."

Sonya strode on ahead.

"Come on." He softened just a little, something else he never did with other women.

Sonya took a few more steps and stopped.

"Literally, it means 'merciful girl.'"

"Really?" Amused, Chance thrust his hands in his pockets and ambled up to her.

"He's a fool." Sonya had not softened with him.

"I'll say. Wrong on both counts."

Sonya flashed surprise at the jab. "And so are you."

"That so? Maybe you got us mixed up back there. I'm a drunken Kraut and your plane jockey is headed to Moscow." Chance jerked his head over his shoulder.

"Moscow is that direction." Sonya pointed to her left.

"He's a fool. Like you said." Chance walked on ahead.

"Repeat after me: *Bitte, Verzeihung.*"

"What's that?"

"Say it. *Bitte, Verzeihung.*"

"Bitte, Fersei-ing...ung."

"Not bad." She fell into step next to him. "It is a useful phrase. One you will find, as you say, very handy."

"What's it mean?"

"'I am sorry.' Practice it."

She was ahead of him, smiling. She glanced past Chance to see where the *contradiction* had gone.

"Bitte, ferseiung." He tried it faster.

She smiled broader and held out her hand.

"You're right. Pretty useful." He took it.

His fingers enveloped a still unfamiliar hand. Chance realized this was only the fourth time he had touched her since they had met. He knew her scent, her voice and her appearance, but now his whole being focused on his right hand. When she took his hand in the bombed-out store, his instinct was preoccupied with staying alive. Now he wanted to know what he had missed.

Her skin was warm and soft; not at all like he had expected. Chance's mind wandered around like the chivalrous drunk, trying to remember just what he had expected and why.

His experience with women had been physical and perfunctory. Since he had hopped a freight in Cairo, Illinois in 1938, he had always had the feeling that wherever he was, he wasn't staying long. Towns were places he passed through or flew over. Women he just passed through. Mostly. He had formed attachments exactly twice. The second time he kicked himself for not learning the first time and swore there would never be a third. But the hunger was back, calling out of the black inside. He couldn't help it and, worse, he didn't know what it wanted. Sex and a laugh were things he easily understood, but this was something that didn't have a name.

Chance had thought about that a lot in the past few days. It filled the time in the sky. Eight times a day he had one hour to think, staring at the blue or the stars while Rossi kept the wings mostly level and the nose on the horizon. What bothered him was that he couldn't think. It wasn't like planning an air route to London from Rhein-Main. There were no waypoints, no compass. He just knew where he was, flying by instinct.

She squeezed his hand. He pulled her to a stop and toward him. Her smile welcomed him. Chance pulled her closer and the smile vanished into surprise and then something else. Faces inches apart, she turned and the scar stopped him. His head cocked back on reflex. Her face tightened and the scar gaped raggedly.

He kissed it.

He was tender and unhurried. Her skin was warm and he could feel the unevenness of the wound. He pulled back slowly.

Her head spun back to him, a blur becoming twin volcanoes staring at him over parted lips. Anger threatened to overflow from the cauldrons. But something else was seething with it.

He kissed her lips.

A tremor shook her and was gone. Her hands came up and stopped. His hand on her back felt the tension leave her body as if she had passed out. He still expected a slap.

The anger was gone. Sonya's face showed the shock as her bottomless black eyes searched his. She walked away out of his arms. Her hands were still up, frozen in mid-push, ready to shove him away. She took several steps before they flopped to her side.

Chance let her go on, moving after her, watching her walk. For a while, she seemed to be sleepwalking. But the more elegant, confident step slowly returned. Chance lengthened his stride until he was next to her.

They reached the edge of the crowd. Some were dancing slowly, saving their strength. Chance could see only a few feet into the throng. Sonya stood on tiptoe trying to see farther as the swing music echoed in the skeleton ruins. The *Trümmerfrauen* had stopped for the day, watching like vultures on the heaps of rubble around them.

"This way." She hooked her arm in Chance's and led him through the fringe of the crowd.

They careened through a blur of hunger. Faint smiles flickered on hollow faces. The crowd surged and rebounded around little clearings where some Berliners danced half-heartedly. In one, Chance spotted an older couple swaying in place, the shopping bags with their week's rations always snug between their feet.

They were in the shadow of the modern *Columbushaus* office building at the north end of the square when Chance realized they were steps from the Soviet Zone. No groping Russian soldiers marked the border, but two groups of four stood outside the burned-out office building just feet away. One eyed Chance and then shifted his attention to Sonya. Chance's mind raced with his reaction if the Russian wanted to search Sonya. The Russian took a step toward her and Chance moved around to intercept. They got close enough for Chance to smell beets on the man's breath.

"Howdy." Chance smiled.

The Russian froze, trying to decode what Chance had said, assuming it was German. Chance pushed Sonya west by the small of her back, leaving the concentrating soldier behind.

"Stop, please. I know where I am going," Sonya protested.

They walked west and Chance felt her pressing against him as they bumped through the listeners and dancers.

A bony man appeared from nowhere and fell into step next to Chance. He was so thin, Chance almost didn't notice him at first. Chance only turned when he noticed Sonya's eyes widen at something behind him. Two larger men were shepherding the thin, old man toward the stage. Chance turned back to Sonya, feeling her pull on his arm again.

"We can listen from here."

The band struck up "I'll Be Seeing You" and vague homesickness slipped into the back of Chance's mind. There was no vocalist, but the echo of the words in his head competed with Sonya's presence. He put his arm around her and she leaned into him, swaying slightly with the music. There was no room to dance. Chance felt everything about her and had the strange sensation that he had known her a long time.

Sonya stopped swaying as a taller man passed near her. The big man looked as if he might say something to them, but the song was winding down and he moved toward the west, disappearing in the crowd. The big man looked ahead with a purpose, ignoring the music. Sonya watched the man out of the corner of her eye and four years of keeping himself intact on a daily basis made Chance track him until he vanished.

The song wound up with a flourish that was too much for the small band. The Germans cheered then hushed. Chance could see the band was standing and hopping off the truck bed. At the back, men were trying to help someone up. It took several tries and then the thin, old man that had passed Chance in the crowd straightened his clothes and moved to the microphone. The Germans went wild. Sonya cheered and clapped.

"Who is he?" Chance yelled above the roar.

"Michael Neumann. A great man."

Michael waited for the crowd to die down and then for a C-47 to thunder over on its way out from Tempelhof, which produced a new wave of cheering.

"*Meine Freunde.*" Michael's voice rumbled out of the square toward the east.

"My friends," Sonya whispered and then stopped as two other men pushed past them on their way toward the stage.

Instead of watching them, Sonya spun around. Chance followed her gaze on reflex and noticed immediately that the Russian border guards had disappeared. Ten thousand volts seemed to flash through his body and the crowd like a wave. The mood changed from excitement to fear. For a split second Chance held his breath with the rest of the crowd. Neumann still spoke but echoed from miles away.

Something terrible had happened. Animal panic had swept through the throng looking for a place to take root. A single scream came from somewhere in the center of the crowd. A herd of zebra surprised by a lion, five thousand Berliners began to stampede.

CHAPTER 39

Potsdamer Platz, Occupied Berlin,
June 29, 1948, 10:14 P.M.

Chance was drowning in an ocean of arms, legs and terror. Hands clawed at him. Waves of bodies broke over him. He was two steps from Sonya and being pounded away from her. The streetlights went out. Seconds later the lights near the truck stage flickered and died. Panicked people ran into him blindly. Chance turned sideways and launched himself toward where he had last seen Sonya. He rammed through a young couple, splitting them apart and sending the young man ricocheting into the darkness. The girl stood for a second, screaming a name before she was knocked down.

Chance did not recognize Sonya when he reached her. She lashed out with arms and legs at an out-of-place hulk who swung what looked like a police baton. A woman was crumpled against her leg, her face a bloody river delta. The woman held one unsteady hand on her head and flailed around with the other. Sonya's eyes were locked on the big man as he raised the club again.

Someone collided with Chance knocking him back. Helpless, he watched the baton come down at Sonya. She leaned back, turning her head to avoid it by millimeters.

The move exposed the other woman and the baton slammed into her skull. The crack was audible even in the riot. She pitched forward like a sack of airlift flour.

Sonya kicked the man in the hip, throwing him off balance. The impact sent her spinning to the ground on hands and knees. Chance screamed from the darkness inside and went for the man. The baton was already on the way down. He blocked it with his left forearm and his hand went numb as lethal pain shot up his arm. His right fist came up and glanced off the hulk's jaw.

The big German merely turned his twisted face on Chance and wound up again. Chance could see another man with a baton hacking his way toward his fellow attacker. The thug caught an old man full in the face, smashing him out of the way. The thug stepped over the bloody heap of the woman and the old man as the hulk brought the baton down again.

Chance reached for the arm with both hands as his foot lanced toward the knee of the second attacker. The smaller man screamed as his knee snapped backwards and he careened to the right before going down as the leg gave out completely.

The hulk's baton felt like a freight train as it hit Chance's hands. He let the momentum bring it down as he slid his left hand to the man's elbow. The man reacted by trying to pull his arm back. Chance shoved his left hand forward and pulled back with his right. The man bellowed as his elbow dislocated. His grip on the baton went limp and Chance ripped it away.

He wasted no time using it. The hulk's scream became a gurgle as his mouth filled with blood and broken teeth. Stunned, he was bounced away into the panicked crowd.

Sonya was slipping below the mass of people. She could not get up before being knocked flat again. Only a few feet away, Chance lost sight of her again. He planted his left foot against the impacts of dozens of Berliners and reached into what seemed a river of boulders. He found a familiar softness and pulled a dazed Sonya almost to her feet. The crowd immediately began to carry her along. Chance lost his grip on her and clawed his way through the tide of people to get to her.

He wrapped his arm under her shoulders as flashes lit up the square from the east. A split second later, the crack of gunfire turned the crowd on itself.

The thugs had driven almost half the crowd east to where the Soviet soldiers waited for their cue. Chance recognized the crack-whang of the Russian rounds over his head from Ziewald. He turned west toward the dim outline of what he hoped was a way out of the square. He could not be sure if he was heading for a *Strasse* or the dead end of rubble where a building once stood.

Many in the crowd were brought to a standstill, the fear of the truncheon-wielding thugs balanced by the distant terror of gunfire.

"There." Sonya's voice was strained with fear, but still held a command as she nodded toward the south.

They collided with dozens of Berliners, each in their private hell of panic. Their eyes danced around them, seeing no one else, looking for new danger.

Chance heard screams and the crowd parted like a wall. The hulk stood in front of him, his mouth a bloody maw that pinched into a sneer as he saw Chance again. He pointed at Chance and waved to his friends nearby who were herding the crowd east.

The other thugs drew up behind the hulk as he screamed curses sloppily, spitting blood, his right arm bent at an impossible angle. Chance pushed Sonya behind him. Four men armed with batons and one crazed monster bent on revenge made for very bad odds. Practically in step, they closed on Chance and Sonya.

Chance started looking for targets in what would be a short, hopeless battle.

"*Zusammen!*"

Michael's raspy voice thundered over the loudspeakers. Chance waited for the hulk to be in range. He expected the big man would fake left and right, distracting Chance and allowing his comrades to look for an opening.

"*Alle zusammen!*" The words rippled through the mob again like a bomb blast.

Clutching the microphone, Michael's bony arm stretched out over the crowd and pulled them together by thin fingers.

A frantic man bounced off Chance and turned toward the stage. Other Berliners came out of their blind panic. The crowd stilled to whimpers of pain and the calls for help.

"*Wir sind ein Volk!*"

The monster opposite him twisted a thick neck toward the silhouette on the truck bed. The other thugs stopped swinging their clubs as their victims no longer ran from them. The fallen got to their feet, helping others up.

"*Und ein Leben haben wir zusammen.*"

Chance pulled on Sonya but she was caught in the spell. Even without understanding the words he could feel their electric effect.

"*Zusammen!*" crackled like lightning over their heads.

Around them, the crowd's mood swung again. They found a focus and fear twisted into anger.

"*Zusammen!*" Sonya shrieked and pointed at the group of thugs. The word was taken up by the crowd.

The monster whirled back on Chance and lunged. The American waited for him to get close. A small man with a torn jacket came out of nowhere and grabbed at the monster's muscled arms and was flicked off. But the monster could not swing the baton again as a woman grabbed his arm. She held on as he tried to shake her off. More Berliners came out of the dark, leeching onto the thugs, tangling their arms and clawing at their faces. Like ants on elephants, the people brought the big men down. Their batons were ripped away and their confidence evaporated into surprise, then terror. The crowd wanted its blood.

The monster managed to hurl off dozens of enraged citizens and tore his way to within feet of Chance. He reached out with both bloody hands and Chance brought the club down square in the middle of the neanderthal's head. The impact sounded like another gunshot. The monster's knees crumpled and he was crushed backward by the charging mass of Germans before he could hit the ground.

Chance reached back for Sonya and pulled her close again as they surged west. They did not stop until Chance realized they were running down a dark street alone.

"Are you hurt?" he panted.

Sonya shook her head between gasps. She reached for Chance's face and wiped away blood. Her fingers searched his hair, bringing his face close to hers. For the second time in an hour, something moved deep inside of him. Her confidence and strength were unsettling, yet very attractive.

"You are also unhurt." Her voice betrayed relief as her hand lingered on his cheek.

"Now, I must cross back. They may close the border."

"Why go back at all? Those guys were Reds."

"They were policemen, to be exact. Markgraf's men. Sent to make trouble and scare the people." She wiped back her hair and began to walk. "As you see, they operate in the West when and where they want."

"Stay."

"You will protect me?" The mock in her voice was unmistakable.

"Yes."

"Not in Berlin. You are also not safe. It makes no difference."

She moved toward the East. Chance stopped her.

"What did that guy say?"

"*Zusammen.* Together. The Russians and you want us worried about surviving. Each thinking only of ourselves." Sonya walked a few more paces. "It makes it easy for you to get what you want." She looked back toward square.

"What I want isn't easy."

"No. We both think only of what we need."

Sonya stared at him for an uncomfortable eternity before turning up the street. They had walked 500 meters in silence before Chance noticed they were not heading east.

The hotel was blacked out. A uniformed doorman stood outside with a kerosene lantern. He tipped his hat with a smile as Sonya led the way in.

For five U.S. dollars they got one candle and a key.

JITTERBUG LIFT

The room was on the fifth floor with a view into the Russian half of Berlin. It was oddly quiet for such a large city. Only the low growl and rumble of the occasional streetcar or a single car horn reached them.

Chance hurried across the room after locking the door, guided by the tiny sparks of light in her eyes. But they stopped him before he reached her.

"What will you do if I cannot find Max?"

"I'll keep looking. I'm not going back without Nevada."

"Then you are never going back. The Russians do not practice 'forgive and forget,' as you say."

"Remind me of that when hell freezes over. I'm leaving here with Nevada and you."

Chance moved toward her again, but she turned toward the city.

"I also cannot leave without…something."

"They won't come after you. Not where I'll take you."

"Home? Where is home, Chance?"

"Wherever you are." The answer exploded out of him, reaching his consciousness when he heard it. A million tons left him. It felt right. For the first time he knew exactly where he was going.

"I cannot… I will not leave without… It is more valuable than any treasure. I have risked everything for it. I could have left Germany before the war. But I didn't. I will not leave without it."

"What the hell is it? And where?"

"It will fit in your airplane." She turned, her arms slid up to his neck. "With it safe, I will go anywhere with you." Her face was moving toward him when the world ended.

"But it is in the east."

Suddenly, she couldn't breathe. Chance was holding her ribs. Not crushing them, but steel bands were not allowing them to expand.

He threw her toward the bed. She bounced off the side to the floor.

"You will never get Nevada!"

His answer was a strangled, animal growl. He lunged and she put up an arm to protect herself. But all she felt was a blast of air as he passed her and was gone.

Sonya combed her hair without meeting her own gaze in the mirror at her apartment. At the crossing, the young soldier had checked her papers carefully. He then checked a list of names on a beat-up clipboard. The flimsy list fluttered, annoying him. He slapped it flat and frowned. His face could not conceal the surprise as his eyes stopped half way down the page. He looked at her without raising his face from the list. She could not tell if there was a smile trying to form there. Then he did something odd. He gave her a furtive salute, his fingers just touching his helmet before they pointed into the East.

Sonya heard him making the phone call before she had gone five meters.

She had thought quietly in the dark since she had gotten home. She knew it would not be long, so she tried to clean up. She could almost do it without looking in the mirror and was grateful when the power went out.

The power also went out in the Russian Zone – a little fact that they tried to conceal. Poor maintenance and spare parts disappearing into the East made outages a regular occurrence.

Ten minutes later, she heard the tread of boots on the steps and stood. Running her hands through her unwashed hair she went to the door and paused. The knock startled her. She toyed with the idea of ignoring it for a moment.

She opened the door to Ivanoff and stood back.

He strode into the room and surveyed it carefully.

"So." He had managed to perfect the German pronunciation of that pregnant word. He turned and carefully studied her in the kerosene lantern light from the hallway. Her face was a treasure with the scar in half-darkness.

She looked across the hall. The door to the nosy neighbor across the hall remained shut, but a shadow moved in the light seeping under the door. Now she was sure. It never opened when the Russian came.

She saw Ivanoff staring at her and closed the door. He was in the dark and completely blind. She knew he and other pilots hated that.

The match hissed brightly to life. The candle was dimmer. A long trail of soot snaked above it. Ivanoff watched how her face changed with the light.

Sonya's frame shuddered slightly. Her face was grotesque in the light from below. She kept her scar toward him like a talisman against evil.

Ivanoff's eyes scanned the shelves behind her and locked on something. He moved near the bedroom area hidden behind a draped blanket in the corner. He pushed back the blanket with one finger and noticed the bed was still made as he stealthily sniffed the air.

"What kept you tonight? Another blackout?"

"Markgraf's idiots. I wanted to hear the music in the *Potsdamer Platz*. I am lucky to be here alive." She sensed he had seen something and spotted the bowl with a handkerchief draped over it. She had been angry and foolish.

"Markgraf is following orders. You should tell me about where you are going. It can be very dangerous in the West just now. Especially at these propaganda stunts," Ivanoff said evenly. "Have you some coffee?"

"Only Ersatz."

"Pity. It will need sugar."

"I have some."

She watched the simple fact detonate in his head. Her calm admission would emasculate him. He held a death sentence over her head and she behaved often as if the situation was reversed.

She set the bowl on the table and went to heat the water on the alcohol stove. He pulled off the handkerchief and his eyes widened almost imperceptibly. The flame lit with a weak whump and she blew out the match. He would know everything; only the Americans have their sugar in granules. The British have it in lumps.

"Black market?"

"What?"

"The sugar."

"An American gave it to me."

She enjoyed churning his insides with the bald statement. She was not even trying to hide a sin she had not committed.

"Then he brought you coffee as well."

"No. Just sugar."

Ivanoff spat a laugh. "A cart with one wheel. What did he expect for that?"

"What you expect for nothing." The scar gaped like a ragged shell hole in a fighter.

"For nothing? Your life is nothing?"

"You don't offer me my life! You offer me a hell." She heard the words as if someone else was screaming them.

Ivanoff calmed. He stared at her and she wondered if he looked that way when he killed. Then his face softened and flexed into a frown.

"I saw you at the hospital." He tossed the statement at her like a ball of razor blades.

"I was doing what you asked. I had heard the rumor about the dead pilot and thought…" She shuddered to a stop, seeing Ivanoff's eyes burning at her.

"You thought?"

"The American you are looking for would be there looking for his friend."

"Yes." Ivanoff tossed the handkerchief back on the sugar bowl. "You do not have to meet any more Americans."

He shoved the blanket dividing the bedroom from the table back completely and ripped the top cover back, leaving only the bare white sheet on the bed.

CHAPTER 40

*Approaching Tempelhof, Occupied Berlin,
June 30, 1948, 11:28 P.M.*

Despite the rain, Chance and Rossi could easily see the burning aircraft in the Berlin street below. Lightning seared the cockpit and ruined Chance's night vision again. It would take five minutes to get it back fully, but he would be trying to find a runway in the dark downpour in four.

The rain could not erase the acrid smoke pall rising from the side of an apartment building. The C-54 had been on approach two planes ahead of them. Chance had heard the ground approach control talking to the four-engine cargo plane. The ground controller had warned them that they were below the glide slope, an invisible line painted in the soaked sky with radar and the radio, and ordered them to pull up. The pilot had acknowledged, but a few seconds later approach control repeated they were still below the glide slope. Then he almost begged them. There was no acknowledgement this time. The next plane had seen the fireball in heavy rain and reported rough up- and down-drafts in the thundershower.

Normally a crash would have closed the field, but that would have stacked up over 30 aircraft in bad summer weather. And more people would have died – nameless Germans who were now welcoming the break in the sweltering heat. They heard the line of planes constantly overhead, one every three minutes. The heartbeat of a starving city.

"Following aircraft, tighten your girdles, guys. It's rough coming down." The pilot of the plane ahead sounded shaken and the violation of the otherwise professional radio procedure emphasized the point. Ground control switched them tersely to the ground frequency – a sign that they had landed.

"5534, continue descent. Downdrafts reported one half mile from runway." Now it was PIE IN THE SKY's turn. Chance thought the new ground controller sounded calm. He was in the radar hut parked just off the runway threshold. Worst thing that could happen to the controllers is the hut would get struck by lightning – or they would guide in an aircraft that crashed. The man who had just spoken to two dead pilots was probably out in the rain, asking himself a thousand questions all beginning with *What if I had…*

"5534, continuing descent." Chance was not so calm. He had landed in bad weather many times before. But seeing the wreck rattled him. The smoke smelled of meat.

A fist slammed under PIE IN THEN SKY. Chance felt his butt press hard into the seat. The thunderstorm's updraft – a river of air being sucked into the clouds to power the rain, lightning and, in turn, pulling in more air – jerked the C-47 up almost one hundred feet. It was the natural equivalent of a jet engine – but almost two miles across.

"5534, you're above the glide slope." The ground controller spoke like a cop getting people past a traffic accident and went immediately on to the other aircraft behind Chance, lining them up.

"We know. We know." Rossi sounded dry as he checked the engines. "Hows about we go around on this one?"

"I'm not flying all the way back to Frankfurt in this." Chance pushed the yoke forward as the plane bucked.

Inbound planes were tightly choreographed, spaced-out in three minute intervals in good weather, five minutes in bad. The planes flew in, staggered in altitude, in the northern and southern corridors from Hamburg and Frankfurt. The empty planes would fly back in the central air corridor to Hanover just as narrowly controlled. No aircraft was allowed to circle. Any plane that missed approach or wanted to go around had to fly all the way back west, refuel and start again. The skies over Berlin would remain clear.

Except for the weather.

"5534, back on glide slope. Continue descent." The ground controller sounded satisfied; as if he alone had dragged the rebellious PIE IN THE SKY back onto the straight and narrow.

Chance knew it was far from over. Now he could feel them sinking and going down faster, despite pulling the yoke hard back.

The C-47 had moved out of the updraft to the storm and into the falling air being pulled down by the tons of rain. And they were not going straight down. The dump of air from above fanned out over the ground like water from a fire hose. The air pounding the ground swirled, eddied back into the sky and then curled back down. As Chance flew through the maelstrom, it felt like PIE IN THE SKY was playing bumper cars with a bunch of Tulsa roughnecks on a Saturday night.

"Power." Chance knew Rossi had anticipated the order. The engines revved to over 2500 RPM.

"5534, you are below glide slope." The ground controller still sounded annoyed with his errant child.

Chance hated that. Demons clawed the yoke as he brought it to his chest. Chance had the sense he was drifting right, but could tell nothing for sure. Rain was flooding the windshield and no lights appeared from below.

"We're goin' right," Rossi tossed his opinion in and flicked his eyes over at Chance. Chance's eyes strained for the line of lights on metal crosses in Neukölln's graveyard that pointed to the runway threshold.

"5534, you are right and well below glide slope."

"Power!" Chance knew they were trapped. Their only hope was to feel their way out of the downdraft. But he had no fingers to reach out in the dark downpour and there were no signs in the sky, written in Fraktur, German or English saying Exit or *Ausgang.*

His eyes darted to the altimeter. They were just above field elevation. Tempelhof was a wide grassy oval, a giant plate where almost anywhere was a runway.

"Gear down!"

"Gear down," Rossi repeated.

The graveyard with its row of welcoming crosses was only two hundred feet wide. The wind had blasted PIE IN THE SKY completely off the runway heading and they were now dropping toward the row of buildings north of the cemetery.

"Go around, 5534! Pull up and go around!" The ground controller was finally nervous.

Chance wished he could. He jammed his fist over Rossi's on the throttle levers and shoved them to the stops. The C-47 was still sinking; its engines could give no more.

A hammer slammed into the right wing. Chance knew they had hit something. It cost them airspeed and the plane was wrenched into a fatal flat spin. There was no recovery at this altitude, only trying to salvage the plane and maybe their lives.

PIE IN THE SKY's right landing gear was not fully extended when it caught the roof of *Leinestrasse* 98. The apartment building was one of hundreds put up by Hitler around the airport to impress arriving allies and intimidate future foes. The roof cracked and the jolt sent plaster into the apartment of Heinz Herbstman, narrowly missing where he was entertaining his neighbor, Getta Klein. She took the noise as a sign from God and never saw poor Heinz again.

The impact tore off the PIE IN THE SKY's right tire and jammed the gear in the half-extended position. Part of the support gear shattered and pushed up into the wing, fouling the control cables to the right aileron. Chance now had only partial control of the spinning aircraft, unable to bank fully right or left.

Chance's instincts took over again. Years of flying mixed with an almost spiritual understanding of what keeps planes in the air moved his hands and eyes. He saw the RPM gauges for both engines were still reading positive and the right landing gear light was red. The plane was yawing right, in seconds it would be flying backwards. The right engine was already at the stops and he cut the left back to idle. The power imbalance slowed the spin to a stop with the C-47 sliding in toward Tempelhof, left wing first.

Chance kicked the rudder over hard. It would do little good but it might make the difference. PIE IN THE SKY began to turn back left. Heavily loaded, it waddled like a drunk.

Ground lights from some taxiway flashed past. They had only feet to go. He cut the right engine as the left gear banged into the soggy grass. PIE IN THE SKY crabbed hard as the mud sucked the left tire down. Chance forced the wheel left against the jammed aileron cables, hoping to keep the right wing from plowing in.

It only worked for a second.

The mangled right landing gear caught a slight rise in the field. The broken struts stabbed into the muck and slowed instantly. The left side of the aircraft kept going, the inertia of the load and airframe spinning it around the right gear.

Thinking of Sonya, Chance reached for the fire extinguisher controls. His head carried on straight ahead and slammed into the window frame as the plane spun around.

CHAPTER 41

*Tempelhof Military Hospital, Occupied Berlin,
July 1, 1948, 5:39 P.M.*

Shanley and his exploding head were back. He was warning Chance that he was going the wrong way. He was being fooled. The horizon was playing tricks on him. Up was down. Down was up. He was lost.

"Trust me," Shanley's mouth begged as the rest of his head disintegrated.

Chance tried to reach for the pieces, but his arms were weighed down.

"Stop it." The voice was a man's, but Chance didn't recognize it. It wasn't Shanley.

"Please, stop. You will hurt yourself." Sonya's voice had immediate effect and Chance stopped trying to catch the pieces of Shanley's head. They were gone anyway. But he found the weight was off his arms. He reached up and touched his forehead.

"Ah-ah. Bad boy. No playing with the bandages." The male voice was back.

"Please, behave." Sonya sounded tired.

Chance thought she was working awfully hard trying to appear in his dream. She was very fuzzy at first and then began to take shape. A shape he liked. Then she got fuzzy again.

"*Bitte, Fersighung.*" Chance found his voice meandering around, looking for Shanley.

"*Macht's nichts.*" Sonya's voice caressed his face like a woman's breasts. She became clearer now, her breasts just a few inches away as she touched his face.

"Well, hello, flyboy." The orderly was black and smiled easily, his bulk eclipsing everything else in the hospital room.

Chance guessed he had been the weight on his arms.

"You're gonna behave now, right?"

Chance nodded but his forehead throbbed him to a stop.

"Ain't no li'l frawline here. So don't get lost chasing after her."

Chance remembered the spinning plane. The right wing digging in and then nothing.

"Rossi?"

"Oh, he's fine. He's been raising a stink about your airplane. Seems somebody wants to junk it for parts. He thinks it's private property. Raising a holy stink."

The smiling orderly tossed the last sentence over his shoulder as he stepped out. Chance heard a Dakota on approach and tensed. The last few seconds of the crash played out again in his mind.

"What is wrong?" Sonya was close again.

"Nothing. Just trying to remember what happened."

Thinking and saying that exhausted him and he fell back on his pillow. But the pillow wasn't there. It seemed like he would never stop and he fell forever in the black night with flashes of lightning. He panicked and threw out his arms to catch himself. He gasped.

"I am here." Sonya hadn't moved. But the room was dark now. "You were sleeping. Did you have a bad dream?"

"No… Yeah. What day is it?"

The planes were still just a few minutes apart. Chance could not tell if they were coming in or going out.

"Thursday."

"What date?"

"You have been out of your head all day."

Chance touched the bandages on his forehead. Sonya took his hand away and held it in hers. Chance remembered thinking about how much he would miss her as he saw the runway lights spinning out of control.

"Who is Shanley?"

"He was my bombardier. He was killed in the war. I have nightmares sometimes. Did I talk much?"

"Sometimes. Most I did not understand."

Chance zeroed in on her. Something was wrong. "How'd you get in here?"

Sonya found something to study on the tips of her fingers in her lap. "You called my name so much. You would not be quiet." She looked up. "You're German has improved."

"Hey." Rossi talked right over her. "Just me here."

"You kept saying '*Bitte, Verzeihung.*' What are you sorry about?" Sonya was the only person in the room.

"Lots of things." Chance shook that off. "It's all I know."

"I will teach you more. You will have time now."

"I want to see the plane." Chance started to get up and the pain hit him from nowhere. A pike was being driven through his forehead. The impact sent him flying. He fell backwards, away from it. Back again into the darkness. He waited until he hit bottom, but there was none. Even Shanley left him alone.

Still falling, he opened his eyes and saw Rossi hunched uncomfortably in the chair.

"Sonya."

Rossi leapt up and was at his side. It was so fast, it made him dizzy.

"It's me." Rossi's New York accent was hard to miss. "You see me?"

Chance turned to him and tried to focus. Sonya moved behind him – or, rather, through him.

"Not so loud. Please." Sonya was all control, a protective side Chance had never seen. She turned back to Chance.

"You passed out." Sonya and Rossi were a duet.

"It felt like a hammer." Chance remembered when a chain spinning loose on an oil drill in Tulsa nearly took his head off. That was a love tap compared to this.

"Does it hurt?" Rossi was all alone.

"Yes. Real bad. What day is it?" Chance found he could focus on Rossi in the dim light.

"Just after midnight. Friday. You've been out for several hours."

Sonya brushed his cheek with her hand and was gone.

"Chance. Chance. Come back. Come back. Just follow my voice."

"How can I miss it?" Chance thought that was funny but he was afraid to laugh. "What's with the plane?"

"Bastard vultures want it for scrap. Say it's a hundred spare parts they won't have to fly in here."

"Where is it?"

"Right where you parked it so gently."

"In how many pieces?" Chance fought back the fatigue.

"Just one," Rossi shrugged.

But Shanley had warned him in the dream. He was scared again. It was like falling into the darkness that now waited right behind him. His feet were on a crumbling cliff and the hunger was calling out of the abyss. He thought about parachute training at Eglin Army Air Base. The hopeless freefall.

"Don't pull your cord until you are below ten thousand feet. Otherwise, you'll suffocate and the enemy might just use you for target practice," the sergeant had cautioned the class.

Chance wondered if there would be some line painted in the clouds to tell him where ten thousand feet was.

"Chance." It was Sonya calling from the back of the Quonset hut.

What the hell is she doing here?

"Chance, please." Sonya was in front of him again.

Rossi looked concerned and a doctor who was doing his best to imitate Elmer Fudd was looking into Chance's eyes.

"He blacked out," he pronounced, stating the obvious with all the conviction that years of medical training and more years of patching holes in pilots' heads allowed him. "Keep him quiet."

"What's going on with my head, doc?" Chance asked Elmer's back. It seemed he was always talking to the medical staff's backs here.

"Youse cracked it on the window when we hit." Rossi was only a little less matter of fact than Dr. Fudd. "Yer brains are scrambled."

"That's not new." Chance was waiting to fall backwards again. He was determined to hold on this time. "When can I go see the plane?"

"When youse can stand up without fallin' down."

"I can do that now." Chance threw back the sheets and swung his legs over the side of the bed.

"Chance, this is foolish." Sonya was getting angry. "Stop him."

But Rossi still leaned against the window. Chance thought Rossi smiled like he knew something. Then Chance had that uneasy feeling the black abyss was opening behind him. He stopped.

"We'll go tomorrow." He fell back into the bed and let sleep take him away. He hoped Shanley wouldn't follow but Sonya would.

CHAPTER 42

*Tempelhof Airport,
July 2, 1948, 1:29 P.M.*

PIE IN THE SKY looked like it was sinking. The right wing had pushed up the soft sod on the rainy night of the crash. A green-black wave appeared to be sucking down the aircraft. The right propeller was bent back and Chance could see the mangled landing gear below it.

Chance moved his hand along the skin as he slowly made his way around to left side. The plane was still alive and it gave him hope. From this side nothing appeared out of place. Only the plane's list hinted at its wounds.

There was something familiar about the tock-tock of bricks bouncing off each other. In the bright sun, Chance could see a group of *Trümmerfrauen*. They were paving a new 5,000-foot runway across the broad oval of the airfield. Berlin was consuming itself. Behind them, 13,000 cubic yards of cannibalized German rubble already supported 4,987 feet of American pierced steel hard top. A parade of aircraft landed, taxied, were unloaded and returned to the sod runway parallel to the hardtop within a half hour to take off again. But the old runway had to be repaired constantly as the drumbeat of cargo aircraft hammered its surface every few minutes. The women were laying crushed bricks and concrete eighteen inches thick with garden hoes and their bare hands to form the foundation for the new runway.

One *Trümmerfrau* was looking over at Chance and Nevada's crashed dream. Chance thought of the blonde who shrieked at him with the accusing finger in Frankfurt. The spindly woman wiped sweat from her face and went back to shoveling crumbled buildings with the other women. They moved like zombies, despite the fact that working on the airport got them an extra 500 calories a day. No one was strict about it. They ate pretty well. And so did their children.

Across the airport, behind the non-stop runway traffic, Chance could make out the small crash truck with its scorpion tail crane. The vultures were gathering to dispose of PIE IN THE SKY. Nearby, fresh rubble came out on a wheezing Mercedes truck. Chance met Rossi by the right engine.

"Will she fly again?"

Rossi kicked a clod of dirt thrown up by the crash. "You got about ten grand?"

"They've paid us for the first week. About fourteen hundred."

Rossi only shook his head before looking up behind Chance. Chance turned and saw a cloud of dust drifting toward them. A loud roar was behind it. The cloud tasted bitter to Chance. When it cleared he could see the Mercedes heading back to the edge of the field, leaving a mound of shattered bricks about fifty feet from PIE IN THE SKY's left wingtip.

The Mercedes passed a second truck heading out from the terminal building with another load of rubble. It sped past the women working on the new runway and piled its load next to the first pile of debris.

"Here comes trouble." Rossi spat out dust, nodding toward a military green Packard racing out behind a third truck full of the crushed bones of Berlin. The Packard driver had to swerve to avoid the second truck heading back, honking his horn believing it would do something.

An Army colonel stepped out of the Packard and went for Chance as if what was about to happen had been scripted.

"Colonel James Van Buren. I run field maintenance. The wreck has to go. It's interfering with traffic."

"She's not a wreck. And we're 500 feet off the runway." Chance defended his lady.

Van Buren blinked. Someone didn't learn their lines. He charged on anyway, hoping the unseen audience wouldn't notice. "Today."

"Where are you going to tow it to?"

The Colonel's laugh became a sputter as they were enveloped by another dust cloud. "Tow it? We're breaking it up. You've flown in about 200 spare parts." The Colonel futilely tried waving the dust away and gave up. "They've ordered these old taildraggers phased out anyway. Can't load them fast because the floor's tilted." He tilted his hand to show Chance he really knew how a Dakota sat.

"No. It's my airplane." Chance felt the black abyss opening behind him.

Rossi saw Chance weave slightly and moved behind him. "Maybe we should chat about this some other time. Chance got banged up in the crash. I gotta get him back to the hospital."

Chance almost smiled at Rossi's newfound diplomacy.

"We settle it now. We're fixing it. I'll make arrangements to have her moved off the field."

"With whom, Mr. Mitchell? Berlin's blockaded. I control everything that moves on the ground here. And I don't have the time or resources to help you."

He spun around toward the Packard, but staggered, lost in another cloud of ground up Berlin.

"Give me a break, damn it!" Chance could not feel what was holding him up. There is no ground effect for toppling pilots. He coughed and winced away plaster and mortar scratching his eyes.

The cloud cleared and the Packard was already making for the terminal building. Chance noticed the workers were dumping the rubble in a neat line near PIE IN THE SKY.

"Maybe they'll just bury her. Better than lettin' them hyenas at her." Rossi dryly tried to spit out a third mouthful of dust and moved Chance toward the jeep he had sort of borrowed from the motor pool.

Chance did not look back at his airplane until they reached the edge of the terminal apron. He thought as hard as his rattled, angry brain would let him. He came up with nothing as Rossi pulled the jeep to a stop, clear of a taxiing C-54 Skymaster, the new giants that could fly in 40 ton loads.

Rossi said something lost in the thrum of the Skymaster's props. Chance still stared at nothing on the jeep's dashboard so Rossi shoved his arm and pointed across at PIE IN THE SKY.

Above them, Major McKane waited until the last load of rubble was dumped. Watching from the roof of the gigantic Tempelhof terminal building, he counted the minor eruptions of dust. The wrecking crane had just started to move away from the maintenance area toward Chance's aircraft when two dump trucks raced past it to PIE IN THE SKY. They dumped their loads before the crane crossed midfield.

McKane pulled out his binoculars as the crane circled the ring of rubble completely surrounding the wounded Dakota, looking for a way in to begin feeding on the plane's carcass. The crane doubled back, expecting the rubble to have dissolved into the grass. McKane replaced the dust caps on the binoculars as the frustrated crane headed back to the terminal.

On the terminal apron, Colonel Van Buren was screaming at a German man in dusty clothes, backed up by three *Trümmerfrauen*. McKane didn't need his binoculars to see that the colonel was unhappy. The German only shrugged, hands lifting slightly.

PIE IN THE SKY was safe. For now.

CHAPTER 43

*Soviet Army Headquarters, Karlshorst, Berlin,
Soviet Zone, July 3, 1948, 3:22 A.M.*

The staff in the basement communications room was getting their first night's rest in days.

They had been secretly annoyed with Colonel Ivanoff. They didn't dare speak to each other about it, even when off duty. But they all knew each other's minds. Over the last three weeks Ivanoff had become as permanent as the light-green paint on the walls and the damp, musty odor from the hole where over a thousand phone lines entered the windowless room. It was one thing to have the insomniac eternally upstairs. Then they could rely on the Tempelhof bell to wake them if he got a call or made one in the middle of the night. But he had been around their necks for almost a month.

The only non-regulation motion in the room had been Ivanoff himself, stretching to keep his scarred back supple. No one had spoken except to report a contact or pass information. They even tried not to cough.

The call had come in just after 2:00 A.M. and lasted five seconds. The private taking the call almost did not realize its import. The woman reporting had sounded tired and relieved.

JITTERBUG LIFT

"Our cousin is in the hospital. He is being well taken care of. I am going to bed."

The last sentence was not part of the message, but Ivanoff forgave the operative for the unprofessionalism. He called her back personally and asked if "our cousin" was expected to survive. The woman sleepily, but sharply replied yes, not realizing who she was talking to.

The crash of the aircraft ahead of PIE IN THE SKY in the thunderstorm rated one column inch in *The Times* of London. But an operative in Frankfurt had to look no further than the front page of the *Mainz Allgemeine Zeitung*. At the end of the story about the plane crashing into the apartment building short of Tempelhof was a single sentence about a second crash landing at the airport the same night. The pilot, a civilian named Chauncey Mitchell was hospitalized with a head injury. A picture showed the charred remains of the apartment building and the jumble of melted metal with a few parts recognizable as an airplane. A smaller picture was inset showing PIE IN THE SKY tilted on the field, although the name was not clear enough. After buying a dozen newspapers, the operative found one with the clearest picture and enlarged it to get a partial tail number.

It was a woman who worked as a cook in the Tempelhof hospital that finally found Chance. She had offered to spy for the Russians as soon as the blockade started. Living in the West, she told herself that she was merely hedging her bets. The cook's contact had made the call to Ivanoff as soon as she retrieved the slip of paper the cook had left on the shelf of the *Apothek* near the rubble that had been Gestapo headquarters. It was inside a box of stomach remedies for people who had overeaten.

Ivanoff had merely nodded as he received the full report. However, the private who gave it to him noted that his face changed. It frightened the soldier. The fighter pilot's eyes narrowed, the lion had found its prey. Ivanoff's voice was even and low as he ordered them not to leave.

He left the room and returned a half hour later with a single order to be phoned into the West. Once the order went through and was confirmed, he closed the door on the staff without saying thank you.

It took them almost two hours to realize he was not coming back.

Despite the heat, Farber seemed at ease in Michael's tiny office at the Berlin city hall. The ADN reporter had breezed through a few easy questions like a child hurrying through vegetables to get to dessert.

"What will be your position on the vote?"

"If you are unsure, you may listen to my speech in a few minutes." Michael glanced at his watch. "Honestly, Herr Farber, I am disappointed in you. I would have expected more of an effort to extract some non-truth from me. Or are you just going to make the whole thing up?"

Farber stood and folded his rumpled suit coat over a sweaty arm. "We are close to finding your daughter. Would you care to comment on that?"

Michael smiled. "Just now? Just as I am to speak and the *Stadtparlament* is to vote in a few days on giving in to your masters?"

"You are not eager to know? My readers will be so disappointed."

"Then tell me. Where is she? My reaction would make quite a story."

"I am sorry. The vote takes precedence over such personal matters. Perhaps after the vote."

"Again Herr Farber, you and this cheap trick disappoint me. You dangle hints of nonsense before me and expect me to sit quietly while the Russians take over."

"Germans will take over. Loyal Germans."

Michael waved the canned political speech away like stale smoke and picked up his papers.

"I cannot say I look forward to speaking with you again…"

Farber blocked the door. "You see, we were looking under the wrong faith. That is what took us so long. I do look forward to hearing your speech. *Guten Tag, Herr Neumann.*"

Michael did not breathe again until Farber and his sneer were gone. Throwing the speech on his chair, he closed the door in the airless office and dialed Sonya's number. Their system was that she would disconnect the phone if she was unable to talk. Sonya answered immediately.

"Sonya, it is Uncle Martin."

"Hallo, Martin. How are you?" Sonya followed the script, sounding animated. "I cannot talk just now. I must go out."

"Please, call as soon as you can." Michael hung up.

Michael tried not to think of what he was asking of Sonya while he waited for the phone to ring. He concentrated on his speech. The Berlin papers with pictures of the crashes were still scattered on his desk. He wanted to remember the names of the dead and injured pilots in his speech.

The phone rang as he was forcing the image of Sonya with the young American in *Potsdamer Platz* from his mind for the third time.

"They may know where she is."

Michael heard only the crackle of damaged phone lines for several seconds.

"Are you sure?" Sonya's calm whisper was soothing. "They are bluffing."

"They said they had been looking under the wrong faith."

The crackling lasted much longer this time.

"We must do something now. The vote cannot be delayed." Michael drew a long breath. "I do not know if I can be strong."

"You can be. You will be."

"You are my strength, S..." He stopped from saying her name over the phone and winced away tears. "Please let me know when."

"I will. Do not worry."

The crackling died with the connection. Michael felt he was letting go of a lifeline as he put the phone down.

When he stood in the *Stadtparlament*, the chamber went quiet. He looked up at the gallery and saw Farber in the front row, directly opposite him.

Michael looked down at his empty hands; he had left the speech in his office.

"*Wir leben noch.*"

The simple sentence produced applause from some, grudging nods from others.

"Yes, we are still alive. Some are not. Two Americans died a few nights ago to feed us. Others have already died." Michael brought his gaze squarely on Farber. "If foreigners can make such sacrifices for Berlin, then I can. And shame on anyone of us who cannot."

The floor was shaking when he sat down. Even the grudging cynics were applauding.

Sonya knew she was completely trapped as she hurried back home from the hotel where she had called Michael. Safety dictated that she never called him from the same place twice. She had chosen the *Junkerhaus* this time because it was far from her apartment. She had to be sure that she was not followed.

She had lost Chance completely. She had planned to go back and beg him to understand when his name had leapt out of the paper. Michael would soon learn that she had lied to him. It would crush him, he would give up and Berlin would give up, too.

Ivanoff would certainly know where Chance was by now. He could simply send in an operative to kill him in his hospital bed, but he needed his prize alive. Eventually he would catch Chance and he or Nevada would give her up. The paper had said that Chance was still in hospital but was expected to be released shortly.

It would be soon, very soon.

And she would fail her mission. She had given up years. She had not run. She had given up everything. Almost everything.

She saw the crack of hope only a few meters from her apartment. She turned around and headed for the *Alexanderplatz Hotel*. The pieces were all there, but would have to be brought together delicately and it would require razor-thin timing.

And it would cost her everything this time.

CHAPTER 44

*Felsenstrasse 17, Soviet Occupied Berlin,
July 3, 1948, 6:02 P.M.*

The afternoon had been hot and sticky. Sonya had stripped naked, but the sheets still clung tightly, trying to suffocate her in bed. She peeled them off and stood by the window, lifting her hair off her neck. A trolley rolled by on *Felsenstrasse*. The shadows had lengthened but there was no breeze. The oppressive haze promised more heat.

Ivanoff stopped at the door as if he had hit a wall. His eyes scanned the provocative pose. Sonya made no effort to cover herself, dropping her arms and moving only slightly away from the window into a shadow behind the armoire.

"I have found him." Ivanoff almost smiled. He quickly gave up the unnatural act. "Help me."

Sonya gently pulled the tunic off. The shirt was stained with blood.

"It is bad this time."

"Be quick."

Sonya was, but she made a point of never being quick enough. Pain gurgled in Ivanoff's throat as she ripped the cloth away from the oozing scars. She was relieved. There would be no need to go to the place inside herself.

JITTERBUG LIFT

"Are you sure?"

"The plane crashed here in Berlin."

The stone that formed in Sonya's stomach threatened to choke her. Ivanoff flopped face down on the bed. His wounds tempted her. But she needed him.

He left before dawn and the day had reached furnace heat by the time she reached the crossing. The barbed wire told it all. It lay unbroken across the street. The guards waited out their duty in the shade of the small shack. There was no one to search. One waved Sonya back as she approached. His terrible German told her the border was sealed. No exceptions. Still she lingered there for several minutes, standing exposed in the sun.

She hurried to the other crossing and found the same answer. Her world had shrunk to half a city. She spent some time talking to the guard, asking how long the closure might last.

"Until you come to your senses." This guard's German was better. He laughed and translated his barb to his brothers, who joined in.

Sonya raced the two kilometers back to her flat. It was afternoon and she hoped she was not already too late. She picked up the phone and stopped. This would mean more contact with her former enemy. She still had other, easier options, but she had promised.

The man who answered the phone sounded weary from the heat.

"This is Ballerina, please listen. I have a message for Max. The American pilot is in danger. They know he is in Tempelhof Hospital."

"I do not know what you are talking about. And I do not dance." The laugh was forced.

"I knew Drummer and Clown."

There was a long pause with a distant breath on the line.

"They died well."

Sonya choked the memory from her voice. "Please, tell Max."

The line went dead. She heard the door creak closed across the hall and saw her own door was still open. She closed it quickly.

She had thrown a pebble over a wall and hoped it would trigger an avalanche.

CHAPTER 45

*Tempelhof Airport, US Occupied Berlin,
July 4, 1948, 8:47 P.M.*

The note had simply said Chance could find information about his friend at the *Student Café* in the *Hinterhof* just off the *Grossbeerenstrasse* north of Tempelhof. He would go there and ask for Erik.

The skinny German laborer who had delivered it left nothing but his fingerprints in coal dust on the envelope. And he would only say "*Verstehe nicht*" when Chance tried to question him. And he had turned down the dollar bill Chance offered him – enough to buy three days ration of bread on the black market. The loading captain and the arrival of a Skymaster full of twenty tons of dried potatoes had ended the conversation.

Chance tried to find Rossi but gave up after searching in the rain for fifteen minutes. He was sucked into a world of gray as soon as he cleared the field gate.

Dimitri waited in the bullet-cratered doorway of the apartment building across from Tempelhof, hoping not to have to tail the lanky American today. His wounded leg had warned of the coming rain a full day before. He was hoping the storms would finally break the heat, but knew the next few hours would be agony. First, he groaned audibly when Chance appeared at the field gate. Then he cursed out loud when he realized the pilot was in a hurry.

The pain in his leg almost distracted him from noticing the black Opel Admiral four-door sedan trailing Chance. After the limping man in soaked clothes recognized the auto for what it was, he had to admire the technique of the driver. Instead of slowly moving to keep behind the charging American, drawing attention to the tail, the driver would actually dart ahead of Chance and wait. After the pilot had passed, the car would patiently mark time, engine running, until he was almost out of sight. Then the driver would repeat the maneuver, appearing lost. But Dimitri knew these tricks. He had been taught them, too. Something about that made him think. It was going to be hard to figure out, but he welcomed the diversion from the pain.

Chance was unaware of Dimitri, the Opel and the other eyes watching him. The rain fell harder and the city would smell fresh for a while. Chance had noticed before how the city was clean just after the rain. But in a few hours the summer heat would simmer out a fetid reek of rotting wood, wallpaper and fresh garbage.

That thought never fully formed in his brain; he was already overwhelmed by the tantalizing possibility of finding Nevada. He ran a few steps and trotted. He barely noticed the rainwater trickling down his back. His clothes clung to his legs making him feel as if he was wading through mud. He had no idea of how he would get to the cafe and what he could do with the information once he got it. Chance's instinct dragged his foot one step forward, not pausing to celebrate before performing the miracle again with the other leg. His injured body was giving up. The temporary chill of the rain bit into his muscles. He tried to think of getting to the cafe without crossing over into the Russian sector. Then his mind wrestled with the question of which of the two streets ahead would bring him to the *Grossbeerenstrasse*. Then it wandered off to think of Sonya without an answer. He stumbled.

Fifty meters behind, Dimitri stifled a yell, delighted he had thought of the answer about the Opel. The driver never shut off the engine as he waited for Chance to charge ahead. They could not be black market thugs with such an extravagant waste of petrol. He would include that in his report. It would impress someone. He began formulating the logic in his head and stopped when he realized that both the Allies and the Soviets had petrol; the Russians having as much as they wanted. A frown crossed his face, catching raindrops in the deep creases in his cheeks. Perhaps he was not supposed to notice this. Still it could be the Americans. Perhaps they were becoming clever and using the old German autos instead of their obvious Packards and Chevrolets. On the other hand, the risk was there. He needed more information.

He took a step to his right, sending another spike of pain up his leg. A Mercedes truck, held together by rope and scraps of fence chain, blocked his view of the street. He glanced at Chance and then hobbled back toward the black Opel, moving toward the street behind the truck and pausing. The tailing auto had stopped some tens of meters behind him, the windshield wipers twitching like beetle antennae.

The front of the car rose as it lurched forward. Dimitri cursed himself for making the unforgivable and basic mistake of revealing that he was watching a target. He had spooked the driver.

Dimitri's heart clenched as the Opel swerved toward him, skidding sideways on the wet cobblestones. He noted the rear window was rolled down part way. In this weather that was foolish. The spy winced as he jumped back from the curb and landed on his bad leg. Agony tempered his relief as the Opel veered away toward Chance, who was now at the corner of the next street.

As the racing auto closed on the oblivious American, Dimitri wondered how he would explain all this in his report without making himself seem a criminal fool. The Opel cut the corner too close and he saw Chance dodge the sedan. But it sped on, the roar of the motor fading in the hiss of the rain.

Dimitri pondered if that had been an assassination attempt. His masters had said to keep his reports short. But today's would take several pages. Dimitri stopped at that. He did not know his masters. Not really. A man he knew as Andrei spelled out his orders in educated, almost refined Russian. He was paid by the same man. Actually all he knew was the deep voice on the phone. He picked up his money at a letter office for refugees in the West. Dimitri mulled over who he was really working for.

He decided to stop thinking about that. He had enough to worry about. The American had gone around the corner. Dimitri damned the Soviet surgeons and limped after him.

Chance did not hear the car until it jumped the curb, his still dazed mind focused on Sonya. Even if he found out who had Nevada, he would still need her to get to Max. But, more than that, there was something in him that she was pulling on. He had begun to realize it was actually something of her in him and he did not care. He wanted to be with her, despite that she may only want him for a smuggling run in PIE IN THE SKY. The noise behind him almost did not overcome that drive welling up inside.

Chance's shoes skidded on the wet stone paving. His right leg slipped behind him. Off balance, he barely had time to move to the right. It was enough to help his left leg which thrust him out of the way of the bumper and headlight of the hurtling car. He felt the air pushed out of the way by the vehicle and the heat of the engine on his face as it passed. He never had his footing and stumbled against the concrete façade of an office building. His right shoulder hit the wall and his head snapped to the right, bouncing off the wall. Chance found he was outside of himself, watching, detached from the scene. For a moment he could not form a thought. He had only a sense of fear; something was wrong but he could not quite put his finger on it.

The car passed ahead and spun in the street. The driver missed a gear and Chance heard them grind. He knew he had to get to his feet. But what he was going to do after that was a mystery. The blackness was opening up behind him. His fingers clawed the wall of their own volition.

The Opel jumped the sidewalk about fifty feet ahead of him. The headlights were blinding.

Chance tried to think of a way out of this, but he simply could not. He found himself lurching to his left, away from the building. The curb and the safety behind a Volkswagen seemed miles away. His legs carried him and his arms flew forward as he half fell, half dove for the street.

He hit the cobblestones the same instant the Opel hit the Volkswagen, driving the pre-war car back a foot and over Chance's back. The wheels on the car were flat and kept it from rolling over the American. Chance barely heard the Opel bang off the Volkswagen and roar away down the sidewalk; he was almost unconscious.

The whole scene became unreal. He saw a man limping across the street to where he could study Chance. Chance tried pushing himself up on his elbows, but he could not bring his feet under him.

Dimitri feared he would be out of a job after writing only one more report about the target's death. He felt genuine relief that the American was still alive and not obviously injured. However, the American seemed dazed and Dimitri fought the urge to point the way to safety. He surprised himself with his concern for the pilot. He had been told to watch Chance without being told what to think about him. No one said he was an enemy. He was merely a target. Maybe this was an exercise to test Dimitri and refine his skills as a spy. Maybe his masters had bigger plans for him. Maybe he could get his leg fixed. But did such things happen to all the American pilots?

Dimitri heard the engine racing toward him and looked down the street to where he last saw the Opel go around the corner. It wasn't there. He realized his mistake and turned to see it coming from the opposite end of the block. The spy was confused. He was certain the black sedan had disappeared around the corner to the south and yet it was coming from the north. It could not have circled the block in a few seconds, no matter how much petrol it had.

Chance had no idea what was happening, beyond that the black car was coming back. He tried to get up. His legs moved this time and he got to his hands and knees, but the bent bumper on the Volkswagen snagged his flight jacket. He knew he had to move. They were coming back to finish him.

The Opel went past Chance and skidded to a stop. Chance heard the driver grind the gears as he rammed it into reverse.

JITTERBUG LIFT

The car leapt backward and the brakes squealed as the rear door flew open, bouncing on the hinge stops.

There was only the sound of the rain and the engine winding down. A voice with an accent called out of the blackness inside the car. Chance heard what the man said but didn't believe it. A hand beckoned, its arm disappearing in the shadow toward the voice. The voice commanded again.

"Get in, quickly!"

CHAPTER 46

*Hagelbergerstrasse, US Occupied Berlin,
July 4, 1948, 9:14 P.M.*

Dimitri worried no one would believe him.

He was focused on the American on his knees behind the Volkswagen when the Opel squealed to a stop, blocking his view. He waited for the sound of a gunshot, his shoulders hunching on reflex. Instead he heard a voice in the auto. He could not make out the English words. Dimitri strained to hear, knowing they would be important for his report. The voice called again, but a louder motor was drowning it out. It took the spy a second to find the source of the interference as the first Opel came racing up from the south.

Chance's fogged mind could not figure out how to save itself. The face came out of the shadow of the back seat of the Opel in front of him, looking forward at the oncoming twin car. Automatically, Chance turned toward where the man was looking and saw the other car. His mind cleared for a second and he had that awful lost feeling he had when Nevada and he took the check ride in PIE IN THE SKY. Chance turned back to the man, hoping he would just explain what the hell was going on.

"Get in, now! They will kill you!"

The racing Opel was only sixty feet away when Chance began to move. Safety was on the other side of the street, some fifteen feet away.

Chance stumbled, then lunged. The open door of the Opel was not getting close enough. He heard the engine noise swelling in his ears. He was between the two cars. Something hit his right foot, twisting him in the air.

The side window of the stationary Opel spider-webbed into splinters. Dimitri plainly heard the tumbling pistol round buzz past his ear like a raging bee.

Then the spy heard a man scream. No, it was more of a yell. A single syllable. The wheels of the standing Opel spun on the wet street and the vehicle began to move. A second shot cracked from the skidding Opel, the muzzle flash lighting up the driver and a second man in the front. A third man was firing the pistol from the rear seat. The dazzling image burned into Dimitri's eyes.

The Opel with the bullet-shattered window raced off, followed by the second. A third shot echoed as the two cars disappeared, leaving Dimitri soaking wet and confused.

He decided it would be best to tell the truth in his report – no matter how long it was.

Chance's first thought was how bad the man's shoes were. His rescuer was slightly hunched and looking back as if his stare could obliterate the chasing car. Chance's foot was pinned in the half open door of the sedan. He started to twist around to free it and something cold and hard caught the back of his neck.

"*Geht's nicht.*" The voice had genuine menace and emphasized the metal pushing Chance firmly back down.

"Don't be stupid, Herr Mitchell." The man's stare stopped Chance with more force than the pistol at the base of his skull.

The eyes flicked behind Chance to the other German in the back seat. "*Pass auf!*"

Chance felt the weight leave his neck and the twin concussions of the .45 fired above his head. One of the still smoking casings pinged off the shattered window and landed between the bad shoes.

"*Links! Links!*" The bad shoes twisted as the voice hissed above. The door holding Chance's foot flew open as the Opel made a hard left. Chance could see the blur of a bombed out building in the flash of a street lamp between his legs and yanked his foot in.

Chance almost missed the sound in the roar of the engines and the gunfire. It sounded like a stone hitting the rear window followed by a dull "Uh" and a gasp from the front seat. Glass landed on Chance's neck.

"*Bin getroff'n.*" The driver's voice was young and girlish. It reminded Chance of Jimmy, his dead radioman.

"*Wo?*" Worry was in Bad Shoes' question.

"*Nichts ernst,*" the driver forced through clenched teeth.

The .45 lit up the interior like lightning. The blasts hammered Chance's head and back. The shots ended in an all too familiar click with the action back.

"*Muss laden.*"

The empty magazine landed on the seat between Bad Shoes and the shooter. The shooter's knee pressed into Chance's back as he searched for a new one.

"*Fahr langsamer.*" Bad Shoes was pleased.

"*Was?!*" The driver was not.

"*Langsam!*"

Chance heard the motor slow. He had recovered enough to think about escaping. The door of the Opel had not closed. He could push himself up and be out the door on the next curve to the left – if there was one.

The knee lifted from his back as the shooter shoved the magazine in place. The bad shoes moved as the leader reached across to the shooter.

"*Warte.*" The man was calm, but Chance heard more than that. He was about to deliver a punch line.

Chance heard the motor of the other car roar closer and the sharp intake of breath of the impatient shooter with the knee in his back.

"*Zu eng!*" he complained.

"*Unnnnnnnndddd... Los!*" Bad Shoes commanded as two more rounds banged inside the car.

Chance was flying again over Germany. It was the one thing he could never do — shoot back. That was left to others as shells would tear through his aircraft. He had spent the entire war without firing a weapon. He flew one, but he still felt helpless.

The .45 jerked Chance back to reality, banging out five bullets toward the trailing car. The shots ended with cheer from the shooter.

Bad Shoes did not join in the celebration, he patted the driver on the shoulder.

"*Schnell. Nach Hause.*"

The knee left Chance's back and he pushed himself up slightly.

"The danger is over, Herr Mitchell," Bad Shoes pronounced. "But, please, stay down. Just in case."

"Who are you?"

"You may call me Ernst and this is Nicki. We work for Max." His face brightened as he saw the recognition in Chance's face. "Yes, the same."

"Thank you for saving my ass."

"You are most welcome."

"What do I have to do to get Nevada back?" Chance rubbed the back of his head.

"Your wound is bothering you? From the crash?" Ernst cocked his head at Chance to Nicki.

Nicki frisked Chance roughly and shook his head. Chance recognized him as the crazy man who steered him away from the Russians when he brought Sonya the sugar.

"*Nichts.*" He did not sound at all crazy now.

"You fly with the angels. Your stealing the plane back was also a miracle, not?"

"Angels got nothing to do with it. How do I get Nevada back?"

Ernst watched a couple of men on the sidewalk as they passed them. "Max has a way," he said to the window before turning back to Chance. "I must say I admire your loyalty — to a point."

Chance did not like Ernst's faint smile one bit.

"So." It was that damned little word the Germans loved to use. "She has not told you?" The smile widened almost to a sneer. "Then I admire your loyalty completely."

Chance was seeing red when one eyebrow lifted and started to heave himself up. Nicki's foot was on his chest before he could raise his shoulders above the seat.

"I told you, Herr Mitchell. It would be very dangerous for you to get up just now." Ernst's eyes conveyed more menace than the foot on his sternum.

The car lurched violently. Ernst looked up. The car heaved again. They had run over something. He grabbed the driver's shoulder.

"*Freddi? Was ist los?! Pass auf!*" Ernst lunged over the seat. "*Freddi!*"

The car hit something hard and stopped. Nicki's foot jammed up to Chance's chin as the German was thrown forward against the back of the front seat. He cursed and tumbled on top of the American.

Everything stopped for half a second. Then Ernst slid back and climbed out of the car.

"*Freddi!*"

Nicki pushed himself off of Chance, as if the pilot was part of the floor, and was out the door.

Chance wondered if they had ditched him someplace and whether it was safer to stay in the car or try to run. He pulled himself up and noticed the car was cocked at an angle. They were up against a building.

"*Tot?*"

Nicki's voice brought Chance's gaze around to the front of the Opel. The blonde head of the driver lolled against the top of the seat as Ernst let go of it. Chance could see pain in the man's face.

"*Ja.*" The word was clipped and final. His eyes flicked to the American.

"*Was soll' wir denn?*" Nicki was nervous and did not even notice Chance get out of the car.

As he moved around to the driver's door Chance could easily see the all too familiar dark stain on the driver's shirt and pants.

The source was between two budding breasts. The girl could not have been more that sixteen. She was white, her eyes half closed, seeing nothing.

"She said it was nothing," Ernst bored into Chance. "She kept driving and saved our lives. Your life, Herr Mitchell."

"*Komm. Sie können es nicht ändern.*" Nicki touched Ernst's arm gently.

Chance recognized the same hopeless phrase he had heard at the border crossing into East Berlin. The Germans had used it when they pulled him away from the Russians groping the woman.

Ernst nodded almost invisibly, studying the girl. Her beautiful face was relaxing into a sack over a skull.

Chance stared, too. It was not the first dead teenager he had seen. But a girl made things very different.

"We must go. Immediately." Ernst leaned in to Freddi again.

Nicki bent to help and they pulled the body from the Opel.

The rain had picked up again. Ernst tenderly laid the girl's head back on the pavement. Nicki hopped into the front seat of the Opel and backed it away from the building onto the street. The one remaining headlight threw the dead face into hard relief.

"Get in. Now, Herr Mitchell."

Chance started moving and had the coat off before the German could stop him. Other arms took off the garment and laid it on the face of the girl. They were attached to Chance but moved on some other will.

They looked down at the body.

"*Fur dee leicke.*"

Ernst did not hide his surprise at the butchered German phrase.

"*Danke.*"

He did not wait for Chance to get in the Opel, but stepped in, confident the American would follow.

CHAPTER 47

Hagelbergerstrasse, American Sector, Occupied Berlin July 4, 1948, 11:22 P.M.

A few people standing on the wet sidewalk caught his attention as Dimitri entered the street from the south. He was soaked to the skin, but the good-soldier-turned-spy limped on. The rain had sputtered to a stop and the air was saturated near the pavement still warm from the day. Layers of fog slithered along the sidewalk as he came up on the tiny knot of onlookers. The few murmurs died away as the group noticed their new member with distrust.

Dimitri's shoulders sank as he realized his assignment had ended. The American's coat covered the upper body completely. There was no blood to be seen. He bent to pull back the coat and a woman gasped.

"*Lassen Sie das. Polizei.*"

The woman's companion moved between her and the view of the body. Dimitri hesitated and partially straightened up. The group relaxed until the spy suddenly bent back and flicked the top of the coat away from the girl's face. A chorus of disapproval did nothing to dampen his elation. His report would be very long today.

He had passed the abandoned Opel Admiral that had tried to run the American over several blocks behind. The windshield and the driver's window were shot out. Blood was clearly visible inside. He lingered only to record the auto's number, along with the one for the other Opel that had rescued Chance, on a disintegrating notebook page before making a call to his master. A woman had answered and took the message that the American target had been abducted. Only his luck and thick-headed determination led him up the right street to the body.

The sound of motors coming from the south alerted him and the crowd. He did not bother to look and headed north away from the approaching jeep and trailing Packard. His eye caught the glass and metal frame from the smashed headlamp, and the scrape on the bricks of the shoe store with three pairs of shoes widely spaced in the window display.

The Americans had beaten the *Stadtspolizei* for the simple reason they had vehicles and Berlin's police force traveled on foot or used the *S-bahn*, which snaked through the city, taking them briefly over into the Soviet Sector and causing them inevitable delays.

McKane exploded out of the Packard before it stopped. The crowd parted as they would for an elephant, leaving the major plenty of space. McKane's MP trailed behind, backed up by two others from the jeep. McKane stopped abruptly, but the crowd still surged back as if hammered by his shockwave. He took in the remains of the Opel's headlamp and his eye carried on to where Dimitri was a hobbled shadow hurrying away.

"Want him?" McKane's pet MP had followed his gaze.

McKane shook his head and pulled back Chance's jacket. His reaction was a short grunt. He looked at the black stain and the girl's white skin.

"They're using girls now. Bled a lot." The MP turned toward the crowd.

"But not here," McKane said to no one.

The brief exchange invited the Germans to loosen their tongues. The crowd closed on the MP with short phrases and gestures.

"Three men left her here about a half hour ago. One took off his jacket to cover the body. It was pouring rain," the MP translated without editorial. "The car had come off the street real slow and hit the building. The men left in the car."

A flash lit the scene with a soft "whump" that died to a crackle. The MP popped the bulb from the Speed Graphic camera and it sizzled on the wet pavement.

"Ask 'em if the man who left the jacket was forced back into the car." McKane gently laid the flight jacket back over the girl's face.

The MP translated and McKane heard several *neins* as he turned back toward the Packard.

"Wake up the file girls and find out who she was. And let the local Krauts look but not touch. This is all ours." The cement mixer was grinding hard as McKane heaved himself back into the Packard.

Ivanoff hoped the rain would not stop. It would mean anyone out would be desperate, like the American pilot. He would be easier to spot alone on the street. The Russian colonel looked out at the crossing from the building across the square. Frau Belinger's apartment had a perfect view of the checkpoint. She had just explained to him for the fourth time that she had never liked Hitler and was not a Nazi. She offered him tea for the fifth time. He shuddered at the thought that she might offer something else.

He dismissed the thought and went back to the two problems drawing his attention from the gnawing pain in his back. He expected that his team of kidnappers would appear at the crossing at any moment, confident the American pilot would be with them. He had been a guest of Frau Belinger since shortly after noon. The snatch team had promised him nothing would happen before then. Ivanoff wanted to be at the crossing to take charge of the pilot as soon as he was brought across. Mitchell would be little use to him dead and he wanted no mistakes. He disliked having his future entrusted to others. He wanted the joystick in his own hands. He could not risk crossing into the West on an illegal mission, so he had to wait here in this silly woman's flat until the kidnappers brought him the American. He would ensure the crossing went smoothly. He even had a backup plan in case the Allies sealed their side of the border. Marksmen on the rooftops across the street would pin down the Allied soldiers with scattered fire. No one was to be hit unless they approached the car. The large Opel would easily crash through the Russian barbed wire into the East. He would be rehabilitated and once again General Zukushev would bring him coffee himself.

The second problem was new and more disturbing. Frau Belinger had only told him once how she hated the Nazis when Ivanoff noticed a form approaching the crossing that he knew intimately. Sonya's familiar gait and figure stood out like approach lights against the other Berliners. Ivanoff knew she would have tried a kilometer to the north and then walked through the heat knowing it was most certainly futile. What could have been so important? He thought of the sugar. But even if she bolted, a phone call from him would ensure she never left Germany.

But that is not what bothered him.

He had begun to realize what Sonya had become. Jealousy was a new and, consequently, raw emotion for him. He would not let her go so easily to some American with sugar. He wondered what he might sacrifice to keep her.

Frau Belinger was sidling up behind him again when there was a sharp knock at the cracked apartment door. She gave the same short, startled cry that she often did when lightning struck nearby.

"*Voydity'!*" ordered Ivanoff and Frau Belinger cried out again.

The Soviet sergeant was in the room and at attention in one step. His boots clicked together with a rifle shot as he fixed his stare on the opposite wall and began his report with his pedigree of rank, company, platoon, etc. before Ivanoff cut him off.

"Your business," he demanded in Russian, keeping his pronunciation piano wire taut compared to the lazy, rural drawl of the sergeant.

The sergeant began his report with all the rehearsed details. Ivanoff's head went up in obvious irritation, although he did not face the long-winded sergeant. The sergeant dared to flick his gaze at the back of the annoyed colonel and finished the report in three short sentences. The last one had only a subject and a verb.

Ivanoff looked at Frau Belinger who trembled, thinking they were talking about her fate. A mumbled, pleading *bitte* rose to her lips just before Ivanoff hurled a question at the sergeant over his shoulder.

"*Da.*" The sergeant learned very quickly.

Ivanoff waved him out. Frau Belinger watched as he stood at the window for a moment, silhouetted by heat lightning to the north.

"Your telephone." Ivanoff's educated German impressed her as she fetched the phone.

CHAPTER 48

*Somewhere in Occupied Berlin,
July 5, 1948, 1:26 A.M.*

Chance had no idea where he was. Nicki wove through the streets of Berlin for almost a half hour before ducking into a warehouse garage. The tall, thin Ernst had carefully checked the street behind them before closing the door. Silently, they had exited through a doorway to a building that was missing its upper half.

The factory consisted of scattered islands of light with a few figures busy at each. The air was heavy with the sharp, mixed smell of sausages and lubricating oil. Voices murmured out of the darkness. Chance felt as if he had entered a small village cut off from the city around it. Despite the fact that it was the middle of the night, the hustle was from a market square at noon. He could distinctly hear the sound of someone hammering on wood, but could not see the source.

Ernst had disappeared into the darkness without a word, leaving Chance in a little pool of light, feeling as if a hundred pairs of eyes were on him. One pair belonged to Nicki, who hovered at the edge of the pool of light, smoking a cigarette. Now and then he looked at Chance as if he wanted to say something. He finished the cigarette and threw the butt on the floor.

"It is craziness, you know." Smoke trailed out of his mouth into the damp darkness. "This air bridge." He pulled out a crumpled package of Lucky Strikes and poked into it looking for another. After a moment he sucked a breath through his teeth and tossed the pack at a box in the corner with his left hand.

The gun was in his right hand before the pack bounced off the wall.

"Do you think it will work?" He lazily pulled the action back and began to clean the chamber with his handkerchief.

Chance suddenly remembered he was in the middle of something bigger than himself, Sonya and, yes, Nevada. During the war, he never thought about if they were winning against the Nazis. Only if he was going to survive the next five minutes, if they were flying, and if he could sleep, eat and maybe fuck if he was on the ground. The war, just like the airlift now, was somewhere else, happening to someone else.

"Don't know." Chance also realized this was only the third German he had had anything like a conversation with. "Who was the girl?"

"Freddi? An orphan, I think." The shooter snapped the action closed with a round in the chamber and popped the clip out of the .45. "Ernst liked her, I think. What about the other pilots?"

The dangerous way Nicki was cleaning the weapon interrupted Chance's answer. He hadn't spoken much with the other pilots, except about the weather, Russian fighters and food. There were no social events. The mess hall was for inhaling food while your aircraft was being refueled or so you could get to sleep as quickly as possible.

He shrugged.

"Herr Mitchell does not care about the airlift. He only wants to find his friend." Ernst's eyes appeared out of the darkness, targeting Chance. "Is that not right?"

He stopped right in front of Chance, searching the American's face.

"Yeah. And go home." Chance stood, making Nicki nervous. The American and his boss were evenly matched in size and intensity. "How do I get Nevada back?"

"You Americans are not on speaking terms with the Russians at this moment." The smile on Ernst's face was somewhere between amusement and *you poor fool*. "However, Max is."

"Then he can get him back."

The smile reached full amusement and went right on to ridicule. "Herr Mitchell, that will cost Max a lot."

"How much?"

"More than you will make if this silly airlift would last two years. And it will not last even one."

"You got him over there."

Nicki got even more nervous. Ernst calmed him by turning his head slightly toward him without taking his eyes off Chance.

"He went over there himself. Max employed him to do a job and he lost his way." Ernst took a step toward Chance. "That was his risk. For which he would have been paid."

Nicki saw Chance's right fist ball and start up. Ernst was faster.

"Think, Herr Mitchell." But he already saw Chance was not thinking. Ernst's left arm flashed out of his pocket. Chance felt a sharp pain in his bicep and then his arm went numb. He caught only a glint of metal as the German's hand disappeared back in his coat pocket.

"Try thinking again." Ernst's tone was fatherly.

Chance obeyed as the feeling slowly returned to his hand.

"If I do the job, can you get Nevada back?"

The German smiled only with his eyes. His face lifted slightly.

"Excellent suggestion." He retreated to a bench with several clocks on it. "Your plane?"

"Banged up a bit. Right landing strut is broken off. They want to scrap it." Chance cocked his head. "But you knew that."

Ernst brightened. "You will have anything you need. Dollars, deutschmarks – east or west. Even Rubles." A frown lined his thin face. "But even Max cannot bring a new landing strut into Berlin."

"Maybe Rossi'll come up with something. But I gotta get back there to do it."

"Then we have a deal, not?"

"Only if Nevada is there to talk me down on the radio. If I don't hear him, I don't land."

Nicki looked to Ernst, whose smile never wavered.

"We agree."

The German offered his hand.

"Where and when?"

"You will be told when we are ready."

Chance finally shook the German's hand.

Ernst nodded to Nicki who vanished into darkness. The German became the congenial host, extending his hand for Chance to proceed. Chance wasn't feeling so congenial. He stood where he was.

"We are running out of time, Herr Mitchell. The piles of bricks hiding your plane are disappearing. We have only a few days."

"So that was your idea."

"Oh, no. I must say it was inspired. But not our idea. Someone else. You seem to have many friends. You should be careful about your friends, Herr Mitchell." His gaze reached into Chance. "Even Sonya."

"Sonya knew Nevada." For some reason it still was almost a question.

"Yes." Ernst was matter of fact, hiding his amusement at the naïve American. "Rather well, I think. He was looking for cash and she brought him to us."

Chance blinked the jab away. "She work for Max?"

"Sometimes. I do not know who she really works for. If anyone. Like most Germans these days, she works primarily for herself."

Chance nodded. "Yeah. She wanted me to do a job for her."

"To her credit, it was she that contacted us about you." Ernst blocked the doorway out to the Mercedes, idling in the alley. "But do not let your feelings for her cloud your thinking, Herr Mitchell."

"I want to bring her out." Chance surprised himself. He had said it, but almost didn't believe it.

Ernst still blocked the door.

"It is not possible. Or wise. Do the job and you will get Nevada."

"I want her, too."

The amusement flickered back into the German's face for a moment and then it was hard again.

"It is not possible. You may have one or the other – which one is of no matter to us. I would say she would be easier for us – but for you a waste. She will not go with you."

Anger leapt from Chance's face, but Ernst was not intimidated. "You must choose. Now."

It was almost a whisper. "Nevada."

CHAPTER 49

*Gardenerstrasse, Soviet Occupied Berlin,
July 5, 1948, 3:47 A.M.*

Nevada was elated. But not because he was in the back of a windowless van which might be taking him to the West. And not because this was the fourth time he was moving in as many days.

He had seen the moon.

The guard had fumbled with the lock on the black van and given Nevada time to look out the long tunnel and catch the waning crescent moon rising. It was sunlight. Reflected sunlight, but sunlight. The first he had seen since watching the sun set back in June when he took off for the East.

All the places he had been kept were designed to keep him from knowing the time, whether it was day or night. He rarely saw the faces of the guards. The summer heat did not penetrate to the damp basements or windowless rooms. Even the food was always the same.

Almost always.

Nevada had noticed that for two meals a day the porridge would taste pasty. The cook, if he could be called that, was stretching the glop with flour. Then one meal would be normal. This would happen six times and then there would be three normal meals. Nevada figured the cook worked a day shift for six days. He counted the three normal meals as a "weekend" and kept track of the weeks.

The voice had hinted about someone looking for the plane, but he guessed it was now July and Chance had given up finding him.

Nevada's bulletproof optimism sank to a new low when he realized that he might be heading for another stretch of interrogation. The first stretch lasted three weeks and stopped abruptly. For hours at a time, he had stood before a wall as a man – or his twin – paced behind him in the darkness, asking questions in perfect English. The man was clever, asking him about the past, then shifting the focus to the present and back again. Several times, Nevada was jolted awake by a bucket of ice water and dragged to the room with the pacing man. The man would talk as if Nevada had already confessed to being a spy. But Nevada wasn't a spy. At least he was pretty sure he wasn't.

The first round of interrogation had ended with a van ride across town to a new cell. Then a week – maybe more – later, the questions started again. Nevada figured something had happened. He could hear the tension in the man's voice. He couldn't figure out what it was, but the questions focused more on who he was working with.

The van stopped and reversed. They were inside a building or garage; he could hear the engine noise echoing off the walls. He recognized the echo and doubled over. The pain was excruciating. He had promised himself he would not get his hopes up and yet he had. The fall was hard and jolt at the bottom crushed his soul.

He could sense the wall in front of his nose as the guard placed him there – even before he pulled the hood off. The guard hadn't showered and his body odor was pretty ripe.

"You may go home now." The English of the familiar voice behind him was perfect. The accent, foreign. The meaning, electric.

In the silence, Nevada's core resisted taking the bait like a dog that had been choke-chained back too many times for chasing after a rabbit. All of him wanted to, but one part knew it was false. But, like the dog, he couldn't help himself.

He edged toward the only door he could see. The guard didn't move. There was nothing but silence from behind him. His ears strained for something. He could not even hear the man breathing.

He stopped at the door.

Out of the corner of his eye, the guard still leaned, impassive, against the dull green paint.

The handle was ice cold and stuck. Nevada twisted it and the latch released with a squeak that almost hurt his ears. The door was open and the guard still leaned.

Nevada stepped into the darkness on the other side. His footsteps echoed off the walls and there seemed to be no hall. He noticed how long his fingernails had become as he felt along the walls. The same dull, green paint cut under his nails as he clawed at the prison surrounding him.

His mind flailed for a hold on sanity. *How had they done it? How had they brought him in and bricked up the way in so quickly?*

He was completely trapped. There was no other way in. Or out – except past the voice.

"Who are you working for? The OSS? Nazis?"

Nevada heard someone sobbing as the voice moved closer. Tears dripped from his nose, wetting the wall. His mind wanted to push through the brick, but knew the only way out was the voice.

"Who was the woman…?"

"Who was the woman you knew in Berlin?" Nevada joined in, his voice cracking. "Who paid for the plane to be repaired?"

Nevada knew all the questions by heart, choking out the litany between sobs.

But for the first time, he wanted to answer them. He knew it was wrong, but he saw in himself the sobbing bastard who wanted to give the answers.

And he knew the bastard would win.

CHAPTER 50

*Tempelhof Airfield, July 5,
1948, 2:58 P.M.*

Chance thought he heard someone outside PIE IN THE SKY. The wheel well had turned into an airless furnace in the afternoon sun. Chance had checked the mount of the right landing gear and found that the brackets that held the gear to the main wing spar had all been bent. The wing spar itself seemed intact, but would have to be inspected with a fluoroscope. A dye that glowed under a ultra-violet light would be smeared on the metal, collecting in any invisible cracks that might be there. The cracks would glow brightly under a special UV lamp.

Chance tallied how long this would take and how he would find the special equipment in the middle of the panic of the airlift.

The Allies were worried. The summer weather had been normal, causing the lift to stop on four different occasions for longer than a day. And countless times for an hour or two here and there. Efficiency and tonnage had been slowly rising, but they still worried how they would feed and heat the city at the same time during the winter. Coal would be worth more than gold in a few months, so they were laying in as much as they could in advance of the coming fall weather with its inevitable fogs followed by winter ice.

And it still looked hopeless.

Chance hoped that Rossi would think of some way or know some source to scrounge the needed parts. But the chocoholic New Yorker had only grimaced whenever the main gear X-strut was mentioned.

Chance had his arm deep inside the hot wing feeling for the fuel tanks when he heard the voice again. He pulled his arm out, snagging his elbow on the jagged edge of the torn away brake line. He jerked his arm back and scraped his knuckles on the wing rib. For a moment he had an image of Rossi finding him, bouncing around inside the wheel well like Harpo Marx, banging his head on this or that and flinching. Only to hurt himself elsewhere and start the process all over.

He managed to calm down, avoiding further injury, and came out into the painful sun.

The voice was soft and soothing. He lost it for a moment in the dusty, humid air and the landing of a Skymaster. His head throbbed and he mentally looked behind him for the abyss. He had been feeling better – mostly because he felt he had a real shot at getting Nevada out. But hallucinations would be a real setback.

The voice was there again, drawing him around to the other side. He waded through the overgrown grass to the left wing and almost missed her. The brown hair was hidden in the shadow under the wing. A woman was sitting in the grass and looking down. She murmured again in the same motherly tones.

"Hey!" Chance's voice cracked. He hadn't had anything to drink since Rossi left over an hour before.

The brown head shot up and another joined it out of the grass. The brunette didn't move, but the other woman, gray hair peeking out from a kerchief, stood.

"*Bitte...*" the sitting woman started to plead. Gray-hair cut her off with a wave of her hand.

"Our friend is not vell." Gray-hair did not plead, looking Chance squarely in the eye. Her thin legs swam in ridiculous cutoff trousers, with black-and-blue blotches on her knees. A bony arm wobbling in a sweat-stained man's shirt minus the sleeves pointed to the sitting woman.

"What's the matter with her?" Chance charged in the last few feet and saw a third woman lying in the lap of the brunette. She looked twenty going on a hundred, barely reacting to Chance's presence. The gray dust had caked on her face with a line along her brow where her kerchief had protected her skin. She was dressed in an unbuttoned man's shirt. Her waist was lost in trousers that could have held all three women. Two men's shoes lay by her feet. Her arm flopped up to her forehead and the shirt slipped off her chest exposing a shriveled breast. Chance turned away to the older woman as the brunette rebuttoned the shirt.

"She is not having... It is zu varm. Not?" Gray-hair's spindly arms stirred the suffocating blanket of summer air. "Here is the only..." Gray-hair searched for the word and pointed to the shade of the wing. "Shadow...?"

Chance dropped to one knee next to the sick woman. She tried to focus on him and smiled weakly.

"*Bitte, Verzeihung.*"

"She says..." the older woman started.

"I know what she says." Chance found himself starting to smile at the sick woman, but her head lolled away. He noticed there wasn't a drop of sweat on her face. He and the other two women were bathed in it, although the other women looked like they were drying out, too. "Tell her not to worry."

Gray-hair translated as Chance unsteadily got to his feet. The sick woman mumbled something and slowly came to a stop.

"She has heatstroke and needs water. Pronto."

"*Ja.* Ze are fetching vazzer."

"*Er ist verletzt!*" cried the brunette suddenly, staring at Chance's elbow.

"You are hurt?" Gray-hair reached for Chance's arm. She hesitated a moment before taking his forearm as Chance started to lift it. A rivulet of blood ran from his elbow to the heel of his hand. "I will see," she volunteered.

Chance let her.

"It stopped. But you must vash it," Gray-hair pronounced.

"I've had worse." Chance remembered Nevada roughly feeling the back of his head. But the woman was gentle and her touch warm, despite her rough-skinned fingers that felt like metal files.

"Do not vorry. Ve vatch ze plane," Gray-hair tossed in with a faint smile. "Nobody touch."

Chance heard the jeep coming. "Good. Thanks," he said over his shoulder as he came out to Rossi pulling around the dwindling mounds of rubble. A red-headed *Trümmerfrau* clung to the seat and dash, her white knuckles bright as landing lights in the sun. Rossi killed the engine and hopped out before the jeep stopped. The woman gave a short cry of fear before the suddenly driverless jeep rolled to a stop.

"Saw her coming back out here." He jerked a thumb back at the redhead climbing out of the jeep with three canteens. Chance recognized her as the spokeswoman from the premature Fourth of July. "How's Erika doin'?" He looked past Chance at the sick woman.

"Heatstroke." Chance felt a twinge of surprise that these formless women had names. They were everywhere in Berlin and cities all over Europe. But so were streetlamps.

"Yeah. Give it to her slow," Rossi said to the redhead hurrying past him to her friend.

The German women huddled around the sick woman. Rossi offered Chance a cool canteen, US ARMY plainly stenciled on the olive drab canvas cover.

"You could use some, too."

"What'd you come up with?" Chance asked before drinking.

Rossi ran his hand through his black, sweaty hair and wiped it on his overalls before pointing back at the jeep. "Hydraulic lines, cables, shocks, bushings..."

"Okay, great," Chance was impatient. "What about the strut?"

"Even found that."

Chance brightened.

"What's left of it," Rossi added. "These Germans are something. Bunch of 'em hauled it over here and *retoined* it to us. All proud of demselves." He started a laugh as Chance looked into the back of the jeep. PIE IN THE SKY's broken wheel lay in the back. Chance could see plaster dust on it and part of a roof tile impaled the tire.

The sick woman's moans became louder and she coughed. A chorus of German tried to calm her, but she threw up. She thrashed on the grass, her heels digging into the sod as she arched her back. The women watched, helpless.

Chance knelt down and poured his canteen over her forehead and then all over her clothes.

"Don't force her. She needs to cool off first." He emptied his canteen on her. Gray-hair translated to the others.

Chance went back to the jeep and closely examined the broken strut. He had a sense of revulsion as if he was examining the dismembered arm of a friend or a child.

"I can fix 'er. All but dis." Rossi nodded at the shattered strut and started to open a chocolate bar and found the wrapper was all that was holding it in shape in the heat.

"Any chance of flying one in?"

"Truman couldn't even get one in here. The colonel's got everything buttoned down. Only food and coal's comin' in. Anything that can't fly outta here is scrap."

"Okay, we fix it."

"It's an aluminum alloy casting! Youse can't weld it 'cause youse set it on fire and then youse can't put the fire out."

The sick woman moaned again and Chance glanced at her. He tried to think. His mind went in circles, stopping only for occasional, irresistible diversions for an excuse to see Sonya. He would apologize or say anything. Maybe she knew someone who could help him. He was frustrated, hot and dizzy, standing in some foreign country probably walking distance from his only friend, with a crippled plane and a throbbing head.

"You come out of ze sun, please." Gray-hair came around to face him.

Chance did not look like he was going to obey.

"At zis moment. Please." Gray-hair took his arm and led him to the shade. She took her kerchief off and rinsed it in the water from the canteen Rossi had brought. She started to wash his elbow.

For a moment Chance studied her sun-dried face. Despite age and the ravages of war, echoes of beauty were still to be enjoyed. She caught him looking and cracked a smile.

"Okay, tough guy. You vill lif." The smile vanished when she noticed the bruise and cut above his left eye. "You have much problem, not?"

"I hit my head when I crashed this."

"Oh!" Gray-hair translated quickly to the others. Red-head shot something back like she knew all along. Gray-hair tied the still wet kerchief back on her head. "It fly again. *Ja?*"

"No. What do they say? *Kaputt.*" Chance looked to Rossi for help.

"*Ka-poot.*" Rossi threw away the melted chocolate bar and jerked a stained thumb toward the terminal. "And they could get that scavenger crane out here any time now. That rubble is almost gone."

"Ze veel is broken?"

"Yeah." Chance was getting annoyed at Gray-hair for talking about honored dead. He could easily see the terminal over the piles of shattered bricks. Through the waves of heat, the scorpion crane swelled and wavered like it was breathing. He almost didn't hear Gray-hair over the departing Skymaster.

"Mine friend. He help. He is good mit autos."

"No...thanks. He wouldn't..."

Gray-hair wasn't listening. She darted to the still intact landing gear. "Zis. Is broken, *ja?*"

"Shut up." Chance's frustration threatened to blow out the top of his skull.

"I not shut up. He can fix." Gray-hair stood her ground, slapping the strut. "He make new."

Chance walked out from the wing, fist balled.

"Tell her to shut up!"

"Then she'll be in pieces day after tomorrow," Rossi shrugged, running his hand on the aileron.

It took them three hours to loosen the remains of the strut and get it out from under the wing. The healthy women dug a trench to bring it out as Chance and Rossi removed it from the mangled mountings. The *Trümmerfrauen* even helped lift it into the jeep. Each one of them could have been blown away by a hot breeze, but together they were able to carry more than Chance.

Gray-hair sat on the pile of jagged metal, directing them through the maze of rubble-lined streets to a section just west of Tempelhof on the other side of the rail yards.

They arrived at no more than two-and-a-half walls of what had been a stable. Gray-hair hopped down and called for someone named Jürgen as she charged into the ruin. Chance followed her, not finding what he expected. In the center of the roofless room was a block of bricks with what looked like rocks on top. Chance recognized the coal clinkers and the blacksmith's tools arranged neatly on a crate still bearing Nazi markings.

"We're crazy. Fuckin' crazy."

Rossi was more fascinated with the predecessors of the tools he used. He snorted a laugh.

"These are all homemade."

"Great." Chance rubbed his pounding temples.

"But done real nice. They've been heat-hardened."

Chance turned and thought he was in full hallucination. In the corner, a pale woman stepped down from an ornate, covered, horse-drawn carriage – minus the horse. Two children peeked out of the carriage windows. They were obviously living in the antique.

"*Hallo, Ulrike. Jürgen ist nicht da,*" she whispered to Gray-hair, her eyes flicking nervously between the two Americans. She picked at the bathrobe which had been sown together in front, as if she could somehow make herself more presentable to the unexpected guests.

A short conversation followed. Chance guessed Gray-hair was explaining what was going on. He couldn't decide if he or the pale woman was more incredulous.

"Jürgen is at home in a short time," Gray-hair finally pronounced. "Zen is all fixed." She clapped her hands together as if that would rejoin the metal.

One of the children was crying and the pale woman climbed back into the carriage. Rossi went to the carriage door and waved a floppy chocolate bar at the child. He gave it to the pale woman after the crying stopped.

Chance discovered he needed to take a leak and went over to Gray-hair who was sitting in the carriage door playing with the older of the two children.

"Where's the…toilet?"

Gray-hair pointed toward the back of the ruin where the rear wall petered out. Chance walked back and found himself in what had been an alley. Large holes marked where the buildings along the alley had been. Two apartment buildings still stood on the other side of the craters. Chance could see people enjoying the cooling of the evening in the windows about fifty feet away, but he could see nothing that resembled a toilet.

His nose led him to it. A clump of torn newspapers hung on a broken rod sticking out of the wall. A stain of urine and feces marked the spot. Chance wondered if anyone was watching, but realized in Berlin, this was probably more normal than indoor plumbing.

He heard Gray-hair talking excitedly when he came back around the wall. A wiry man in filthy pants that were inches too short, and a shirt that was more Chance's size, was trying to follow what was happening. He fingered a threadbare cap with both grimy hands, as he eyed Chance and Rossi, who was struggling to get up from the dirt floor. Chance figured this was Jürgen and could tell the little man was exhausted. As Gray-hair finished her explanation, the pale woman joined them, placing her hand on Jürgen's elbow. Distracted a moment, he produced a tiny parcel, wrapped in brown paper from behind his cap and gave it to her. She carried the treasure immediately to the children.

They went out to the jeep in the twilight and with pantomime and Gray-hair's translation, Chance and Rossi explained what they needed. Jürgen's eyebrows shot up several times as he gave a hopeless sigh.

The pale woman came out with a small cube of cheese. Jürgen smiled wearily, shaking his head.

"*Gib' den Kinder.*"

"*Die Amis haben ihnen Chokolat gebracht,*" the pale woman nodded at Chance and Rossi.

The little man took the cube and said something low to Gray-hair.

"He says: Excuse me. I eat dinner. And zank you for the Shocolat."

"Youse is welcome." Rossi found something in the broken gear to study.

"Go ahead. Please." Chance didn't know what to look at.

The little blacksmith nibbled at the cheese as he looked at the shattered strut. He examined the broken ends carefully and finished the cheese as if savoring a fine steak.

"*Ja. Ich mache es,*" he finally pronounced confidently.

"He vill fix it. See, I told you!" Gray-hair clapped her hands together.

"*Ich würde mich geehrt fühlen,*" he added and bowed slightly.

Gray-hair couldn't figure out how to translate that and fiddled with her kerchief, frowning. She brightened.

"It honor him."

"Great." Chance nodded back slightly. "When?"

Jürgen anticipated the question and was already answering it to Gray-hair. He shrugged. Fatigue crushed the answer down to a whisper. Gray-hair hopped and drew a deep breath, clapping her hands together again.

"Ve do it now!"

CHAPTER 51

*Schmiedhofstrasse, Occupied Berlin,
July 6, 1948, 2:28 A.M.*

They could see the smoke rising out of the ruined stable for blocks before they got back to Jürgen's. The undulating, orange glow was the only light in the ruins and the smoke was held low by the inversion layer. It would brighten and dim every few seconds in a steady rhythm.

The claustrophobic, still night had been little relief from the summer heat and the day promised to be humid – the air cool, but thick.

Several eyes flickered outside the low walls, turning as one to Rossi and Chance pulling up as if they were Truman and Churchill stopping to visit. They were curious, but showed no other emotion in the pulsing light.

Chance had finally learned Gray-hair's name was Ulrike on the ride over, but they had not spoken of anything else. He wasn't sure what he would find and had only asked Rossi if he thought Jürgen could pull it off.

"If he can't weld it, maybes I could try." Rossi did not sound optimistic. "But dese Krauts know their stuff," he added to Chance's haggard, gloomy face.

They had been gone for little more than an hour, bringing some tools that Jürgen had requested through Ulrike. They also brought three loaves of bread, sugar and coffee from the mess. Rossi had managed to produce a large sausage from someplace.

A few of the Germans muttered as Chance and Rossi strode into the blacksmith's work area. They found Jürgen stripped to the waist, working with two other, larger men. All were sweating profusely in the heat from the forge. Two boys took turns working the bellows which had been cobbled together out of two doors, some canvas, wood and drain pipe.

Chance noticed a pile of coal had appeared next to the forge. His silent question of its origin was answered when a woman came in with a basket that had few lumps. She added it to the pile and Jürgen smiled a thank you. She grinned at the two Americans as she joined the group at the walls. Evidently, coal was the cost of one ticket to the show. It hit Chance just how much that pile represented. In a few months, that little pile would be one day's defense from freezing for the whole neighborhood. It seemed inconceivable that someone could freeze in a modern city, but during the first post-war winter of 1945-46, thousands froze in Berlin. And then coal could flow into the city.

The woman and the others were gambling their lives to save an airplane.

Chance's airplane. And Nevada's.

Chance looked for the strut. The entire wheel assembly had been disassembled and laid out on a canvas tarp that had served as the awning for the carriage the day before, preventing it from becoming an antique oven. Jürgen and the two other men brought a bracket to where they could see it under a kerosene lantern hung on a bent coat pole near the forge. He murmured something to his apprentices, pointing to a bend. His battered, grimy fingers ran over the surface like a surgeon's. The apprentices moved off with the damaged piece as the little mechanic peeked into the forge. Chance thought he had missed the strut in the dark. Then he spotted the X-form lying in a box near the forge. Rossi spotted it about the same time. It appeared intact.

"They fixed it already?" Chance's excitement came through his night-heavy voice.

He knelt down and tried to touch the strut. It wasn't there.

"*Lassen Sie den Fingern weg!*" The little man darted over. "*Nein! Nein! Stop!*"

Ulrike appeared. "You must not touch."

Chance's eyes were playing tricks on him. In the dark he had seen the form, but it was an impression in damp sand. The little man examined where Chance had touched the mold.

"Where the fuck is it!" Chance crushed Jürgen's shoulder.

The mechanic backed away, frightened and pointed at the forge.

"Holy shit," Rossi whispered. "He's melted it down and is casting it."

Staring at the dazzling forge, Chance's eyes adjusted to the glare. He could just make out the glowing cauldron, a liquid seething inside like molten lava.

"You said it would burn," Chance accused Rossi.

"It should."

The New Yorker looked around a moment and found something. He strode over to a corner of the ruined stable. Broken glass clattered as he poked a pile with his foot. He laughed.

"Dis guy's a genius."

Jürgen brightened and trotted over.

"*Ja! Es schützt.*"

"It protects it," translated Ulrike.

"Glass melts on top and keeps da air out." Rossi could only shake his head.

Jürgen squinted into the dazzling cauldron of molten metal. He made a disapproving sound.

"*Es geht nicht.*" He held a hand before his eyes and peered between his fingers. "*Nicht fliessend ist es.*"

"It's not melting enough." Rossi was behind the little mechanic.

Jürgen grabbed more coal and heaped it around the cauldron. He snapped his fingers at the two boys on the bellows. "*Schnell, Junge! Mach schnell!*"

JITTERBUG LIFT

The boys' thin arms worked faster, but all their exhausted effort brightened the forge only slightly.

Nevada's future was in that cauldron. Without one hundred pounds of alloy in the right shape, PIE IN THE SKY would not fly again. At least not in one airplane.

Chance grabbed the shovel handle that levered the bellows. He pulled up with all his strength as the winded boy staggered backward. One of the larger Germans took the other boy's place. Rossi and Jürgen heaped coal from the meager pile onto the forge.

It took only minutes before Chance's arms screamed. Dizzy, he waited for the black abyss to swallow him whole. Another German tapped his shoulder and Chance let him take his place. He peeled off the soggy tangle of his shirt. The effort was almost too much. Rough hands helped him. He turned and found Ulrike behind him.

"Ve vill do it!"

Chance glanced over at Jürgen who was still not so optimistic and shook his head in the glare. The German who had replaced Chance on the bellows was flagging already. Chance wondered when any of them had had a full meal. He tapped the man on the arm and took his place. Another man from the crowd pulled off his shirt and spelled the other man on the bellows.

Chance furiously worked the bellows. He was flying. Moving his arms kept him in the air. He had to keep pumping.

The growing heat he felt on his right arm and face was a comfort at first. Then it burned more than his muscles. The part of the door that made the top of the bellows closest to the forge began to smoke. The paint blistered and charred. The German on the other side of him fell back with a curse. The heat was too much. Chance kept working until he could smell his singed hair.

Somehow he found himself farther from the fire. He refocused and Ulrike stopped him from going back.

"You are burning!"

Jürgen pointed at the bellows and tried to explain.

"Ve make ze...ze... *Blasebalg* new. Farser avay," Ulrike pleaded.

Chance almost bought that idea. The fire was cooling and he looked for the coal. Only a few lumps were left.

"More coal?"

Jürgen looked around and asked the crowd. Sad eyes only peered out of the dark.

"*Gibt's nichts mehr.*"

Chance didn't need a translation.

"Water. Throw water on me!"

Ulrike called to the Jürgen's wife who produced a pot. Ulrike doused Chance over his head and he bent back to the door. The water smelled of something putrid.

"The bellows, too!"

Everything was on the line. Chance decided pain didn't matter.

Water splashed from somewhere on the door and sizzled away in seconds. Another splash lasted marginally longer. A third hit his back.

One of the other Germans joined him. They fell into a rhythm. Water cooled them every third stroke. Chance could see it steaming off the arms of the German who was farther from the forge than he. Chance began to understand what a boiled egg felt like.

Chance heard a voice behind him. It seemed perfectly normal that Sonya was there. Her voice pushed away the pain. He wanted to turn around but there wasn't time. Sonya called again, but was interrupted by a gout of water.

The rhythm changed. He found Rossi huffing on the end of the shovel handle and the German staggering back, wiping his face. Chance couldn't stare at the forge for more than a second. The heat and intense glare blinded him. He felt a surge of hope.

The forge was a breathing beast, ready to give birth. One of the big Germans tapped Chance's arm to relieve him. Chance shook him off. Rossi accepted the relief and drank water Ulrike brought him.

The American mechanic watched Chance. Chance's world shrank to his arms and the see-saw motion of working the bellows. The water dousing came regularly now. No one organized it. People just helped where they could. Ulrike darted in and offered him water in a soup can. He paused only because the abyss was forming behind him, complete with Sonya whispering to him to let go and fall in. He poured the rest of the water over his head. Ulrike took the bent soup can and scurried back to the relative cool of the night.

Out of the corner of his eye, Chance could see Jürgen and a spent Rossi folding the halves of the mold together. He could no longer look at the forge at all. The white heat was searing his arms and shoulder despite the near constant water.

Somehow Jürgen could see into the cauldron and nodded. He whistled to the other Germans.

"*Es geht!*"

He grabbed Chance's arm.

"*Sofort!*" He motioned toward the mold.

In seconds, wet canvas was over Chance's shoulders. The other big German and he were shielded against the unbearable heat, each hold one end of a long bar with hooks for holding the cauldron of molten metal. Jürgen motioned for them to lift. Chance heaved with as if pulling PIE IN THE SKY out of the Tempelhof mud.

Nothing moved. The cauldron was stuck.

Jürgen yelled for something as Chance's mind wandered in search of anything outside this hell. The hammer rang as Jürgen smashed the front of the forge. The little mechanic was destroying his livelihood, but the exposed coal fire and white-hot cauldron doubled the heat. The small crowd was lit up now and fell back from the intense light. Water flew in from farther away, re-soaking the canvas. Some splashed toward the cauldron, but never reached it. It flashed into steam long before it reached the surface.

They had only seconds before they would cook where they stood. Jürgen swatted out his smoldering pants and motioned for them to lift again. Still nothing moved.

Shanley was there. Sonya. Nevada smiled from the east.

Chance found himself staggering forward toward the mold, the cauldron free of the forge.

"Halt!" The little mechanic was all business.

Chance thought they were too far from the mold, now clearly lit by the glowing crucible. Jürgen ran over and nudged Chance slightly left, then signed he was to stay put.

The crucible was now bright red and Chance began to worry. One of the young boys handed Jürgen a long steel rod. He hooked it onto a peg on the bottom of the crucible and began to tilt the crucible forward. Red-hot glass spilled from the crucible onto the ground.

It was as if a thousand flash bulbs were going off. Exposed to the air, the alloy left in the crucible began to burn. The entire neighborhood was suddenly visible.

Chance's stomach sank but Jürgen squinted and motioned them a few steps forward to the mold. He held up his fist to stop them and hooked the rod onto bottom of the crucible again.

Lightning flowed out. The liquid metal, dazzling as it burned in the air, poured into the mold. Steam and fumes roared out of the vent holes, followed by sparks and flame. The mold heaved on the ground, twisting in agony as it contained the white-hot metal.

Chance's eyes gave up and he had to close them. The weight on his arms lightened quickly and the roar died away to a sputtering sizzle. Chance coughed from the acrid smoke and let himself be led to the wall.

Hands guided him down to a blanket on the ground. Voices whispered in German. He opened his eyes to see Ulrike working on the blisters that had risen on his arms and shoulders. Other men and women tended to the big German who nodded over to Chance. Rossi appeared.

"It'll take a while to cool. Youse should take it easy."

"How will we know it worked?" Chance's own voice was miles away.

"We'll test it the way dey've been testin' castings for a thousand years."

Rossi said something else, but Chance let the abyss take him.

It was getting light when Chance awoke to Jürgen gently shaking him. He handed Chance a pair of large tongs and headed to the smoldering mold. The forge was still too hot to approach and they detoured around it.

Sensing something was happening again, the Berliners at the edge of the stable roused themselves and pressed in on the walls.

The young boys had already broken away the wooden sides from the mold and were prying away clumps of sand with wooden sticks. A large hunk fell away, exposing one end of the strut. It smoked and glowed a dull red, just visible in the pre-sunrise. Jürgen waved them away and pointed to Chance.

Chance grabbed the end of the strut with the tongs and lifted. Clumps of the mold clung to it as he pulled it free. His arms ached from the effort and his skin stung from the burns, but he lifted with hope.

The hammer flashed in the first light of the sun and struck the metal. It rang. Mold sand fell away revealing the pure, silvery metal. Jürgen grinned for the first time.

Dimitri was walking away when he heard the bell note followed by a cheer from the crowd. He knew where Chance would be going next.

And he had another long report to make.

CHAPTER 52

*Tempelhof Airport,
July 6, 1948, 11:38 A.M.*

The day lived up its threat of heat in the night. The wheel assembly lay in the back of Rossi's commandeered jeep. Jürgen had hand-filed the mating surfaces until they fitted together as if made of one piece. Rossi reassembled most of the wheel in about an hour. He left the brake lines off; they could only be done when the wheel was back on the wing. The arteries would be connected once the bones were rejoined.

Chance stood before the wounded side of PIE IN THE SKY. The scorpion was coming. He saw it leave the terminal and head straight at him. Only the steady flow of aircraft in and out was holding it up from crossing the runway.

He had asked the crane crew to help lift the airplane wing and they had refused. Their orders were clear: gut PIE IN THE SKY and salvage as much as they could. The new runway layout put a taxiway straight through where Chance's only hope lay wounded on the grass.

The rubble that protected it had all but disappeared. *Trümmerfrauen* had hauled it away over the past few days. It had amazed Chance that these women who moved so slowly and seemed so weak had shifted the huge piles of broken Berlin.

JITTERBUG LIFT

Rossi got up from a jumble of wood beams he had scrounged from the terminal. They had been used to hold in place generators, motors and other large cargo the Skymasters had flown in.

The scorpion pulled up through the opening bulldozed through the remaining heaps of bricks. The sergeant driver planted himself in front of Chance and was to the point.

"You got everything you wanted off of her?"

"No."

The driver didn't blink. "They said you could be trouble."

"They were right."

The sergeant cocked his head to better see the broiled half of Chance, studying his singed hair and blistered arms as if trying to figure out just how a man could be cooked like that and still be belligerent.

Rossi sized up the three other privates hopping off the scorpion, matching each of them to a suitably sized piece of shoring.

The sergeant planted himself square in front of Chance, hooking his thumbs into his belt. "Look, bud, you've had a rough time…"

"I've filed a flight plan."

The sergeant's head rocked back slowly. Chance wasn't sure if he was nodding or recoiling from the verbal slap.

"With who?"

"Some dumb sergeant. You can't touch this aircraft until it closes."

A grin almost made it to the sergeant's cracked lips. "To where?"

Chance was tired of Twenty Questions and went to the pile of shoring.

"Most you'd get is two hours to Frankfurt." The sergeant opened the door of the scorpion. "I'll wait."

He said something to the privates and they picked out relative cool spots in the shade of the crane.

Chance hated having the vultures perched so comfortably nearby and tried to ignore them. He failed.

"Give us a hand with this wing."

The sergeant answered for his men. "You're sun happy. Three men ain't gonna lift no wing. Thirty ain't either."

"Maybe you could help and make it four."

"Maybe I got orders otherwise."

Chance didn't hear Ulrike show up.

"Is fixed, not?"

"Not."

Ulrike wiped a pint of sweat off her forehead with the back of her hand and nodded.

"Da Ving is too low."

The sergeant laughed and Rossi shook his head.

"Not?"

The sergeant laughed louder. Ulrike marched over and faced him.

"You help."

"Get back to work."

"I work. I…"

"Beat it." The sergeant grabbed Ulrike's wagging finger and shoved her toward the distant runway. "Lousy Kraut."

"That's enough." Every part of Chance that didn't hurt wanted to strangle the sergeant. The rest of him wanted to help throttle him anyway.

Ulrike glared at the sergeant and walked off in a huff.

Chance went back to Rossi.

"It's useless," Rossi gently whispered. "With fifteen guys we couldn't lift da wing."

"We'll rig something up."

"What?"

"Think of something!"

Chance pushed up on the underside of the wing. It moved a fraction of an inch. Frustrated, he shoved harder and the wing rose further. Surprised, he found Ulrike had returned and was pushing with boney arms. The brunette and redhead followed in short order. In less than a minute, over forty *Trümmerfrauen* joined Chance under the wing. They waited, silently watching the tortured American.

Ulrike said something to the others and turned to Chance.

"I tell zem dat it is your airplane."

"Tell them I need it to get my friend."

"Ver is he?"

"In the East."

Ulrike's sunburned eyebrows rose. She translated to the other women, who whispered, excited.

"Ve help."

"This I gotta see." The sergeant made himself comfortable.

"Tell us venn, please."

Chance looked at the gaggle of German women, swept from every corner of Berlin. They were barely holding themselves up.

"On three."

"*Vertig!*" Ulrike commanded. The women found their places. A sea of reeds pushed up on the underside of the wing.

"One, two, three!" Chance heaved and for a moment nothing happened.

"*Eins, zwei, drei, alle zusammen!*" And the women pushed. They groaned and grunted, "*Zusammen!*"

And the wing lifted.

Rossi charged in with the shoring and fumbled it. Chance was afraid to let go, but did. The wing sank back a fraction, but the *Trümmerfrauen* held. Chance and Rossi got the shoring in place. One of the privates stood, unconsciously moving to help. The sergeant was too stunned to stop him.

"Okay!" Chance breathed and the women relaxed, some sinking to the ground.

Chance and Rossi both stared at the spindly group as they rubbed their aching hands and arms.

"*Danke.*" Chance nodded to each. "*Danke.*"

CHAPTER 53

*Tempelhof Airport,
July 6, 1948, 2:17 P.M.*

Just to have PIE IN THE SKY moving again was exhilarating.

When Chance had flipped on the instruments in the baking cockpit, he still wasn't sure if he was seeing the plane come back to life or watching its final heartbeats. Rossi had been outside with the fire extinguisher, watching number one. Chance punched the starter and the motor had protested before beginning to spin. It caught after two revolutions and Chance felt the vibrating plane push at his back, eager to move. He could see Ulrike and the *Trümmerfrauen* cheering and hopping behind Rossi. He gunned the engine for effect, and to be sure the sergeant got a face full of Berlin rubble. He grinned and then laughed when the scorpion appeared in front of him, scurrying for the terminal.

He left number two with its bent propeller alone and nodded to Rossi. Rossi moved to the other side. Chance had told the *Trümmerfrauen* not to push, but some of them braved the flying gravel to run around to the right wing roots. Rossi kept them from pushing on the flaps and a couple darted behind the right gear to midwife PIE IN THE SKY's rebirth.

It had taken two more lifts by the *Trümmerfrauen* standing on the built-up shoring to get the wing high enough. The right wheel was still in the hole dug under the wing to reattach it. Ulrike and the other women had scraped a short ramp out while Rossi and Chance worked on making PIE IN THE SKY whole again. With the left engine straining, the Dakota wanted to pull to the right badly.

But, the engine, the women, Chance's skill and even Jürgen were just enough.

Chance felt the plane lurch level as it began to plod out of its grave toward the terminal.

"Tower, 5534 taxiing."

"5534, clear to taxi. You're late."

Chance grinned at the jibe.

"Sorry, tower. We've had some trouble with the right gear."

"5534, we know."

Chance lumbered the plane to the far northeast edge of the field to avoid having to cross the busy runway. He had a nagging fear that the right gear would collapse directly in front of some arriving Skymaster. Then the scorpion would claim its victim for sure.

When he got PIE IN THE SKY to the terminal, the lack of right brakes and no right engine made the plane a handful in negotiating the other taxiing aircraft. Chance bounced all over the cockpit, checking right and left, throttling up and back, trying to steer with the tail wheel and sometimes pushing his shoulder against the frame – as if that could help.

He was drenched in sweat when Rossi crossed his arms over his head, telling him to stop. Chance rode in the cockpit as his plane was pushed into the maintenance hangar. Not because it was required. He was just plain beat.

Rossi had asked for the socket wrench for the fourth time before tapping him on the shoulder. The big New Yorker was working on a ladder, stuffed inside the wheel well and hooking up the brake lines.

"Why don't youse go close yer flight plan?"

Chance looked up from the tool cart as if woken from a dream.

"You ain't helpin' here. I'll get one of the guys to spot me da tools. Youse a million miles away."

Chance fumbled around for the wrench. Rossi nudged him with his foot.

"We ain't goin' nowheres 'til tomorrow."

Several heads turned his way when Chance announced his call sign in the flight office. That kind of fame wasn't good. One of the other jockeys was asking him where he got the spare parts as Chance plowed out of the suddenly crowded room.

He didn't plan to go to her. It wasn't conscious. He simply walked out of the airport.

CHAPTER 54

*Soviet Military Headquarters, Karlshorst,
July 6, 1948, 11:22 A.M.*

Ivanoff snapped to attention, keeping the pain from his face. General Zukushev's driver opened the rear door of the ZIS-110 limousine and the pale officer stepped out. Zukushev paused to put on his red banded cap almost in slow motion. He carefully smoothed his tunic before the driver handed him his briefcase. Looking forward at nothing, Zukushev walked at a funeral gait through the stone pillars into the stucco building. Even the porter could not resist a glance as he held the door open an eternity before the general reached it.

Zukushev never looked at Ivanoff. Nor did he return his salute.

Sonya almost did not recognize Ivanoff's desperate tread on her apartment building's stairs. She flew at him as soon as the door opened, clinging to his shoulders until he winced.

"You must leave! The MVD was here looking for Nevada. They think you and he are working together and I was hiding him here."

Ivanoff took her hands off of his shoulders and held them, bending them back slightly.

"Do you not understand?" The scar gaped on her twisted face.

"Yes. I understand."

"You have to move him to another place. If they take him, they can make him say anything."

"When were they here?" Ivanoff's eyes were locked on their target.

"Not more than an hour ago! You must hurry."

Ivanoff held her hands for several seconds more, twisting them painfully and then let them fall. He turned and was out the door in a single step, closing it behind him.

But Sonya never heard him on the stairs. Instead there was a knock followed by the low murmur of voices across the hall. She stood still in the stifling air, listening. Then there was nothing.

Her door opened slowly and Ivanoff stepped back in. He took his cap off and behind him the door across the hall clicked shut. Ivanoff handed her his cap and locked the door.

"So. Why have you lied?"

Sonya's finger lanced toward the door. "That little snitch will say anything…"

"Tell me the truth! Now. You are gambling with both our lives. You cannot save yourself without me." He gripped her neck. She could feel the scars scraping the sensitive skin under her chin. "I know you called to save the American pilot Mitchell."

His hand tightened a little, but Sonya kept fear from her face.

"The first thing you learn as a fighter pilot is not to fixate on your target. You will fly into the ground." His hand tightened again. "Or miss the enemy that kills you."

Ivanoff stroked her hair with his left hand, almost choking her with his right.

"You never asked me the name of the other American. It is an interesting name, do you not think? You know it. Say it."

"Nevada. Chance told me." Sonya met his gaze.

"But you never asked me. When I asked you to find out who was looking for Nevada, you never asked me his name. I never told you or you would have said that." His right hand now held her tightly under her jaw. "There is a man here in Berlin. A sadist. If he does not hear from me in one hour and every hour – whether I am arrested or killed or simply cannot get to a telephone – he will find you. And he is to kill you. His way."

Ivanoff pulled her to the phone and dialed. Sonya could hear two rings before the call went through. Ivanoff said his name and hung up.

"Now, you have one hour more."

It took her fifteen minutes to tell him everything. Everything about Michael and his child. Everything about Max. And almost everything about Chance.

"It will happen tomorrow. But only if Nevada is there."

"How does Max propose to get Nevada?"

"I told Max you are hiding him. I was to convince you to move him. And they would ambush you."

Ivanoff was behind her. She was facing the open window.

"Were they to kill me?"

"Only if you resisted."

He came around to face her.

"And the landing site?"

"I do not know yet. I will find out later today."

"Why would they tell you?"

"They will want to be sure you have not been alerted."

Ivanoff's scars crackled as he tensed. The leathery hand stroked her neck again.

"Remember I will always have you."

This time she heard his boots on the stairs when he left. It was a slow, meditating beat that faded and was gone.

The big MVD man was surprised. The short one was not. Just after midnight, Ivanoff had led them to a house off *Charlottebergstrasse* in northeast Berlin.

"Blindfold him, Comrade Colonel." The little man handed Ivanoff a hood before they entered the basement. "And not a word."

"The men under me are loyal. They were following my orders."

"We know." The little man pulled a leather strap out of his pocket and handed it to the larger one.

Nevada could sense he was outside. The sound was different. This had to be a new trick. He knew he would tell them this time. He hated himself and tried to think of a way, but he knew he could not last.

There was no stinking guard this time. The seat was soft and the car smelled of cigarettes and sausage. They accelerated, but the car rode smoothly, making two sharp turns before there was a cry from up front and a violent impact. Nevada bounced off the seat in front of him and toppled back onto someone riding with him in the back. He could feel shards of glass under his bound hands. Whoever he landed on pushed him off, cursing in Russian. There was a single shot followed by two more. A groan was followed by someone falling on top of him. Raspy breathing by the man on top of him slowed and the man's bulk muffled the quick voices closing on the car. Someone in the car was pleading. Doors opened and the weight of the man on him vanished. Two sets of strong hands yanked him from the car on orders spat in German.

Nevada felt himself carried into the cooler night air again. His feet dragged on the ground. He felt a shoe fall off. Then he was in another car, squeezed between two men with the shoe tossed in his lap. The car's motor was already running and it hesitated as the driver floored the accelerator. A short exchange was silenced by a voice of authority. The car began to swerve and Nevada quickly lost track of the rights and lefts.

This was a very good trick. And a waste of time. He was going to tell them anyway. But something had cracked inside of him now. He was confused at first and then realized he was angry. For the first time in months, he was angry. It was a good feeling. He decided he wasn't going to cooperate anymore – no matter what they asked him.

CHAPTER 55

Spree River, near the Oberbaumbrücke,
July 7, 1948, 12:47 A.M.

The water was colder than he expected.

Before dark, Chance had walked along *der Grobenufe*, a narrow park on the southern and Allied side of the river, shortly after leaving Tempelhof. The stone steps down to where Berliners had strolled aboard the river boats in happier times were still there. He had also spotted the ruined *Brommystrasse* Bridge five hundred feet down river toward the center of Berlin. The span from the east side of the river tilted down into the water like a boat ramp. Unfortunately, the nearby *Oberbaum* Bridge had been a popular crossing point into the East for foot, car and train traffic before the blockade and was now heavily guarded. Chance could see the large lights that would light up the bridge and spill into the river.

Now well into the night, Chance was thirty feet from the Allied side and breast stroking straight across, while the current carried him toward the bombed-out bridge. He had left on his dark shirt, hoping it would hide him in the glare of the Soviet checkpoint. The water smelled of the city – human filth, oil, garbage and decay.

JITTERBUG LIFT

Chance heard a shout on the bridge behind him, but resisted turning around. His face would be a beacon – and easy target – against the black waters. The shout repeated and Chance gulped air thinking he would soon have to dive in this sewer to escape Russian bullets. The shout was answered by a tired voice and the conversation faded in the sound of the water.

Chance's muscles began to stiffen in the cold. The effort of moving in the wet clothes was becoming too much. Chance saw that he was being pushed along by a swift current. He guessed he would reach the bridge span in another few minutes. It occurred to him that he really had no idea how long it would be before he could climb out of the cold Spree. He began to shiver uncontrollably. It struck him that he just might freeze in the river at the height of summer and promised himself that he would plan the next harebrained attempt at suicide more carefully.

The area near the bridge was either blacked-out or ruined buildings. No lights showed. There was just enough glow from the rest of the city to see the half-sunken barge barely breaking the surface about fifty yards ahead. When he had scouted the crossing earlier in the afternoon, the river had been swollen from a recent line of thunderstorms. The river had dropped in the last twelve hours, exposing the barge. It was acting as a check valve, narrowing the current and causing it to race faster away from the safety of the tilted bridge span. Chance realized that, once clear of the barge, he would have to swim like Tarzan to cross the current and get to the broken bridge. He could already see the lights of the next downstream crossing over the Spree. Russian soldiers were clearly visible on the bridge and the river itself was brighter than a Yankee Stadium night game.

The current slammed him into the metal hulk and he kicked off, only to be rammed back into it. He kicked off again and found he was weakening fast. The cold, the crash and fatigue were plotting his demise.

He thought of Sonya.

When things were bad on bombing runs, he would turn to his favorite dream of letting himself down from APPLE PIE at the end of the final mission and just sitting in the grass – if it wasn't raining or they weren't trying to pull out his wounded crew.

He never got the chance to do that, but he used the idea to keep him going. Now he hoped he had something more than a moment in the grass. He also hoped it would be enough.

Chance cleared the barge and began to swim, not trying to hide his stroke. He was late out of the gate and losing ground. The eddy from the current off the barge was pushing him back toward the Allied side and he tore at the water to pull himself east. Suddenly, he was on the other side of the swirl and the eddy reversed, sucking him back into the wrecked barge. A rat's nest of steel cable and jagged, torn metal snared him as the current pulled him under. The water rushing past the barge was hell-bent on filling in behind the tilted hull.

Chance tried to claw his way back to the surface, his lungs starved. A thousand knives and needles cut into his flailing arms and hands. He could see nothing and wasn't sure if he was trying to pull himself up or down. Fighting panic, he stopped. He had a handhold on part of the wreckage. He tried to pull himself up against the current and felt the frayed steel cable snagging his shirt and flesh like talons.

His oxygen-starved mind wandered, looking for an escape from the terror. Chance dragged it back to focus. He had seconds to figure something out.

He swam down. Fighting every instinct screaming from the abyss, he moved downward into the hulk. The current lessened and he felt a deck or bulkhead. He moved, feeling the water trying to yank him back up into the death trap. The surface tilted up, but his brain was shutting down. He was flying with Sonya. She was already there with him and he was free. He felt so good.

A shred of him shook off the vision and pulled on. He found a hatch and went in. The current was gone and the space was empty of debris. He let himself float up and hoped.

His face broke the surface but he was afraid to breathe; afraid it was another hallucination. His lips sensed the air and he gulped it in. It wasn't so much air as a fetid stench. But there was air in it and his mind cleared.

He saw a dim glow above and behind him. A door was high up on the bulkhead. He paddled over to it and figured it was about three feet out of the water. He felt nothing to push off from below, and the bulkhead was bare. No ladder or anything he could see to grab onto. He lunged for the door and fell short. He tried again and was even lower. The cold and oxygen starvation made his efforts pathetic. The water level was also going down. He could not rest.

He thought of Sonya again and put everything on the line. He clawed at the bulkhead, ripping his fingers on rusted metal. It got him an inch more and it was enough.

Chance pulled himself up into the doorway, got his bearings and realized he was facing the Soviet side of the river. The span of the *Brommystrasse* Bridge tilted into the water about a hundred yards away. He let himself rest a few minutes in the warm air. Then he slid into the water and headed for the bridge.

The cold came back quickly, slowing him, but the current was with him this time and he reached the span in a few minutes.

The roadway was tilted steeply and he pulled himself along the sidewalk railing, slipping often. At the top he found a jumble of stone and concrete. Carefully creeping up to the lip of the road, he peeked out into the street. A rail yard cut off the street ahead. The street along the river was empty and no lights shone in any of the buildings above him.

He pulled himself up and stood on the road. His legs were still numb and he stumbled as if drugged, moving north and west. He had no idea what time it was, his waterlogged watch had stopped at ten to one.

She stopped kissing him. His glacial rage had numbed her lips. Her hands moved from the back of his head to the dried blisters on his cheek. Sonya pulled back in her doorway, dark eyes discovering the burns on his face and his soaked clothes.

"My god, what has happened to you?"

"Why the hell didn't you tell me you knew Nevada?"

Chance charged into the apartment, shouldering her out of the way. Sonya closed the door quickly and he grabbed her shoulders.

"I want to know one thing, now."

Her obsidian eyes seemed part of the darkness. He desperately wanted to see inside.

"Did you just want me to get your stuff out or was there something else?"

She winced at his anger and moved away. Two Dakotas had rumbled over the west before she lifted her eyes to face him. By then he was wrestling with two demons from the abyss.

"I wanted Nevada to do the flight for me. But he just wanted money. I contacted Max who would pay for another job. I hoped later he would do something for me." Her head tilted slightly to the left. "If I had told you, would you have wanted me? Would I have been any other use to you?"

"Yes!" The floor groaned as Chance closed the distance in a stride, looming over her. "And if I don't fly for you, can I be anything else to you?"

Sonya lifted her chin and her bottomless, twin weapons stabbed his eyes as she held her ground in front of his convulsing chest.

"In another time. In another life. You would be everything." Pain stretched the scar. "There are things I cannot tell you. Ugly, terrible things."

"You want me to feel sorry for you?! Nevada's in the East, not you."

"You forget where we are."

"You can get out."

"No." The weapons waivered. "Not without you."

Her scent reached him with her warmth, easily detectable despite the warm night. He knew what he was going to do. It was only a matter of time.

"I'll get you out."

The night had clouded over, reflecting lights and turning the city gray. Sonya did not let him pull her from the shadows.

"You did not come here to tell me that."

"I wanted to know why you didn't come clean with me."

"That did not bring you here either." Only half of her face was visible now. "You had another question."

She let the shadow swallow her as a Skymaster thundered over the West. Chance's eyes searched the ceiling as if it held the answer.

"Nevada and I…" Sonya's voice was soft and embracing, drawing him into the darkness.

"Stop it!"

"If you bring him out, it will not change…"

"Shut up!"

Chance's anger recoiled off the fact that she was right. He stood, fists balled, in the only light left in the room.

"You're pretty good at reading me."

Sonya's voice seemed to come out of nowhere. "It is not hard."

"Then someday, you'll explain *this* to me."

He lunged into the shadow and wrenched her toward him. He cut her cry of surprise short with his mouth covering hers. He sensed every curve in her body as he mashed it to his. His arms and hands surged up her back. Buttons rattled on the hard floor. Her body convulsed and he stopped. She twisted her face away. Terror bled from her eyes. Her mouth gaped, afraid to provoke him with a sound. The scar screamed silently.

His breathing slowed to deep gulps of air and he brought his hand up to her face, still holding her securely at the waist. He traced the scar lightly with his fingers.

Something else had come out of the abyss with the hunger, pain and jealousy. Something meant for her.

His lips brushed her cheek as his hand pulled her face close. He let her down and surrounded her with his mass, protecting the shredded front of her blouse with his chest. One hand guided her hips, his other hand slipped inside, wiping away the remains of her clothes.

The dark eyes watched him, as if seeing something for the first time, or at least, something almost forgotten. He was patient, waiting for her to relax, and then join him. He brought her along, shielding her. Surrendering and then surging forward.

Finally, she closed her eyes and gave herself to the long, slow cry.

CHAPTER 56

*Felsenstrasse 17, Soviet Occupied Berlin,
July 7, 1948, 3:45 A.M.*

"Can you be ready to go tonight?"

The tension went out of her, the same way when he kissed her for the first time. Her lips parted and she tilted her head to the left just a little as her shoulders eased.

"Oh, you are a fool. But I am glad we both are," she smiled as she whispered.

"But I don't know how to give you the heads-up. The border is sealed. They've cut the phone lines and I won't have time for another swim when he gives me the word."

She frowned a little, trying to decode *the heads-up.* "Do you know where?"

Chance hesitated. "Don't worry, I'll get you there."

"If you tell me now, I can be sure to get there."

He held her. "Trust me. You'll get there."

"It must not be far."

"I gotta go."

"Yes, it is almost light. There is a bombed building one hundred meters north of here. In the basement you can get to the U-bahn."

"How?"

"At the north end. Promise me you will be careful."

"I will."

He was almost gone and barely heard her.

"I love you."

He stopped, wanting to say a thousand nothings and do everything.

"Go!"

He hurried down the stairs and was out on the street before he realized the distance between them was opening – maybe never to be closed again.

Ivanoff had been walking for fifteen minutes in the warm darkness. As usual, his driver had let him off blocks away. His wounds had been very bad recently. Ivanoff wondered if, in the end, the scars would win, twisting him into a warped troll from a Russian fairy tale.

He saw the figure coming out of Sonya's building silhouetted against the heavy air, dimly lit by a distant streetlight and the breaking dawn. He had already encountered workers hurrying off to factories, bakeries and shops and the man could not compete with the pain. Ivanoff went back to the thought of the coming action.

It surprised him that more of his energy had been diverted to Sonya since this crisis began. Normally, he could shut out the petty distractions, but he wanted to conquer her – own her completely. He chided himself for being so foolish. To do either, he had to survive, his position intact.

With a foot on the steps to Sonya's block, he looked up *Felsenstrasse* after the man. He could barely see him, but something in his hunter's instincts made Ivanoff watch him. There was something wrong about the figure, the purpose with which he moved. There was also something familiar about him.

Ivanoff forgot the pain and found himself moving after the figure. The figure passed under a streetlight and Ivanoff could make out the clothes. They were dirty and stained, but distinctly American.

Ivanoff began to hurry and then stopped as the figure did. The fighter pilot pressed himself against a wall as the figure turned to check behind him. Ivanoff could not believe it, but here was his enemy. A thousand rages exploded in his mind as the figure darted into a ruin. Ivanoff cursed himself for hesitating as his anger overwhelmed him. He drew his sidearm and ran after the figure.

The Russian reached the ruined building in seconds. It was a crater filled with a jumble of concrete and bricks. Farther from the streetlight, he could not detect anything moving. Peering over the edge, he checked to be sure he was not silhouetted against the streetlamp or the now velvet blue sky and listened. To his left he heard the man picking his way slowly through the debris. The prey was unaware of the stalker.

Afraid he would lose the man, Ivanoff moved away from the street along a narrow walkway that had once served as a delivery entrance. One side was a brick arch, half of the tunnel-like hallway. The other side fell off into the crater.

He caught something moving out of the corner of his eye and resisted looking at it directly. The figure was in a shadow. Ivanoff used the night-fighter's trick of keeping the target at the edge of his vision, where it was more sensitive in the dark.

He tried to figure out where the American was heading. Perhaps he was going to hide there, waiting to try crossing the next night. But that would be risky. He raced through what he knew about the neighborhood. None of the Soviet commanders, officials or officers lived there. They were in the nicer suburbs to the east – although one actually lived in the West. It was near the crossing to the West and there was a subway line leading to the city center. A subway line that had run under the river to the west until a bomb had collapsed the tunnel!

Mentally calculating the run of the line, he moved to the north wall of the crater, knocking a lump of concrete loose from the walkway. It tumbled down into the crater. The figure stopped. Ivanoff froze, hoping his dark green uniform would be invisible in the brightening dawn. The figure was still, but his form stood out against the lighter colored concrete. He was no more than twenty-five meters away and down ten. The figure began to move again, searching along the north wall, peeking into openings in the rubble. Ivanoff saw him stop and pull back a board. The Russian lunged to the edge of the crater.

"Halt!"

Chance turned. He got a good look at the Russian and Ivanoff aimed at the man who threatened his position and even his life and was now the key to saving both.

But he still fired.

CHAPTER 57

*Felsenstrasse 17, Soviet Occupied Berlin,
July 7, 1948, 4:13 A.M.*

Sonya had just found it when she heard the shots.

The cracks echoed between the buildings and she jerked. She could see nothing from the window to the north in the near sunrise light. She had heard no police or military sirens, although she had the vague sensation of a shout.

The pre-war touring map showed a familiar area. During the war, the Allies would drop supplies to the Resistance in Germany, flying the "milk wagons" in formation with the bombers to cover their tracks. The Russians also had a favorite secret landing field, not far south of Berlin, flying in spies, weapons and supplies right under Hitler's moustache.

The shots clenched her heart into a stone of pain. A flood of horrible images of what might have happened to Chance crowded her mind, but years of practice made her force the emotions away and detach herself from the situation. She might have only minutes, if not seconds. She would not pack. Dozens of betrayed Resistance fighters had been caught with a suitcase on the bed or in hand during the war. She would take only what she needed – food and water. She dumped out a brandy bottle and poured in what remained of Chance's sugar, swallowing tears and driving herself forward. She filled it from a bottle of water, corked it and grabbed a kitchen knife. She snatched up the map, her coat and was out the door in just over an eternal minute.

She only made it to the first step before the street door opened. The tread of boots was unmistakable. She had been hearing it for three years since another hot, summer day. The rhythm was becoming more and more off-time because of the scars. The boots hurried and she waited for them, planning. The obvious was to dart back into the apartment and hide the bottle and knife. But that was a dead end. It would only make her coming pain have no purpose.

She could smell the cordite from his sidearm even before he reached her. His tunic was tracked with dust. She backed against the door which opened with a squeak, still unlocked.

"He was here. I was coming to tell you."

He smiled. Then he punched her.

Her mind cleared. She was in a heap against the wall. Her hands were cut from the shards of glass and china in the splinters of the shattered shelf. She tried to sit up and hit her head on a dangling shelf. The room writhed like a ship in a hurricane.

She needed a plan, but it depended on what had happened to Chance. Ivanoff had stripped off his tunic and shirt. He had shoved the dresser and bed against the far corner of the alcove that served as a bedroom. All the chairs but one were tossed on top of the bed. The table had been turned over, its legs in the air. It took her dazed mind a moment to realize that it was intentional. She had heard of the Russians using this technique to interrogate captured German officers. It told her Chance was alive and Ivanoff still needed her information. She allowed herself a moment of elation, realizing what this meant – before preparing herself for the worst.

Chance kept to the wall for two reasons. One, it helped him orient himself in the total darkness and, two, it kept him on his feet.

He had smelled the dank air of the subway just before he heard the chunk of concrete fall. He spotted Ivanoff darting for cover, but recognized him only as a Russian officer. A single floorboard lay across the opening to the subway tunnel. It would take him a half second to kick it away and another to dive into the tunnel. He figured the Russian could get off one shot if his reflexes were normal. The odds of Chance being hit at this range by pistol fire were small.

The first shot came an instant after Chance's foot hit the floorboard. He heard it whizz past his head and thwack into the rubble behind him. The Russian's reflexes were much better than normal. So was his aim.

The second shot caught Chance under his left arm as he dove for the opening. It felt like a stabbing punch, knocking the wind out of him. The round broke his rib as it glanced off, stopping just behind his left pectoral muscle. A third shot bounced off the rubble and clattered like a pebble in the darkness.

Chance stumbled into the opposite wall and could see debris from the collapsed building partially blocked the tunnel to the left, which he figured was west. He had less than ten seconds before the sure-shot Russian would be coming through the same opening. Floorboards and beams had collapsed down, forming a shelf holding up the remaining bricks and concrete rubble. He saw where the main floor beam rested on the side of the tunnel wall and tried to shift it. Pain seared through his chest and shoulder, making him feel faint. He pulled his arms down and put his right shoulder to the beam. Chance could hear the Russian picking his way down the crater. He gave it everything and hoped it would be enough. The beam shifted and a tearing sound roared in the tunnel. Dust choked him and the tunnel went dark, bricks bouncing off his leg as he scrambled out of the way of the falling rubble. He kept moving, fighting the growing pain in his left upper chest. He went about fifty yards before stopping. The avalanche had sealed him in. He coughed up dust, pain wrenching him over to the left. He felt under his arm and found the area wet with a large lump a few inches below the armpit.

Experimenting as he went, he found a position for his left arm that was the least excruciating. He had no idea how far he had half-stumbled, half-crawled before he saw a light ahead. Chance hoped the Russian had not seen him come out of Sonya's and moved toward the deserted platform.

Sonya knew it was time again. The burning in her chest was too much. She gathered her strength and pulled with her arms. As before, Ivanoff let her pull herself up only so far. She got half a breath. A taste, but never enough. Her wrists were tied to the ends of the table legs, as were her ankles. She was nude and face down, suspended in the air – the air she needed so badly. Her own weight forced her rib cage open and apart. To breathe she needed to pull herself up, exhausting her muscles and costing more energy than she gained from the breath. It was an elegant, losing battle.

She felt Ivanoff's boot on her back, pushing her down. She gave in again and sagged between the table legs. This was the all-too-familiar instruction phase, where the prisoner learns on a primitive level who is the master, who controls life and pain. The real question would come later. Not too much later. Her former lover would want her weakened, but not on the edge of death. It was a delicate game and she would have to play it carefully. There was a shred of hope. She would cling to that.

It was time for another breath. The torture chamber prepared, Ivanoff was closing the window and drawing the drapes. She pulled at her limbs carefully, hoping to steal a complete, delicious gulp of air. The table gave her away, creaking. Ivanoff pretended not to hear and then she heard him make an animal sound as he brought his belt down on her back. She screamed only a second, swallowing the rest. She would not give him the satisfaction. He would have to work harder.

"Do you realize why I cannot trust you?" His voice was low, the German consonants sounding like an electric arc. She lifted her throbbing head slightly. The map, the brandy bottle and the kitchen knife were on the floor in front of her. The boots moved away. "He risked everything – even the whole mission and his friend's life to come to see you. You must have given him a very good reason. Perhaps he gave you a very good reason to betray me as well."

The apartment quickly became an airless oven. Sonya watched the sweat dripping from her face. Dehydration would be the next enemy. Her body would betray her; its basic, mindless hungers Ivanoff's allies.

"Dear Sonya, you are at the center of all this."

The boots moved around her.

"Where is the landing to be?"

"I do not know," the words seeped out between short gulps of air.

"He has told you. Otherwise why would he have come?"

Sonya allowed herself a smile and the memory of brief pleasure. Then the pacing boots stopped. She tensed for another blow.

"You need only tell me where."

The game was set. That was the key to saving her mission. And she would give in to him eventually. But not too soon. He knew her all too well. Her strength had been a challenge to him at first. Now it would mean hours of agony, buying Chance and the mission time. Then she would surrender. She began to rehearse how it would take place, formulating the words, the emotions. Once that was done, she would flee to that place she had been so many times before. He would go after her there, ripping her to pieces along the way, gutting her. She would let him do that for her mission.

Would she do that just to save Chance? She had known him such a short time. Was he worth it? The answer surprised her and gave her something to take with her.

She tried to breathe again and the belt lashed down. She felt it even in the refuge. She heard him by the wall. He smashed the lamp to the floor. He picked out the cord and tore it from the socket. He leaned down and showed her the bare wires.

"Tell me. Tell me now and I will..." He cut himself off. She had heard it in his voice. There was something still there. Something she could use.

Chance had laid a five dollar bill on the counter of the apothecary. He had recognized the drugstore by the green cross on the sign and the bottles in the window. The girl behind the counter had screamed when Chance brought the bandage to the counter. The entire left side of his shirt was wet with dark blood. That brought an older man, maybe daddy.

"You must go in hospital."

"I need a shirt. Now."

The five dollars had friends by the time the daughter arrived with the shirt. In the back, Chance peeled away the bloody rag and started to wrap the bandage around his chest and shoulder.

"Stop." Daddy pharmacist moved to help. He said something to the girl whose face never lost the look of horror. She returned with a dark bottle. The pharmacist dabbed some liquid around the wound. It burned. He poured more on the gauze and had Chance hold it in place.

"I do dis in de var. Right out zer in der street." He nodded out toward the front of the store.

"Did it work?"

The pharmacist did not understand the question.

"Did they live?"

"Many times not." The pharmacist eyed Chance over his glasses.

"I am a pilot. With the airlift."

"You must not fly. For some time."

He helped the American into the shirt; Chance could not lift his left arm above his waist.

"I do not vant your money." The pharmacist slapped the money into Chance's right hand. "I vill say no ting mit *Polizei*."

Chance was weak from hunger and loss of blood by the time he reached Tempelhof. He was shivering, not able to get warm despite the July sun. He straightened himself and waved lazily at the MP at the gate. Clear of that hurdle, he leaned against the doorway into the flight office. It had taken an enormous effort to walk past a bored MP.

Bluffing a non-comm was one thing, but there would be no fooling gravity and nine tons of airplane.

CHAPTER 58

*Tempelhof Airport, July 7,
1948, 7:38 P.M.*

Chance saw the German walking across the apron toward PIE IN THE SKY and knew this was it. The man had been helped down from one of the scurrying trucks carrying German laborers to unload the endless stream of aircraft. There was something very familiar about him. The blast of the taxiing Dakota almost blew the thin man away like a piece of tissue paper.

Chance had stayed in the cockpit for the three missions they had flown since he got back to Tempelhof. Rossi had known Chance had been stabbed or shot as soon as he saw him.

"Nobody walks like that unless dey's been really hurt. Lemme see."

Rossi had whistled softly as he looked at the wound.

"Bleedin's stopped. Youse is black and blue all over here." He pushed in on Chance's side gently, making him see stars and suck in his breath.

"Youse got a fever and shouldn't be standin' much less flyin'."

Chance had explained why that wasn't going to happen and they worked out a system to have Chance stay in the cockpit during loading and unloading, with Rossi helping out with takeoff and landing. At lower airspeeds, the pilot has to move the yoke more to get the aircraft to respond.

Chance hadn't asked Rossi about flying into the East. Something about the way the big New Yorker talked about how they would divide up the flying time told him that Rossi was in all the way.

The pain and the waiting for the message from Max made Chance forget his concerns about landing on Jürgen's recast landing strut. He had remembered that as he saw the man fluttering toward PIE IN THE SKY. The strut had survived six take-offs and landings. It just had to last two more of each.

Chance could see the man talking to his copilot, motioning toward the front of the plane. A moment later Michael leaned into the cockpit as Rossi trotted into the terminal.

"Good evening, Mr. Mitchell. I am Michael Neumann. We should go immediately."

It was agony for Chance to turn, nonchalantly shake his hand and take the paper with the destination, waypoints and times.

"You show this to anyone else?"

"No. Not even your copilot."

Chance compared the flight instructions with his air chart.

"Are you planning on coming along?"

"Of course."

Chance looked up from his work.

"It is very necessary." Michael leaned on the doorway as if he had run a million miles. "But we should go. Time is very short."

"As soon as my copilot gets back aboard. You're going to have to ride in the back."

Chance ran through the engine start-up list and punched the starter for number one.

Dimitri knew that things had reached a critical point. The man on the phone had been emphatic – almost desperate. The good soldier-spy felt that things hinged on him. He was the center of the battle. But he still hated getting sunburned. It took longer now to cook his leathery skin, but it still cooked.

He had been so proud that he noticed the repaired PIE IN THE SKY parked in the hanger east of the terminal at the north end of the large oval of Tempelhof the day before. He surmised that the big American's plane was about to rejoin the constant flow of cargo into the besieged city. Dimitri had timed the turnaround during an idle moment. He was amazed to see that the four-engine Skymaster had been off-loaded in less than twenty minutes from the time its propellers stopped. The engines restarted and the plane was airborne again in less time that it took him to eat the bread and cheese he had brought for lunch.

A few hours later he was crushed when he lost Chance by the Spree River. He saw the American enter the narrow park by the *Oberbaum* Bridge and Dimitri purposely came around to the other end of narrow strip of grass and weeds, so the target would not realize he was being trailed. But Chance had vanished.

He had given up finding him and decided not to be too self-critical in his report. It was dark after all.

The Russian knew Chance could only come back to the airport by one of two streets and would have to enter the main gate off the *Columbiadamm* from *die Züllichauerstrasse* to avoid the bomb craters. He returned to the street just north of the field to wait out the night.

In the early morning sun he could tell immediately the American was hurt. He had seen more than a few walking wounded during the war – desperate men who had to keep going or die where they fell. Chance leaned to the left as if carrying a heavy load, his left arm swung listlessly. Dimitri was happy that he would not have to be self-critical in his report – there wasn't room for it.

He called in to report that the American was wounded and the voice was very excited. He was to keep watching.

It was late afternoon when Dimitri recognized the Opel that had rescued Chance from its smashed bumper and missing headlamp. What got his attention was the thin man dressed as a laborer getting out of the pre-war luxury sedan about one hundred meters from the entrance to the airport. The man walked to the gate and entered the airport. The auto drove ahead past the gate and Dimitri. He pulled out the smeared notebook and double checked the license number. Dimitri felt this was critical information and made a second call. There was no answer.

His relief that the sun had finally set was interrupted by a jeep squealing up to the gate from inside the airport. Orders were barked and the gate was quickly closed. MPs were running everywhere.

Chance felt the plane shift. McKane filled the cockpit door.

"Kill the engine and both of you come with me."

"What's going on?" Chance made no move to do either.

One hand on the ceiling, McKane leaned over and poked a finger into Chance's upper left shoulder. The pain instantly twisted Chance's smile.

"I can do that all day."

Chance glanced out the windshield. He could just make out the distant taxiway in the last glimmer of twilight and the airport lights. A C-54 taxied slowly by in front of PIE IN THE SKY. He turned left and saw Rossi with two MPs. Two more were moving toward the rear door of Chance's airplane.

He reached for the ignition switches and watched McKane hunch over to head out the cockpit door.

"You know much about flying?"

"No." McKane still faced aft.

Chance left his feet on the brakes and shoved the number one throttle full forward. The engine protested the bad mixture, but accelerated. McKane tried to twist his bulk around in the narrow space and despite his frail size, Michael made it very difficult for him. It took time and gave Chance the second he needed.

The major pushed Michael aside like a snowflake and lunged for the ignition switch as Chance popped off the brakes. Suddenly unfettered, PIE IN THE SKY leapt forward and Chance heard

McKane bounce backwards in the tilted Dakota, unable to find a handhold in the empty aircraft. Michael had been tossed into the copilot's seat and was pinned to the bulkhead.

Chance had to use both hands now and punched the starter for number two with his left hand while he set the flaps for takeoff with his right. The abyss behind him opened up in the pain. He clawed his way away from the edge, holding onto the agony to keep going.

It was Ziewald all over again. This time he had no time but plenty of space – if he could get off the apron without plowing into the scramble of airlift traffic. The Skymaster had moved slightly left, opening a way to the field, but an incoming Dakota was taxiing into the gap. Chance punched the landing lights as number two caught. He set the mixture on both engines by feel and firewalled the throttle. It would be very close.

He could hear banging in the back and knew the door was still open. He mentally crossed his fingers that somehow Rossi had gotten back aboard and was sitting on McKane, but knew it was more likely an armed MP.

McKane's giant fist grabbed the door frame. Chance set the props to takeoff pitch and felt PIE IN THE SKY surge forward. He bounced off of the apron into the grass. Now anything could happen. At least the *Trümmerfrauen* were gone for the night.

McKane's other hand grabbed the cockpit door. The plane bounced up as it crossed the first runway. Michael twisted McKane's fingers, just enough for the giant intelligence officer lose his grip with one hand for an instant. Chance needed five more seconds before he was committed and he hoped that McKane was smart enough to realize it when it happened.

PIE IN THE SKY lurched again. Chance thought of Jürgen and hoped the repaired strut could take the punishment. They were back on the grass and closing on the second runway. Chance caught the landing lights of a Skymaster touching down on his right. A panic of distorted voices rang out of the earphones in his lap. The Skymaster was crossing a mere fifty yards in front of him.

He hauled back on the yoke, the pain forcing the world into a narrow tunnel before his dimming eyes.

A loud whang echoed in the Dakota as her left wheel snagged the radio antenna strung between the tail and cockpit on the Skymaster. It missed the left inboard propeller by less than a foot.

"Pull that lever up!"

Michael seemed amazingly strong as he clawed his way forward and pulled the landing gear lever up.

Chance turned right and headed for the air corridor. The gear motors had just stopped whining when McKane reappeared in the cockpit door. Chance was sweating and kept blinking to focus on the instruments.

"Turn us around and put it down." The major had his best command voice on.

"You don't know how to fly and my friend here only knows about the landing gear," Chance said through his teeth. "So you know the score."

Chance adjusted the mixture badly, causing the engines to miss before he corrected.

"But you're both gonna have to learn fast."

CHAPTER 59

*Felsenstrasse 17, Soviet O1ccupied Berlin,
July 7, 1948, 7:56 P.M.*

Sonya barely heard the phone ring. She knew it was late, hopelessly late.

Ivanoff answered the phone before the second ring. He had been expecting it. He was exhausted from the torture, but she could hear the excitement in his voice. Something had happened. He slammed the phone down. It protested the abuse with a single ding.

The floor shook and she felt the unmistakable steel barrel behind her right ear.

"Where? Tell me now. Where is he going?"

Even her dazed mind could piece together what had happened. Chance was on his way. There was still hope – even if not for her.

"I will tell you nothing."

She summoned her strength and turned her head to face him and his pistol. "Shoot me if you wish."

The pistol trembled and was gone. Then there was a weight on her back. The table legs creaked under the strain of her weight and his. Her ears rang and she opened her mouth. Air was tantalizingly close but unreachable. It would not come. She had tasted hell a few years before. This was deeper yet. Her chest burned and she began to shake. She wanted to scream, but could not. Ivanoff pressed harder.

The room began to shrink in front of her, the edges turning blackish red. The sound in her ears became a siren.

She nodded.

"You will have one breath. Use it well."

The weight lifted and his head was next to hers.

"South. Not far," she gasped more than spoke.

"Where?"

She could barely whisper the name.

The weight was gone.

"Resistance landing field? From the war?"

Sonya nodded slowly, defeated.

Ivanoff was on the phone. Her mind had given up. He ordered his plane. Fully armed. He made a second call, asking for the general. She heard him slam the phone down, unable to get through.

Then nothing.

CHAPTER 60

3,000 Feet over Central Air Corridor, 48 miles West of Berlin, July 7, 1948, 8:21 P.M.

McKane still hadn't said anything. Chance had finished running down the landing procedure, pointing out the landing gear handle, mixture levers and flaps. The major hadn't taken his eyes off Chance except to briefly glance at the main gear lever between the pilot and copilot seats when Chance had pointed it out. Michael had paid attention, too. Missing nothing.

Chance felt good having the bigger man under his thumb for a change. He would have felt better if he wasn't running a fever and could forget the jack-hammering pain under his left arm.

"You know this is kidnapping."

"Close but no cigar. You're a stowaway. And so are you, Mr. Neumann. Sorry."

"We weren't going to stop you. We just wanted to keep Mr. Neumann from being stupid with you."

Chance scanned the air chart and adjusted their course slightly.

"You know, if I were Max, I would know all about this stunt by now." McKane craned over to look at the chart. "I wouldn't be there. Neither would Nevada. Of course, he wasn't going to be there before, anyway. And Max never was going to be there."

Chance slipped the chart back under a rubber band on the yoke, pretending not to hear.

"Nevada will be there, Mr. Mitchell. You can be assured of that," Michael pronounced.

"Will he? I got news for you both. Max Fäder is dead. He has been dead. He was caught and killed by the Nazi's in 1945." McKane looked square at Michael. "I've seen the report."

The engines were out of sync, rattling the airframe. Chance tweaked the throttles and they settled back to a smooth drone.

McKane leaned across the narrow cockpit. "Sonya has been working for the Russians since the end of the war. But she's also been a contact named Anna for the Nazi underground. She made this whole Max thing up. Remember Freddi? Her daddy was Otto Saskin, head of the Berlin SS and she's been a courier helping the bastards escape. You're not very good at this, Mitchell. And you're not getting any better. You're a dupe with an airplane."

Chance leaned out the mixture and checked left to see if the exhaust on Number One had dimmed.

"Take a look out at the engine and tell me when you can't see orange in the exhaust."

McKane glared at Chance who grimaced as he reached for the mixture controls on Number Two.

"Unless you want some Russkie hot-shot to flame us in five minutes." Chance's pain pulled his voice tight.

McKane turned his bulk and peered out into the night.

"What about it, Mr. Neumann?" Chance left his hand on the mixture controls but watched Michael carefully.

"Max is not dead…"

"Have you met him, seen him?"

"Once. Before the war."

"I've never met him."

"Sonya would have nothing to do with Nazis. They killed her father."

"What is your Max going to do about the moon? New moon was yesterday," McKane threw over his shoulder.

The night was clear. A thin crescent hung low ahead of them. Highlights glared off the silvery aluminum airframe.

"It'll be gone in a few minutes. Watch the exhaust."

Chance adjusted the mixture back.

"It's gone." McKane spun in his seat. "Think! Why was Nevada captured? You think the Russkies have troops sitting around in fields all over Germany? They were waiting for him! Sonya set this whole thing up. You're delivering the leader of Free Berlin right into the claws of the Russians in exchange for a Nazi, Chance. They're letting him go, to get Neumann. That's all. PIE IN THE SKY's a good name for this heap. That's all this has been. Pie in the sky."

"But I was not with Nevada, Major. How do you explain that?"

Chance eased the Dakota into a gentle descending turn.

"Looks like I don't have to." McKane glanced out the window as the moon moved around. "Now you've got some sense."

Michael grabbed Chance's arm. "Please, Mr. Mitchell! I have known Sonya since she was a child."

Chance shook off Michael's grip like a dry leaf and brought the nose up on the artificial horizon, flying a bearing of 172.

McKane tried to stand but couldn't in the cramped cockpit.

"You're flying south!"

"Yup. And if you see anything out there, sing out." Chance's voice was hoarse as he flipped off the navigation lights. "Welcome to Soviet airspace."

CHAPTER 61

*Felsenstrasse 17, Soviet Occupied Berlin,
July 7, 1948, 8:07 P.M.*

Sonya realized she was still alive as she felt someone shaking her. Her mind stopped wandering and she found she was trembling, but alone. Still suspended between the upturned table legs, her breathing was not enough to keep her consciousness from drifting in and out of focus. During coherent moments, she would find herself struggling against the strips of cloth tying her limbs to the table legs. The exhaustion and lack of air overwhelmed her and her thoughts melted away like smoke.

She thought her right arm was free, but woke to see it was twisted with the bed sheet strap cutting off the circulation to her hand, making it numb. She tried turning it the other way and found the strap was loose. But her efforts could not bring it over the end of the table leg. She tried pulling on all her limbs at once, springing her upward, but shooting pain up her extremities to her battered torso. It lifted her slightly but she fell back still short of pulling free. She breathed as deeply as she could, knowing she could not function without air. She tried again and the agony was worse as she flopped back down hard. Wood splinters now sawed into her wrists and ankles. They meant more pain, but they perversely gave her a better grip on the table.

Ivanoff could not bring himself to kill her. His sadist would take care of that. Or he would be back when he found out she had lied. It would cost him more time, which was part of her plan. But her tries had become weaker. She knew that there was no other way out. The snitch across the hall would hear any cry for help and fetch Ivanoff. This would be her last chance.

She wrenched her body and yanked against the straps. For a moment she rose up and held her place before gravity started dragging her down. She pulled her right arm back unnaturally over her shoulder and she thought she had failed.

Her face slammed into the bottom of the table top. The impact stunned her. Now she had a chance; her right arm was free, but the effort had come at a cost.

She did not know how much time had passed when she woke again. She had more oxygen, but it only sharpened the pain. It took her an eternity to free her other arm. Then she tried her legs and found it would be impossible without turning over. Hope faded again until she tried pushing out with her right leg, her arms holding onto the table top.

She passed out again before she managed to snap the table leg. It took her only a moment to untie her other leg. Then she began to crawl toward her clothes in the bedroom miles away. She could not figure out why the floor was coming up so fast. Her face hit hard and the floor opened into blackness.

CHAPTER 62

*Soviet Military Headquarters, Karlshorst,
July 7, 1948, 8:15 P.M.*

Zukushev held his pen off the paper, not noticing the blob of red ink dangling from the nib.

"It is out of my hands."

The office was silent except for a murmur of voices from the common area for the adjutants and secretaries. The typewriters sounded like woodpeckers. Zukushev finally raised his eyes to the disheveled war hero.

"Too much has happened, Comrade Colonel. The first incursion. Which you attempted to hide." Zukushev pointed the pen at a photocopy of the doctored phone log. The drop of red ink stained the page where the operator had dutifully logged the calls to and from Ivanoff. "And then the theft of the aircraft. After that, they offered me a way to salvage the situation." Zukushev's eyes wandered away from Ivanoff. "At least partly. But now…"

"I know where they are going, Comrade General! We will catch them. Even the MVD cannot argue with that. We must hurry."

The general put the pen down "So you say."

He slid a sheet across to where Ivanoff stood painfully straight, his tunic still dusty from the bombed-out building.

"Twenty minutes ago, the MVD received a report that a plane was circling south of here. They happened to have a unit in the area watching a convent. Most of the unit went to investigate the plane. There was no plane. When the unit returned to the convent, the two men they had left were dead." He nodded his pale head toward the paper. "Do you recognize the name of the place where the plane was supposed to be?"

Ivanoff could see it clearly in both the Cyrillic and Latin script. Then he had difficulty seeing anything.

Zukushev reached for the phone. "You and I both know that such things do not happen by accident, Comrade Colonel." He paused, still holding the receiver. "I must report this. In deference to your..." He had trouble with the word. "...heroism in the Great Patriotic War, I will wait five minutes."

Zukushev finally met Ivanoff's eyes. "Consider your options carefully, Comrade Ivanoff."

Ivanoff saluted sharply, painfully twisting the scars in his back and goading his anger.

Only one secretary had the stupidity to watch Ivanoff march through. Hypnotized by the predator's eyes, she watched him stride past, his boots echoing like cannon fire in the silence.

His driver still waited outside, but was surprised to see Ivanoff burst out of the headquarters, checking the action of his sidearm. He tore the door open on the Horch before his driver could reach it. The driver snapped to attention and saluted. Ivanoff returned the salute automatically, his burning gaze catching the flickering heat lightning to the west. He ignored the scars and leapt into the front seat.

He would not be denied one final kill.

CHAPTER 63

*Felsenstrasse 17, Soviet Occupied Berlin,
July 7, 1948, 8:31 P.M.*

Sonya knew Ivanoff would be waiting. Her wandering mind was convinced he was calmly waiting just outside the door, letting her torture herself with the fairy tale that she could somehow escape him. She pulled on the door handle as she had thousands of times, but it stuck. She wrenched at it, a small cry of frustration echoing in the hallway. Finally it gave and the night air floated onto her face, clearing her mind.

She looked half-dead as she clung to the front railing of the apartment building. She picked her way down and then fell hard on her knee, twisting her body into a heap on the stone stairs. She looked around for the muzzle and the hunter's eyes aiming it carefully for the base of her skull. Her imagination smeared them together out of the shadows. She was almost disappointed he wasn't there.

The street was silent and the streetlights blacked out. Some light filtered over from distant parts of the city and lightning played silently over the western horizon. The end of the block was another planet away. Coming down the stairs she had thought about dying. The world would end quickly and probably with no more pain. It would end her hopeless struggle. She could never be with Chance. But she wanted the hope anyway. And she was determined not die at Ivanoff's hand. He'd had her on a leash since he had spared her.

She was still for over a minute before an arm flopped down on the step and she tried to get up. She failed twice, then found her feet and stumbled down the steps.

Two sets of arms lifted her powerfully. One held her as a long coat was thrown around her shoulders and an outrageous hat slammed on her head. Sonya struggled against the mad hallucination.

"*Ruhig!* We are your friends," the voice whispered roughly, and Sonya heard the wariness.

"Chance has sent us," a second, smoother voice interrupted.

She looked up into Harald's face as if seeing an angel.

"What has happened to you, dear lady?" Harald was angelically aghast.

"A Russian. He attacked me. We must go. He will be back," she gasped, the warning sapping her strength.

"Enough!" Peter was not good at being an angel and pulled Sonya forward, her feet dragging on the pavement.

"The beast. Try to walk as fast as you can. We have a car nearby." Harald was still pleasantly proud of their heroics.

Peter and Harald carried most of her weight, her new hope bore the rest. They had gone several meters when Sonya stumbled, a new panic seizing her.

"My god, he always comes this way. Always!"

"We shall take care of him," Harald bragged.

"He is a Russian officer and armed."

Harald swallowed his bravado and Peter went on alert.

"Faster!" Peter commanded.

"If you would, please." Harald was still polite.

They reached the southern end of *Felsenstrasse* at the same time Ivanoff raced around the corner on the opposite side of the wide street. He careened across to the curb in front of Sonya's building, not fifty feet from the trio. He was fixated on wrestling with his next task. Part of him worried he would not have the courage to shoot Sonya. The rest of him focused past the pain as he climbed from the Horch, pistol in hand.

The streetlights came on suddenly, eliminating the sheltering shadows. Ivanoff spotted the trio down the street with Harald gaping back at Ivanoff's uniform and drawn sidearm.

Then Harald laughed. It was as if one of them had told a joke. He slapped Sonya on the back. It turned her away from Ivanoff and propelled her toward the car, now just thirty meters away down the side street.

"You are too funny, *liebchen!* Just too funny." He laughed drunkenly and loud, resisting the temptation to see how his performance was being received. Peter could not resist and kept looking over his shoulder at Ivanoff who was slowly moving down the sidewalk toward them. They turned the corner and lost sight of Ivanoff.

"Keep going past the car." Peter urged them on, keeping them ahead of the Russian.

Ivanoff reached the corner just thirty feet from where Harald was putting on his best party drunk, weaving just enough. He stared at the trio. Harald's acting was too much for Sonya and she tripped, falling forward. Peter lost his grip. Harald was off balance from his act and Sonya's extra weight began to drag him down. He barely got a foot under himself and hauled her back up straight. Peter caught up with them and glanced back at Ivanoff. They were well past the car and even if they darted back to it, the Russian would reach it before they did.

Ivanoff took a step toward them and his scars burned. He turned sharply and disappeared down *Felsenstrasse* toward Sonya's apartment.

"He's gone," Peter whispered. "Get to the car."

Harald dropped the curtain on the performance of his life and brought Sonya around as Peter raced to the old Mercedes. He was now eager to leave and not so gentle with Sonya.

They were almost at the point they were going to sneak over the border before he stopped shaking.

And Sonya gave them a new destination.

Standing in Sonya's apartment, Ivanoff knew he could call in an alert, but no one would listen to a dead man. He was halfway down the stairs when he realized there was still a way to have his kill. And several more.

CHAPTER 64

800 feet over Apolda, Soviet Occupied Germany, July 7, 1948, 8:37 P.M.

Chance had been watching the heat lightning ignite the western sky for the last half hour. A line of severe thunderstorms was boiling up in the July heat and beginning its onslaught to the east. The solid wall of flickering orange flashes meant that there was little hope of avoiding it.

"There's something all lit up off to the left." McKane had his face pressed to the windshield.

Chance found the pool of light easy to spot. He brought the wheel over and began a slow turn to avoid the town just a kilometer to the southwest.

"We're coming to 068." Chance answered McKane's curiosity so the big Major wouldn't burn a hole through the compass by staring at it.

"East," McKane spat.

"East north east," Chance corrected. "This leg is another forty-five minutes. Let's go over the landing and takeoff procedure again."

"Aren't you afraid I'll learn how to fly this thing and turn you into 180 pounds of pain?"

Chance grinned at the now familiar bluster. "Not a chance."

"That I'll learn to fly or that I'll make you wish you were never born?"

"Both."

"Major McKane, I will do everything in my power to prevent you from doing that." Michael glared unafraid from cockpit at the bulk of the Army officer.

McKane snorted at Michael's reed-thin frame.

"I have already survived much."

"Alright. Everybody play nice," Chance cut in. "Landing, from the top. Mixture back to auto rich…"

They finished the entire procedure in two minutes. McKane showed he was a quick study, only forgetting how to put the props into full fine, which Michael was all too pleased to remind him about.

"We may have walked away from that one. We would have been going pretty slow by the time we hit the trees."

McKane still didn't look pleased. "Let's do it again."

Chance was happy the Major was at least practical. But he frowned anyway.

"Was it your idea to dump the rubble around my plane at Tempelhof?"

"No. It was somebody who needs this plane more than you or Mr. Neumann."

Chance thought about that for a moment and gave up with a shrug.

McKane snorted a laugh at Chance's ignorance. "You may have forgotten about them in all this. Took me a while to figure it out." McKane looked back at the lightning chasing them, now bright enough to light up the cockpit. "It's easy when you think about it. The most powerful force on earth. Mothers." The seat squeaked as he bore back into a surprised Chance.

"*Trümmerfrauen.*"

CHAPTER 65

Soviet Air Base Werneuchen, Soviet Occupied Germany, July 7, 1948, 9:42 P.M.

Ivanoff's weapon was cleaned and ready.

He assessed the power it gave him as he strode across the apron. He still controlled it for at least one more night. The slow-grinding Soviet Military system would emasculate him of it, leaving him a cripple in a rough green uniform with a trinket on his chest.

They would even strip him of that. His record would be "corrected." No one whom Stalin had blessed could have screwed up so badly. In any court martial – if there was one – his military record would be "lost" or "immaterial." With a wave of his hand the judge would wipe out years of service, sacrifice and agony.

What had he done wrong? Had his dalliance with Sonya distracted him? Or was he up against a superior foe? He ground his teeth thinking he couldn't even hit the man with a pistol at close range.

His rage sliced back to Sonya. He had had her, but never possessed her. Her black eyes defied him out of the shadows. She had stared down his weapon and lied. Lied to save the man who did truly possess her.

JITTERBUG LIFT

The radio crackled over the dynamotors whining in the YAK-9U. Control gave the special weather warning again. Thunderstorms threatened heavy turbulence, hail and lightning. All but emergency flight operations had been grounded after 2130 local time.

Ivanoff saw a lightning flash from behind him glint off his weapon. It was time to use it before it was stolen from him forever. Fortunately, the Soviet Military system moved just slow enough. No word of his disgrace had reached the airbase sixteen miles northeast of Berlin. He punched the starter. The three-bladed propeller began to turn as the starter motor screamed. The 12-cylinder Klimov VK-107A engine thundered to life, rocking the airframe and surging forward like a beast against its chains.

He did not ask for permission to taxi, he *told* the tower he was taking off. The tower warned him about the weather and Ivanoff retorted with an announcement that he was rolling. A black car raced away from the hanger area as a new voice from the tower ordered him to stop at once.

Jets of orange lanced the night from his exhausts as the huge fighter roared down the runway. As soon as his nose came level he fired a quick burst. The tracers blazed down the runway, a ray of hot metal that fended off the puny car. It bounced into the grass and impotent flashes of pistol fire sparkled from the windows.

Ivanoff jerked back on the stick and was quickly at five hundred feet. He checked his fuel gauges. Four hundred liters meant he could find any enemy within 675 kilometers.

He was not concerned about coming back.

CHAPTER 66

*700 feet, 22 miles west of Lommatzsch,
Soviet Occupied Germany, July 7, 1948, 9:48 P.M.*

Chance checked his watch again and noticed his shivering was worse.

"We gotta climb."

To avoid low hills, they had to come to 1000 feet fifteen minutes before making the turn at the rail line running north out of Lommatzsch. Chance's air chart showed they would be coming *up* to the minimum safe altitude for this part of Germany. They had been flying 100 to 200 feet below it since leaving the air corridor, and the same low hills had been hiding them from the Soviet radar net.

"Put the mixture to rich." Chance pointed at the control when McKane hesitated, a punch of pain under his left arm reminding himself that he was still very much wounded. He pulled back on the yoke and pushed the throttles forward.

The small, flickering yellow dot on the radar screen in Sachsen went unnoticed for almost thirty seconds. The Russian lieutenant on watch was more intent with Allied traffic near the border, over one hundred miles to the west. The traffic had dwindled and now a ghostly smear showed the front lines of the approaching bad weather. He waited only for the sweep to show the blip twice in a row before reaching for the phone.

Ivanoff was hunting a single deer in a dark forest and he knew it. The odds of him spotting a low-flying Dakota in over 120,000 square kilometers of night sky was close to impossible and getting closer by the minute. The YAK bounced as if hitting boulders. Giant bubbles of steamy air were boiling up in the unstable sky ahead of the storm front. They slammed into Ivanoff's fighter several times a minute, throwing the artificial horizon and temporarily disorienting him in the moonless sky. They were the opening skirmishes in the coming battle that only a fool would fly in. The lightning would illuminate aircraft for a split second, but also night-blind pilots, dulling their retinas like a giant photoflash. The thermals were throwing up clouds, lowering the ceiling and making the sky a jungle that could hide a fleet of Dakotas. The rain and turbulence would also blind radars.

Once he found his prey, Ivanoff could not let them slip away.

Radio static had been building on the Control frequency. A chorus of frying pans spattered the spectrum with explosions and crashes of energy.

"Alpha 28..." the transmission began before being trampled by a megawatt blast of noise.

Ivanoff strained his ears despite the painful static. The Alpha call sign was used for fighters. Control might be vectoring the hunters to him. They would know he was listening and it would be in code. But he knew the codes and would be more than a match for anyone stupid enough to come after him.

"Control, Alpha 28." The other aircraft was still in the air. The drone of the fighter's engines was clear on the strong signal.

"Alpha 28 say your position."

Ivanoff realized Control was already having trouble seeing what was in the air in the clutter from the thunderstorms.

"Control, Alpha 28. I am ten miles east of Beacon 45."

There was a long pause. Ivanoff checked his air chart. The other fighters were far to the east. Anything closer to the thunderstorms was already on the ground.

"Alpha 28, come — bearing 236. Unid—aircraft fly—bearing 070. 20 kilo— 120 degrees—Leipzig. Repeat..." The rest of the transmission was lost in the static.

Ivanoff quickly sketched the vectors on a chart, the lines jagged from the pounding turbulence. He pulled a high-g turn, shoving the throttle forward.

"Control, what is altitude and speed of aircraft?" he grunted into the microphone. He was giving himself away, but he would not be denied his kills.

"Al—28— un— fly..." Control confused him with the other flight but the transmission was mutilated beyond recognition.

He didn't need their help. It was the same pattern: the aircraft was flying low and had ballooned up to clear the hills southeast of Leipzig. He assumed it was the Dakota and calculated the intercept. It would take him fifteen minutes to reach it. He would have to guess the wind and, with the growing cloud cover, the planes could completely miss each other only a quarter mile apart.

But he had already beaten slimmer odds.

Chance was trying to keep track of the train signal lights in the rain showers and lightning. PIE IN THE SKY was groaning and creaking in the violent air.

"There they are again."

McKane shot a glance at him. Even in the darkened cockpit, pain twisted on Chance's face with every bump of violent air. They had turned several minutes before, over a small town, and they picked up the train signals immediately. Chance was counting the villages along the line to navigate. But more than one shower had made them almost lose the line. On top of that, the cloud base was lowering, forcing them closer to the invisible ground. Only the train signals gave them any sense of where it was. Chance estimated they were at about 200 feet, while McKane was convinced they would be smelling manure any second.

Rain exploded on the windshield as the plane hit a severe downdraft. They had been racing the edge of the weather until they turned north and now they were flirting with the ragged edge of the storms.

"Was that the one we turn at?" McKane seemed worried.

"Not sure." Chance was worried. There would be no go-around on this flight. One delay, any poor navigation or missing a light and the game was over. "Damn. We might have missed the last one."

"Should we turn around?"

"No, let's assume we missed it. Look for the light. We'd never find the landing area without it." Chance wasn't enjoying McKane being helpless anymore as he brought the plane onto the approach heading. Michael wasn't much better, but he seemed to be willing them forward with some hidden strength.

They scanned the darkness. Chance wondered why he hadn't given up long ago. He could have been back in New York by now – hating himself.

Lightning blazed to the left, reflecting off the clouds and turning the world an electric blue.

"Shit, we're in the clouds again."

McKane tensed as Chance pushed the Dakota lower, the yoke twitching to keep the plane at the proper attitude.

"There! See it!" Michael screamed.

Chance forgot his wounds as their goal flickered brightly ahead of them. "What's our heading?" He refused to take his eyes off of the dot.

"319. Plus or minus. I don't see… No. I got it! I got it!" McKane was actually getting excited.

Chance banked PIE IN THE SKY left, the nose pitching up suddenly as they hit an updraft. He keyed the radio on the pre-arranged frequency.

"Nevada, come in."

Nothing but static came over the radio.

CHAPTER 67

*Jüterbog, Soviet Occupied Germany,
July 7, 1948, 10:01 P.M.*

Nevada wasn't going to fall for it this time. But he had to hand it to them. It was a very good trick.

Ernst keyed the microphone in the cab of the small truck and shoved it at his face.

"Answer him!"

The lightning distracted the American. After months of darkness and silence, the world had exploded back. The sun had hurt his eyes and the real food had made him queasy. Now he imagined that he heard a child crying.

A mile away and 500 feet above, McKane looked very smug.

"Let's get the hell out of here."

They had heard the signal come up and someone said something, but Chance wasn't sure he was hearing anything but ghosts in the static.

"It's a trap. Let's go." McKane loomed in the cockpit.

Chance keyed the mike again. "Nevada! It's Chance. Answer me or I'm not going to land!"

Again the signal came up, but there was no voice.

"Now!" McKane thundered louder than the storm.

Chance put the microphone down and picked up the air chart. He almost didn't hear Michael.

"The Russians have had Nevada for three months. He cannot believe he is free. He cannot trust anyone."

"He's not there, Chance!" McKane tried to drown the raspy voice.

Chance turned to Michael. Lightning flickered off his hollow face and seemed to be coming from inside his eyes. Michael pulled up his sleeve. The tattoo was dark against his pale, thin forearm.

"I know about these things. Tell him something, a secret only you two would share."

Chance picked up the microphone again. "Jennifer in Romsey. I'm the only one that knows about her besides you and her."

"Who the hell is that?" McKane spat.

"Mayor of Winchester's granddaughter."

The signal returned briefly, but there was no voice.

"Try something else! Something that changed your lives," Michael's voice wavered as the turbulence threatened to bounce him off the ceiling.

"We're out of time!" McKane was already on the ceiling.

Chance keyed the microphone again.

"I killed Jimmy Vernon." Chance paused, his voice ragged. "I hit him in the head with the fire ax."

McKane sat back down. The only sound was the convulsions of PIE IN THE SKY.

The signal came out of the static. Nevada's voice was soft, but clear.

"You had to, Buddy. You couldn't save him. You can't save everybody." The signal dropped for a moment and came back. "But I was beginning to think you had forgotten about me." Nevada's voice became stronger with every word and a weak laugh came at the end.

"Sit tight. We'll be down in a minute." Chance put the microphone away. "Start looking for the red and green lights."

Thunder was audible in the cockpit an instant after another flash of lightning.

"Are we gonna be able to take off again in this?" McKane had already moved on to the new obstacle.

"Ask me after we have taken off." Chance pointed just left of the nose. "Bingo! Got the green. And the red! Damn! We're too high! Flaps! Mixture!"

The two lights shimmered in the rain soaked windshield. Ahead, three bright white lights brightened out of the dark. Beyond them two dazzling points flashed at the threshold of the runway – a generous name for the stretch of wasteland they were going to land on.

Chance pulled the throttle back.

"Full flaps. Shit!"

The plane was all over the sky. Updrafts and downdrafts collided in shearing winds that wrestled and tossed PIE IN THE SKY like a broken toy.

"Gear!"

Chance locked onto the two lights at the end of the landing area. They gave him a horizon for the last, critical seconds. The gear motors whined and Chance resisted thinking about Jürgen again.

"Brace!"

McKane shoved his arm on the top of the instrument panel. Michael carefully searched for a place in the doorway. Chance felt for the fire extinguisher releases. If he pulled them, he was just trying to live another day before going to a Russian prison.

Chance pulled the yoke toward his chest and throttled back. McKane played his part and put his free hand on the propeller pitch controls.

They hit hard, a downdraft blindsiding them at the last second. The plane dug in and slowed, the nose pitching down. Chance yanked the yoke back. At this speed, it barely made the difference and PIE IN THE SKY settled back on her tail.

"Unlock the tail wheel."

McKane searched for the lever and Michael lunged forward and pulled if for him. The airspeed fell off the dial at 30 knots. Chance pushed his toes forward to brake and was relieved to see there were no trees. He spun the plane around and stopped with the propellers turning over slowly.

McKane scanned the soaked darkness.

"I can't see anyone."

CHAPTER 68

*Jüterbog, Soviet Occupied Germany,
July 7, 1948, 10:10 P.M.*

"I must say I am surprised to see you in this weather. You fly with the angels." Ernst blinked away rain splashing his face. He had surprised them by banging on the rear door while Chance, McKane and Michael were searching the night from the cockpit.

"I'm surprised to see me, too. Where's Nevada?" Chance blocked the rear door of PIE IN THE SKY.

The German turned to the darkness. "Nearby."

"Let me see him."

"Patience, Herr Mitchell."

"Let me see him. Now."

"Or you will leave?"

The rain and darkness did nothing to hide the derision in the German's eyes.

"Yeah." Chance started to close the door.

"Moment." He used the German accentuation on the second syllable. "Please."

Ernst waved into the rain and mist. The Opel Admiral squatted about seventy feet away in the mud. The rear door opened and Nicki switched on a flashlight, shining the beam on the figure next to him. Nevada winced in the intense light.

Chance's heart wanted to climb out of his throat.

"Nevada!"

Nevada reacted sluggishly, coming alive.

"Chance!" He still sounded drugged.

Chance forgot his wound and climbed down. Ernst stopped him with a hand on his chest.

"In time, Herr Mitchell."

"What's wrong with him?"

"The Russians are terrible hosts. But he will be all right with some rest."

Chance moved toward the car again and the German's steel baton jabbed painfully into his left side, making Chance stop. Nevada said something but it was lost in the wind. The flashlight went out as the door closed.

"It will be soon. This rain is not good for the ground, not?" Ernst looked down.

Chance could see his feet sinking into the dampening sandy soil. The sound of a truck pulling from behind the Opel and struggling through the muck just made it over the wind and thunder. Ernst's baton went immediately back into his pocket. Chance climbed back aboard PIE IN THE SKY, using his right hand only, which was painful enough.

The large BMW stake bed heaved its way over the uneven ground, its headlights hooded. Chance stole a glance toward the cockpit. The door was closed. McKane and Michael were being good boys. The truck pulled up near the tail and Ernst had a brief exchange with the driver and waved the truck back until its tail was near the door to PIE IN THE SKY.

Three young men hopped down from the truck and quickly began to unload the crates into the aircraft. Chance thought it was odd that the crates were sturdy, like those he had used to haul heavy machine parts into Berlin. But the men moved them easily. Almost as if they were empty.

"Tell them to tie them down. It's going to be rough going back."

Ernst smiled. "Of course." He moved to climb aboard.

Chance hesitated and stepped back. Ernst put one foot on the mud-slick floor.

"It is good to get out of the rain." He reached up and grabbed Chance's left arm to pull himself back up. The pain on the American's face told him everything.

"You are injured?"

"Pulled a muscle the other day. I'll be fine."

Ernst smiled again and looked at the crates. Chance thought he was very interested in them. An exchange of German and the crates were lashed down tightly to the cargo ties. One of the young men asked something and Ernst shrugged.

"He would like to see the cockpit. He has never seen an American aircraft."

"No dice. If that's all of it, let's get Nevada aboard."

"It is not all of it. We must wait a short time." Ernst smiled again. Chance did not like that the tall German was much too pleased with himself.

"No. *Bitte, Verzeihung.*" Chance looked straight at the young man.

The young man was surprised with Chance's German. Ernst smiled again and cocked his head toward the door. The young German nodded and hopped out. A moment later the truck started and rumbled off into the storm.

"How much longer?"

"A few minutes."

Nicki came to the door and whispered something to Ernst. Ernst was not happy. He replied with a terse order. He turned back to Chance and never smiled again.

"Remain here at the door, Mr. Mitchell. Our guests have stopped across the field and are looking us over. They have much reason to be afraid."

Rain sounded like marbles on the skin of the Dakota.

The lightning was flashing more often and the thunder rumbled closer. Ernst was closer to the door and heard the truck first. It was not the BMW, but a smaller Mercedes truck with a covered bed picking its way across the rolling ground, its engine racing as it slipped in the mud. Lightning made it easy to see as it came around from the tail of the plane. It stopped and, for a long minute, nothing happened.

"What are they waiting for? This ain't gonna let up."

Ernst did not react to Chance, but watched him carefully, his hand moving slowly back to his coat pocket. No lights showed from inside the truck.

The passenger door opened and two figures climbed down. They wore fedoras and rain coats. A third figure got out of the driver's side, leaving the engine running. All three studied the plane for a moment, standing still in the rain. Then one barked something to the others in German and they began to approach PIE IN THE SKY, one struggling to hold an umbrella over the center man. The center man could have carried his own umbrella, but he was carrying a briefcase with his only arm.

Chance had seen enough officers to recognize the military bearing of the three men. They marched in step toward the rear door, with the lightning keeping time. They looked inside to where Ernst and Chance stood.

"*Schön guten Abend,*" the man with one arm clipped out smartly.

"*Abend.*" Ernst was more relaxed, but Chance saw something new in his penetrating eyes. He could not quite place it as fear, respect or both.

The maimed German turned to Chance. "Good evening. I am Martin Lauter. Will we be able to fly in this weather?"

"It'll be rough."

Lauter nodded and ignored assistance from the umbrella bearer in climbing aboard. He straightened inside and resumed his military posture after removing his hat and shaking off the rain. About fifty, he had close-cropped gray hair and a starfish-shaped blue blotch just forward of his left ear, probably earned at the same time he lost his left arm. He smiled, actually more of a grimace, showing bad teeth under a precisely trimmed pencil-line moustache.

"Open the crates." He was almost laughing as if there was a joke in them.

Ernst produced a crowbar from somewhere and jimmied the lid of the largest crate. The musty smell of ten years was detectable in the damp air. Ernst pulled back a coarse blanket, revealing a white cloth with stripes along the edges. Chance could see it held something like two incendiary bombs and was surprised when Ernst pulled back the cloth.

Blue velvet with gold fringe encased the two masses. In the lightning, Chance could see the Hebrew script embroidered in gold on the velvet. Separated by padding was the base of some other gold object.

Lauter noticed Chance craning.

"Jewish relics." He said 'Jewish' as if it was a disease. "They do not weigh much." He cocked his head toward the cockpit. "Perhaps Herr Neumann would like to come out and see them. And find his child."

Chance stared at the man for a long time. McKane had a lot of it right. Chance was behind the curve and falling back fast. Flying upside down in fog was no problem. But he was facing an obvious Nazi on the run who was asking about the child of the leader of free Berlin, a Jew sitting in the cockpit of his plane loaded with Jewish religious stuff sitting in some muddy field in the Soviet Sector.

"Michael," Chance's voice finally boomed over the crates.

The cockpit door opened and Michael slid out, careful not to open the door any wider than he had to and closing it behind him. He moved aft, pausing briefly at the open crate. As he passed Chance, tears were on his cheeks.

Lauter pointed outside, his face set. Michael sat on the floor and painfully tried to get down, but none of the other Nazis helped him. Chance pushed past Lauter and helped Michael from inside the plane. Chance climbed down after them, regretting it instantly as his wound throbbed. Lauter got down with some effort, refusing the help of the younger Nazis.

They walked to the back of the Mercedes truck. The tarp over the bed made a black cave. In the lightning, Chance could just make out the shoes and legs of several people.

"Which one is yours, Neumann?" Lauter commanded.

"Sarah?" Michael almost screamed above the storm. "Sarah! Come here, please."

There was a murmur of voices – children's voices.

"Do not be ridiculous, Neumann. They were infants when you gave them up."

Lauter barked an order and the umbrella bearer lit up the interior with a flashlight.

Seven children, four boys and three girls, ranging in age of ten to twelve years old, cowered from the light.

Michael whirled on Lauter. "How do you have them? Where is Max?"

"Which one, Neumann? Quickly. We must go." Lauter was used to giving orders.

Michael seemed to grow a foot. Chance thought he was shivering with the cold, but Michael's face told him it was rage. Raw, animal rage.

Then it vanished to a smile.

"All of them."

"That was not the agreement!" Lauter was also used to having his orders obeyed. "You pick one and the rest stay! That is the arrangement. One child for each group of us."

An argument erupted among the Germans, but Michael cut it short.

"*Alle! Zusammen!*" his voice carried above the storm. "I made no agreement with Nazis. All of them. Together!"

"That is unacceptable. Sonya agreed to this." Lauter waved Michael away. "Pick one or they all stay." He turned to Chance. "We shall go."

Chance stood his ground. "Hang on. You forget whose airplane you're going in. If he says they're his, then they all go." He pointed his finger right at Lauter's dripping nose. "Or you stay."

Chance turned toward the plane and then whirled back on Lauter. "You'll be lucky if I let you go. I don't like Nazis and I especially don't like Nazis using kids to bargain their way out for themselves or their friends."

"Then this Nevada does not go either."

Chance turned to Ernst. "I'm tired of getting shoved around here. I'm taking Nevada and the kids. If you try and stop me, you're going to have to kill me." He bore back into Lauter. "And then nobody gets out."

Ernst did not move. Lauter straightened and then shrugged. "As you wish. The weather is getting worse and we have wasted much time." He strode off toward the rear door of PIE IN THE SKY.

Lauter and his acolytes did not help Michael or the children aboard. The children were difficult. Some resisted. Michael quieted them with a soft, fatherly tone, telling them they were going for a ride or cooing a quiet word. One girl had been crying and Michael asked for her name.

"Maria."

Chance saw Michael force a smile and the frail man seemed to have the strength of McKane as he hefted her aboard. Chance stayed outside.

Lauter pushed his way back to the door. "Where will you have us sit?"

"Right here." Normally, Chance would have them forward of the cargo, but he wanted nobody wandering up to the cockpit just now. "The children go forward."

The younger, umbrella man was aboard and heard the exchange. He made a disapproving noise as he scanned the cold, dimly lit cabin with its floor smeared with a paste of flour, coal dust and mud.

"*Aber...*"

His protest was cut off by a wave of the leader.

"We shall be quite comfortable. Let us be off." He sat down on the metal floor and the umbrella holder and the driver followed.

"Hang on. I'm getting Nevada." Chance grabbed a flashlight from its holder by the door.

PIE IN THE SKY'S twin motors were still turning over about 180 revolutions per minute, but the sound of another motor reached Chance. It rumbled like a plane, flying low. He tilted his head, trying to locate the sound. But the storm and the Dakota's engines made it impossible. Rain was flooding into his ears.

"Herr Mitchell!" Ernst's voice came out of the darkness. He was just outside the door and pointing north, away from where Nevada was.

In the lightning, Chance saw a figure coming across the open ground. He began to run.

CHAPTER 69

*Jüterbog, Soviet Occupied Germany,
July 7, 1948, 10:38 P.M.*

"What are you doing here?"

Sonya cried in pain as Chance pulled her to him with his good arm. He found he was holding her up. She still wore the ridiculous hat Harald had put on her in Berlin.

"What's the matter?"

Sonya gulped air. "It is nothing. I will explain later. Ivanoff... the Russians know you are making the flight tonight. There may be not much time."

Chance brought her the last few steps toward the plane, the mud and her weakness making her slip.

Ernst shook his head with a smile and helped Sonya aboard. She turned to Chance. His mind was trying to sort out a thousand little facts and nuances. Somewhere from the abyss was a warning cry. He had learned a long time ago to always listen to that voice. But time was short; the storm was becoming a riot.

Chance raced toward the Opel. The door opened and Nicki stood outside, squinting in the rain.

"He is very weak. It may..."

The rest was lost in the roar of the diving YAK and ripping noise of the nose UBS machine guns. The bullets tore through the hood of the Opel, sending sparks everywhere. Nicki's head was obliterated and the body toppled backwards as an orange fireball blossomed from underneath the car. Chance grabbed Nevada and pulled him into the mud.

"McKane! Go! Go!" Chance screamed at the plane.

He could see the YAK's twin exhausts disappearing in the rain as he got to his feet. A fragment of his mind counted the seconds before the fighter could finish the turn and come back for another run. The pilot would have the burning car to line up on and illuminate the field.

Nevada was struggling to get up. Chance grabbed him under the arms and pulled him free of the mud. He wasn't sure where the YAK was, the wind was twisting the sound.

Ivanoff was amazed he had found them. He had calculated that Sonya had told him a half-truth and knew that there were only a handful of resistance landing sites close enough to Berlin for her to escape. He flew the last radar vector back and forth, almost giving up hope when he spotted the tiny lights in what should have been wasteland. His delight was confirmed when the Opel blazed up and he saw PIE IN THE SKY, propellers spinning nearby. But he was already committed to his run on the car and could not veer over to catch the Dakota.

The blazing car became pulsing blur in the rain and clouds as he made his turn. But he was confident he could easily line up on the light again.

PIE IN THE SKY was taxiing slowly, moving away from the burning car. Nevada was weak and slipping in the muck. There was no way he and Chance could catch the plane. Chance moved toward the Mercedes truck, still idling where the Germans had left it.

He heard the YAK screaming toward the field. He threw Nevada into the passenger side of the truck and hopped into the driver's seat. It took precious seconds to find the gear lever and clutch. The YAK was close as Chance got the truck moving.

He held Nevada with one hand while ignoring the torture of steering with his wounded arm. The YAK opened up right over him. The shells tore up the ground and converged on the Dakota. He saw the flashes as the tracers hit the fuselage between the wing and tail, angling across the opposite wing. No fire showed, but he knew PIE IN THE SKY and those onboard had been hit badly.

Chance hoped McKane wouldn't panic and think he could do more than taxi at about ten miles an hour. He also began to calculate just how much of the landing area they were eating up. He floored the accelerator and raced ahead of PIE IN THE SKY, honking the horn to get their attention. The rear door was still open but he couldn't make out anyone inside. He slid the Mercedes sideways to a stop about one hundred feet ahead and to the left of the lumbering plane and ran around to where Nevada was trying to get out. His legs were on the running board and he was leaning back on the bench seat.

"Can you make it, buddy?"

Nevada only shook his head weakly. Chance gauged the run to PIE IN THE SKY. The plane would pass them in seconds.

"Go," Nevada gasped out.

"Okay." Chance began to move without thought. He bent down and put his wounded shoulder into Nevada's gut and grabbed his copilot's left arm with his right hand.

"Not without you."

And he lifted Nevada with a scream.

His first step doubled the pain and the abyss yawned below him. He felt he was trying to run uphill in the mud as the chasm widened. The plane was coming even with them. Chance saw a hand at the back door and the holes stitched along the roof. He lost his footing for a split second and went down hard. The plane was passing them. He groaned to his feet and moved forward.

"Take him!" He flopped Nevada into the moving door and hands pulled him inside. Chance fell again and the tail passed over him. He struggled to his feet and slogged after PIE IN THE SKY. He reached the door and saw Sonya, her arm out. He grabbed on and, together, they pulled his weight aboard.

Chance heard the YAK closing again.

"McKane! Mixture! Power!"

The Dakota's engines throttled to a roar and the plane surged forward. Chance struggled forward against the acceleration. The floor was slick with mud and blood. The Nazi driver was a heap of blood and ripped flesh near the crates. Michael was trying to quiet the screaming children.

Chance only had seconds before the plane would try to fly on its own without a decent pilot at the controls.

He reached to door and McKane looked all-too-glad to see him.

"Flaps!"

McKane obeyed as Chance threw himself into the pilot's seat. The agony made the instrument panel a blur. He would have to judge their speed by feel.

"Hang on!" he screamed to the rear and jerked the yoke back.

PIE IN THE SKY lurched up as Chance heard the YAK's shells slam into the airframe.

"Gear!"

McKane was on the ball and yanked the lever up as Chance flipped the plane left out of the stream of shells, his left wing tip missing the ground by inches.

Rain blasted the windshield and turbulence controlled the Dakota's flight path more than Chance did. In seconds they were in the low clouds which strobed electric blue several times a second.

"Get Nevada up here."

McKane was happily out of the seat and went back aft, bracing himself against the doorframe. Chance busied himself getting the aircraft off the takeoff heading and steering an evasive course to lose the YAK in the storm. Actually he was steering southwest and the storm was making his course very evasive.

Nevada appeared at the door, half carried by the major.

"I need somebody who knows what they're doing. Strap in."

Nevada nodded slowly and McKane guided him to the right seat, the turbulence pushing both men on top of Chance more than once. Nevada buckled in and adjusted his seat.

"Good to be back home."

Even the blasts of pain could not keep Chance from grinning.

"What's our altitude?"

"Two thousand."

The plane hit a violent downdraft and Chance put on power.

"Give or take."

PIE IN THE SKY wasn't responding as it should. Chance checked the mixture. Lightning appeared to flicker off from the right, but it wasn't blue or purple. Chance saw Nevada staring out the right window.

"Number two is on fire."

CHAPTER 70

*Somewhere over Soviet-Occupied Germany,
July 7, 1948, 10:53 P.M.*

Ivanoff damned his luck.

On his second run he had definitely hit the slowly taxiing Dakota. On his third, he had holed it again just before losing it in the low, boiling clouds. He thought his best opportunity had passed. He would never find the plane in this weather.

He assessed his situation. He still had ammunition, including the entire load of the lethal 20 mm ShVAK cannon. He would keep going until he was out of fuel. He thought like his prey. They would run for the west, trying to avoid the towering thunderstorms. The weather would hide the Dakota, but also narrow its escape paths.

Then he saw the orange light just for an instant at 10 o'clock and slightly low. Instinctively, he brought his fighter onto the bearing. It was moving, acting like a beacon as he lost it and found it again in the canyons of clouds.

There was Sonya and her American lover. He would be in range in a few seconds and he would be sure of his kill this time.

"Fuel cutoff! Ignition off!" Chance ran down the engine fire check list.

Nevada flipped the switches and watched the fire.

"It's in the cowling. Not on the wing."

"Extinguisher." Chance flipped the switch that would send a blast of carbon dioxide into the engine to douse the flames. They had one chance. The bottle of compressed gas would be empty in seconds and there was no more. If the fire spread to the leaking fuel in the wing tanks, there was no stopping it.

"It's...dying, I think."

Ivanoff saw the fire clearly from just under three kilometers and then entered a churning cumulous cloud. A second later he came out into clearer air and could not find the target. A flash of lightning blazed overhead and he saw the Dakota to his left. He was going to overshoot. He jammed the rudder and threw the YAK into a sideslip, angling his guns while still moving forward, like a skidding car. The Dakota was almost in the center of the gun site and he pressed the trigger.

Chance saw the tracers flash past the windshield. He twisted PIE IN THE SKY left away from them, pulling up at the same time.

"This guy's persistent."

"Very. And he will not stop at the border." Sonya was in the door.

Nevada looked up at her.

"Hi, beautiful! Someday you'll explain to me how you managed to get on this roller coaster."

Sonya managed a weak smile and stared forward while Chance focused on the instruments, bringing PIE IN THE SKY level again. Nevada was not too far gone to notice their expressions.

"If we live that long," Nevada forced, and went back to check the engine fire. "We're still hot over here. Just a few flames. Nothing big yet."

"Might as well have a searchlight on us. Power," Chance commanded. "We're going to need some room to dance."

Nevada pushed the throttles forward. PIE IN THE SKY lumbered up.

Ivanoff searched the angry sky for any sign of the Dakota. He tuned the radio and heard only screaming static. St. Elmo's Fire, an eerie green glow from static electricity, danced along the wings and slipped into the air. The constant discharge allied with its giant brothers to deafen the radio. Without contact with Control, he was blind. He wondered if they were back there watching the yellow blips darting around the screen or if they were also blinded by the weather.

The lightning was the key, lighting the clouds and showing the gaps between the thunderstorms. The giant arcs also showed the centers of violence that needed to be avoided by the hunter and the hunted.

"It looks a lot calmer over there." Nevada pointed right.

"I know, but for now we'll keep out of sight."

"It's where he would expect you to go." Sonya braced herself in the cockpit door against another round of turbulence. "Colonel Basily Ivanoff wears the Order of Lenin and is an ace fighter pilot." The next jolt nearly sent her out of the door. She pulled herself back. "He won't stop. Not until he brings us down."

She looked behind her. The two Nazis were eyeing the uniformed McKane.

"You brought the Army?" She cocked her head aft. "The Nazis may make trouble."

"They ain't getting anywhere without a pilot."

"The younger one was a pilot in the SS. He rescued his master by landing his plane on a Berlin street at the height of the Russian attack."

"How do you know all this?"

"It is not important. Do you have any weapons?"

"Only Major Blutto back there. McKane, Army Intelligence."

The yoke lurched forward out Chance's hands, sending them into a hard dive.

"Guns! Guns!" Nevada yelled.

He had been checking the engine fire when he caught Ivanoff's gun flashes as the YAK pounced from above. Chance grabbed the yoke back and the world went crazy. Giant fists punched the plane sideways. Something flashed white in the cockpit and sparks flew out of the instrument panel before it went dark, three loud explosions deafened Chance and the last one stunned him.

The abyss opened, but he refused to let it take him. He heard Nevada hiss in pain.

"Are you hit, buddy?" his own voice echoed in his head. He wasn't sure if he had just thought the question or actually asked it. There was a smell of cordite and burning electrical wiring. Nevada was flipping out the circuit breakers. His arm flopped back down.

"I may have run into something." He tried to grin but it was lost in a convulsive shiver.

Chance got the plane level and Sonya reappeared at the door. She checked Chance.

"I'm fine. Nevada's hit."

"Where?"

Nevada stopped her.

"Leave it. We gotta ditch this bully. That fire's leading him to us every time."

Chance scanned the canyon of clouds ahead of him. They had only seconds.

"Find someplace safe and brace yourself." He knew Sonya wouldn't obey, but said it anyway.

He last remembered they were at 4,500 feet and tried to remember the minimum altitudes from the list. He gave up any fancy calculations. There was no time. He steered for the largest thunderstorm, bristling with lightning.

They entered it, or rather it inhaled them.

Ivanoff had lined up for another run. He could not believe this plane would not die. He came up on their tail in the clear air between the raging storms. He had them dead in his sites this time. Pressing the cannon trigger, he watched his tracers arc across space and was stunned as suddenly the Dakota wasn't there.

The updraft ahead of the storm lifted PIE IN THE SKY like a picnic napkin. Chance felt like he weighed 400 pounds. He could barely keep his arms on the yoke, his left arm and chest screaming pain. He saw tracers rocketing under him and tensed for the slam of shells. He pulled the throttles all the way back.

"Feather One!"

Nevada hesitated, then punched the red button on number one.

PIE IN THE SKY stopped flying in three seconds. Chance was at the complete mercy of the storm and Chance knew thunderstorms had no mercy. Ivanoff flew under them and passed them into the cleared air in the center of the storm.

"Unfeather One!" Chance commanded.

The effect was barely noticeable in the violence of the storm. The one good propeller bit in again, but the updraft began to toy with them, the eddies of air wrenching PIE IN THE SKY like a mad wrestler tossing a child. Ahead, Chance followed the brightening exhausts of the YAK. Ivanoff was giving it all the plane had.

An invisible hand threw the YAK down, Ivanoff still had the power on. Chance knew in seconds it would be their turn. He did not even have that long.

Only a quarter mile behind the YAK, PIE IN THE SKY was ripped downwards. Something came loose in back. Chance heard a crate slam into the fuselage. It would be like an elephant loose in a roomful of eggs.

"Hang on!"

To what? The plane was solid but writhing in a torrent of air heading straight down at ninety miles an hour. They were on the edge of the rain, which was dragging the cold air downward. He could easily see the YAK spinning down ahead of him. They seemed to be slowly gaining on him. Chance wished he had a weapon, but it would only waste time. They were both fighting for their lives now.

His experience at Tempelhof had given him an idea of how to get out of these downdrafts. The temptation was to put on power and pull up. But that was like a swimmer trying to swim against a rip tide.

A lightning bolt seared past them and struck the trees below. The splintering tree flashed bright orange and told Chance how close death was.

Ivanoff saw the flash too. He had pulled the nose up and pushed the throttle to the stops. The engine was screaming, but the stick felt limp. The storm was still in control and there was nothing he could do.

It was the worst feeling in the world.

The YAK hit the forest tops at eighty-five miles an hour. The trees cushioned the blow, and Ivanoff felt the impact cut the shoulder straps into his shoulders. His spine snapped just above his pelvis and his legs went numb. The right wing tore away, bathing the area in burning fuel. The plane came to a stop when a branch punched through the canopy and pinned his chest to the seat. The tail had broken off and arched over, jamming the canopy. The fire reached the cockpit quickly and he could smell his flesh cooking, but it was a long time before it reached living nerves.

Chance caught only a glimpse of the fireball from the YAK. The yoke shuddered as he flipped the plane on its wing. The desperate maneuver put less surface against the powerful downdraft and turned PIE IN THE SKY hopefully toward the way out of the river of plunging air. It also brought the right wing tip to the tops of the trees. Chance wasn't sure if it was turbulence or if the wing caught something, but the airframe groaned and the cargo shifted again. Chance came out into clear air and leveled the plane. Only a few hundred feet away, the updraft seized the plane again and hauled the nose straight up.

Lauter had been watching the crate crashing around the cargo bay. When Chance put the plane on its wing, he fell, landing sideways across the cabin. As PIE IN THE SKY caught the updraft, the crate slid aft, catching the German in the chest. His head struck a rib of the plane, one hundred fifty pounds of Jewish tradition breaking his neck as cleanly as a hangman's noose.

The storm sucked the Dakota up to the thin cold air at nine thousand feet before Chance wrestled it free. He found clearer air and leveled off.

"Nice flyin'." Nevada sounded weak, his voice was an airy rasp.

"Thanks. Sonya!"

She appeared in the doorway.

"The chief Nazi is dead. One of the crates came loose."

"Check Nevada."

Nevada let her open his jacket. She flipped on a flashlight and found she did not need it. The wound was on his upper shoulder and bleeding badly. Sonya found the first aid kit and pressed a bandage to it.

"Do you know where we are?"

Chance scanned the stormy sky ahead of them.

"Vaguely."

"Leipzig is to the southwest. It should be fairly well lit. Fly a bearing of 186 when you get there. Approximately 84 miles. And look for a flashing red and white light."

She looked down at Nevada.

"There will be help waiting there."

CHAPTER 71

1 kilometer West of Viershau, American Occupied Germany, July 7, 1948, 11:34 P.M.

Nevada smiled when their wheels touched down. Chance braked and could see that they had landed on nothing more than a wide country road.

Sonya opened the rear door and the young Nazi got up.

"*Setzen Sie sich!*" McKane ordered and put his foot into the German's chest. The young man shoved the foot away and received the other in his teeth a second later.

A truck roared up to the plane and Chance heard Sonya shouting commands.

"Are we home?" Nevada whispered.

"Yeah. We've done our bit."

"Thanks for coming after me. I knew you were…just pig-headed enough."

A bearded man appeared in the cockpit, dressed all in black. He examined Nevada without a word

"You will live. Get to a hospital. It will need stitches." He turned to Chance. "You should go with him."

Chance came aft to where the truck crew was off-loading the last crate. Five large men reverently carried off the cargo and covered it with canvas on the truck, pausing only to gaze on the wrapped Torah. The rain had stopped, but more heat lightning played across the western sky.

They came for the young German last and bound his hands with a one-inch rope. Sonya saw him off the plane and into the back. The men also handled the unconscious man carefully.

Sonya returned to Chance.

"He will tell us where the others are hiding."

"You organized this whole thing."

"Yes."

"Who are you? Really." Chance swayed. The night and last few days were catching up to him. Sonya gently steadied him.

"I have told you. Sonya Ziegler. My father was a baker in Treptow before the war."

She led Chance to the rear of the truck.

"That is the Torah of Solomon and the treasure of seven synagogues." She turned to where Michael was herding the children together. "And they are the treasure also. Max, whose real name was Joshua Fäder promised to hide it and them. I promised, too. Max and I fought in the resistance here in Germany. Lauter headed *Amt Sechs* and hunted us. He killed Max and found the treasure and the children near the end of the war. They were to be Lauter's price to freedom. At the end of the war, I found Anna Niederhauer – she worked under Lauter. I became her and waited for him to surface. I helped some Nazis, but eventually I found him and the children – they were hidden in a convent near Jüterbog."

"Jitterbug." Chance shook his head. "Why were the Russians waiting for Nevada?"

"It was to be, as you call it, a dry run. We thought the MVD had penetrated Lauter's network. I wanted to be sure they would think they had correct information so we could deceive them. Nevada was waved off at the last minute, but he did not see the signal. But it meant we could fool them tonight."

"You were helping Nazis."

"Yes."

Chance shook his head slowly. "Must have been tough. That one anybody important?"

"One of hundreds. He had his share of evil and loot. He financed everything." She glanced at the canvas covered-body in the road. "I am glad to be done with him."

"Why could you not tell me this?" Michael had come up in the dark.

"How would it have looked if the Russians had found out you were dealing with the Nazis? And for security. I could not trust… I did not think I could trust the Americans."

"Nevada didn't give you away to the Russians. If he had, you'd be long dead." Departing lightning flashed on Chance's face.

"Yes, I will always be grateful to him."

"Sonya, it is time," one of the men in the truck called.

Michael grabbed her arm. "Please. I have seven children now. They will need a mother."

"I still have to keep my promise. There are many mothers without their children. Or a husband. They will need you. And they will help. Maybe…" She stopped and kissed his cheek.

"Your father once told me that he had been born half a Jew, but he would die a whole one. You should be proud of him. He would be very proud of you." Michael squeezed her arms.

"Thank you."

Michael went back down the road toward the truck where the children were already loaded.

"So this is it." Chance reached for her and she let him pull her to him. "Nevada and I were just…"

She put her finger to his lips.

"I did what I had to. Nevada was a pilot I needed. But you…" She kissed him. "…I will always need. *Bitte, Verzeihung.*"

The truck started and she climbed in. Michael rode in the back with the treasure and the children.

The sound of the truck had long faded before McKane came up to Chance, looking out at a handful of lights across the fields.

"I'm going to walk to whatever *dorf* that is over there and wake somebody up."

Chance walked back to the rear door of PIE IN THE SKY. He helped Nevada down and together they walked to the rain-wet grass.

"We owe a lot to a little mechanic, two guys from the black market and some skinny women."

"That so?"

They sat down and were there when the sun rose.

EPILOGUE

Michael stood in the snow-covered field. Soft mounds showed were some of the huts had stood. A rough marker in Hebrew, German and English identified this spot as hallowed ground.

"We will say Kadish for your mothers and fathers."

He started slowly, tears filling his eyes. He stopped, unable to go on and heard the children softly saying the words. He later asked Maria how she knew the prayer.

"The nuns at the convent taught us."

The western part of Berlin voted to remain free. The Allied Airlift lasted through the winter of 1948/49, flying coal, milk, flour and hope until May 12, 1949. The Soviets realized they could not starve the city. Berlin remained divided with the Soviets erecting a wall that stretched across the reviving city like a scar. It fell in November 1989 with the reunification of Germany.

Dimitri was a good spy for almost his entire life, answering the calls and following orders. When the Berlin Wall fell, the calls stopped. He never really knew which side he was working for.

Sonya Ziegler escorted the Torah of Solomon to the fledgling state of Israel. She became one of the founding members of its intelligence service. She was killed in 2008 in the garden of her Nahariya home when a homemade rocket fired from Lebanon exploded only feet away.

Chance, Nevada and PIE IN THE SKY flew over one thousand airlift loads into Berlin. They never made it home, but went on to fly relief and rescue in and out of beleaguered and war-torn areas around the globe.

They disappeared over Africa in 1968 while flying medical supplies to Biafra.

Sonya directed a search for them that lasted two months.

ABOUT THE AUTHOR

Jay Flynn, Kaenan Oliver and Dominic Oliver write together as Oliver Flynn. They all reside in Los Angeles. For more information, go to: oliverflynn.wordpress.com